KT-501-518

# THE
# BRIGHTON
# MERMAID

Dorothy Koomson is the award-winning author of fourteen novels including more than twelve *Sunday Times* bestsellers. Her books have been translated into more than thirty languages and she continues to be a method writer whenever possible. She wrote *The Brighton Mermaid* in part as a love letter to the place she's called home for more than ten years. And she hopes you enjoy it.

**Dorothy Koomson in order:** *The Cupid Effect, The Chocolate Run, My Best Friend's Girl, Marshmallows for Breakfast, Goodnight, Beautiful, The Ice Cream Girls, The Woman He Loved Before, The Rose Petal Beach, The Flavours of Love, That Girl From Nowhere, When I Was Invisible, The Friend, The Beach Wedding, The Brighton Mermaid.*

Bromley Libraries

30128 80386 025 6

# Praise for *The Brighton Mermaid*

'Another brilliant, suspenseful read from a master storyteller'
*Candis*

'With a cracking plot to boot – this **brilliant read will hook you from the start**'
*Fabulous*

'This will **creep its way under your skin** and stay there long after you finish the final few gut-twisting chapters. **Brilliant**'
*Heat*

'**Tense** and **emotional**'
*My Weekly*

'**Thrilling**!'
*Take a Break*

'Koomson is the queen of the big reveal, and takes her time slowly building the tension in this **truly gripping** read'
*Sun*

'Has all the classic elements of the big beach novel. It adds **extra depths to the whodunit** in terms of characterisation and emotional impact, and races to a conclusion that had me **turning the pages as if they were on fire**'
*Viva*

'A hot read'
*Woman*

'Just when you think you know what happened and you have your suspects a turn of the page will prove you wrong. This novel is **fast paced** and a great read'
*Woman's Way*

'The novel **simmers with tension** and **an undercurrent of darkness**'
*Daily Express*

'*The Brighton Mermaid* is a **breathtakingly brilliant**, twisty belter of a book and you need to read it!'
Miranda Dickinson, author of *Somewhere Beyond the Sea*

'**Fast-paced, dark** and **simmering** – can't recommend this novel enough'
Caroline Smailes, author of *The Drowning of Arthur Braxton*

'**Gripping, twisty, scary** and **uplifting** in spite of it all . . . thriller lovers, this one is for YOU'
Cathy Cassidy, author of *Love From Lexie*

'A big, meaty read with a **complex, multi-layered plot**'
Vaseem Khan, author of the *Baby Ganesh Detective Agency* series

'All the twists and turns and characters in the story **totally engaged me**'
Trisha Ashley, author of *The House of Hopes and Dreams*

**What the bloggers are saying...**

'A bloody awesome read! I have **been on the EDGE of my seat**!'
*Random Things Through My Letterbox*

'A brilliant exploration of the **dark side of human nature** and the secrets people hide'
*Life Has A Funny Way*

'Emotive and thrilling this **makes for a compelling read**'
Charlene Jess

'It was an excellent, **absorbing read**, and there's lots of content to sink your teeth into'
*Bookbag*

'If you're looking for a book where you won't be able to guess where it's heading, where you are on the edge of your seat and **cannot guess the ending** then this is the book for you!'
*Needing Escapism*

'I'm convinced it's this intimacy between reader and character that makes Dorothy's stories so gripping. In the case of *The Brighton Mermaid* **the suspense, thrill and fear was palpable**'
*Tiger Tales*

'I've been **left reeling** from this book that packs a humongous punch. The story builds steadily at first but when I sat down for the last 30% this evening, I didn't expect anything like what I read'
*Rachel's Random Reads*

'As always Dorothy Koomson **uses a number of hard-hitting issues** in *The Brighton Mermaid* but all are deeply woven into the story-line, not one appearing placed for effect alone'
*Cleopatra Loves Books*

'The premise for this story is clever, intriguing and a perfect hook. The **lingering sense of threat** and **ominous atmosphere** builds gradually . . . kept me gripped and on the edge of my seat'
*Bibliomanic*

'Wow this is one of the best books I've ever read. It was **mesmerising** from beginning to end'
*Sincerely BookAngels*

'**Plenty of twists** and turns that kept me **on the edge of my seat** and unable to put the book down'
*Opinionated Emz*

# THE
# BRIGHTON MERMAID

# DOROTHY KOOMSON

arrow books

1 3 5 7 9 10 8 6 4 2

Arrow Books
20 Vauxhall Bridge Road
London SW1V 2SA

Arrow Books is part of the Penguin Random House group of companies whose
addresses can be found at global.penguinrandomhouse.com

Penguin
Random House
UK

Copyright © Dorothy Koomson 2018

Dorothy Koomson has asserted her right to be identified as the author of this
Work in accordance with the Copyright, Designs and Patents Act 1988.

First published in Great Britain by Century in 2018
First published in paperback by Arrow Books in 2019

www.penguin.co.uk

A CIP catalogue record for this book is available from the British Library.

ISBN 9781784755423

Typeset in 10.98/14.5 pt Baskerville MT Pro
by Integra Software Services Pvt. Ltd, Pondicherry

Printed and bound in Great Britain by Clays Ltd, Elcograf S.p.A.

Penguin Random House is committed to a sustainable
future for our business, our readers and our planet. This
book is made from Forest Stewardship Council®
certified paper.

To those who are missing and those who love them.

# Prologue

*Saturday, 2 June*

The ground is uneven and crunchy underfoot, and I stumble when I hit it. But it takes a microsecond to steady myself, to force myself upright and then to start running.

I make it off the gravel driveway, through the gap in the hedge and then out into the fields that surround the farmhouse. In this inky blackness, in the distance, I can just about make out shapes – bushes, hedges, a line of trees far, far down over the fields. I need to get to the trees. If I can get to the trees, I can hide.

*Thud, thud, thud, thud!* The world around me is full of their foot-steps, moving across the earth, chasing me down.

My legs are stiff from where I've been lying in the same position for so long, and they protest as I try to pick up the pace, attempt to run faster over the uneven, soggy ground.

*Thud, thud, thud, thud!* The noise . . . the vibrations . . . They sound horribly closer now.

*Thud, thud, thud, thud!* There's a fire in my chest where my lungs should be, and my eyes are struggling in the darkness as it constantly changes the shape of the horizon. But I can't stop, I can't even slow down, I have to keep moving.

*Thud, thud, thud, thud!* Nearer and nearer.

*Thud, thud, thud, thud!* I need my legs to go faster. I need them to call up the muscle memory of when I used to do this, when I had to literally run for my life. I can do this. I *have* to do this. I have to reach the trees. I'll be safe there, I'll be able to hide there.

*Thud, thud, thud, thud!* fills my ears. *Thud, thud, thud, thud!* They're right behind me. *Thud, thud, thud, thud!* My ragged breathing, the whistle of the wind, the creak of my bones are all drowned out by it. *Thud, thud, thud, thud!*

I have to go faster. I have to—

# 1993

## Nell

'Maybe she's asleep,' I said to my best friend, Jude.

We were both staring at her. She looked so soft, lying there on top of the pebbles, half in, half out of the water, her face serene. Even with the foamy tide constantly nudging at her, trying to get her to wake up, she was still; tranquil, lifeless.

'She's not asleep,' Jude said. Her voice was stern, angry almost, as though she couldn't believe I was being so stupid.

'I know she's not asleep,' I replied. 'But if I pretend she's asleep then she's not the other thing.' I couldn't bear for her to be the other thing and for me to be standing there in front of her when she was the other thing.

'She's not asleep,' Jude repeated, gentler this time. 'She's . . . she's not asleep.'

We both stood and stared.

From the promenade, I'd spotted her down on the beach, the light of the almost full moon shining down on her, and said we should check to see if she was all right. Jude had wanted us to keep going, getting back to her house after we'd sneaked out was going to be tricky enough without getting back even later than 3 a.m., which was the time now. But I'd insisted we check. *What if she'd twisted her ankle and couldn't get up? How would we feel, leaving someone who was hurt alone like that? What if she's drunk and has fallen asleep on the beach when the tide was out and is now too drunk to wake up and pull herself out of the water? How would we live with ourselves if we read in the paper in the morning that she'd been washed out to sea and had drowned?*

Jude had rolled her eyes at me, had reminded me in an angry whisper that even though our mums were at work (they were both nurses on night duty), her dad was at home asleep and could wake up any minute now to find us gone. He'd call *my* dad and then we'd be for it. She'd grumbled this while going towards the stone steps that led to the beach. She was all talk, was Jude – she wouldn't want to leave someone who was hurt, she would want to help as much as I did. It wasn't until we'd got nearer, close enough to be able to count the breaths that weren't going in and out of her chest, that we could to see what the real situation was. And I said that thing about her being asleep.

'I'll go up to the . . . I'll go and call the police,' Jude said. She didn't even give me a chance to say I would do it before she was gone – crunching the pebbles underfoot as she tried to get away as fast as possible.

Alone, I felt foolish and scared at the same time. This wasn't meant to turn out this way. We were meant to come to the beach and help a drunk lady and then sneak back to Jude's house. I wasn't supposed to be standing next to someone who was asleep but not.

*She must be cold*, I thought suddenly. Her vest top was soaked through and stuck to her body like a second, clingy skin; her denim skirt, which didn't quite reach down to her knees, was also wringing wet. '*I wish I had a blanket that I could pull over you*,' I silently said to her. '*If I had a blanket, I'd do my best to keep you warm.*'

It was summer, but not that warm. I wasn't sure why she was only wearing a vest, skirt and no shoes. *Maybe*, I thought, *her shoes and jumper have already been washed out to sea.*

I leant forwards to have another look at her. I wanted to make her feel more comfortable, to move her head from resting on her left arm at an awkward angle, and stop her face from being pushed into the dozens and dozens of bracelets she wore on her arm. Thin metal ones, bright plastic ones, wood ones, black rubbery ones, they stretched from her wrist to her elbow, some of them not visible because of where her head rested. I wanted to gently move her head off her arm and lay it instead on my rolled-up jacket. I didn't dare touch her though. I didn't dare move any nearer, let alone touch her.

Her other arm, the right one, was thrown out to one side, as if it had flopped there when she'd finally fallen asleep. That arm had only one slender silver charm bracelet, hung with lots of little silver figures. That arm's real decoration, though, was an elegant and detailed tattoo of a mermaid. My eyes wouldn't leave the tattoo, which was so clear in the moonlight. Usually when I saw tattoos they were a faded greeny-blue, etched into peach or white skin, but this one was on a girl with the same shade skin as me. Deep black ink had artistically been used to stain and adorn most of her inner forearm. I leant a little more forwards, not wanting to get too close, but fascinated enough to want to have a better look. It was truly beautiful, so incredibly detailed it looked like it had been carefully inscribed onto paper, not rendered on skin.

I could see every curl of the mermaid's short, black Afro hair; I could make out the tiny squares of light in her pupils; I could count every one of the individually etched scales on her tail, and I could see droplets of water glistening on the bodice, shaped of green seaweed, that covered her torso. The mermaid sat on a craggy grey rock, her hands demurely crossed in her lap, smiling at anyone who cared to look at her.

I couldn't stop staring at her. She was mythical, she was a picture, but she was also like a siren at whom I couldn't stop staring. In the waters beneath the mermaid's rock, there were three words in a swirling, watery script: 'I am Brighton'.

# Now

## Nell

*Friday, 23 March*

'And I'm sure you will all join me in wishing Nell good luck with her next venture,' says Mr Whitby, manager of the London Road branch of The Super supermarket chain. I have worked with him there, latterly as his assistant manager, for nearly eight years. Eight years. I hadn't intended staying that long but somehow I never got around to leaving until today. I've finally saved up enough to take twelve months off paid employment, and, hopefully, at the end of it, I'll have solved the mystery that has haunted me for nearly twenty-five years. Hopefully, at the end of it, I will be able to walk away with my family still in one piece.

We're in Read My Lips, one of those 'hot' new bars that seem to pop up every few months in Brighton. It's a short walk from the Pier and we're in our own cordoned-off VIP area downstairs with brightly coloured squashy seats and mirrored tables. The lighting is the darker side of 'muted' and the music is the wannabe side of grime. And it is packed. Ordinarily there would be no way for us to get in here, but Mr W, who suggested we come here for my leaving do, said he had 'connections' that would get us in. The twenty of us who've come out tonight have been impressed so far. Even more so when he insisted on buying the drinks – completely out of character for a man who usually leaves dealing with customers and staff to his assistant manager. (He seems to have issues with not letting his true feelings – not caring – come through.)

In the slightly brighter corner that we've been allocated, Mr W peers at me over his wire-rimmed glasses. 'I think it's fair to say that ever since we welcomed Nell into our Super family many, many years ago, we have nurtured and cared for her. We have overseen and, may I suggest, been fundamental in helping her to grow up into the vibrant young woman she is today. Obviously we are all a little sad and disappointed that Nell has chosen to leave us in the run-up to Easter, one of our busiest times, but we can forgive her. That is the nature of the family we have created here at The Super. And it is also the nature of our Super family to be willing, when Nell comes to her senses and realises where her future truly lies, to let her know that there will always be space on the clocking-in board for her.'

I stare at him, shocked. The other people who have come to celebrate with me stare at him, shocked. Not only has he spoken many, many words without doing his usual of breaking eye contact or allowing his tone to reveal how dull he is finding speaking to you, he has delivered a masterful example of passive-aggressiveness. I'm shocked that he has it in him.

The music in the bar could have been designed to accompany his speech – in the gap that follows his words the music crescendos, dramatically underlining what he's said. It then drops away again as Mr Whitby raises his glass. 'To Nell,' he says happily.

Part of the assistant manager's job at The Super was to let people know it was perfectly normal to feel unsettled and slightly anxious when they dealt with Mr W, so I pull a smile across my face, to tell everyone that despite what he said, it's OK to raise their glasses too. 'To Nell,' my former colleagues chorus before they sip their drinks. I love these people, they make me smile. We at the London Road The Super are oddballs, there's no pretending we're not, but I adore them and I'm touched so many of them have come out tonight, especially when most of them have to be up early tomorrow to work a full shift. I'll miss them.

'In all the leaving speeches in all the years, I have never heard one like *that*,' Janice murmurs to me when everyone breaks off into smaller groups. She has worked at The Super longer than almost everyone here except Mr W. 'I mean, that was the equivalent to him throwing himself at your ankles to stop you leaving.' She smirks. 'He's going to miss you.'

'You mean he's going to miss the person who's been assigned his quota of unused words?'

Janice smirks some more. Even I know I talk too much.

'When I first resigned, he didn't say a word. Not one word. I had to repeat it because I didn't think he'd heard me and I thought that if he was going to break his usual silence it would be then. But no, he stored it all up for tonight. To tell me I've dropped you all in it with Easter and "mark my words, you'll be back".' I shake my head. 'Anyway, I need something to wash away the lingering taste of passive aggressiveness. Want something?'

Janice raises her nearly full flute of prosecco. I turn to the others. 'Anyone want a drink?' I ask above the music. As a group, they look at me as though I'm crazy – until Mr W stops supplying the drinks, no one is reaching into their pockets. 'Fine,' I say. 'When you talk about this night in weeks to come, though, just remember that I offered, OK? Nell offered to buy drinks even though she isn't going off to another paying job.'

The bar itself is lit up like a multicoloured beacon in the dark space but not many people are waiting to be served. I rest my bag on a padded stool and reach in for my purse.

By the time I stepped out of the Super building for the last time ever tonight, I was Nell again. As soon as I clocked off my final shift I shed my assistant manager persona and donned my usual T-shirt-and-red-jeans look, slotted in my various earrings, and pushed on my bangles, which go from forearm to wrist on my right arm and all the way up to my elbow on the left. Once I took my mobile off its waistband holster and slipped it into my jacket pocket, that was it. I was me again.

Once I am me again, of course, the messages start again.

Despite the music, the thrum of conversations around me, I hear the *bleep-bleep-ting* of a message tone from my mobile.

*His* tone.

It goes off in my pocket, but echoes in my chest.

*Don't read it*, I tell myself even as I'm reaching for it. *It can wait till morning*, I remind myself as I pull my mobile out of my pocket. *It'll ruin your night*, I state as I bring up the message.

I know before looking what it's going to say, but I still have to take a deep breath before I look. It says the same thing every time – it uses the same five words to control me. Sometimes I think I look in the hope it will be different, that the screen after that message tone will say something else. But no, it's the same as always:

**He needs to see you.**

The same five words as always, the same full stop as always. The same lack of greeting or sign-off. *He needs to see you. He needs to see you.* It bounces on the edges of the music, thumps on the beats of my heart. *He needs to see you. He needs to see you. He needs to see you.*

I want to type: *'I don't want to see him'*, *'Leave me alone'*, *'Go away'* . . . anything . . . *anything* that will put an end to this. But I can't, of course. I am where I am, I am who I am, and saying no to him is not an option. The clock is ticking and I can't escape that.

Swallowing the emotions, pushing them deep, deep down, I shove my phone back into my pocket and return to taking my purse out of my bag. I turn towards the bar, to the rows and rows of drinks, sitting like shimmery escape pods to the point of oblivion I suddenly desperately need to visit.

My eyes run over the names, the labels, the bottle shapes, the liquor colours, and nothing appeals. Nothing catches my eye and tells me it will take me to where I need to be right now – away from the reality of my life.

I turn to the person on my right, hoping for inspiration. He has a fancy and expensive-looking bottle of beer in his hand and a faint sneer that broadcasts how much better he thinks he is than everyone in the place, possibly on the planet. *Nope, won't be taking inspiration from him.*

I turn to my left. The man who stands there, leaning on the bar, is watching me with his head tipped slightly to one side. When I make eye contact he smiles. I grin back.

'What are you drinking?' I ask him, not looking at the glass he has on the bar in front of him.

'Tequila from God's own country.'

'You're Mexican?' I ask.

'Nope. I just like to say that.'

'Tequila it is then,' I say. 'Will you have one with me?'

He grins a little wider. 'It'd be rude not to.'

# 1993

## Nell

*Saturday, 26 June*

Jude looked spooked when she came back from calling the police.

She explained over the sound of the waves and her footsteps crunching on the shingle that she'd had to call 999 three times before anyone would believe her. They had told her the third time she was going to get into trouble if she called again. 'All right then, I'll keep calling until you come and get me.'

That's when they'd believed her. Told her to wait by the phone box but she'd said she wasn't going to, she was going back to the dead body on the beach. 'You actually said that?' I asked her. 'Those actual words?'

'Yeah, course,' she replied. 'Why?'

I didn't answer because I couldn't imagine ever saying something like that, let alone to a police person.

'It's really creepy up there,' she said, shivering. 'There were a couple of men who were really dodgy-looking. I was scared of what they might do.'

I stared at Jude, thinking, *Of course there are dodgy-looking men out there – it's Friday night in Brighton. What's actually weirder is that there aren't more people down here on the beach. That we're the ones who found her.*

My eyes darted from Jude to the woman and I couldn't stand to look any more. Anyway, Jude was back – I didn't have to look any more.

I turned away. Rotated until my back was to the sea and my vision was filled with the rise of the sea wall, the pebbles that lay in undulating mounds up to the promenade, the shapes the darkness made of the ornate railings. I didn't know if Jude had looked away like me or if she'd taken her turn standing and watching over the woman who, I had realised, wasn't actually that much older than us.

It wasn't long before a policewoman and a policeman were crunching over the pebbles, their faces like thunder. That's when it became real. That's when I realised that someone had died. Someone had died and it was going to turn out like it did on the television. We were going to find out that she had been murdered. That her last minutes were awful; full of terror and pain. I looked into the faces of the police officers, saw how angry they were that we were wasting their time like this, and knew our lives were never going to be the same again.

# Now

## Macy

**05:13**

I stand, mobile in hand, and watch the clock on the cooker, waiting for it to click onto the right time. Once it hits the specific digits I am waiting for, I'll be able to call. She'll answer and things will flip into their correct places. Saturday will start, the whole day will be a perfect dream and the rest of the week will be wonderful: none of us will oversleep; we won't need to rush any morning; I won't have to shout; the children will get gold stars and certificates; I'll manage to appease even the most difficult clients that are always sent my way; and Shane might even hear about that long-promised promotion.

**05:14**

Shane and the kids, snuggled together on the sofa, laugh at me from behind the icons on the lock-screen as I stare at my mobile. Everything I do, I do for them. Every call I make, I do it with them in mind.

Today's call, like all the other calls, is not like it was back then when I made the first call. *Then* I'd been desperate.

I had been up all night. *All* night. Shane had tried at various points during those hours to get me to go to bed. He'd come downstairs more than once, had watched me pace the kitchen, doing the only thing that would stop my mind racing, and he'd asked me again to follow him up to bed. *Try to rest; try to sleep*, he'd begged. I'd ignored him. And kept ignoring him until he'd given up, snapped at me that he was going to bed so that one of us would be capable of looking

*15*

after the children in the morning. I could hear his frustration, could see he was holding back from screaming that this sort of stuff was driving a wedge between us, but I couldn't stop his anger, nor my pacing. I kept going, even when I heard him leave the room.

Walking the lines of the edges of the black and white tiles of our kitchen floor was the only way to stop my mind hurtling backwards and forwards through time. Moving along each line, straight and perfect, was a way for me to externalise what was going on inside, kept me tethered to the moment. But, that night, even walking the lines couldn't stave off the quiet terror. It all kept bubbling up inside; struggling, fighting, battling to let itself out. I was constantly dragged back to that night and the moment my life changed, then I was flung forwards, to the hell that would be unleashed if I told.

All night. *All night* I was thrown about through time, struggling to deal with what happened and its potential consequences.

*I have to confess*, I'd finally decided as light started to climb up over the horizon. *I have to tell Nell.* I'd kept the secret for twenty-five years, and I couldn't keep it any longer. Yes, it would destroy her. Yes, it would decimate our family. Yes, it would unleash again the hell we'd all barely lived through last time. But I couldn't keep it in any longer. Staying silent was literally driving me crazy and I had to tell.

I'd looked at the cooker clock and it had said 05:14. Too early to call, but far, far too late in terms of confessing. I'd found my mobile, slipped down the side cushion of the kitchen sofa as usual, and started to dial. Then stopped. Then started again. Then stopped. By the time I actually dialled her number, it was 05:17.

## 05:15

Nell had answered after the third ring. 'Are you all right?' she'd asked. I could hear in her voice that she hadn't been to bed yet. She obviously wasn't working that Saturday so she'd been up all night, on her computer, searching and searching as usual. This was why I had to tell her. It would get her to stop. It would make her realise why what she was doing was dangerous to all of us.

'Yes,' I'd said, 'I'm fine.' And, as I said the words, I realised I *was* fine. The terror, the thing that had seized and driven me all night, that had caused me to pick up the phone to reveal all, was gone. It was hearing her voice. It was the normality of Nell that had done it. When we'd both spent so much time being anything but normal, hearing the natural, ordinariness of her tone even at that time of the morning was enough to calm me down.

I felt my worries – a tight little bundle that sat in the middle of my chest, resting heavily on my heart – untangle; become transparent and manageable.

'So what you doing up at this time?' Nell asked. I'd heard her stifle a yawn. 'One of the kids ill or something?'

'No, no,' I said. I felt ridiculous, then. I'd been up for hours, walking the lines, trying to hide from what I'd seen a quarter of a century ago, and now these worries seemed small, even ignorable for a while. 'You need to come over,' I told her. 'Clara has a football match and Willow has a gymnastics competition. You need to pick one to go to.' I sounded bossy, like I was telling my big sister what to do. But you know, now I felt less panicked, I remembered the many things that *really* irritated me about Nell. I loved her, but I did not love the part of her that sat up till the small hours searching for people on her computer. *Computers*, because she needs more than one of them to search for people. Nell wasn't married because she was always searching for people on her computers. She didn't have kids because she was always searching for people on her computers. Everything about Nell and the way she lived her life was about searching for people on her computers. She would be a different person with a real life, a real family, if she'd just stop searching for people. Yup, when I remembered how Nell had ruined her life because of something that was, at best, a hobby, it made me cross and it made me bossy. I often thought I could shock her into living in the real world by forcing her to take part in family life.

On the other end of the phone line, Nell had taken a deep breath, had stayed silent for a second and then said: 'Sure. Fine.

When do I need to be there?' She'd showed up on time, she took Clara to her football match, during which Clara had scored the winning goal. Then Nell had made a huge fuss of Willow on winning a medal for the first time in any of her gymnastics competitions, and then she'd stuck around to help Aubrey with his ever-expanding model replica of Brighton Pier.

It'd been an amazing day, and that had turned into an incredible week: no lateness; Shane was promoted then given the nod for another huge promotion; I came up with a concept that a difficult new client loved; and the children came home with five different gold stars and reward certificates.

## 05:16

I bring up Nell's number, ready to hit 'call' when the time comes.

After that first week I had cast my mind back, tried to find what had been different about that week which could have caused our good fortune, and I realised it was the phone call with Nell. It was the only thing that had been different, out of the ordinary.

The next Saturday I did it again, I called her at exactly 05:17. Spoke to her. Asked her to come and be a proper part of our family life after work. And the week went brilliantly again. Even better than before. When it happened again for the third week, I realised that it *was* the phone calls. Something about connecting with my sister at that time of the morning on a Saturday, about bringing her over to our house, made all the difference.

I've been calling her every Saturday at 05:17 for nearly nine months. And those nine months have been as darn close to perfect as we can get. In all that time, she has answered every single call. Guilt, of course. Every time Nell picks up the phone to me at that time of the morning, she does so out of the guilt she should rightfully feel.

## 05:17

I press 'call' and start my weekend.

# Nell

*Saturday, 24 March*
*Ring, ring, ring.*

It's 5:17 on Saturday morning. I know that because my phone is ringing.

*Ring, ring, ring.*

It's 5:17 on a Saturday morning and my phone won't stop ringing until I answer it. I have a few more seconds before I need to pick it up so I don't open my eyes, or reach for the offending item, I just let the sound jangle through me, tap-dancing on every single nerve in my head.

I never want to answer the phone when it rings at this time every Saturday, but I always do. It's a compulsion; a force outside of my will that makes me raise my hand, pick up the phone and then give myself over to the words, thoughts and needs of the person at the other end.

'Are you going to get that?' the voice beside me asks.

Even though his voice has startled me, I stay perfectly still and keep my eyes closed. Usually when the phone rings at this time on a Saturday I'm alone. I'm home and I'm alone. The fact that I'm not alone also means I am not at home. That means I need to fake sleep until I remember as much of last night as possible.

'Hey! Nell!' the man beside me says loudly. He knows my name, which is a good sign. A *great* sign. It means we must have talked at some point before we came back to his place. 'Are you going to answer your phone?'

'No,' I croak. 'I am not going to get that.' My voice is battered, my throat furrowed by dry spikes. I was either smoking or I was talking loudly and singing even louder. I groan at the thought of it, hoping it was the smoking rather than the singing.

'All right, can you *please* get that,' the man says. 'It's too early and too Saturday for that noise.' Despite the irritation in his voice, he sounds nice. Like a nice man I had a nice conversation with before we came back to his place.

I open my eyes and roll towards the sound of my phone. Beside my bleating mobile is a small glass of water, and a hotel telephone, notepad and pen. OK, not his place – a hotel.

As I reach for my phone, the rows and rows of bangles on my arm clink together as they pool at my wrist. *You're too loud for this part of my hangover*, I tell them silently. *Too, too loud.*

I jab at the 'cancel' button to the racket, then press and hold down the power button until my phone is off. Because it *will* start ringing again as the caller desperately tries to connect again during the sixty seconds of 5:17 a.m.

I clatter the phone back onto the bedside table. I should turn it off more often, but I don't. I can't. I fear what I might trigger if I do.

'There. Better?' I say to the man on the other side of the bed without actually looking at him.

'Yeah. Much. Thank. You.' He says this as though he is forcing each word out through his teeth.

OK, so maybe he isn't that nice after all.

# Macy

She didn't answer.

She cut off the call and didn't answer. And now she's turned off her phone.

I've called back three times now, trying to get her to speak to me before the cooker clock flicks from 05:17 to 05:18, and each time it goes straight to voicemail. I can't believe she's turned off her phone. *How dare she!*

*HOW DARE SHE!*

She *knows* why she needs to answer, it's an unspoken agreement between us – I call, she answers. She doesn't even have to talk for long. If she picks up, listens to what I need her to do, everything will be OK. How dare she do this!

I lob my mobile across the kitchen. It lands, quite by chance, on the cream leather sofa by the door and bounces unceremoniously on its cushions before coming to rest.

In the past, if she doesn't answer first time, she always picks up the second time I call. If I need to ring again, it's always still 05:17. She *never* turns off her phone. *Never.*

I watch the cooker clock flip from 05:17 to 05:18. And that's it. My chance gone. If I hadn't already done so, I would throw my phone across the room in the hopes of hearing a satisfying smash as it hits something solid. '*What have you done to us, Nell?*' I ask, with my right thumb knuckle wedged in my mouth. '*What have you brought down on us?*'

# Nell

I throw my arm over my eyes as I ease myself back onto the bed. I'm reaching for the blurry, ethereal strands of last night that float around my mind like clouds in a still sky. I need to fuse those strands together to make one coherent timeline because certain things aren't really making sense now. Like the fact I'm fully dressed. I'm in bed with a man and I'm fully dressed, right down to my odd socks and multiple bangles.

*Last night* . . . Last night was my leaving do.

*Last night* . . . We went to Read My Lips, the hottest new bar in Brighton.

*Last night* . . . Mr W made a passive-aggressive speech. I went to the bar. I got the 'He needs to see you' text.

*Last night* . . . I talked to a man and bought him tequila.

Last night . . . I *think* I came home with the man I drank tequila with.

*This morning* . . . I've woken up next to the man I think I drank tequila with – fully clothed.

'Was that your husband, boyfriend or girlfriend calling to find out why you didn't come home?' The man – whose name I'm desperately trying to remember – asks now the room is silent.

'None of the above,' I reply.

'Yeah, right.'

'It was my sister,' I say to him. 'She calls me at five seventeen every Saturday morning for a chat.'

*What* is *his name?* His voice is sounding familiar, so I think it is him from the bar, but his name is drawing a complete blank.

'Why?' he asks, clearly not believing me.

'All sisters call at that time on a Saturday morning,' I reply.

'Mine doesn't.'

'Well, aren't you the lucky one?'

'And aren't you just the most darling ray of sunshine?' he says.

'There's no sunshine when I hurt this badly.'

'Poor you,' he coos. 'Imagine how you're going to feel when the effects of room service booze kick in.'

*Oh God.* Last night . . . *I threw myself on this bed, picked up the telephone and in an ultra-posh voice ordered a bottle of tequila and 'your very finest champagne'.*

'I'll pay for it,' I say with a groan.

'Uh-huh,' he replies.

Even though I can't remember his name, I'm forced to look at him then, to underline what I am saying by making eye contact. I can't speak for a moment because he's gorgeous. He's propped up on two white pillows facing me, and he's divine. The set of his features, the slice of his cheekbones, the gentle slope of his brow, the curve of his chin, the bow of his lips, the smooth, hairless lines of his head, the eyebrow-free openness of his face, the eyelash-less emphasis of his gaze, work together to make him simply beautiful.

Zachariah. *Zach.*

His name is Zach and last night I kissed him in the bar. When Mr Whitby had departed, when other people had left and we'd had three more shots in quick succession, I leant across and kissed him. He'd kissed me back, our lips tingly with lime and salt and long notes of tequila as they moved together. Kissing Zach made the tequila more potent; it swirled in my bloodstream, twirled in my head. With every shot, chased down with a long kiss, things seemed a little better. I forgot about the sheer terror of what I was undertaking in the coming year, I shrugged off the worry of how what I was doing would reverberate through my family, and I managed to shove the 'He needs to see you' text message to the back of my mind.

Zach had told me he'd moved to Brighton *that day* for work and hadn't sorted somewhere to live yet so was staying in a hotel. I'd asked him if his room was nice, and he'd said he'd show me if I wanted. I did want. And I had obviously made liberal use of his room service menu.

'I *will* pay for it,' I say, about the tequila and champagne.

'OK,' he says, still looking sceptical. 'Fine. Whatever.'

We stare warily at each other for a few seconds. His lack of facial hair, I realise, makes him seem completely open, since he doesn't get to hide behind the expressions that are emphasised and nuanced by eyebrows and eyelashes. I haven't met many men who are completely hairless, but to be fair, I haven't met many men who are as good-looking as him, either.

'Did we . . . *you know* . . . *do it?*' I ask, because I'm still intrigued about why I have my clothes on.

'We did not,' Zach states.

I'm surprised because of the kissing. In the bar, where neither of us cared who saw us. In the lift, where we missed his floor more than once. Even on this bed . . . The kissing seemed to be a promise of lots of . . . *you know* . . . *doing it.* 'Any particular reason why we didn't?' I ask.

'You were very drunk. I don't have sex with drunk women.'

'OK. Good policy. But I should point out that I don't usually get that drunk.'

'I'm glad to hear that you don't usually get that drunk,' Zach replies flippantly.

'You don't sound very glad,' I say.

The world swims in front of my eyes suddenly. *I'm going to pass out. Or vomit. Or both.* I have to slam both hands flat on the bed to steady myself. As I do so my bangles and bracelets come together and sound again like a loud crash of cymbals rather than the tinkle of metal on plastic on metal.

'You make a lot of noise with those bangles,' Zach comments.

'Yes, I suppose I do.'

'If you were ever in a life-threatening situation where you had to hide, I wouldn't think much of your chances.'

'Well, thankfully, I've never been in such a situation, and hopefully I will never find myself in one.'

'Yeah. Thankfully.'

I crank my head round to look at him askance. 'Seriously? *Seriously?* We were *that* off our heads we thought going to bed together was a good idea?'

With a small shrug he replies: 'I guess I must have been drunker than I thought.'

'What's *that* supposed to mean?'

'It means I agree with you – you and me without booze doesn't seem to be the best idea.'

'Yeah, well, it sounded like you were saying you wouldn't have looked twice at me unless you were drunk.'

'I wouldn't *dream* of saying something like that.'

'Watch it, you, or I'll . . . "room service" you again . . . but this time *I won't pay for it.*'

A smile nudges at his lips and he turns his head away before it becomes a real grin. 'All right, all right, truce?' he says.

'Truce,' I reply grudgingly.

'Now we've cleared that up, you fancy sex?'

'Hell no!' I shudder at the thought of it. I have morning breath and hangover hair, plus neither of us has exactly covered ourselves in glory in these last few minutes.

'Fair enough,' he says with a shrug.

Oh. *Now that I've turned him down for sex, does that mean I have to leave? Because I don't think my legs will work if I try to use them now. Actually, I don't think I can move very far without chucking up.* 'Erm, you know how we're not going to have sex?' I begin.

'Yes?' he replies.

'I was wondering, kind of hoping, actually, that I could go back to sleep? Here? I know it's a bit cheeky – well, a lot cheeky – and

I know the last few minutes haven't been the most fun of your life, but I am so very tired I have to swallow my pride and ask you, beg you, if necessary, to let me catch a couple of hours of sleep. I promise I'll be no trouble, I'll just close my eyes and go to sleep. I'll even take off my bangles so as not to disturb you.'

He is silent for a few seconds. His eyes roam over my face like curious fingers learning and mapping out my features. 'All right. Fine. Go to sleep. But only if you don't plan on staying all day when you wake up.'

*Charming.* 'As soon as I wake up, I will leave. I'm already dressed so I won't even need to go near the shower. I can walk straight out of here and right out of your life.'

'*Eurgh!* You've got to use the shower. What sort of filthiness is that?'

'I was just trying to make sure we keep this as short as humanly possible.'

'Yeah, well, there's short and then there's filthiness. You have to have a shower before you go. In fact, I insist on it. Don't commit a crime against your fellow travellers by being *that* commuter.'

'I'm not going to commute anywhere – I live in Brighton, remember?'

'Fair enough. But you still need a shower.'

'All right – shower, dressed again, outta here.'

'Sounds good.'

I chance a glance in his direction to find him staring me, a small smile on his face – he was smiling at me like that at the bar, just before I spoke to him, I remember that.

His smile makes me beam at him. More and more of our time together last night is seeping in now: the firmness of his body against mine, the way his hand felt resting in the small of my back, the soft sigh of wanting more and more of his kisses.

'See you later,' I say.

'Yes, Nell, see you later.'

# 1993

## Nell

'Tell me again what you two were doing out so late?' the policeman asked us.

Jude and I were sitting in a little room with three chairs at a table, two on one side and one on the other. We held hands, trying to comfort each other but in reality we both seemed to take it in turns to shake so violently we made the other quake with us.

I was cold. Really cold. My lips felt coldest, or maybe it was my fingertips, or maybe it was the centre of my chest where my heart was. I was cold and shaky.

Every time I blinked I saw her: the untroubled face, the motionless body, the detail of her tattoo. Every time I breathed I realised that the woman with the Brighton mermaid tattoo wasn't going to do that ever again. Every time I looked at my hands I saw the remnants of the black ink they used to take our fingerprints, and was reminded that they thought we'd done it. The police thought we were responsible for what had happened to the woman we found on the beach.

Their behaviour since they'd taken us from the beach – the policewoman sitting stonefaced between us in the back of the police car – right up to this moment showed that they thought we were guilty of a crime. They'd said they were taking our fingerprints to eliminate us from the investigation, but it felt as if they were actually checking in case we'd been in trouble before. They'd said they would call our fathers but it felt like hours since

27

we'd been there, and they hadn't arrived. They said they wanted to know what had happened, but whenever we explained they didn't seem to believe us.

And this police officer, he kept coming back to this room. He was the one who had asked us the most questions. The others kept coming and going, some of them standing by the door, arms folded, keeping an eye on us, others coming to sit down opposite us and start up the same battery of questions: '*Who is she?*' '*Are you sure you don't know her?*' '*What were you doing out there at that time of night?*' '*Were you drinking?*' '*Taking drugs?*' '*Engaging in sexual acts?*' Over and over, on and on. They were hoping, I realised, that we would slip up. This officer, though, out of all the other ones, seemed most determined to prove we had done something.

'I've got a child about your age,' he said when neither of us spoke to answer his question. 'He'd catch all sorts of hell if he was out behaving like you two at that time of night. Unless he had a very good reason.' He had a hard edge to his voice now. 'So tell me, what were you two doing out at that time of night?' He folded his arms across his chest. 'What very good reason do you have for being out there at that time of night?'

This policeman acted like a man who was taller, wider and more imposing than he really was. His dark blond hair was cut severely at the sides, his shoulders were slightly hunched, which made him look thinner, and he had a scar on his cheek. Whenever he spoke his eyes narrowed and his lips became distorted with a sneer. It was him, I was sure of it, that was keeping us here, stopping us from seeing our dads. I didn't even care that I was going to be in huge amounts of trouble with my parents – I just wanted this to be over.

'You're going to tell me,' he said. 'Whether you want to or not, you're going to tell me what you were doing on that beach with that girl. You're going to tell me which one of you hurt her. *Killed her.*'

Jude broke down. She couldn't take any more. She clung on to my hand, bent her head forwards and started to cry. Her shoulders were shaking and she made small gulping sounds that I'd heard before but not very often. Jude was the strong one, the one who took risks, the one who'd convinced me to lie to my parents and say I was staying at hers for her birthday. Once her mum had gone to work, her dad had told us not to stay up too late because he was heading to the club in Brighton to meet his friends, as he did most Friday nights. We'd told the police this. We'd told them that when her dad had gone out, we'd got ready and gone to a party a sixth-form boy from school was having.

We'd been invited last minute, and Jude liked the boy even though I thought he was far too full of himself. He over-gelled his hair, sprayed on too much aftershave and kept commenting on girls' 'juicy butts'. But when he'd found out Jude's birthday was on the same day as his, he'd come up to her – right in the middle of the canteen – and said, 'Come to my party, if it's your birthday too. Bring your mate with the juicy butt.' And he'd winked at her and then at me and walked away. Everyone around us had just stared and Jude had told us we were definitely going to go.

I hadn't wanted to go. But Jude had persuaded me. Had said it would make us two of the popular girls at last. *No, Jude*, I should be saying to her right then. *It has made us two girls sitting in a police station being told off by a police officer.*

I wanted to cry. But I knew, even if I didn't know anything else, it would make this man happy if we both started crying. He hadn't managed to catch us out, so now he wanted to make us cry. And he'd succeeded with Jude. She was the strong one, usually, but I was the stubborn one – always.

I stared at the man's scar, a dark pink curve that turned his cheekbone into an oval. He glared at me for staring at his scar, and I could almost see him decide it was my turn to cry, too. Jude was probably wise to get it over with, but I wasn't going to let him do that to me. I hadn't done anything out of the ordinary – other girls sneaked out of the house all the time and often did properly wild things. They didn't go to parties and stand at the edges feeling out of place amongst the other people who were drinking and chatting and fitting in with each other – everyone at the party had seemed to know how to be together and we hadn't. The sixth-former who'd invited us to his party had been super-nice – offered us drinks, told us to have some snacks, told us we should go upstairs and play Spin The Bottle if we wanted. But Jude and me, we weren't like them. We were different, younger, and we didn't really belong there.

We'd stuck around for a bit longer, daring each other to try the punch, to try a beer, to try something bright blue that people were downing from small glasses. But neither of us was brave enough. We sat on the sofa and watched the older kids get drunk, then we'd both eventually decided without actually saying anything to each other that it was time to go home. Jude hadn't known what time her dad would get back from the club, so we'd decided we'd have to sneak in and pray that he was still out or asleep. And as we'd been coming home, there she was . . . The girl we found.

And now here we were, the two girls being broken by a policeman.

*I'm not going to cry*, I thought. *I. AM. NOT. GOING. TO. CRY.*

He could see that I wasn't going to give in. 'You two are a couple of those dirty girls, aren't you,' he said quietly. 'You act all good and prim for the parents, but really you're always out, catting about. You can't keep your legs shut. You're dirty girls. Dirty little sluts.'

His words were vicious and cruel, like arrows fired rapidly from a bow, and they made Jude cry more, her weeping loud and uncontrolled. Those words, nasty as they were, made me even more determined. I gently let go of my sobbing best friend's hand and sat back in my seat, folded my arms across my chest and stared right at him. Right at him.

His eyes flashed outrage, and his lip curled as he accepted the challenge – the gauntlet that I, a weedy little teenager who was already in huge trouble with her parents, had thrown down in front of him.

*I am not going to cry*, my face told him.

*You think you can take me?* his nasty smile replied as it slimed wider and wider on his face. *You really think you can take me, little girl?*

He came to the table and slammed his hands down, leant forwards, right into my face. It felt at that moment that it was just him and me in there. Just the two of us about to fight it out. He'd win, but only after a long battle. I wasn't going to make it easy – I wasn't going to cry at the first drop of his toxic words. It would take so much more than he realised. His lips drew back as he loaded more of his poison-tipped words into his bow, ready to fire them at me. I stared straight into his eyes; I was not looking away. He'd made Jude cry, and that was not right. I might be young and I might not know very much, but I did know what he was doing was wrong. We were, at best, witnesses. He had no reason to think of us as suspects, to treat us like convicted criminals.

He snarled: 'How many—'

The door flew open, and suddenly, standing there, big, tall and muscly, was my dad. He seemed to take up the whole of the doorway. I looked down from the policeman and stared at the table because *now* I was going to cry. Now my dad was here, I was going to break down and sob. I couldn't remember a time in my life when I had ever been so happy to see my dad. Now he was here, this policeman would stop.

Straight away the policeman stood upright and backed away from the table.

'Tell me you were not questioning my daughter without an adult present,' Dad said. His voice – outraged but authoritative – sounded amazing to my ears.

The policeman looked at my dad with so much hatred, so much anger. He probably didn't like being stopped mid-flow; he probably hated someone speaking to him with such authority. 'She – *they* – didn't need an adult because I wasn't questioning them,' the policeman replied.

'I am not stupid,' Dad said. 'Judana is crying and my daughter is shaking. What were you doing to them?'

'This is a police station,' the officer replied, suddenly irked that my dad had taken control of the situation. 'I ask the questions here.'

'Not if you will not tell me what you were doing to my daughter and her friend,' Dad stated.

The policeman smirked nastily. 'Are you going to cause problems?' he asked. 'Are you going to need to cool down in a cell and think about how you're talking to a policeman . . . in a police station?'

'I will talk to you however I deem necessary,' Dad replied.

'I think we should all calm down,' Mr Dalton, Jude's stepfather said. The man Jude always called 'Dad' was standing behind my dad, but I hadn't noticed he was there. He was a big man – not as tall as my dad, but still bigger than the nasty policeman with the scar. With him was the policewoman who had left the room earlier, right before the horrible policeman had started calling us sluts.

Jude, who'd stopped crying when Dad walked in and started talking, began to cry again when she heard her dad's voice. Now she was crying because she was in trouble for sneaking out to go to a party. *This* was what we were meant to be crying and shaking about; this was why we were meant to be scared. We weren't supposed to be sobbing about being called names and being made to feel less than human by this horrible man.

'I think it's fair to say this has been a less-than-ideal evening,' Mr Dalton said, 'and I think we would all be better off going home and sleeping on it.' Mr Dalton was a solicitor so I knew he talked to the police all the time. He'd probably spoken to this policeman before. He sounded polite and calm, as though he knew that if everyone was reasonable, everything would be cleared up in no time.

'They are not going anywhere,' the policeman said, but the snarl had left his voice now that he was dealing with Mr Dalton, a white man who was also a solicitor. 'We still have to take their witness statements.'

'Enelle, we are leaving,' Dad said. I didn't need to look at him to know that although he was talking to me, he was staring down

32

the policeman. Despite how Mr Dalton was trying to manage things, Dad's disgust at how we were being treated was not going away, and he was not backing down.

I didn't move. I watched the policeman's face become a red, inkblot-like Rorschach pattern that would scream 'hatred' to whoever looked at it. I had never seen a look like that on anyone's face. It was clear he wanted to hurt my dad because my dad was doing what I had been doing – not giving in. Just like I wasn't going to cry, my dad wasn't going to be intimidated.

'Enelle. Get. Up. We. Are. Leaving.'

The policeman didn't say anything this time and I jumped up, suddenly remembering how much trouble I was in with my father.

'Judana,' Dad said in a slightly softer tone – because she was crying and because she wasn't the daughter who he was going to punish until the end of time – 'we are leaving. Come on, we are taking you home.'

'We do need to talk to the girls,' said the policewoman beside Mr Dalton. 'They're witnesses to a very serious crime.'

'Well, as they are witnesses, you can come to our homes to interview them, with an adult present, when they have had time to sleep and start to deal with what they have experienced tonight.' Dad didn't take his eyes off the policeman as he spoke.

The room was charged; electric, terrifying. Jude's dad looked worried: his eyes moved quickly between my dad and the policeman, clearly wondering what would happen next.

Jude scraped the chair as she stood up, the sharp sound breaking the atmosphere and allowing the policeman to look at the table and Dad to focus on me. He put his arm around my shoulders, this one gesture saying: *I'm here. You're safe.* The look on his face adding that I was in so much trouble I wouldn't be leaving the house to do anything but go to school for the next fifty years.

Jude and I left the building with our dads' arms around us, but I knew it wasn't over with the policeman. I knew that it was a long, long way from being over with him.

# Now

## Nell

'Are you going to call me?' Zach asks. He's sitting up in bed, watching me finish getting dressed after a long, indulgent shower. From the angle he sits at, I can see the top half of his body and it, like the rest of him, has not a single hair anywhere on it. His skin, without hair, was as soft as it was smooth. And I'd delighted in exploring his body without coming up against any 'roadblocks' of hair or stubble.

A couple more hours of sleep transformed how we were together: the kisses turned into caresses turned into the type of sex you pull out for exes who you want to spend years regretting letting you go.

'I gave you my number early on in the evening,' he states when I say nothing to answer his question. 'Are you going to use it?'

The men I've slept with, especially ones I've met in bars, are not usually this direct afterwards. We've both got what we wanted – sex – from the encounter and they can generally leave it there. After all, a woman who goes home with them isn't exactly marriage material in their minds. If they do want to hook up again they'll ask in roundabout ways, often checking their phone or switching on the television, while mentioning giving me a call sometime. The number of men I have met in a bar who later ask me if I'm going to call has, so far, amounted to one: the man in front of me.

He continues to stare at me as I push the rest of my bangles over my hand and up onto my wrist.

Zach has a tattoo. I remember the first tattoo I saw on dark brown skin was on the Brighton Mermaid. Zach's tattoo is very different to hers, of course. His isn't one single tattoo, but a collection of small symbols, curls and lines that stretch from the centre of his chest, over his left pec, capping his left shoulder and spreading down over his left bicep. He must have spent hours sitting still, having the needles inject all that ink into him. Earlier I traced over every millimetre of it with my finger, as fascinated by it as I had been with the Brighton Mermaid's one.

'This silence is starting to drag into awkward,' Zach says. 'Are you going to call me or not?'

I shrug on my jacket. 'I wouldn't wish me on anyone,' I state.

'Well, it's a good thing I'm not you, isn't it?' he replies.

He is gorgeous, there's no escaping it. He is quick-witted and funny. Decent enough to not have sex with me when I was drunk and hadn't explicitly consented. And when we did get to have sex, it was out of this world.

Slowly, I walk to his side of the bed and sit down on the edge. 'Listen—'

'What job is it that you're going to do?' he cuts in.

'Sorry?'

'You said last night that you've been saving for years and finally you're in a position to leave your job as assistant manager of a supermarket to do another job you've been doing on the side for years.'

'I told you all that last night?'

'Yes.'

'Oh.' It's unlike me to be so open with anyone, let alone a complete stranger.

'So, what is it?'

'I find people.' I know how it sounds when I say it out loud. How ridiculous and fanciful, but that is what I do.

'You find people?'

'Yes, I find people.'

'What, you're like a private detective?'

'Not quite. I use genealogy methods to help people find out if they have family out there. I do it by creating a family tree, looking through old records, searching online databases.' And DNA. I also use DNA to help create a fuller picture of a family's history and composition, but that can freak people out. (I learnt *that* the hard way: one guy I'd been seeing for a few weeks thought I'd had sex with him purely to collect the DNA in his semen. Even when I explained it would have been easier to get a skin scraping or to pluck a couple of hairs than to keep a condom, he insisted on checking my bag to make sure I hadn't secreted away the condom – that he'd flushed down the toilet – with his precious seed in it. Unsurprisingly, I didn't see him again – despite him calling me many, many more times.)

Zach nods slowly. 'Right, sounds interesting. Why do you do it?'

I shrug. 'I like doing it.'

'How many people have you found?'

'Over the years? Quite a few. But I've *helped* find more. What I do most of is help people to link things together so they get to the missing parts and strands of their family. I don't regularly go looking for a specific person, like a detective would. I just try to find the unseen leaves on the different branches of a family tree, if you see what I mean?'

'I do see what you mean.'

Being so close to him, I can't help eyeing up his tattoo again. The whorls and curls, shaped and expanded by his firm body, are spectacular and I want to feel connected to them again. I reach out to touch a thick black line that sits on the brow of his shoulder and he catches hold of my wrist to stop me making contact.

'You haven't answered my question,' he reminds me. 'Are you going to call me?' His eyes, without eyelashes, are an intense brown. He's making it clear I'm not to touch him if I don't want anything else to do with him.

I lower my hand. 'Maybe,' I reply.

'Not a "yes", not an outright "no", but clearly a "no" without actually saying the word. Fair enough.' With that, he raises his hands and knits them together behind his head, clearly waiting for me to leave.

Oh.

I should feel better about this, shouldn't I? He didn't try to convince me to ring him; he didn't seem that hurt I wasn't going to call; he accepted what I said with good grace. I should feel good that I didn't actually have to say no and there were no complications, no angst or passive aggressiveness from him. So why don't I feel happy, relieved? Why do I, instead, feel monumentally stupid?

'See you then,' Zach says with a hint of a smile on his face when I don't move.

'Yes, see you,' I reply. Why didn't I say yes? What is there about him not to like? We had a laugh from what I remember of last night; we had brilliant kisses, amazing sex. It isn't like he's proposed marriage and he hasn't treated me like I'm a slag because we had sex without dating. What exactly would stop me from calling? Why exactly would I say 'maybe' when it should be an emphatic yes?

I collect my bag and slip on my shoes, feeling more stupid with every passing second.

I drag my feet when I leave the main room, and head down the short corridor past the bathroom and the wardrobe towards the door. 'I'll pay for the room service downstairs,' I call to him when I'm at the door.

'Cool,' he calls back.

I unhook the chain and place my hand on the handle. *Last chance, Nell,* I tell myself. *Last chance to say you will call.*

'It's a shame you're not going to call,' he says loudly. 'I think we could have had a lot of fun together.'

*Thank you, Zach!* I think as I smile to myself. He's giving me an out, a way to say I will ring him.

'I said I'd maybe call,' I respond.

'All right, I'll wait for your maybe call, Mermaid Lady,' he says.

My blood thickens in my veins all at once and my heart skips several beats. Mermaid Lady? *Mermaid Lady?*

Swallowing the bitter taste that has pooled at the back of my throat, I turn and move stiffly back to the main area of the bedroom. He is still sitting in the same position as before, that same smile on his face. I look around the room, try to see if there's anything that will give me a clue as to who this man is. I know nothing about him, but he seems to know something significant about me.

There's nothing on display in the room – he has put his clothes away in the wardrobe – only a suit jacket hangs over the back of the chair by the desk. The curtains are partially drawn, but even if they were wide open there would be nothing else to see – everything is out of sight. He's either a very neat person – or a man with something to hide.

'What did you say you did again?' I ask him.

'I told you last night.'

'I don't remember much from last night. What was it you do?'

He frowns. 'I'm a teacher. I'm about to start a job up at Surry Hills High, the private school on the way out of Brighton. Near the Marina thing.'

'Yes, I know it,' I say. We all knew the kids from Surry Hills High growing up. They were ultra-posh, even posher than the other children who went to fee-paying schools. 'Bit of an odd time to start a teaching job? It's March, and it'll be Easter in a week or so.'

'One of the teachers left suddenly, didn't work their notice. They called me because I'd previously applied for a job there . . . What's this all about, Nell?' he asks. 'Why all the questions?'

'Why did you call me Mermaid Lady?' I ask in return. I stare directly at Zach as I wait for his answer.

It's been nearly twenty-five years since Jude and I found her on the beach. At the time it was a big thing. Then after what happened to Jude, it became an even bigger thing. Then for two more years it kept getting dredged up as talk of a serial killer haunted all of us who lived down on the south coast.

It died away eventually, submerged under the surface of the constant churn of everyday news. But it's resurfacing, I can feel it. The twenty-five-year anniversary is piquing people's interest. There was a series of articles online about it a few weeks ago, a mention in the paper last week. Talk of a possible reconstruction, see if it would jog anyone's memory from all that time ago to identify her or find out who might have killed her. If that threw up anything, there could be grounds for an exhumation and re-examining of the forensic evidence. All the articles had mentioned me, had talked about what happened to Jude, had stirred up the stuff about my dad's arrest . . . I'd seen each of these articles and had felt sick, actually on the verge of throwing up, because it was all coming back to haunt me again.

Yes, I quit my job so I can concentrate on the mystery of the Brighton Mermaid, but I want no part in someone else's investigation. I don't want to be newspaper fodder again. And I certainly don't want to find out I've slept with a journalist who's writing a story on the Brighton Mermaid, or a ghoul who might know who I am and is trying to sell a story on it.

Zach had been watching me when I spoke to him in the bar, had just been standing there on his own, and now we're in a hotel room rather than his own place. He could be anyone. Right now, I observe him intently, wanting to see every reaction for even the slightest hint of a lie or subterfuge.

'I called you Mermaid Lady because it's pretty much all you talked about last night,' he says. 'Even in your sleep you were mumbling stuff about mermaids.' His frown deepens. 'Was I not meant to call you that?'

I should laugh it off. Dismiss it as nothing; say he can call me what he likes and I won't mind. But I can't. I *do* mind.

'No, you shouldn't call me that. Ever. *Ever.*'

Zach removes his hands from their link behind his head and instead raises them in front of him in surrender. 'I will never call you that again, ever.'

I'm shaking. It must be the alcohol, the after-effects of going so completely over the top last night. It's nothing to do with the visceral pain – the awful, twisted agony that comes from having to talk about this. In my head, on my computer screens, it's OK. When it starts to cross boundaries into real life, it hurts. Quite simply, it hurts.

'Look, I'd better go, leave you alone,' I say to Zach. 'I honestly will think about calling you. But this morning was great. Good. Fun.' All the pleasant words are being wheeled out to smooth things over. He doesn't know anything. I'm just being paranoid. This anniversary stuff is getting to me. I shouldn't take it out on Zach.

He nods. He's clearly not going to risk speaking.

'And I really *will* think about calling you,' I repeat.

Another nod. Although now he looks like he'd rather I didn't call thank you very much.

'I'll see you,' I say.

A third nod.

Now I feel completely ridiculous.

'Yep. I'm going. This is me leaving.'

He raises his hand in goodbye and I practically run to the door, throw it open and leave. How many more times is my connection to the Brighton Mermaid going to have this effect on my life?

# Macy

'Let's do something,' Shane says as he comes into the kitchen.

I look up at him from my phone, which I've been sitting and staring at for hours now. I've done other things, of course, the children have had breakfast and are dressed and settled with books and games and TV, but all the while I've been looking at my phone, willing it to ring. Actually, I've been willing time to go backwards so it can be 5:17 a.m. again and I can call and she will answer her damn phone.

'Do what?' I ask.

'Something. Anything. Let's just get in the van and do something. It looks like it's going to be lovely out today. Let's get out there.'

I glare at my phone again. It's when she does things like this that I want to tell her. I want to tell her what I know so that she can be the one with this burden for once. She can be carrying this secret and all the worry and fear and sheer blinding terror that goes with it. It's when she pisses me off like this that I want to see how she would deal with what I saw twenty-five years ago. No, I didn't see a dead body like Nell did, but what I did see was horrific. How would Nell handle that type of horror? How would she cope with a nightmare much closer to home?

'All right. Let's do something,' I concede.

'Oh, come on! You could sound at least a little more excited about it. We're spending time together as a family. That's what weekends are for, aren't they?' Shane is like the super-keen ambassador of fun at a holiday camp sometimes – he seems to have boundless energy to get everyone up and at it when we need it.

'OK, OK. Let's go do something,' I say as I get up, pocketing my phone. Anything's got to be better than sitting here thinking of ways to understand my sister.

# Nell

*Saturday, 24 March*

**He needs to see you.**

There are five of those messages when I turn on my phone again.
Nothing from Macy.

I read each one, knowing they say the same thing, knowing they
are not only summoning me as though dropping everything to go
and see him is what I am supposed to live for, they're reminding
me that the clock is ticking. I do not have all the time in the world
and if I can't get it right, get this done in the time given, my life is
going to fall apart again. Scratch that: *everyone's* life is going to fall
apart again.

I stand outside the hotel – one of the ones on the seafront. Zach's
room didn't have a sea view, but once I leave the hotel I'm on the
main road, with a view that is endless sea, forever sky. The hotel is
a bit further into Brighton than where we found *her*. That's probably why I started talking to Zach about mermaids. When alcohol
loosens my tongue, anything that reminds me of her makes me
talk about her.

*So what do I do now? Who do I choose to go and spend the afternoon with?*
Macy or him?
Him or Macy?
I look left, towards the Pier. I would love to go there right now,
to blend in among the crowd that has already flocked there, many
of them having got the early train down to make the most of their

day by the sea. On the Pier I would be anonymous, possibly another tourist who's come to experience one of Brighton's world-famous landmarks.

Beyond the Pier, beyond Surry Hills High school, beyond the rolling greens is *him*. Sitting in his wheelchair, waiting. Nothing about him dulled by the passage of time, nothing tamed or relaxed.

I look right. To King's Lawns, the multicoloured beach huts, the 1930s block of flats that starts the run of seafront buildings into Hove. Beyond that art deco seafront building is her. Macy. She's most likely bordering on hysterical by now because I haven't answered my phone. Not only that, I turned it off. If she's called again and hasn't been able to get hold of me, in Macy's mind, this will mean something terrible must have happened to me.

Usually I don't rebel against her anxiety. Usually I answer the phone when she calls, I talk to her, then get to her house as soon as possible to take my place in her family's life. I've ignored her this morning, so if I go and see her now, she will fall apart with relief, then she will snap at me in indignation, then she will slide away from me. She will hold herself in a semi-normal state, only speaking when spoken to, only engaging when it is to get something she needs. Other than that, she will stare at me, hurt at me, and Macy's hurt is something I cannot take.

Macy or him?

Him or Macy?

It has to be one of them.

Because if I choose the third option of 'Nell', which is really just choosing neither of them, I know I'll pay for it double next time.

Macy or him?

Him or Macy?

I've just spent £140 on room service booze from last night. ONE HUNDRED AND FORTY POUNDS. I've budgeted very carefully to get the year off work, and in one night I have blown nearly a fortnight's worth of food shopping. I'm a mess sometimes. An absolutely bloody mess. No wonder Macy regularly side-eyes me.

Even though she's four years younger than me, there's no way she'd do something like this.

Macy or him?

Him or Macy?

Macy. Of course Macy. I was never going to choose anything else.

# Macy

From the top of the hill at Tilgate Park, I stand and watch Willow, Aubrey and Clara tear down the steepest part. Their limbs are flying every which way, their clothes flapping behind them as they race to the bottom. Tilgate is a huge place, rolling hills and greenery, designated outdoor adventure centre, outdoor gym, nature reserve, ponds and lakes.

We've just arrived here and whilst there's glorious sun, there's a nip to the air – spring is almost here but winter seems to be clinging on, sending out its chills to make sure we don't forget it too soon. The clocks will be springing forward tonight, the already lighter evenings will be officially acknowledged. There's change coming – not just a hint of it, a very definite line seems to have been drawn between the recent past, the present and the future.

I don't know what the future will bring. I feel sick sometimes at the thought of it. At the change I feel in the air, at the shift I can sense in my life.

I watch the children run and feel like that is what my life is going to be like from now on. Now Nell has potentially broken the run of good luck we've had by turning off her phone, things will become uncontrolled. That could mean wild, fun and free, and it could also mean unpredictable and terrifying.

There was a series of articles online recently. The person obviously wanted to write a novel, the way they punned and used flowery descriptions, but the net result was this: people looking at me oddly at work because Okorie is not that common a surname; me suddenly being 'friended' on social media by numerous people who knew how to get around my various ways of locking down my accounts (I only ever accept requests from people I've met more than once in real life); and me having that constant sickly feeling of having to tell Nell what I saw twenty-five years ago.

At the bottom of the hill is a wide path and then the lake. I watch the children run, not a care in the world as they race each other to the bottom, and I have to bite my tongue. I want to yell to watch out for other people, to slow down so they won't be catapulted into the water, to watch out for dog poo, to just be so damn careful nothing bad will ever happen to them. Biting my tongue, curling my fingers inwards then digging my nails into my palms – causing myself actual, physical pain – is the only way to stop myself pushing my fears onto them.

Shane doesn't understand – he gets mad with me and tells me to stop putting adult limits on children's natures. It's more a case of adult insight into children's natural ability to seek out trouble, I'd say.

'Aren't you glad we didn't just hang around the house waiting for Nell to grace us with her presence?' Shane asks. He's been to get himself a coffee from the nearest café and checking the sports scores on his phone, no doubt. If I didn't know how much he adores sport and how it's on round the clock in his office at home, I'd be suspicious of him always being on his phone.

'We don't wait for Nell to grace us with her presence,' I reply, because I won't have him rewriting history. I can get annoyed with her but, for many, many reasons that he knows, he can't.

'You know what I mean,' he says.

'If I know it, then say it.'

Shane stops himself sighing, resists rolling his eyes, and instead slings his arm around my shoulders. He buries his face in the nape of my neck and nuzzles a kiss on my slightly chilled skin. 'I love you,' he says. 'Truly. And I love our family being out like this, doing something different, using up the hours on a Saturday for more than competitions and matches and the games your sister plays with the kids.' He pulls away, his bright blue eyes staring into my brown ones. 'That's what I mean to say. Sorry. Now I've said that properly, I understand how what I originally said sounded.' He presses a kiss onto my cheek and I can smell the bitter warmth of espresso on his breath. 'I didn't mean to diss your sister. You know how I feel about her.'

I draw back, out of his hold, and raise unimpressed eyebrows at him.

This time he does groan and he does close his eyes. 'You know what I mean,' he says.

'Kids!' I shout and start to stride down the hill towards where my children are starting to get too close to the water's edge. They managed to stop themselves before they went running into it, but that's no guarantee they'll stay dry. It's nice being out, but Shane convinced me a while back that I don't need to carry a change of clothes for all of them now they're older, so if they get wet now, they stay wet till we drive back home. And I couldn't stand the whole day of them in damp clothes while waiting for the colds that would no doubt arrive once we're home and drying off. 'Willow! Aubrey! Clara! Come away from the edge.'

'I didn't mean it like that,' Shane calls after me. He doesn't care if the people nearby hear him, he just wants me to understand.

'I know what you meant,' I reply over my shoulder. I do, as well, I know *exactly* what he meant.

# 1993

## Nell

Apart from school, Jude was allowed to come to my house and that was it. Me, I wasn't allowed out except for school. Mum and Dad hadn't even bothered saying it – I simply knew it.

After the shock had worn off, after the police had come to take our witness statements at home, it was business as usual for my parents. And that business was punishing me for sneaking out from Jude's house. Secretly, I was pleased. I wasn't like Jude, I didn't mind staying in. I didn't need to be constantly out. The world felt very different. I'd been near a dead body. I'd stood and waited with a dead body. People all over the city knew that I'd seen a dead body. Kids at school whispered about us, giving us a wide berth. It bothered me, a lot more than it seemed to bother Jude.

Although, today, Jude had been over for a while and there was something odd about her.

She kept walking around my room with her hand clenched in a fist. Then she would sigh and sit down. Then stand up as if she was going to do something important. Then pace around the room again.

Jude had started to dress like the woman the police and everyone else called the Brighton Mermaid. The young woman was around nineteen, they said, and had been strangled before being left on the beach. And in the time since we found her, Jude seemed to want to inhabit her persona. She'd stopped wearing make-up, she wore vests and denim skirts, and went barefoot whenever possible. She had stopped plaiting her hair in two neat cornrows like I did, and instead wore it in a cute Afro style with a headband. And the bangles. She had managed – in the time of being grounded – to get herself an armful of bracelets that sat from wrist to elbow on her left arm, so she now jingled when she walked.

The Brighton Mermaid's face and body and tattoo were painted onto the inside of my head, they fit like filters over my eyes, so sometimes when I turned too quickly or from the corner of my eye would catch a glimpse of Jude, my heart would stop. I'd think, just for a second, that the Brighton Mermaid had come for me. It truly gave me the heebie-jeebies, Jude dressing like a dead woman. The only things Jude hadn't copied were the tattoo on her right arm and the charm bracelet that had been the only jewellery on that same arm.

'What did you do, Jude?' I asked her.

It was obvious she'd done something and I was sick of her not settling, of her walking around with a clenched fist, of me seeing her from the corner of my eye and having a shock.

'I had to do something,' she said. 'I had to find a way to keep her with me.'

'What did you do, Jude?' I repeated, a little quieter because now I was scared. She was going to get us into trouble. Huge trouble. I knew her parents were all cool and laid-back, but mine weren't. They still looked at me with disappointment and anger about the fact I'd been out that night. And fear. As well as being let down and annoyed with me, the whole thing had terrified them. Not only because it could have been me instead of that girl without a name who'd ended up on the beach – they were horrified and shaken that I was capable of lies and subterfuge. They'd thought I was different, but I was like all those other teenagers out there who did things behind their parents' backs.

The fact that Jude was allowed out meant that her parents weren't still checking the windows in her bedroom were locked every night, and her mother wasn't still considering giving up her job as a night nurse so she could be in every night. Dad had grocery stores along the coast, and when he had to open up at one of them, he would usually stay there the night before so he could start early. In the last week he'd had to leave the second Mum walked in from work. Yesterday, a staff member had called in sick over in East-bourne and he'd had to leave the shop shut. Their lives were now about being at home, making sure I didn't try to do anything like I had done again.

Our lives had been upended, but that didn't seem to be enough for Jude. She wanted more awfulness to find us because she had done this thing. I knew all of a sudden what she had done and it was terrible.

'Please tell me you didn't,' I said to her. 'Please.'

Slowly her fingers uncurled and there it lay on top of the network of dark brown lines that laced across her palm like branches from a tree. There it lay, the silver charm bracelet, adorned with several different, intricate mermaids, some loops hanging empty as though they had lost their mermaid but were patiently waiting for her to swim back.

I put my hands first on my face, then they covered my mouth. I wanted to scream at her to throw it away, to take that thing out of my bedroom, out of my house because it was most likely cursed.

'Why did you do that?' I said from behind my hands. 'Why?'

I was hot, that feverish type of heat I got when I had chickenpox and I couldn't keep myself upright for very long. I felt sick, that seesaw type of nausea I'd had constantly the last time I had a stomach bug.

'I had to have something of hers. *We* had to have something of hers,' Jude quickly corrected herself. She needed to bring me in on her crime so what she had done wasn't too bad. '*We* need something so we'll never forget, never give up trying to find out who she is.'

'They'll probably lock us up when they find out what you've done,' I said. She had done it, but I would get into trouble right along with her. 'How did you do it?'

She looked unsure of herself then. She glanced at the door that she'd closed behind her, pausing as though someone might have their ear pressed against it, eavesdropping. To be fair, Macy probably *was* out there doing that.

Jude came closer and then sat on the edge of my bed, near where I had pulled up my legs to my chest, trying to comfort myself. 'When I came back from the phone call, you turned your back and I took it then.'

'Oh my God, Jude!' I screeched.

'Shhhh,' she hushed desperately. 'Shhhh.'

'You touched a dead body to steal from it!' I was shaking. Uncontrollably quivering. I started to bite the large knuckle of my thumb. The pain of my teeth pushing on my skin almost hard enough to draw blood was comforting in a perverse way – it kept me focused on my pain rather than the craziness of my best friend.

I hated Jude sometimes. She was my best friend and I loved her, but she was constantly doing things like this. She was always acting first and then I was paying the price later. I hated her. So much.

'You've robbed from the dead, Jude,' I said to her. 'That's the lowest of the low.'

'No it's not,' she snapped. 'What's lowest of the low is that no one cares any more.'

'Who doesn't care?'

'Them lot out there,' she said, and waved her hand at the windows. 'It's not even on the news any more. They've stopped caring that she doesn't have a name and that we don't know who she is or if anyone cared about her and is searching for her.

'She looks like us, Nell. That could be me or you strangled – and probably raped – on the beach and no one would care after a couple of weeks. It's not right.'

'But you can't change that by stealing from her.'

'I'm not stealing from her. I'm borrowing it. Once we find out who she is and where she comes from, I'll give it back. Until then, we have to keep it to remind ourselves to never forget.'

I couldn't forget, and I had tried. I had tried so hard. But her face was the one I saw every time I closed my eyes; her tattoo was what I saw when I put lotion on myself after my bath; her hair was the style I suspected my hair would be in if I didn't plait it every week. I couldn't forget her, and even if we did find out who she was, what her name was, where she had come from, I knew that wouldn't change. I knew I would keep on seeing the Brighton Mermaid for ever.

'I promise,' Jude said to me in my little bedroom, 'I will give it back as soon as we find out who she is.'

# Now

## Nell

They were out.

After bracing myself for Macy's hurt, I'd arrived at their little corner of Hove to find Shane's people carrier gone, and the door went unanswered. They'd managed to organise a perfectly good Saturday without me, apparently, and it was only the lingering remains of my hangover and the fact that I'd had to go past my flat to get to their house that caused me to have a kick of irritation about it. In the main, it is good that I don't have to spend the afternoon apologising to Macy and avoiding Shane.

I shut my blue front door behind me and lean against it for a second or two, just drinking in the space, the only area of this whole planet that is mine, all mine.

That's part of the reason why I usually go home an hour or so after I've been with someone. I love walking through my front door and knowing that whoever I have been 'out there' – worker, friend, lover – is not who I have to be in here. Whichever mask I am wearing comes off at the door and I can shed the persona I put on for the outside world and just be me.

I want a shower. I had a long one earlier in Zach's hotel room, but I want another in my own home, with my own soap and body lotion. Then I want to put on my fluffiest pyjamas, top them with my furriest dressing gown, and then pick at leftovers from the fridge. I know I should get right at it, go straight to my desk and start this renewed search, but I can't face it. Yes, I've been thinking about the Brighton Mermaid and I've been thinking about Jude, but the will to work at it is absent.

I shed my jacket and shoes, and this simple act causes a wave of exhaustion to crash over me. It's not just being up late, or drinking too much, or even the physical stuff with Zach earlier. It's the other thing. The thing that clings to *every*thing that I can't shake off.

# 1993

## Nell

*Thursday, 15 July*

'Enelle, wake up,' Dad's voice said.

I could tell by the way he said it that he'd been calling me for a long time. I'd hardly slept in the weeks since we found *her*. Every time I closed my eyes I kept seeing her face. Sometimes it was all right, her eyes were open and she was laughing. Her face was warm, her smile was wide and her happiness danced in her brown eyes. Other times – most times – she was cold and still; there was no smile on her face and her brown eyes were unstaring and frozen. I couldn't take those dreams. When I clawed myself away from them, forced myself into wakefulness, I would lie still in the dark and pant away my fear. Then I would bury my face into my pillow to cry. I hadn't told anyone that I battled sleep to avoid the dreams; I hadn't confessed that I cried and cried into my pillow to stop myself running out into the dark to try to find out who she was and where she came from because that would be the only way to stop her haunting me.

I couldn't tell anyone what was going on because Jude seemed fine with it. She didn't seem upset and bothered, and I wondered, more than once, if that was because she had the mermaid charm bracelet and it kept the bad dreams away.

The last two or three nights, though, I'd slept. I'd gone to bed at normal time and woken up when it was light outside. Each time I'd felt almost ashamed at that: as Jude had been so mad about a couple of weeks ago – a poor young woman had been murdered and I was starting to put it behind me.

'Enelle,' Dad repeated, 'are you awake?'

'Yes, Daddy?' I replied, and struggled to sit up.

He put his finger over his lips, to tell me hush and, I guessed, not wake Macy, whose room was next to mine. 'Get your dressing gown and come downstairs,' he said quietly.

'What time is it?' I asked.

'Don't ask questions,' he said. 'Just get your dressing gown and come downstairs.'

His voice, even though it was quiet, sounded very serious and it set my tummy spinning. I hadn't felt this sick with worry since I'd seen that Jude had stolen the mermaid charm bracelet. Maybe that was it. Maybe the police had found out and had come to ask me about it. I *knew* it would get us into trouble. Jude had started to wear it, hidden it among the other dozens of bracelets she now wore on both arms, and I'd told her the police weren't stupid, that they'd eventually come knocking on our door because they'd find out somehow, and that she would probably be arrested if she got found with it. *That* had got through to her and she'd started to keep it in her pocket instead.

I pulled on my dark blue dressing gown over my pink nightdress and followed my dad downstairs, both of us walking quietly on the perpetually creaky stairs. What was I going to do if they asked me about the bracelet? Would I lie and say I didn't know where it was? I didn't though. I mean, I knew Jude had it, but I didn't know where it was right then. Maybe I could say that? I could say I didn't know exactly where it was and just hope they didn't ask me if I knew *who* had it.

In the living room, Mum, dressed in dark brown, was sitting on the settee, right next to Jude's mum, Mrs Dalton, who was also dressed in dark brown. They sat so close together, Mum with her hands covering Mrs Dalton's, that it was almost impossible to see where my mum began and Jude's mum ended.

Jude's mum was sobbing. Not loudly, but definitely. Her shoulders were rounded and shaking, her body stopping every few seconds to quake, and her fingers were gripped tightly onto Mum's hands. She looked like she was clinging on to Mum for dear life.

Mr Dalton stood in front of the fireplace, looking greyish-pale, his blue eyes as dull as his complexion. I had barely stepped foot over the living room threshold when Mrs Dalton virtually threw herself out of her seat and launched herself at me.

'Where is Judana?' she demanded, grabbing hold of my arms. Through my dressing gown I could feel her fingers digging into my soft flesh. Mrs Dalton's eyes were wild, unfocused, puffy from the sobbing, as she pushed her face right into mine. Her usually neatly curled hair stuck out at all different angles, matching her ferocious expression. This was so unlike Jude's mum. Both our mothers were always neat, perfectly made-up and well turned out.

'Lilani, Lilani,' Mr Dalton said, coming over to us. 'Let her go.'

'Tell me where my daughter is!' Mrs Dalton shouted. 'Tell me!'

Jude's dad managed to prise her fingers from me. The tops of my arms throbbed with the imprints of her hands. I rubbed at them, absently. More intense than the pain in my arms was the fear of what she was saying, how she was acting.

Mr Dalton delivered his wife back to my mum on the sofa, and Dad came to stand beside me. 'I'm sorry about that,' Mr Dalton said reasonably. He was the calmest man I'd ever met. Jude was allowed to get away with lots of things I was sure Mrs Dalton wouldn't have let her get away with because he was so laid-back.

'Enelle, now I'm going to ask you a question,' he said. 'Something very, very important. Judana didn't come home from school earlier today. We want to know where she is. Can you please tell me where she is?'

Dad placed his hand on my shoulder. I looked up at him and found he was staring down at me. 'Tell us what you know, Enelle,' he said.

I was sure my eyes widened and I started to bite my lower lip. 'I don't know, Daddy,' I eventually replied.

'You do know!' Jude's mum shouted suddenly.

I stepped closer to my dad. If Mrs Dalton shouted again, I was going to step behind my father and hide.

'Lilani, stop. *Stop*,' Mr Dalton said. This was the first time I'd seen him this upset, and I'd *never* heard him raise his voice, even when he seemed annoyed. I remember Jude saying once that her dad never shouted. Even when she had stand-up screaming rows with her mum (a regular thing), he would step in to calm things down without shouting. Even when she did something bad like sneaking out with me and finding a dead body, he didn't yell.

'I'm sorry, Nell – *we're* sorry, Nell. We just need to find Judana. We thought she went to school today but when she didn't come home, we called the school. We've been waiting for her to turn up. But we couldn't leave it any longer. Do you know where she is?'

I shook my head. I honestly didn't know. When she didn't turn up for school today, I thought she was off sick. I was going to call her earlier in the evening, but then I'd had to do my homework and then it was dinner and then my chores. By then it was after nine o'clock and there was no way Mum and Dad would let me use the phone to call Jude or anyone. *I'll see her tomorrow*, I'd thought as I got into bed. We were the daughters of nurses so it was very, very rare that we got more than one day off school when we were ill. *I'll see her tomorrow, and find out how she managed to get a day off school.*

'Did she come to school?' Mr Dalton asked.

I shook my head. 'She . . .' I began, but my voice sounded croaky and thick, like it'd been dunked in tar. I cleared my throat. 'She wasn't at the end of the road where we meet to go and get the bus, and she wasn't at the bus stop. I thought she was off sick so I got the bus without her.'

Mr Dalton looked at Mrs Dalton and something seemed to dawn on them at the same time. 'I thought she'd got up and left for school early,' Mr Dalton said, because, I assumed, Mrs Dalton would have been at work.

Mrs Dalton's face creased up all over again and she began to rock. 'She wasn't there the night before, was she?' she said. 'She wasn't there the night before and neither of us knew.'

Mum glanced at Dad, and a look passed between them before they both turned to face me. *Is this what you're going to do next, Enelle?* they were both silently asking. *Have you got a plan to run away now you've got experience of sneaking out of the house, too?*

The answer was no, of course. I wouldn't run away. And I'd had no idea Jude was going to do it, either.

'I think we'd better call the police,' Dad said calmly.

That spooked me, scared me. After he'd had to come to the station, after the interview at home, 'I hope that is the last time we have anything to do with the police,' Dad had said to me and Macy. Mostly to me because, of course, it was all my fault they were there in the first place. For Dad to suggest they get involved now, that meant he was frightened. In fact – I looked from one lined, weathered adult face to another – they were all terrified.

My gaze swept over the faces around me again: they weren't simply scared that Jude had run away – they were all scared that she was going to end up like the Brighton Mermaid. I wasn't sure if they knew that right up until she'd left, Jude had looked like her. Was she going to end up like her, too?

'Yes, yes we should,' Mr Dalton said shakily, and I saw him wobble where he stood. Carefully, as though he was drunk and trying not to show it, he moved across the room to the sofa and sat next to his wife. He took her hands in his pale peach ones and then spoke to my dad: 'Could you . . . Could you please call them for me?' He spoke very carefully, very quietly – trying to hide the tremors shaking his words. 'Could you call the police and tell them my daughter has gone missing?'

*Thursday, 15 July*
The awful policeman with the vicious-looking scar on his cheek came with a policewoman to ask me questions about Jude, but he

didn't say a word. He stood by the fireplace and glared at me as I told the policewoman everything Jude and I had done and talked about the day before yesterday.

'*She wasn't upset about anything, no.*'

'*She didn't have a boyfriend, no.*'

'*No one was bullying her at school. Well, no more than any of them had since we'd found, you know, her, on the beach. But no one really said anything. Most of them just stared at us and whispered.*'

'*No, that didn't upset us. We kind of got used to it.*'

'*No, Jude never talked to me about running away. Not ever. We never talked about that sort of thing.*'

'*I wouldn't run away, no.*'

'*No, I'm not just saying that because my dad's standing there. I've never wanted to run away – why would I?*'

'*OK, maybe most teenagers do want to run away, I don't.*'

'*No, I don't know where she'd go.*'

'*The only place we've been to is London a couple of times on the train. Most of the time our dads drive us to places.*'

'*Yes, I know even though Jude calls Mr Dalton 'dad' he is her stepfather.*'

'*I'm nearly fifteen so yes, I know that means they're not biologically related to each other and that's why she's black and he's white.*'

Even though he didn't say anything, I knew the awful policeman was staring at me and in his head twisting every word I spoke, using it to prove to himself that I was a dirty girl, a dirty little slut like he'd marked Jude and me out to be. While he stared at me, I knew my dad was staring at him, making him feel like he was making me feel.

I tried to concentrate, though. This was important. I knew that everything I said could be a clue – *the* clue – that would help them find Jude. Because I didn't like her being away. Because if she had run away, that meant she was far more likely to meet someone who could do to her what someone did to the Brighton Mermaid. Because I needed Jude back.

Jude and I had sort of known each other before we were born. Our mums had met working at a hospital in Hayward's Heath, and had become instant friends. They were very different – Mum was very serious, very considered in all she did. (Dad used to make it his mission to get her drunk on watered-down sherry.) Jude's mum, on the other hand, liked to party and apparently she did a lot of it before Jude's father had died in a car crash in a work vehicle, two months before Jude was born.

Although Jude's mum eventually got a decent pay-out for his death in service, Mum regularly told Dad that Jude's mum would often say, 'I'd give it all back in a second if I could have my Raymond back.' Jude's mum first met Mr Dalton while the death-in-service claim was going through, and then three years later they had run into each other in the street and had hit it off.

I couldn't remember a time when Jude and I weren't together, weren't best friends. We didn't look alike, but we liked it when people thought we were sisters. Even when we fell out – which was rare – we'd make it up really quickly because there never seemed to be much point in being cross with Jude. She was who she was and I was who I was. Even when I hated her, hated the things she did that got me in trouble, I could only do that because I knew she'd always be there for me to love, too. I wouldn't hate her sometimes if I couldn't love her twice as much all the time.

The police had to find her. She wouldn't be safe anywhere else. I knew that. They had to find her.

'Is there anything else you'd like to tell us about, Enelle?' the policewoman asked.

'Like what?' I replied.

From her pocket she produced a clear plastic bag with a silver charm bracelet at the bottom.

I'd wanted to tell them about it. Had wanted to say that she had it and it was cursed and I hadn't told because I didn't want to get her into trouble, but the nasty policeman was in the room with us. I kept remembering how he'd treated us when we had done nothing wrong. The thought of what he would do, say, when we *had* done something wrong had been enough to make me hold my tongue.

'Like this,' she said.

My mouth was dry and I felt sick again, just like I did the first time Jude had shown me the thing. I didn't speak.

'Neither of her parents recognise it. We think it's quite coincidental that she had this hidden away in a book that she used to store articles about the Brighton Mermaid. Did this belong to Judana or the Brighton Mermaid?'

I couldn't speak. I wanted to, but couldn't.

'Was this Judana's bracelet?' the officer tried again. I hadn't thought much of this policewoman when she was questioning me before, but now I could see how sharp she actually was. She'd waited until she had as much information from me as possible before she presented this.

I shook my head.

'Did she take it from the body you both found?'

Hesitant nod; terrified nod.

'Is that why Judana has run away? Did she take it and did you say you were going to tell on her?'

I shook my head quickly. 'I would never tell on her. Never.'

'I see.' The policewoman fixed her gaze on me. 'Do you know where Judana is but aren't telling because she asked you to lie for her?'

'No, no,' I say. 'I really don't know where she is. I wish I did. If I knew, I would tell you. If I'd even heard from her I would tell. I promise. I would tell you. I want her back more than anyone. I just want her back.'

The policewoman nodded. I wasn't sure if she believed me or not but she told me to contact her the second I heard anything and then sat back to look over her notes.

I couldn't help myself now I wasn't talking to the policewoman – I turned my head towards the awful policeman, standing like a malevolent statue by the fireplace. He had a triumphant sneer shading his lip. *I was right about you two*, his nasty, narrowed eyes were saying to me. *Dirty girl, dirty little slut.*

Suddenly Dad was there: he stepped between us, stopped the policeman from what he was doing. I could only see Dad's strong back, but I could tell he had his arms folded across his chest and he was staring at the policeman, glaring at him to let him know that he was going to protect me from anything this man tried to do to me.

*It doesn't matter*, I wanted to say to Dad. *I don't really care what the policeman thinks of me, how he looks at me, what he wants to say to me. As long as he helps find Jude, I don't care much about him at all.*

# Now

## Nell

*Saturday, 24 March*

My office blinds are closed so the room is in partial darkness, the light outside too weak to force its way into the room. There's something comforting about standing in the half-light, looking at the shapes of your world.

I have three computers that I use to find people. One doesn't connect to the Internet, ever, so I keep all my files on there, stripped of all the things that 'tag' you and give away vital information to other people. One computer is solely for the Internet and still runs with pretty high software and data protections. The third is a backup of the other two computers. The backup computer sits on top of the chest of drawers I use to store my files, while the other two computers sit side by side on my desk, Post-its and notes tacked at various points around the screens.

I have large noticeboards all over the room and a whiteboard. Stuck on them are family trees, DNA sequencing printouts, information about the people I'm helping with their searches, newspaper articles, other printouts. There are also pictures that Macy's children have drawn for me over the years.

Right now I'm staring at the photograph of Jude I have pinned up on the noticeboard behind my desk.

I don't have many of her. We were friends and teens before selfies and social media and storing images on mobile phones. We were buddies when not taking your camera film to the shop meant not getting that photo. The picture on my noticeboard

*69*

is one of us on our first day of secondary school but I've cut myself out of it, so it's just Jude standing outside in our garden. She has her hair plaited into neat cornrows, she wears small gold sleeper earrings, and she's smiling at the camera.

Jude and I were so similar, so close, and so very different, too. She made me laugh, made me angry, made me scared, made me jealous when she got something I didn't. And then she vanished.

# 1993

## Nell

'We will have to go down to Blatchington Road to get all your uniform—'

Mum was cut short by the banging at the front door. All of us at the dinner table jumped and then froze, shocked at how loud the sound had been.

No one had ever knocked that hard at our door, especially not during dinner. Dad was the first to recover, to unfreeze and then to move from his seat, ready to go and answer the bang.

And suddenly there was another bang as the front door was, it sounded like, kicked open, slamming back against the wall as it gave way.

Then footsteps – loud and determined; thundering and threatening – were coming down our corridor. It sounded like an army was headed our way, stampeding towards us with no sign of stopping.

Dad was near the door by the time they arrived – six of them, dressed in uniform, all large, all terrifyingly grim-faced. None of them stopped, not one of them broke stride as they barrelled towards Dad.

Macy started screaming, Mum drew back in her seat and I got to my feet. Many hands grabbed my father, pulling him, pushing him, forcing him down onto the brown paisley carpet with such force there was an almighty loud thud as he hit the floor.

Macy's screams tipped over into hysteria, the sound deafening and horrifying. Mum was frozen where she sat, petrified.

I moved. I ran forwards, grabbed at the men who had Dad and started to pull them away. My fingers slipped on their rough uniforms, my body was no match for their strength, but I kept going, kept trying to help my father . . . Except of course I wasn't doing any of that. Macy screamed, my mother sat frozen – and I was rooted to the spot, too shocked to do anything.

Six men pinned down my father: one of the policemen had his knee in the small of Dad's back; another had his hands on Dad's neck and face, pushing them into the floor; a third looked like he was resting all his weight on Dad, trying to cause as much pain as possible.

I couldn't move and I couldn't stop it.

I'd never seen such violence before. It was different from television. This wasn't removed and distant and fake. This was real, this was live, this was brutal. All I could do was watch as Dad's facial muscles were tautened by torture, his body twisted and held in unnatural ways, blood spilling from his mouth. This was brutal and horrifying; cruel and inhumane. We'd heard they could be like this, that the people who had sworn to protect us could be viciously violent, but that was something that happened to other people – to criminals, to the guilty. It didn't happen to people like us who lived in the nice parts of Brighton and had jobs and went to school and paid our bills on time. This sort of thing happened to other people who weren't respectable.

'*Mr* Okorie,' said the policeman with the scar on his cheek and the hate in his eyes as he arrived in the dining room doorway. He looked satisfied with himself as he watched my dad being held down, as though one of his dreams had finally been fulfilled.

I looked at him and I knew instantly what this was – my father had made him feel small, weak and stupid. He knew he could never come up against Dad and have a physical advantage, so he had done the next best thing – he'd found someone else to do it for him.

'*Mr* Okorie,' he repeated, 'we meet again. And I somehow *knew* it would be under these circumstances.' He didn't move from the doorway as he spoke. '*Mr* Okorie, do you remember that Christmas eleven years ago when you were found to be over the limit while driving a car? Oh yes, your solicitor claimed it was eighty milligrams of blood alcohol and therefore simply *on* the limit, but we all know the law is the law. They can't stretch it to suit anyone. Why am I bringing this up? Because that "incident" helped to provide myself and my colleagues with your fingerprints.

'After processing all of the fingerprints from Judana Dalton's bedroom, we discovered evidence that you were in her room. All over it, in fact. Your fingerprints turned up in places where a grown man's hands should not be in a young girl's room. Which has led us to believe that you had something to do with Miss Dalton's disappearance, and that you probably had something to do with the murder of the young woman your daughter so coincidentally found on the seafront.'

'*No! This isn't right! This isn't true!*' I was silently screaming. '*My dad's the most gentle man in the world! He wouldn't do any of what you're saying!*'

Mum's eyes, already round from the shock of what was happening, widened even more. Macy had stopped screaming at some point, and I looked to see if she understood what was going on. She had her face in her hands and her shoulders were shaking.

'It's a shame your family had to be here to see this,' the policeman continued. 'But we were sure a big . . . *black* fella like yourself would resist arrest, so we couldn't take any risks.'

I shook my head. *No, no. This can't be happening.*

'Take him away and somebody inform him of his rights.'

The six uniformed men hauled my dad up and carried him out of there like a side of meat, not like a human being at all. My dad hadn't resisted, he hadn't even said a word, had barely moved.

They did not need to do that to him. They did not need to treat him like that.

The policeman with the scar was staring at me now, controlling his face to hide his glee at the situation. 'See you again soon, Miss Okorie,' he said with a ghost of a smile. 'Very soon.'

He hadn't made me cry, like he'd wanted two months ago, but he had got me. Finally. And, more importantly, he'd got my dad.

# Now

## Macy

*Saturday, 24 March*

The children are eating ice cream from small tubs with little wooden spoons. They chose their own flavours, they were overgenerous with the sprinkles, and now they all sit on the same side of the wooden picnic bench niggling at each other in between mouthfuls. It's not warm enough for ice cream, but when Shane mentioned it – quietly so they couldn't hear – I said yes. Mainly to make up for the rubbish week they don't know they have ahead.

I watch them and think of the times when Nell and Jude and I could be like that. Daddy would take us out somewhere and we'd sit together, Nell and Jude often talking in their secret code, but sometimes letting me be a part of them. Sometimes Daddy would buy us ice cream, but we weren't allowed to tell Mummy because she would freak out about us eating in the street *and* having food from vans when they were basically germ palaces.

Over the years, I've tried to pinpoint where it was that our lives changed. That we stopped being able to do things like go out to the park, or hang out at one of Daddy's grocery shops, or even just be a normal family.

I used to think nothing was the same from that moment when Nell and Jude found the dead body on the beach. I know I'm supposed to call her by that name, but if I do, it makes everything about that time seem vaguely romantic, a mystery that has endured through the ages. And for everyone else, I'm sure it is. But the reality, when you're on the other side of the mystery? Not so romantic. Not so charmingly intriguing.

Nell and Mummy, I'm sure, think our lives were recast when Daddy was arrested that first time. I don't blame them for thinking that. Seeing the barbarity of how the police took him, hearing the voice of that policeman, feeling the terror from Nell and Mummy and not being able to do anything – those were some of the worst moments of my life. But it wasn't then.

'*Mama . . .*' Aubrey says in his well-rehearsed wheedling voice. He's the youngest, the one closest to still being my baby, and therefore the most likely to get whatever he wants, so the other two regularly get him to ask for stuff.

'Yes, darling?' I reply in the same tone.

'Can we have a tiny bit more ice cream?' he asks.

I look from Willow's face to Clara's face to Aubrey's face. They all beseech me: *Let us have this. We don't get ice cream very often so, please, Mum, can we? Can we? Can we?*

'Yeah, sure, why not,' I reply.

*This week's going to hell in a handbasket anyway – why shouldn't they arrive with rotting teeth and high blood sugar levels?*

Daddy had grocery shops called From Our Earth all along the coast, but the one in Hove was the first and the biggest. When people started coming to his shop they were curious about the vegetables and fruits from all over the world that he sold. He told Nell and me that people would come in and spend ages picking up things and saying, 'And how would I cook this?' 'How would you eat this?' 'What does this taste like?'

He held tasting sessions, cooking lessons, would give out recipe sheets. It took him a while, but eventually people started coming to From Our Earth on a regular basis. After nearly ten years in the business, he'd bought the shop next door and expanded, going on to open up places all along the coast. The Hove one took up a substantial part of the parade of shops that backed onto the seafront and was as much a part of the community as the fish and chip place five doors down.

The week after Daddy's arrest, the Hove shop was vandalised. Someone scrawled 'MURDERER' across the front window. The next night someone broke the front window. But it wasn't even then that our lives changed.

Everything was irrecoverably altered when Jude disappeared.

Not the night everyone thinks she left, but the night she *actually* vanished. *That* was the night it went wrong. That was the night when I saw the thing that has been slowly driving me crazy for more than half my life. That was the night when I realised I could never really trust my father.

# Nell

*Saturday, 24 March*

**He needs to see you.**

Five more of those messages this evening. Five more. I read this latest one in bed at 11:30 p.m. What does he think is going to happen? That I'm going to jump into my car and drive over there right this second? *As if.*

I delete the message.

I stare at my phone while it's in my hand. Zach has been on my mind all day. I'd found his number earlier, slipped into the slanted zip-up pocket of my jacket, and I'd typed it into my phone because I didn't want to lose it before I decided whether or not I am going to call him. There's something about him . . . He has such self-confidence and self-possession but not a scrap of arrogance with it. I want to see him again.

I know the clock is ticking, though, and I know, realistically, I don't have a year. I have until the anniversary, so three months, if I'm lucky. But *he* agreed a year, negotiated up from six months. I have to find a solid, tangible genetic link out there that will keep *him* at bay and get me the full year.

So I probably shouldn't text Zach. I probably shouldn't do anything that isn't 100 per cent focused on finding out who the Brighton Mermaid is, and what happened to Jude.

Zach's kisses, though . . . I thought it was the tequila making everything swirly, but it was him. It was all him. I haven't met many men who have done that to me and seemed like decent blokes as well. I haven't met many men who I could quite happily spend the day cuddling and chatting to, should I dismiss that because of what the man who is controlling me might do? Before I can change my mind, I type

**Not quite a call. But will it do? N x**

and hit send.

My phone bleeps almost straight away.

**It will definitely do. Now I get to call. :) x**

I probably shouldn't have done that, but it doesn't have to change anything. I just have to work twice as hard now to make sure I hit my three-month deadline.

# Now

## Nell

*Sunday, 25 March*

*Ring, ring, ring.*

I don't need to look at the clock to see what time it is. It didn't work yesterday, so she's trying again today. Same time, different day. This is the afterwards of finding the Brighton Mermaid, of Jude disappearing. This is what I can't walk away from.

*Ring, ring, ring.*

This is my second chance. An opportunity to make up for yesterday. This is what I am always doing. Making up for yesterday, or yesteryear.

*Ring, ring, ring.*

I don't want to pick up the phone. For some reason I just don't want to. I can't face it. I want to hide away and not deal with anything today.

After the high of yesterday, the reality has come crashing in on me this morning and I don't think I can do it. I can't take on Macy's worries as well as everything else.

*Ring, ring, ring.*

I'm not going to do it. I'm just not.

*Ring, ring, ring.*

# 1993

## Nell

*Tuesday, 12 September*

'You know he was screwing your friend, don't you?'

The awful policeman with the hate-filled eyes and scar on his cheek was called John Pope and he was waiting for me at the bus stop. I didn't see him until I'd got off the 1A with the other children from my school.

When everyone else had gone, dispersed in their different directions, there he was, standing with his arms folded across his body, leaning against the shelter. It'd been two months since Jude had disappeared and the world was skew-whiff, odd-shaped and colourless without her. It'd been just over two weeks since my dad was arrested. He'd been released without charge because the 'evidence' of Dad having been in Jude's bedroom turned out to be his fingerprints on books that had come from my house. Dad often helped us with our homework and sometimes I left my books at Jude's house, sometimes Dad used her ones to help us. Everything that had Dad's fingerprints on had mine on them too. There were no other fingerprints anywhere else in Jude's room, despite what John Pope had said the first time around.

It was a week since Dad had been rearrested. This time because a witness had called to say they'd seen a man matching Dad's description with a girl matching Jude's description on the night she disappeared *and* they had seen him on the seafront the night the Brighton Mermaid was found. The second time they took him in, they'd kept him there for four days, getting the permission needed to do so, while various lines of investigation were pursued. Until they couldn't hold him any longer and had to let him go.

I'd seen John Pope around since that second time, staring at me, watching me – basically stalking my family – but he'd never spoken to me before. Now he was speaking to me, I couldn't walk away. Like when they'd arrested Dad that first time, I wanted to move but my legs would not work.

'You know it's true, don't you? Your father was screwing your friend and he got rid of her to make sure no one found out. Maybe she got pregnant. Maybe she was going to tell. But you know he did it. And you know, deep down, that he was probably screwing that poor girl you found, too.'

It didn't happen: Dad didn't do that – he wouldn't; Jude didn't do that – she wouldn't. I wanted to say that to him, but I knew if I spoke to him he would find something else to say that would smear horrible things in my ears and whittle hideous images into my mind. He just needed me to engage with him once and then he would never let me go.

*You're sick*, I thought. *You're sick and disgusting.*

'How does that make you feel?' he asked. 'To know your father is a pervert. Or did you already know how depraved your father is?'

This was all my fault. I should have said no to Jude that night. I shouldn't have let her convince me to go along with her to that party. I should have said no and none of this would be happening.

'Think about it,' John Pope said as he walked away. 'Think about it.'

*Saturday, 16 October*

'Eastbourne Police say the body of a young woman that was found on the beach in the early hours of this morning is *not* that of missing Hove teenager Judana Dalton. Miss Dalton has been missing from her home since the fifteenth of July. Police are treating the death of this young woman as suspicious and are linking the incident to that of the death of the young woman dubbed the Brighton Mermaid, who was found on Brighton beach in June of this year by Miss Dalton and her friend Enelle Okorie. More details as we have them.'

Silence exploded in our living room. We hadn't been chatting when the news had started, but now a different type of hush fell over us as Mum paused in her crochet; Macy, who was stretched out on the floor in front of the sofa, immediately stuck her finger in her mouth and began chewing at her nail; Dad, who had been completing a crossword puzzle, stopped and looked up at the television; and I curled my knees even tighter to my chest, trying to make myself as small as possible.

*Wednesday, 20 October*
'He was right here with us,' Mum said to the police officers. 'All night. He was right here.'

They weren't in uniform and they had knocked on the door. They were polite – almost respectful – as they asked my father to come in to answer a few questions about the young woman who was labelled the Eastbourne Mermaid.

Another mermaid. Another unidentified young woman who had been strangled; who had been left without shoes; who showed signs of sexual activity that was most likely assault (the papers had hinted that she'd been repeatedly raped); who was found within walking distance of one of Dad's shops ('walking distance' being a good fifteen minutes).

The officers smiled knowingly at Mum because, of course, they'd heard that sort of thing from a suspect's family before, and then they repeated their request for Dad to come in for a talk.

Dad got his coat and we all knew as he shut the door behind him that it was all going to start again. And it was going to be so much worse than before.

\*

*Monday, 25 October*

'Are you Nell Okorie?'

There were a group of them. Ten or so. Mainly boys, a couple of girls. They looked vaguely familiar, most of them being in the sixth form, so slightly older than me. Their pale white faces, cast grey in the falling darkness, all had the same expression: mouths single straight lines, eyes hard and narrowed.

I'd been cutting down across the back fields of school to get to the little pathway that would take me to a bus stop closer to home. I'd started to avoid my usual bus stop on the main road because it felt like everyone was staring at me. Another mermaid, two arrests, one 'chat under caution', 'MURDERER' viciously scrawled across the Hove shopfront several times and countless home raids meant everyone knew who I was. It didn't seem so bad for Macy – she still had her group of friends and she didn't appear to be bothered by the stares and comments and whispers. Maybe it was different for me because I'd found the first woman and because I was Jude's friend. But I couldn't stand it, so I'd started to walk this way after school, and by the time I'd get to the bus stop, a few buses would have gone, most of the children would have got on them and I could get home relatively unnoticed.

I hadn't clocked this lot following me, and now they were all around me. I said nothing to the tall boy who'd asked the question. He wouldn't be asking if he didn't already know.

'Are you Nell Okorie?' asked the even taller boy next to him.

I said nothing and stared instead at the space between them. If I moved suddenly, I could fit between that gap and run for it. I could make it down the path that was a steady downward slope, through the line of trees, through the fence and out onto the main road. They wouldn't do anything on the main road with loads of other people around. If I could make it to the main road I'd be—

The first shove came from behind. The second shove came from behind also and didn't let me right myself so I flew forwards, landed on my hands and knees, scraping away skin on the cold, hard earth.

I moved to get up, and 'Killer!' one of them spat just before pain exploded in my side. Someone had kicked me.

'Killer!' came another voice, followed by another kick.

'Killer! Killer! Killer!' The world was suddenly filled with that word as I threw my hands over my head and curled forwards, trying to make myself really small as they kicked at me and chanted, 'Killer! Killer! Killer!'

'You must not tell your father,' Mum said to me as she wrapped a bandage around my midriff. Nothing was broken, she'd explained, so I didn't need a doctor or the hospital, but because I could barely walk without crying, couldn't breathe without wincing, she was strapping me up.

They'd got bored after a while and had then run away. I'd stayed curled up, cold and in agony for many minutes, wanting to be sure they weren't waiting for me to uncurl so they could continue to hurt me.

'He has so much to worry about, do not tell him about this.'

I knew I couldn't tell Dad this, just like I knew I couldn't tell him that the nasty policeman was still hanging around.

When Mum was finished, I carefully did up my shirt and tried not to gasp every time I moved. Carefully, she put her arms around me but didn't draw me into a hug. 'I'm sorry for what they did to you. It's not fair,' she said. 'But please, Enelle. Please do not tell your father. It will break his heart. And it will cause trouble for everyone.'

'I know, Mummy,' I said with a nod.

When I didn't come down for dinner that night and instead stayed upstairs holding ice on the bruises, Mum told Dad I was coming down with a cold and needed an early night.

*Tuesday, 16 November*
'Are you Nell—'

This boy, a stranger, didn't even finish my name before I was running. I was sore, still, my body ached from the last kicking I'd received, but my legs moved as fast as they could, taking me away from potential danger.

I did that every single time someone approached me and asked if I was Nell – sometimes, I didn't even give them a chance to speak to me at all.

# 1994

## Nell

*Saturday, 12 March*

The knock at the door was familiar. I poked my head out of the living room and stared at the two figures obscured by the frosted glass in the front door.

Police.

Police because there were three others now. Three more 'mermaids' – four in total along the coast. After each young woman was found, the police task force that had been convened to deal with this hideous set of crimes would come to speak to my father. They would take him away, they would keep him overnight – sometimes for two nights – and they would try as hard as they could to eliminate him from their investigation.

Dad had more than one link: these poor young women were found in Brighton, Eastbourne, New Haven and Seaford – places where he had shops; his daughter had found the first one; his daughter's friend had disappeared; and there was a policeman who was convinced he was guilty and was probably pouring all sorts of poison into their ears.

I used to watch my mother after every time Dad was walked out by two police officers. She would exist a little less, disappear a little more, would repeat over and over how he could have been killed the first time he was arrested. It was almost as though she was bracing herself, but I was never sure what for. For the day he wouldn't come back? For the time it would turn out he was guilty? Macy and I took over Dad's chores whenever he was taken: she would water the garden; I would cook and keep the house as pristine as possible. And Mum would sit staring into space. She would take the hot drinks we made her, she would eat the food we brought her on trays to their bedroom, but she would barely engage.

Mum took to her bed every time Dad was taken from her and sometimes also when he was right there. She was delicate. People looked at her and assumed because of the job she did, the nastiness and ugliness she encountered in everyday life and tolerated without complaint, that she was resilient, strong, unbeatable. The epitome of 'The Strong Black Woman'. But she was fragile, really. She got her strength from the certainty of Dad being around – the predictability of always having him there as her soft landing place. All of this was wearing her out. Like the enamel on a tooth being worn away and worn away until all that's left is the exposed soft, pulpy bit that meant everything caused pain, she had been worn away and worn away until everything hurt and the only thing she could do was retire from the world and wait for it to get better.

The knock came again.

Mum was in bed. Dad was in the garden, in his greenhouse, planting and pruning. Macy was in her room, probably sitting on her bed, a book open on her lap, a finger in her mouth as she bit at her already over-gnawed nails, and chewed at the dry bits of skin on her lips.

I had been in the living room, staring at the television, pretending everything was normal inside the house and outside it, too.

None of us had mentioned the 'For Sale' sign that had appeared outside our neighbour Mrs Breers's house, months ago. We'd all acted as though, yesterday – two days after the news of another 'mermaid' – a removal van hadn't arrived and whisked away Mrs Breers and her possessions, even though she hadn't yet sold her house. And we certainly weren't going to mention that we could feel the weight of our neighbours' curiosity about what depravity and wickedness lurked inside our 'ordinary' home.

Another knock. The third one. I had to move then. I walked slowly to the front door to open it. Maybe I'd got it all wrong. Maybe it was someone else.

'Good morning, Enelle. May we speak to your father?'

*Friday, 27 May*
Five in total now. The newest in Peacehaven. Not that much older than me. Treated like that. Left like that. Without a name, without an identity, without a way of proving she – like the others – had existed in the world in any other way than as a body the police now had to investigate.

Jude. This always made me think of Jude. Was she a mermaid somewhere? It'd been nearly a year and still nothing had been heard about her. Was she out there, like these young women had been, but unnamed, or even unfound? I still missed her every day. The loss of her ran like an unstoppable river through everything and the fear of what might have happened to her echoed in its wake.

I wished I knew what happened to her. Where she had gone, even if I'd never find out why. I wish I knew she was alive and safe and well.

Was she a mermaid somewhere? Was that why I hadn't heard from her?

*Wednesday, 1 June*
'The special police task force that was convened to investigate the so-called Mermaid Murders today had a major breakthrough when they arrested and charged a thirty-five-year-old man from Shoreham.'

All our eyes immediately went to Dad.

Even Mum, who spent less and less time downstairs with us nowadays, did what I was doing – checked Dad was sitting beside us when this news came in. That they weren't talking about him. The man who'd been arrested was significantly younger than Dad, he lived miles away from us, but still, after all this time, all the arrests and formal chats and nights away from us, we could only be sure it wasn't him being charged by checking with our own eyes. He was sitting on the sofa, his crossword puzzle on his lap and pen in his hand. He was here and someone else was being charged with the murders.

That meant the whole thing would go away now. Our neighbours would speak to us; the police would leave us alone; *John Pope would disappear.* We could get back to being a family again. We would talk if we all sat in the living room. Mum would spend more time with us. Macy would stop biting her nails, chewing her lips and – the new thing – wringing her hands. If this was the man they wanted, we would be fine now. Just fine.

I was so elated, so relieved, that I didn't even notice Macy's reaction until much, much later. Instead of smiling or even looking relieved, she simply got up and left the room and we didn't see her again until morning.

# Now

## Macy

*Sunday, 25 March*

'Hello, you. Happy Sunday,' my sister says to me.

I'm calling to see if I can salvage something for the week – maybe eke out some good days. And I'm calling to let her know without saying the words how pissed off I still am that she didn't answer yesterday *and* she turned off her phone. But here she is, doing that thing of sounding normal again. She was clearly asleep, but she sounds normal and happy to hear from me and not at all angry that I've called again at this time.

'Hello.' I sound frosty. I don't mean to sound that Arctic, but then I do. Icicles have formed on that one word.

'What you up to today? Shall I come over?' I hate that she's acting like there's nothing wrong.

'No,' I say, adding more icicles for good measure.

'OK, cool.'

'We're meant to be going over to Mummy and Daddy's for lunch. He's harvested some giant leeks and spring greens, apparently.'

'Oh, cool. Send me a picture of Aubrey next to one, please,' Nell says.

*Urgh, she is so frustrating!* 'Yeah, OK. How was your leaving do?'

'Oh, fine. Apart from Mr Whitby saying in his speech that I'd be back at work in no time.'

I laugh because that's what I've been saying to Shane – all this nonsense about being a 'people finder' won't pan out and she'll be back at work in no time. It's good to know I'm not the only one who thinks that. I'm sure she knows why I'm laughing – it's not like I make a secret of what I think of what she does.

'Hey, listen, I'm sorry I didn't answer the phone yesterday,' she says unprompted. 'I was otherwise indisposed.'

'How do you mean?' I ask.

'I was, erm, with someone.'

'How do you mean, "with someone"?'

'How do you think I mean, "with someone"? I was *with someone*. In bed.'

'Ohhhhh, *with* someone.'

'Yes. It would not have been appropriate to start talking on the phone at that moment.'

'Did you spend the whole night with him and sleep over and everything?'

'Yes.'

'Honestly?'

'Yes, honestly.'

I can't help but grin. She once told me she doesn't see the point in sleeping over at a guy's place once they've had sex a couple of times. When she saw how shocked I was at that, she explained that she likes to get out of there before they have to have the awkward 'are we going to see each other again?' conversation in the morning. To be fair, that was just as shocking to me. But clearly something is different with this guy.

'Are you going to see him again?'

'Macy . . .'

'*What?* It's a perfectly simple question.' That will hopefully lead to a yes and then she'll start dating him and then she'll maybe get married and have babies and STOP ALL THE LOOKING FOR PEOPLE ON HER COMPUTERS CRAP.

'A question I'm not going to answer. So what else are you lot doing today?'

'The usual: homework, ironing, getting ready for the week.'

'Are you sure you don't want me to come over? You know how great I am at ironing.'

I was annoyed with her, wasn't I? And now I'm not. She's good at doing that, my sister. 'No, next Saturday, I was think—'

'Tell me when you call me next Saturday morning,' she interrupts. 'You know, in case I forget.'

I smile because she really is good at mitigating my anger at her. 'OK. But are you sure you won't be otherwise indisposed again?'

'Oh, like I'm going to fall for that! I am not answering that question, Mace. I'll talk to you in the week, OK? Bye.'

'OK. Bye.' *Love you*, I say in my head when she hangs up. I'd never actually say it to her. That would be stupid.

'Was that Nell?' Shane asks as he comes into the kitchen. He's dressed in his black running gear – running shorts to his knees, a tight black top, black socks in his neon green trainers, and white headphones snaking up from his music player. Every Sunday morning Shane goes for a thirteen-mile run, training for the marathon he never gets around to signing up for. It clears his head, he says. And running half a marathon every Sunday prepares him for that point in the future when he'll actually do the full twenty-six in front of thousands of other people, including the children and me.

'Yes.'

'Well, you're smiling, so I'm guessing it was a positive call?'

'Yes, it was.'

'Did she say why she didn't answer the phone or come over yesterday?'

I glare at the man who wants to be my husband. Four times he's proposed and apparently he even has the most perfect engagement ring. It's not happening. Not now, probably not ever, especially if he's going to ask about Nell when he really should know better.

'Yes, she did tell me. She was having sex,' I say.

Right on cue his face flushes bright red and he has to break eye contact. He fits his earbuds into his ears and turns to the door. 'I'll see you in a couple of hours,' he mumbles.

'Yeah, see you,' I say and watch him walk away.

*I really am a bitch sometimes.*

# Nell

At seven o'clock I arrive at The Cricketers, a pub on Black Lion Street, which is near the seafront and just around the corner from Zach's hotel.

Via text on Sunday evening, Zach asked where would be a good place to meet for a quick drink on a Tuesday evening and I chose this place. I like it because it's odd. It's a white building that looks like it's been wedged in an alleyway, when in actual fact it's been around for about five hundred years (apparently). Inside feels the cramped side of cosy with red velvet everywhere and framed pictures on the ceiling. It's also the sort of place you would go with someone if you're not sure of their motives. I'd been confused when Zach asked me out for a drink, and I'm none the wiser when I arrive in the bar area looking for him.

I've spent the day trawling through records up on the other side of Brighton, searching for information on Janice from work's extended family. She wants to find out her family tree but has zero interest in actually doing it, so when she asked me for pointers (which was really her way of asking if I'd do it for her), I obliged. I sent her DNA off to the different places last week, and today I got a birth certificate on her mother's side and a marriage certificate on her father's side, while I wait for the results. Her family is proving unchallenging, but with every piece of information I find, I am hoping it will bring me nearer to Jude, to the Brighton Mermaid. To either of them.

I haven't felt this pressure before, I've always been able to search in my own time, but now I'm up against it and so everything I look at is vital, important, *necessary*.

Zach stands as I approach his table, part of a booth by the fireplace at the back of the pub. He has a short glass of amber liquid that looks like whisky or brandy on the table in front of him.

'Hello,' he says with a smile that broadens and deepens when I arrive at his table. He seems unsure whether to lean in and kiss me on the cheek or stick out his hand to shake. I'm on the back foot, too. If I see someone again after sex, it's generally at their house, and we generally dispense with formalities such as how to greet each other, and get on with what we've met up for. It's rare that I'll have a formal date and will therefore be required to know how to say a public hello.

I exhale, give my head a (mental) shake, and decide to treat this as though I am meeting a friend for a drink. 'Hi,' I say to him, like I would a friend, and then lean in to kiss his right cheek. I then lean in to kiss his other cheek, just like I would a friend.

He seems relieved and grateful at the same time as he receives my kisses; his hands linger on my biceps until I step back.

'What would you like to drink?' he asks.

'What are you drinking?'

He grins at the reminder from the other night and says, 'Not tequila.' He picks up his glass and swirls its contents. 'Honey whisky is tonight's chosen poison. Delicious going down, known to give me courage.'

'What do you need courage for?'

'Beautiful woman, first proper date – why wouldn't I need courage?' he replies, staring straight at me.

He kept calling me beautiful the other morning. It didn't sound forced, or insincere; he stared into my eyes, whispering it as though he wanted me to feel it in every part of my body. I was pinned by his intensity at some points, not sure what to make of him – very few men say that sort of thing to me in that sort of way. I redirect my gaze, just as I did on Saturday morning.

'I'll, erm, have a white wine. No, actually, a rosé – remind myself of the summer to come.'

'How can something remind you of something that hasn't happened yet?' he says, smoothly taking up my change in subject.

'Ahhh, easily. You just imagine what it'll be like sipping it when the sun is taking its time to set and the night is so warm every breath feels like a caress.'

'That's quite poetic,' he replies. 'I may even have one after that. Two rosés coming up.'

I watch his besuited form walk towards the bar, and quell the excitement that wants to jump up and down in my chest and my stomach. Yes, he's good-looking and sexy and all of that, but he's also brought me here for a reason, and I don't for one second think it's for a date. I'm wondering if he's changed his mind about us and wants to tell me in person because ghosting isn't his style. Or, worse, maybe he wants to see the look of utter horror and humiliation on my face when he tells me he thinks I'm disgusting for doing what I did with him on Saturday morning.

*Dirty girl, dirty little slut* echoes across my mind and instantly my stomach flips. I couldn't stand it if Zach called me that. I wouldn't let him see my hurt, but it would wound me.

*No, Zach isn't like that,* I tell myself sternly. *Only psychopaths do things like that. How about thinking the best of him until he proves otherwise? How about not letting John Pope infect every single part of your life?*

'So, I guess you're wondering why I asked you out tonight?' Zach begins after we've both taken a sip of the rosé. It's slightly tart, and there's a hint of summer berries – just enough to start thoughts of summer blossoming in my mind.

I nod.

'Well, I wanted to spend some time with you.' He lowers his voice to add: 'Away from the bedroom.'

I nod, but still don't say anything.

'I mean, not that it wasn't nice and everything.'

My eyebrow shoots up at 'nice'. He thought the sex was *nice*? *Quelle horreur!* I had a one-night stand and he describes it as nice.

'I didn't mean "nice" in that way,' he says quickly, obviously picking up on my dismay at his description. 'I meant . . . it was . . . special, I guess. Different from what I'm used to. I liked it a lot. So much so, I wanted to make sure that you didn't regret it or anything.'

'Why would I regret anything?'

He looks at me as though I am being deliberately obtuse; like there is something I am going out of my way to avoid.

'I don't know, I just . . .'

'Are *you* regretting it?' I ask when he stops mid-sentence. 'I mean, is this you needing to get a look at me with my clothes on just in case it might change your mind about not wanting to see me with my clothes off again?'

'Erm, no. The other way around, actually.'

I make a confused face. 'I'm sorry,' I say. 'I'm bright and all, I have a degree and a masters degree, but right now I am completely confounded. You're going to have to spell it out for me.'

Zach sips his wine, then takes a big slug of whisky, almost emptying the glass, and looks directly at me. 'You were very drunk for most of the night we met. You'd sobered up by the time you left on the Saturday morning, but I've been wondering ever since if your initial reluctance to call me meant you weren't as interested in me as I am in you. And if you kind of felt you had to get in touch out of guilt.'

Ah, I *see*.

'So, I wanted to meet up and check in, I suppose. See if you were actually interested or if you'd gone back to not being that keen. I wanted to see if you might be interested in me beyond sex – And now I hear myself talking, I can also hear all my mates laughing at how sincere and earnest I sound.'

'Ahhh, who cares what a bunch of your imaginary mates think?' I say with a laugh. I put down my glass, which I have been gulping from since he started his confession. I reach across the table and touch his fingertips with mine. 'I was being . . . *odd* that morning. I do that because it's very effective at keeping people at a distance. It's a bit of a habit. But I like you. I like you a lot.'

'Even though I look like this?' he replies.

Zach levels his gaze at me across the table and I look right back at him. I *completely* understand now. What he's worried about, why he wanted me to see him in a non-sexual situation – he wants to know if I accept him for who he is without hair, without eyebrows, without eyelashes, before this goes any further. He is worried that it will bother me so he is giving me a way out.

'What do you look like?' I reply. 'Apart from handsome in all the right places, of course.'

He smiles, relieved, slightly elated, I think. The excitement I felt before comes stampeding in again. I want to be alone with him. Not only for the physical stuff, but so we can talk and laugh and cuddle.

'You're just saying that to get me into bed,' he says.

'No, I'm not,' I reply.

'Oh. Why not?'

I grin at him.

'Your place or mine?' Zach asks.

'Yours is nearer.'

'I like the way you think, Nell, I really do.'

*Bleep-bleep-bleep*, goes my mobile in my pocket.

The seventh 'He needs to see you' message today.

I'm going to have to talk to him soon. But not right now, not just yet. I shove those five words to the back of my mind and concentrate on who I came out for instead.

# 2007

## Nell

*Saturday, 2 June*

I saw him from quite a way away, leaning on the back of a bench on the seafront, as if he was waiting for someone. Me, of course. I never worked out how he knew where I was going to be so he could wait for me, but he did it constantly.

John Pope.

It'd taken six months for the case against Ralph Knowles, the man who'd been arrested for the so-called Mermaid Murders, to collapse. The papers said it was lack of evidence, but I always suspected something else had happened. Something so big they couldn't report it without making the police force look bad. I'd had to go and see if I recognised him, if I had seen him on the seafront the night I found the Brighton Mermaid, and they'd all sighed dramatically in disappointment when I hadn't picked him out.

I had been terrified when we first heard the news about the case being dropped. I'd thought they'd reset their sights on Dad, and hell would start up again. But they hadn't come back, hadn't followed up anything. Simply left us to it.

Except for John Pope. He hadn't gone away.

He'd started stalking us again, following us, turning up 'for a little chat', reminding me that he thought my dad was a pervert and killer. No matter how many complaints we made, how many harassment orders my dad's solicitor tried to take out against Pope personally, he hadn't stopped. He hadn't stopped until he had poisoned Brighton and Hove for Dad and Mum. When I went to university, they'd sold their house and moved to Herst-monceux (also known as 'the middle of nowhere'). Dad had shut all his shops, three of them permanently, including the Hove one. That had been his favourite (his first one). But that had been the one that was also subject to the most vandalism. The other three shops he'd kept closed for six months and then had reopened them with different names and different staff, and paid someone to manage them so he wouldn't be associated with them on a day-to-day basis.

When they'd moved to Herstmonceux, Mum had started work in a nursing home. Macy, who'd always been more popular than me, hadn't seemed that bothered about leaving her friends behind. She'd still bitten her nails, chewed her lips and wrung her hands, but she had made new friends in the new area, and seemed to have a full timetable of activities to occupy her time. We had all, in our ways, moved on. Settled on a new life; tried to put all that stuff behind us.

Except I couldn't because John Pope was still around.

The only time I had really been free of Pope was when I was at university and came back to stay at my parents' house. Otherwise he was always there. Haunting me, *hunting* me, it felt like sometimes.

He was dressed in dark clothes, his blond hair had greyed and he was thinner, meaner-looking if that was possible.

'Hello, Nell.'

I stopped, a little thrown – he'd never called me Nell before. Usually it was 'you' or '*Miss* Okorie'. Never Nell.

'What do you want?' I asked without looking at him when he didn't speak again.

'I'd like to talk to you,' he replied, as though he was talking to a human being, not the lower life form he'd always made it clear he thought I was. 'I'd like us to talk without animosity.'

He was clever, manipulative – what he'd just said had neatly rewritten our history to make out that I had been as awful to him as he had been to me. 'What about?' I asked.

His face was impassive, almost friendly. 'I just want to talk. Please.' He indicated to the bench with his hand. Softened his voice to say, 'Please, just sit with me a moment. Please.'

I sat on the edge of the right-hand side of the bench, facing the sea.

Rather than sit at the other end, he lowered himself in the middle, too close for me not to be aware of the shape of him, the reality of his presence.

'What do you want?' I asked when he continued to remain silent.

'I . . . I . . . I need to apologise.'

I froze.

'I was wrong,' he said. 'I behaved abominably. I was so blinkered, so desperate to get a result, I forgot that there were people behind it. People who have suffered all these years . . . because of me.'

I listened to him speak, apologise, humanise my family in a way he never had. I listened to him say the words none of us ever thought we'd hear.

'*Go fuck yourself*,' I said in my head, because everything he said was fake; every word reverberated with an insincerity that reached far, far out to sea.

'You were finally sacked, weren't you?' I said out loud. That was the only reason why he would be doing this. There was no way he would be sitting here with me, calling me Nell, apologising, if he still had the authority of the police force behind him. 'You finally harassed the wrong person, someone they couldn't ignore, and they got rid of you.'

'Yes,' Pope eventually admitted. 'I lost my job. But that's not why I'm here.'

'No,' I said sarcastically, 'of course it isn't.'

'How could you forget about her, Nell?' he asked.

'Forget about who?'

'Your friend, Judana. How could you forget about her? And the other girl, the Brighton Mermaid? How could you carry on with your life as if they never existed?'

'I've never done that,' I said, appalled that he could ever think that. 'I've never forgotten them – I think about them every day. Both of them. They're the first thing that comes to mind in the morning, and the last thing I think about at night. I've never forgotten about them.'

'But you haven't done anything to find them.'

'What am I supposed to do? For years you've had all the police computers and databases and contacts and you couldn't solve anything. How am *I* supposed to?'

'Have you tried?'

Had I tried? I used to go to the library to photocopy posters of Jude saying she was missing, saying there was a reward for any information leading to the discovery of her whereabouts. Those were the words I had used, as well. It had made the posters sound serious, as if an adult had done them.

I would buy newspapers and check the small ads to see if Jude had somehow left me a message because we'd both loved the film *Desperately Seeking Susan* and I thought she might try to contact me that way.

When I first had access to the Internet, and I heard people saying you could find anyone and anything on there, I looked up Jude. I put in her name. I put in her general description. There were so many different search engines back then, and I put her name and description into all of them. Then I would put things in about the Brighton Mermaid, missing black girls, missing girls. All of it gave me nothing.

I had tried, but I had got nowhere. 'Yes, I've tried.'

'How hard?'

'What is it that you want?'

'I'll level with you, Nell. There were several things about the Mermaid Murders that were never made known to the public.'

'Such as?'

'Such as Ralph Knowles, the man we had in custody, had a rock-solid alibi for the night the Brighton Mermaid was killed.'

'What?'

'We had to unofficially unlink the first murder from the others because there were so many things that didn't match. We thought at the time that the later murders began as a copycat. He got the idea from the Brighton Mermaid but didn't know enough to copy it completely. And because they became so notorious, the original murderer backed off.'

'I don't believe you,' I said.

He inhaled deeply through his nose, a flash of anger firing across his face that he quickly hid away. 'I shouldn't tell you any of this, but the Brighton Mermaid was probably strangled by someone wearing gloves, as no fingerprints showed up. With the others, someone used an item of clothing instead. The others were all slightly younger, and they all showed ligature marks around their wrists and ankles, meaning they'd been tied up for quite some time before death. And then, of course, Knowles was in police cells in York the night the Brighton Mermaid was killed. He'd been brawling in a pub.'

I frowned. 'So you think he killed all of the others but not the woman I found?'

'Correct. Except for the Brighton Mermaid, he was in the area where each of those women were murdered around the time of their deaths.'

'Why didn't he get convicted of those murders? All they ever said in the papers was that the case collapsed due to lack of evidence.'

John Pope looked uncomfortable. Was it something to do with him? Was it his fault? 'There was some incorrect handling of the forensic evidence at the time and his solicitor made a big deal of his alibi for the Brighton Mermaid killing. It was clear he had done it: as soon as he was released and he left the area, the killings of other . . . *black* girls stopped. There was nothing we could do to get him, but he left the area and he knew wherever he went the police would be watching him. We still want to get him, but we'll have to wait for more evidence to be found.'

I was reeling but didn't show it. So they weren't linked. The other mermaids weren't really mermaids like the first one, who was only called that because of her tattoo. And there was someone out there who had killed the poor woman I found and inspired another killer while getting away with murder. The thought of that made me feel sick and scared. How many of these evil people were out there?

'You still haven't told me what you want,' I said. 'After all this time, what has any of this got to do with me?'

'We know Ralph Knowles killed the other girls, but with the Brighton Mermaid, with your friend . . . They are still open cases and they are linked, I know they are.'

'No one else thinks they're linked, do they?' I replied. 'It's only you who is hanging on to this.'

'I thought you might be, too, Nell. Since she was your friend. And you found the other girl.'

He knew how to get to me.

'Why do you care so much? It's not as if you like or have any respect for black women or girls.'

'That's not true,' he said without any conviction behind his words. 'Everyone is equal in the eyes of the law. And everyone deserves justice. The Brighton Mermaid and your friend deserve justice. And if you were right and I didn't care, shouldn't *you* at least care about what happened to them?'

'What is it that you want?'

'I want you to work with me. I still have some friends on the force – I'm sure a few of them will help me out with data searches. But I need . . . You wouldn't even have to do much, Nell.'

'What does this not much entail?'

'I'll admit it, I thought your father was involved – more than involved, I thought he was guilty. That he had taken your friend, that he might have harmed those other women. But that's always been because I haven't been able to prove conclusively that he wasn't involved.'

You can't prove a negative; Dad had taught Jude and me that when he helped us with our science homework. You can't prove something isn't there.

'You, Nell, can help me to prove that he wasn't involved.'

'How?'

'Search your parents' house for any clues. We've never had access to their new house, so you'd be searching it for the first time. Look for something out of the ordinary, something that doesn't fit. You may find something that will help us eliminate your father from our investigation. Once we know conclusively that he had nothing to do with your friend disappearing, we can move on. We can find out who else is out there that could have done it.'

I let him speak: he was almost giddy with excitement at the idea that what he was saying might have got through to me. That I was so stupid that I wouldn't realise I couldn't find him the vital clue to show my dad was innocent, and that any 'clue' I did find would only prove the opposite.

John Pope had no idea what his vendetta had done to our family. We'd lost the ability to be with each other. To just be in the same space and not have to think about anything. What Pope had done had sliced away pieces of my father's soul, leaving him diminished. He was still him – he had the same stature and deep, commanding voice. But he was also fretful in quiet moments, distant where before he had been engaged.

What Pope had done had broken my mother. As an adult I understood, now, what had happened to her. When I was fifteen, I had thought it was the shock of Dad being arrested and rearrested and rearrested that had done it. It wasn't simply that, though. I could see now that Mum had been 'good' and polite and had kept away from trouble her whole life. She'd experienced racism and prejudice but she – like the rest of us people of colour – had been lied to, had been sold the promise that good behaviour, obedience, never causing trouble or fighting too hard for your rights, would keep you safe, keep you protected. That promise had been broken in the most violent, pugnacious and cruel way, and Mum had never fully recovered from that trauma.

Thanks to John Pope, I had lost my father and I'd lost my mother. And he thought I would join him in starting that up again? He thought I would search their house and break their trust and as good as tell them I thought Dad was guilty?

I looked him over. Had he ever been a good man? I knew everyone had some good in them – that's what makes us human, what makes people able to say 'well, he was kind to animals' about murderers. But was Pope? Was he ever a good man? Could he even be called a man? Physically, biologically, yes. But everything else that came with being a man – decency, compassion, empathy, strength – seemed lacking in him. Had it ever actually existed?

'I can't help you,' I said. 'My dad had nothing to do with Jude disappearing or the Brighton Mermaid being killed. I'm not going to search their house. I can't. I *won't*.'

He exhaled deeply and loudly in exasperation. '*Fine*. Have it your way,' he said nastily.

The hateful scar-faced policeman was back. His voice, that tone, pulled me back through time to the room he'd questioned us in. *Dirty girls. Dirty little sluts.* I hated that he could do that to me, that he could still make me feel like that. I know most people would expect me to have got over it, would think I was playing the victim by not simply removing it from my mind, but somehow, some way, it had stuck. It had scored itself deep into my mind and I could never completely shake it off.

'I'll have to see if your darling little sister will help me instead. She was *always* far more cooperative anyway.'

It felt, for a moment, that my heart had stopped. The blood seemed not to flow in my chest. If he went near Macy I would lose her like I'd lost Mum and Dad. In many ways Macy was brave and strong, but she was also always on the cusp of self-harming. I had seen the thin faint lines that scored her upper arms; I had noticed the way she had to work hard to stop herself constantly washing her hands. She didn't realise that I knew she had many, many little rituals and habits that helped her to believe she could control her world. Pope had done that. He had brought all that chaos and trauma into our lives on a regular basis, and now he was threatening to do it again because he couldn't get what he wanted from me.

'Go ahead,' I said. 'Talk to Macy, see what happens then. Because, unlike me, Macy will go straight to my father, who *will* engage a solicitor to stop you. And as you no longer work for the police, you can't hide behind them any longer . . . well, I guess we'll all have to see how it pans out. Good luck with that.'

I felt him sag a little in his seat – he'd played his trump card and it had turned out to be a dud. I, on the other hand, had bluffed him and won. It probably wouldn't work again, but it had this time, and that was a small victory worth celebrating when I was far, far away from him.

I stood up, ready to carry on with my journey to Brighton. My mind was buzzing. I was older now; I had learnt how to research in college. I could afford a computer, and I could learn to find people. I could find Jude, find a name for the Brighton Mermaid. I could do this now.

*Yes*, I thought, *I can do this. No matter how long it takes, I can do this.*

'You will help me, Nell,' John Pope said as I began to walk away. 'I promise you, I *will* find a way to make you help me.'

# Now

## Nell

*Saturday, 31 March*

Shane opens the front door and we both miss a beat, stare at each other awkwardly, then avert our eyes. Then: 'Hi,' we both mumble, clear our throats and then say 'Hi' in a normalish voice. Every time we do this. Every. Single. Time.

Macy has lived with him for five years now, they've been together for nearly seven years, and we still do it.

'Who is it?' Macy calls, coming out of the kitchen and into the corridor. I can hear the children in the house – the TV is on in the lounge; sounds of a games console drift down from upstairs.

'Oh. Hi.' Macy says this like it's a surprise for me to be here. She called me at five-seventeen this morning as usual and told me what I had to do today: help Willow with her maths homework; wash Clara's hair; beat Aubrey at chess. 'You are joking, aren't you?' I almost said to her. Almost, then I remembered that last weekend I didn't answer the phone, which meant she was going to punish me this week. Not that spending time with the children was a punishment, it was just that her way of making me pay for ignoring her last Saturday was to immerse me in the realities of family life. So I agreed to everything, then made sure on the way over I picked up Easter eggs for everyone, even Shane.

'Are you coming in then?' Macy asks.

Thankfully she didn't see how Shane and I greeted each other. It's all the more mortifying for the fact we actually do it.

Shane, still with his eyes averted, steps aside to let me in and I try – and fail – to smile at him as I enter.

'Oh, for God's sake,' Macy snaps, 'are you two still doing this? You had sex, get over it.' She rolls her eyes and turns to go back the way she came, flicking her tea towel over her shoulder as she goes.

I can't believe she said that so loudly with the children around. Even if Aubrey doesn't have a clue what sex is (unlikely), Willow does, as does Clara. There are some things children don't need to know. One of them is that Shane was my first. My first boyfriend, my first kiss, my first go at sex . . .

# 1994

## Nell

*Wednesday, 15 June*

'Cheer up, love, it might never happen,' the old man said to me as I approached the counter at the post office. He was holding his pension book and probably didn't understand why anyone could look miserable when the sun was shining outside and he had money in his pocket.

I pulled a smile across my face and kept it wedged in place until he had passed me by.

'I hate it when people say that,' the man behind me said.

I groaned inside. It was clearly a 'talk to Nell' day, which meant I'd spend the whole day on edge, wondering if I needed to run.

Today had already not been a good day. It'd taken me three goes to get my passport photos right. Three lots of two pounds had disappeared into the machine and only one set was useable. I'd had to wait an age before my head teacher would sign the back of them – she was the only person who could do it, since I couldn't ask neighbours and the Daltons had distanced themselves since Dad's first arrest.

Our house had been searched multiple times by the police and after each time, not only did they leave in their wake devastation that we had to clear up, we'd often find – weeks later – that things had gone missing. All our passports had disappeared, probably in one such search. (It was never revealed what they were looking for, but judging by the amount of times they came back, they clearly never found it.) I wasn't going to go anywhere, I just wanted a passport because it gave me the impression that I *could* go abroad if I wanted; that I was a normal girl with normal options.

As someone concluded their business at the two-window counter of the small, crowded post office, on Blatchington Road and everyone edged forwards, the man behind me in the queue said, 'Sorry, shouldn't have spoken to you.' I sighed, quietly, and looked down at the white trainers on my feet. I was definitely going to be running today.

'I'm making it worse,' the man said. 'I really need to shut up. Sorry, sorry, I will stop talking to you. Right now. Well, now.'

As I left the post office, I chanced a look at the man who had been behind me – I needed to find out what he looked like in case he approached me again. I was surprised at how young he was – he must have been about twenty-five at the very most, probably a bit younger. He had shaggy brown hair and a neat beard that emphasised his mouth when he smiled at me. I couldn't help but smile back at him because he seemed nice. And nowadays, I didn't meet many nice people.

*Wednesday, 15 June*

I sat in my seat with an empty popcorn carton until the last credit meandered its way up the screen and the lights came up like a flare being thrown in my face. There'd been five other people in the cinema, and three of them had left as soon as the credits started. The remaining two, like me, blinked and cringed when the lights flooded the place and one of them left. The man sitting three rows from the front stood up, threw his arms out and stretched before he spun slightly to see who was left. He froze when saw me, just like I froze when I saw him. The guy from the post office. I'd seen him on George Street a bit later, sitting outside one of the cafés that I was going to go to. And then he'd been on the bus to come here. I'd got off in case he tried to talk to me. And now he was here. John Pope was still following me – was this man doing it as well?

116

I didn't really see people during the day now I'd finished my exams and was waiting for my results. I would be going to sixth form at the same school to do my A levels, but had to wait a few more weeks to see what my actual marks were. Other people in my class had got jobs, and I'd always spent summers working in Dad's shops, but after the journalist had come in and questioned me, I couldn't do that any more.

'Are you following me?' I asked him. I was sick of this now. Being followed, not feeling safe . . . watching the devastation continue to roll on over our lives. When they arrested that man two weeks ago, this was all meant to be over: Mum was supposed to spend less time in bed and more time with us; Dad was meant to smile and laugh and joke again; Macy was meant to stop wringing her hands; and I was meant to feel normal again. Safe again. Not so guilty all the time. None of that had happened. Our family's life hadn't been magically transformed by Dad being exonerated and I was fed up with it, especially if someone else was going to insert himself into our lives.

'I've been wondering if *you've* been following *me*,' he replied. He looked up at me. 'Are you?'

I shook my head. All the righteous indignation was gone, and suddenly I was shy; I was an uncool teenager talking to an extremely handsome stranger.

'I'm Shane,' he said. 'And I am not following you. Far from it. But I'm guessing since you're in the cinema in the middle of the day like me, that you're between jobs like I am? Seeing as we're bound to end up in the same place anyway, can I convince you to come for a drink *with* me and not just in the same place as me?'

'I'm fifteen,' I blurted out.

'Ahhh, OK. You really don't look it. So, are you waiting for your exam results?'

I nodded.

'How about a coffee, then? I presume you're not too young to drink coffee?'

117

I shook my head again.

'Is that no, you're not too young for a coffee, or no, you don't want to come for a coffee?'

'No, I'm not too young for a coffee,' I said.

He grinned at me and my stomach went all funny, like it was jelly; like all of me was jelly. 'You've got an amazing smile,' he said.

I glanced down at my trainers, knowing we were not going to be just friends. Not at all.

*Friday, 21 October*

'You really are a virgin, aren't you?' Shane said. He'd asked me to put the condom on him seconds earlier and I hadn't known what to do. I'd stared at the brightly coloured square in my hands and had been baffled. I'd been taught the mechanics and biology of sex at school with a heavy dose of 'woe betide you if you get pregnant', but never things like how to put a condom on an erect penis.

He was twenty-three, so not that much older than me, and we'd been seeing each other for four months now. When I went back to sixth form I'd come to his flat near London Road during free periods. Today was the first day that I had skipped a whole afternoon because he'd asked me to.

In his bedroom he had a large love seat in the window bay, it was made of the softest light brown leather, and we often kissed and touched there. Sometimes we'd progress to the bed, but often we'd sit there curled up together, talking in between kissing. Today we'd moved on from the love seat to the bed, and from a few clothes taken off to being completely naked.

Today was going to be the first time I had sex and I'd shown him how inadequate I was at it by not knowing how to put a condom on him. The first time he'd kissed me, he'd had to keep stopping to tell me to relax; the first time he'd put my hand on his erection to show me how hard I made him, I'd snatched my hand away because it hadn't felt hard, it was sort of squidgy and blobby.

And now he'd asked me to put on the condom and I didn't know what to do.

Despite what John Pope had said, I was completely inexperienced, and I was still surprised that Shane hadn't dumped me for that yet.

'Yes, I really am a virgin,' I said.

'Sorry, I didn't mean to upset you,' he said quickly. 'I like it, I'm glad that I'm your first.'

I was glad he was my first, too, because it would make the whole sex thing a bit easier. I'd overheard other girls talking about how it hurt first time, how you might bleed a little, and how you had to make lots of noise and tell him how much you enjoyed it even if it hurt and you didn't really like it at all.

'Hey,' he whispered as he sorted out the condom. 'Relax.'

I closed my eyes and lay back on the bed, tried to relax as I waited for the moment of pain when he put it in. Instead, Shane planted a kiss right in the middle of my chest, between my breasts. I gasped – I hadn't been expecting that. Slowly he kissed just below that, then lower and lower, down and down until he reached the wildness of my black wiry pubic hair. I expected him to stop then, to come back up to my face and kiss my mouth.

'I know how to make you relax,' he said, and kissed me between my legs. I gasped again, louder this time, as feelings I'd never known existed burst through me. Shane's hands grabbed my hips to stop me wriggling away, from unintentionally trying to escape from the pure rush of what was coursing through me.

I arched my back as he pushed his face harder between my legs. I gritted my teeth but I couldn't stop myself almost sobbing out loud as Shane's tongue teased at me. I was making noises, but they weren't planned and they weren't recognisable words, they were just outpourings of the pleasure avalanching through me. I clutched at the white bed sheet, my body convulsing with flood after flood of ecstasy that went on and on and on until I froze and allowed the sheer, bright emotion of what Shane was doing to me to overwhelm me. When it was over, I collapsed on the bed, quivering with what I realised was probably the afterglow of an orgasm. I'd heard of them, but none of the conversations I'd overheard had mentioned having one your first time.

Shane was suddenly over me again, smiling while I became more and more embarrassed. I was sure girls weren't meant to do that. They weren't supposed to be loud and uncontrolled. They weren't meant to experience so much pleasure. In fact, no one who'd talked about their first time had mentioned any of this: enjoying it, or having orgasms.

I think that was why I'd always been a bit suspicious and – I admit it – scared of sex. No one had ever talked about it like it was something the girl was meant to enjoy; it was all about doing it so the guy would stay with you, the guy would like you, the guy got something special. *It's about me as well*, I thought as Shane continued to smile at me. *Sex is about me, too.*

'You know what I love more than seeing you enjoying yourself?' he asked.

I shook my head, blissed out and slightly sleepy now.

'You,' he said, and pushed into me. 'I love you.'

He didn't speak again as he lay fully on top of me, laced his fingers into my hair and began thrusting. I didn't think about what he said, I just gave myself up to the moment, the pleasure he was creating again.

'I do, you know?' Shane said as he flopped down onto the bed afterwards. He was breathing as hard as I was – again. I felt a bit bad: I'd had two orgasms and he'd only had one.

'I like seeing you enjoying yourself, too,' I said, feeling floaty and light; as though I could be carried away on the slightest breeze.

'No, I mean, I do love you.'

'Oh,' I said.

Shane grinned. He rolled towards me. 'That's my girl. I say something meaningful and she replies with "oh".' He brushed his fingers across my cheek.

'I don't know what to say,' I replied honestly.

'Just say what you feel, Nell. It's not hard.'

I didn't know how I felt. Shane was incredible: he had changed my life, he had made everything more than bearable, I loved to see him smile, I adored the flip in my stomach I got when I thought about him. *I'd had sex with him.* Was that what love was? Was it about having sex and funny feelings inside and the particular shape of your lover's smile? But shouldn't love be more than that? Or did all of those things add up to that big thing they called love?

I saw how Dad and Mum looked at each other and I seemed to just know that was what people talked about when they talked about love.

That type of love wasn't only about sex and orgasms and smiles and stomach-flipping. Or maybe it was and, at my age, with my first boyfriend and first orgasms, I hadn't reached that point yet. I didn't know what love was, when it came down to it. The simpler the better, I supposed. Other things conspired to make love difficult and complicated and painful. Maybe, without all the complex stuff, this was what love was all about.

I reached up and brushed at his fringe with my fingers. 'How I feel is that I love you,' I said.

His face creased into his most wonderful smile yet. I'd said and done the right thing. And I just had to keep on saying it for it to feel like I actually, truly meant it.

# Now

## Nell

*Saturday, 31 March*

Macy's ability to get over the fact that I had sex with her significant other has always baffled and impressed me in equal proportions. She doesn't flinch, doesn't seem to dwell. It genuinely doesn't seem to bother her. Me? I'd always be wondering if he compared the two of us, if he was hankering after my sister.

'You two are meant to be adults. You're both older than me and you still act like two teenagers who just looked at each other's bits for the first time.'

Shane looks at me briefly, attempting to be adult about this like Macy said we should, but he can't manage it. He turns his back on me and strides across the kitchen to start filling the kettle.

My sister's three children – Willow, twelve, Clara eleven, and Aubrey, ten – were all fathered by a man called Clyde Higgson, who she was with for nearly eight years. He left when Aubrey had turned one and he hasn't looked back since. It took me no time to find him, but Macy didn't want to know.

After he walked out on them Macy was devastated, so broken by it that I moved in to helped her out. It was then that I saw the reality of what Macy was battling – her anxiety, the thin line of normality and illness that she walks almost every day.

She washed her hands. She straightened and re-straightened anything that was even a millimetre out of place. She did certain things at the same time every week to make sure the following seven days went according to plan. I accept how Macy is sometimes, how sharp and dismissive and bossy she can be, because I know how she battles every day trying to control everything so the children are all right and their world is safe. Macy works hard at creating a stable life by skipping along the edges of normality and pretending she can cope.

Seven years ago Shane walked into Macy's life when she met him on a training course. They hit it off and became an item. When she finally let him come to her home, he saw a picture of me with the children and had to tell her that he knew me, and how.

'Are you two going to be like this for the rest of our lives?' Macy says now we're all in the kitchen. She snatches up her rolling pin. 'Shane and I have been together seven years. Seven years. And, what is it, twenty-two *years* since you two split up. Why can't you act like normal people?' She turns her rolling pin on me. 'Yes, all right, you lost your virginity to him, but it kind of fizzled out just before you went to uni, didn't it?'

I stare at my sister, surprised that she's doing this right here, wondering what has prompted her to bring it up right now.

Her rolling pin is then directed at Shane. 'And you've been with loads of women – why can't you pretend Nell's like one of them?'

Shane may have downplayed our relationship to Macy when he told her he knew me. *A lot.* And by the point when she asked me about it, telling her the complete truth would have ruined her relationship with him, something I couldn't do when she was so happy. Even before she officially told me she was dating, I could tell by how freer she seemed that she had met someone.

'Look, this isn't fair on any of us, you two carrying on like this,' Macy says, dropping the tough-girl act. 'I feel like I can't invite you over whenever I want, Nell, because it'll be awkward with Shane. And Shane, I keep making digs because the way you carry on makes it seem like you still have a thing for my sister.'

She turns to me again. 'Is there something I should know?' She stares at me, eyebrows raised, lips curled into her mouth in a 'tell me everything' smile. I want to blurt out everything, get it all in the open, but that train left the station for pastures unknown seven years ago. Too late now to dredge it all up and see how she feels about how passionate our relationship had been.

'No,' I say. 'No, there isn't.'

'No, not at all,' Shane says, far less convincingly than me.

'Right,' Macy says, 'I am going to leave the kitchen and you two are going to have a normal conversation without avoiding eye contact and nonsense like that, all right? And when I come back you two are going to act like strangers, all right?'

'Yes,' I confirm.

'Right you are,' Shane replies.

She shuts the door behind her and once she's gone, Shane finally turns to face me.

He's looking warily at me because I am glaring at him. I am still so cross with him for putting me in this situation. 'You should have told her the truth from the start,' I hiss.

'I know, I know,' he admits. 'I just . . . I panicked. I know, I know I should have told her everything.'

# 2000

## Nell

*Friday, 18 August*

'Thank you for coming to meet me,' Shane said.

'No need to sound so formal about it,' I joked. 'We're not business associates.' I nudged him and he laughed.

He hadn't changed that much in the four-plus years since I'd seen him. He still gave me a little thrill in my stomach when I'd walked into this little Mexican restaurant by the Lanes and seen him sitting in a booth with a ridiculously over-the-top cocktail in front of him. I remembered how my sixteen-year-old self felt about him, how she'd quivered every time she saw him. Then how she'd ached for him every day for the first term at university. She'd gone out and had fun, but she wanted Shane all the time. She'd cried for him at night, she'd cuddled the bear he gave her, she wouldn't think about anyone else. She'd got over it – *I'd* got over it, but he was Shane and there was a part of me that still got a kick when I saw him. We'd bumped into each other in the street, and he'd asked if we could meet for a drink.

He rubbed his hand briefly along my thigh, then leant in close. 'It's amazing that you're here,' he said. 'I didn't think you'd see me again after . . . after the way I was.'

Shane had spent months trying to talk me out of going to university. He'd wanted me to stay with him, to leave home and move in with him. For us to have babies. When trying to talk me out of going hadn't worked, he'd started crying – sobbing and wailing and letting me know how I was breaking his heart. When that hadn't worked either, Shane had turned nasty. Nothing had been too low to spit at me, nothing had been out of bounds. He'd apologise, only to repeat his insults and worse when a month of phone calls to my halls of residence didn't get me to come home to him. In the end, I'd had to stop taking his calls and returned all his letters unread.

'I did have to think twice,' I admitted.

'I'm sorry. I've felt terrible about it ever since. I was so completely selfish. I was just really jealous, couldn't stand the thought of you not being here and the thought of someone else touching you drove me crazy. Terrible, huh? I can't believe I used to think no one had a right to even look at you, let alone touch you. Thankfully, I've grown up a lot.' He sipped his drink and tried not to look as embarrassed as he so clearly was.

'Think we've both grown up a lot since then,' I replied.

Shane's hand returned to my thigh, a fraction higher this time. 'Is this OK?' he lowered his voice to ask. 'Is it OK to touch you there?'

'Yes, it's OK,' I said. I liked remembering what it had been like to be with Shane before it went wrong. I was a bit lost, coming back to Brighton after over four years away at university. I hadn't got used to being here, and even though I was renting a room in a house, I'd accepted that I'd probably have to move into my parents' house in the middle of nowhere while I got a job and started to save for my own place. Being with Shane was a little bit of home – the Brighton and Hove I actually knew – and I liked being around him for that reason. So it was all right for him to touch my thigh. It was very all right.

'Can I come home with you?' Shane asked outside the restaurant. The owners had tried to get us to leave several times, and then had given up because we kept ordering more tapas so we could stay sitting together in their little booth. Now the restaurant was closed and, outside, Brighton was coming alive. It was Friday night and people were out and about. The air was alive with summer, and people, mainly in groups, moved in different directions, flowing towards the parts of town where the late-night bars and clubs were. Happy chatter rose up as they walked by. Drunk and simply merry people were spilling out of the bars and pubs that closed at normal times and were adding to the thrum that made Brighton a vibrant place.

I wanted to stand in the middle of the road, throw my arms out, tip my head back, then spin. Spin, spin and spin until I took off.

Shane took me in his arms. 'Can I come home with you?' he asked again as he nuzzled my neck. His hands moved down over my hips, resting lightly on my thighs. 'Please?' He slipped his hands up under the hemline of my blue and green silk skirt. 'Please.'

Much as I'd enjoyed this evening, I knew it would be a bad idea to do this with Shane. I didn't want a relationship. I didn't know what I wanted most of the time, but not to have a boyfriend. It wasn't good, either, to go backwards. To look backwards and see where you had been, see *why* you were here because of where you'd been, yes and yes, but it was a bad idea to try to revisit it.

Shane brushed his lips against my neck, his fingers stroked the skin on the inside of my thigh, and the scent of him began to fill my senses. I looked over his shoulder and gasped: standing in the doorway of a baby clothes shop was a man with his hands in his pockets, his shoulders hunched and a scar on his cheek that wasn't visible from where we were standing. John Pope.

I'd tried so hard to forget about him when I was away. I hadn't seen or heard about him in nearly five years, but every time, *every* time I kissed a man, or I had sex, or I even thought about sex, I'd remembered his words: *'Dirty girls . . . Dirty little sluts.'* I'd had to brush them aside. I'd had to stop myself trying to prove him wrong, trying to be a good girl, a clean girl, one who didn't need to be shamed. One who wasn't ashamed to want sex and physical closeness. I'd battled the ghost of his words for so many years. Now when I thought I had won, here he was back in the flesh to remind me that he was still around. Nothing had come of the arrest of that man for the Mermaid Murders. The police didn't come for Dad again, but Pope hadn't let it go. And now he was back to following me around.

'What's the matter?' Shane asked, pulling away slightly to look at me.

'Nothing,' I replied. 'Nothing.'

I tugged my gaze away from Pope, back to Shane. *I'm not a dirty girl*, I reminded myself. I pushed my hands into Shane's back pockets, pulled him closer to me, felt his hardness against my thigh. *No matter what I do, no matter what I don't do, I am not a dirty little slut.*

'Let's go back to yours,' I said.

'I've . . . I've got a flatmate at the moment,' he replied. 'If you came back, you couldn't go into any room except my bedroom.'

'What if I need to go to the loo?'

'Let's just go to yours.'

I glanced over his shoulder at Pope. His gaze didn't waver, didn't drop for a moment.

'It's your place or not at all,' I told Shane.

He moved his hands higher up my thighs. 'OK, my place it is,' he said, and kissed me. Long and slow.

By the time we broke apart, Pope was gone.

*Friday, 18 August*

'I see you've learnt a few new things,' Shane said as we lay entwined later. Out of breath, out of energy, floating on a different level.

'Right back at you.'

'I . . . I never stopped loving you, you know? All those years apart don't have to mean anything.'

I stopped myself from sighing out loud. I knew I shouldn't have done this. Knew it. But seeing John Pope had made me panic. I had to prove to myself that I wasn't a *dirty girl*, and at the same time show that even if he thought I was a *dirty little slut*, I didn't care. What he thought didn't matter.

'We're different people now,' I said to Shane. 'Different people, different lives.'

'Is that your way of saying you don't want to pick up where we left off?' he said sadly.

'It's my way of saying we're different people with different lives.'

'The thing is, Nell, I can't be friends with you. It's got to be all or nothing.'

*Is Pope going to be waiting outside this building?* I wondered as I began to remember where my clothes had landed when we undressed each other. *Or will he be outside my building, waiting for me to come home so he can make me feel grubby and low?*

'I understand,' I said to Shane. I did, I really did. I just couldn't do this with him again.

'Nell, why won't you just give it – *us* – a chance?'

'It's not what I want,' I said. My socks were scrunched up by the door – they were the first thing I'd taken off when he'd ushered me quickly through into his bedroom. My top was probably there, along with my skirt. My bra and knickers he'd taken off when we were on the light brown leather love seat he'd had in the other flat. My bracelets were still on my wrists, thankfully. If I had to sit up and put them all on, it would simply prolong this agony to the point of cruelty.

I *really* shouldn't have done this. He was going to be hurt all over again, and I didn't want to hurt Shane. I'd loved him once. Not now, though. Unlikely to ever love him again.

Shane started to kiss my bare shoulder. 'We could just do this for a bit, maybe? What do they call them? Fuck buddies. We could do that, see how you feel in a few weeks?'

I closed my eyes. There was no way he'd settle for a 'just sex' relationship – he'd simply be waiting for us to get together properly. And when that didn't happen, he'd probably flip out again. I couldn't do that to Shane. We had to end things tonight.

'I better go,' I said rather than answer what he'd said about being fuck buddies.

'No, no, stay. Please? Please?'

'OK,' I said. 'OK.'

\*

*Saturday, 19 August*

I felt bad about sneaking out at 3 a.m. when he was out for the count, but I just couldn't deal with the drama of a morning goodbye. I didn't hear from or about him again until the call from Macy saying, 'You know my new boyfriend? He's called Shane and he says he knows you – intimately.'

# Now

## Macy

*Saturday, 31 March*

Those two think I'm stupid.

They honestly think I have no idea how intense their relationship was. Nell used to sneak away from school to see him. I never saw him or found out who he was, but I remember how different she became. Secretive but happy; then, as the time came for her to go to university, instead of being excited because she was getting out of Brighton and away from everything that had happened to her here, she would regularly come home with red, puffy eyes. Obviously from crying at the thought of leaving her boyfriend, whoever he was. I remember her disappearing more and more as the time to go to university drew closer, and how distressed she looked all the time.

I've given them so many chances to tell the truth. To admit that it wasn't a quick thing, that they were shagging when she came back from university, when she was living at Mummy and Daddy's place. But they don't. Won't. Can't. Whichever. The fact is they haven't. Because they think I'm fragile. Poor Macy, can't cope with the truth. It's them being secretive that's the problem, not the fact they used to go out together.

Well, that and the fact Shane and I haven't made love in nearly eighteen months.

I press my ear against the kitchen door. Will they talk about it?

There's silence. Absolute silence from the other side of the door. They're probably kissing, probably plotting how to be together.

I know they're not. But they could be. It's not that far away from the realm of possi—

'Mama, what are you doing?' Aubrey asks.

That's a very pertinent question. What *am* I doing? I'm listening at my kitchen door to see if my sister and my partner are kissing. Have I lost my mind or something? Sometimes I think there are two people in my head – the one who does ridiculous things, and the other one who doesn't stop her.

'Nothing, sweetheart,' I say and stand away from the door. I place my hands on his little shoulders and his father's face looks back at me.

I love Shane. I love everything about him. But, I hate to admit, I loved Clyde more. I sometimes wonder if that's what it's like for Nell and Shane. People say you never get over your first love, and from the way those two carry on, it's obvious they were each other's.

That's probably why Shane and I can't seem to get it right any more. We used to make love, have sex, fuck all the time. Then he rejected me three times in a row. Four weeks later when he was in the mood, I certainly wasn't. Then when I wanted to be close to him again, he wasn't interested. The seesaw of interest has carried on like that for eighteen months. One up, one down, on and on, never really managing to balance out so we can edge along the central beam of the seesaw and meet in the middle.

We did sort of manage it once, about six months ago. We got all the way to penetration . . . then we both seemed to lose the will and interest at the same time. He rolled off, I pulled the duvet up and we cuddled until we both fell asleep. Neither of us mentioned it again.

Is it because of Clyde and Nell? I look at Aubrey and I see his dad – does Shane look at me and see shades of Nell and know that I simply don't match up?

'You were doing something,' Aubrey says, appalled that I've claimed otherwise.

'OK, I was listening at the door.'

'Why?'

'Because.'

'Because what?' my ten-year-old replies.

'Because what what?'

'Mama!' he says, frustrated that he's unwittingly walked into the what-what loop that gets me out of sticky conversations at least three times a week.

'What?' I reply.

He sucks in air, turns on his heels and marches back to the living room to watch TV and sulk about how difficult I am.

I don't know what to do about my relationship with Shane. I know we have to fix it, but I don't know if we can do that with Nell around. And the last thing I want is for Nell not to be around.

# Nell

*Saturday, 31 March*

Shane and I have made a Herculean effort to be normal with each other. To talk, tease and ignore each other like two people who haven't previously had (a lot of) sex and made many declarations of love. It's been difficult, but done.

Macy looks pleased and relieved and I feel guilty that all this time she's been feeling like this and I've had no idea.

'Oh, Nell,' Shane says as I'm leaving. I've helped put the children to bed, and if I stay any longer I will end up falling asleep on the sofa. Besides, Zach told me to text him when I was free if I fancied going over to his new place in town.

'Yes, Shane,' I reply. I even look him in the eye when I say it, now that we have to do that.

'I was, erm,' he looks over his shoulder at the living room where Macy is and lowers his voice, 'I was, erm, talking to this guy at the gym—'

'Do people actually do that?' I cut in.

'Do what?'

'Talk to people at the gym? I've always thought it was some-where you go to exercise, not to start random conversations with random people.'

Shane looks pained. He's obviously remembering that I can be annoyingly off-topic at the drop of a hat. 'What are you talking about, Nell?'

'Nothing, nothing. Carry on.'

'I was talking to this guy at the gym. He was saying how he wanted some genealogy research done but didn't know where to start. Wasn't going to do it himself, but didn't know who to pay to do it. I said I knew a woman who did that and that I would pass on his number.' Shane reaches into his back pocket and pulls out a slip of paper that is folded in half. He holds it out to me. 'You never know, there might be a few quid in it. He was talking about how it was to do with a will or something.'

'I don't charge people,' I say.

'I know that, but *he* doesn't. And it's stupid not to charge people for your time. Or for the records I'd imagine it costs to get copies of.'

'I manage.'

'Wouldn't it be nice to not have to "manage" for a while though?'

'You sound like my dad. No, actually, you sound like my sister.'

'What are you two doing out there?' Macy calls. 'I'm going to start getting paranoid.'

'I'm just talking to Nell about her work,' Shane says in what seems an uncharacteristic moment of honesty when it comes to something to do with me.

'What work? Nell doesn't have a job any more,' Macy says and dissolves into giggles.

'*Thank you* and goodnight, Macy,' I say. I take the paper from Shane. 'Thanks for this,' I say to him.

'And . . . ?'

'And yes, I'll think about charging people. Goodnight.'

The world outside is darkening and it is glorious. I like the betwixt and between hours when night is descending but it's not quite certain if it will stay. When night could very easily lose its battle to reign over the sky; when daylight could reassert itself.

I don't charge people for looking through records and, especially, for having their DNA analysed because what I do with it isn't strictly legal. I have everyone sign a disclaimer saying I can submit their DNA on their behalf, and that I can get the results. I then interpret those results for people and inform them of the findings. But I . . . I also use the results to scan through all the databases available to see if they are even the slightest of matches to the DNA of The Brighton Mermaid or Jude.

# Macy

*Sunday, 1 April*

On days like today, when Nell's been over and it's been fine, I know without a doubt that what I worry about is stupid to worry about.

I know this. But most of the time I can't stop it. Most of the time it's like I'm trapped behind glass while my mind and body do things I don't want them to do. I don't want to go back five or six times to check I turned the cooker off. I don't want to rewash my hands if I happen to turn the tap off with my fingers instead of my elbow. I don't want to rewash every plate on the dish rack if the water comes out too fast from the tap and splashes a bit of dirt from a pan out of the sink. I don't want to go around straightening everything so it all lines up. I don't want to walk the lines of my kitchen floor. Most of the time, I'm trapped behind glass, shouting and screaming and telling myself to stop it, all the while knowing I can't. I mustn't. Because if I stop, then everything will fall apart.

When Clyde left, things did fall apart. I couldn't do anything. I called Nell, who was at work and never usually answered her phone. I don't know why she picked up that day, but when I told her, calm as you like, that Clyde had walked out and that I was scared of what I was going to do, she came straight away. At the time I thought I'd meant I was scared because I didn't know what to do. But in reality, what I meant was I was scared of what I was going to do to stop the pain.

She'd heard that second version, the real version of my words, and she was there in no time. And she took over, stopped my family from falling off the edge. While she was doing that, she didn't have time for all that other stuff, that obsessing about the Brighton Mermaid, and it was good for her. That's why I try to make her take part in family life: it's good for her.

The thing of it is, Nell doesn't realise she's as damaged as me. She just hides it better. Nell doesn't realise that there's something she doesn't know that means she should stop looking for Jude. If she knew what I know, what I saw from my bedroom window the night Jude disappeared – not the night everyone found out she'd gone, but the *actual* night she vanished – Nell would know she has to stop.

I want to tell her so she'll stop. I know I've been thinking of telling her to hurt her, but the reality is, I can't tell her. If I tell her, she won't keep it quiet like me, she'll immediately confront Daddy with it. And I can't take our family being any more fractured than it already is.

And it would kill Mummy.

# Nell

*Sunday, 1 April*

I see his car from the turn at the bottom of my road.

I live at the dead end of a maze of roads and opposite my building is his silver car. This is what happens when I don't respond to the 'He needs to see you' texts: I get a visit.

I knew I wouldn't get away with it much longer, but it's gone 3 a.m. and I'm only now getting back from a night with Zach after the day with Macy and her family so how long has he been waiting? What if I decided to stay out like I did last Friday night? Would he really have sat there until I returned? The answer is too scary to contemplate.

I stop. *What do I do?* If I go to my building and he sees me, he'll come to talk to me. He'll talk to me until he convinces me. And I do not want that. I do not want that at all. My heart, which I haven't been aware of, becomes a thick, heavy thrum of panic right at the centre of my chest. I should have gone, but I really didn't want to. That's the crux of it. I didn't want to see *him*.

I take my mobile out of my pocket. Call up the last text message, which came through earlier when I was with Zach. I stare at the five words and wonder what to say. I rarely reply to these texts – I get one, I go to see him. So what do I say now that will stop this?

**I can't.**

I eventually settle on this and hit 'send' from my place at the end of my road.

I see him in his car look up and spot me. Instead of getting out and coming over like he normally does, he lowers his head again and seconds later 'He needs to see you' pops up on my phone screen.

**What does he want?**

Can't text it. You know that.

**I can't.**

He needs to see you.

**Please.**

Nell . . .

**Please . . . Please.**

My phone is silent for long seconds. He's struggling with himself, with the position he's in. What my reply is going to mean for him.

All right, when?

**Soon.**

You promise, soon?

**Yes. Soon. Goodnight.**

It's morning, Nell. So good morning.

**OK. Good morning.**

The sound of his car starting up is like a firework exploding in the quiet night air. I'm sure my neighbours will be annoyed, their sleep being broken at this time. He only throws the briefest of glances my way before he turns out of my road and heads back to his part of Brighton.

# 2007

# Nell

*Monday, 3 December*

I stood outside the green front door and willed myself to knock instead of running away as every fibre of my being wanted me to. I had to do this. I had to speak to Jude's parents, even though it had been many, many years since I'd had meaningful contact with them.

After Dad was arrested, Mr Dalton had stopped coming over to drink beer and sit in the garden, and Mrs Dalton had stopped talking to Mum at work. Neither of them had explicitly accused Dad of anything; neither of them had given interviews to the papers about how they'd always known there was something dodgy about the man they'd called a friend and had trusted with their daughter; but they – like pretty much everyone outside of our family – must have had that no-smoke-without-fire thing on their minds.

In the following years, if I saw Mrs Dalton in the street, she would walk past me without acknowledging me. It was like a physical blow each time she did it, because I knew she blamed me. Even at fifteen I had worked out that she had rewritten things in her head; had reimagined Jude in her mind so that *I* was the one always in trouble, always sneaking out, always dragging her daughter along for the ride and something disastrous had befallen her on one of my misadventures.

I had to get over the hurt of her misremembering, though, if I was going to find Jude. I raised my hand and knocked on the door.

'Enelle,' Mr Dalton said. 'This is a surprise.'

'Hello, Mr Dalton,' I said. 'I, erm, I wanted to talk to you and Mrs Dalton, if possible. I won't take up much time. I just wanted to ask you both something.'

'Come in,' he said tiredly. He didn't completely ignore me if he saw me in the street – he'd smile sadly, nod his head, but he'd never speak to me. That was something, though, because he didn't pretend I wasn't there. 'She's in the living room.'

'Hello, Mrs Dalton,' I said. She was sitting on her sofa, watching TV. Mrs Dalton had always been the glamorous one out of my mum and her. They were both always immaculately turned out, but when she wasn't working, Mrs Dalton would style her hair in funky ways, she would wear false eyelashes that made her eyes look huge, she would paint her nails in bright colours. After Jude disappeared, she stopped wearing anything but the most basic make-up; she put her hair back in a bun always; she only ever dressed in dark-coloured clothes. And the weight she lost made everything she wore swim on her. Her daughter had been her whole life, and now it seemed the spark that had made her 'Party Mama' (as Jude had called her) had been extinguished.

Mrs Dalton did a double take when she saw me standing in her house, all grown up and the age that Jude should be. She then glared over my shoulder at her husband, promising him a world of pain for letting me in, before she went back to watching the television that sat in the alcove near the fireplace.

'I'm really sorry,' I said. 'I'm so sorry that Jude disappeared. And I wish I knew where she was because . . . because my life hasn't felt the same without her all these years.' My voice, suddenly overfull with tears, began to break under the strain, cracking up a little more with each word.

I hadn't cried over Jude; I'd gathered up all that emotion, imprisoned it in a bottle made of fear, stopped up that bottle with a lid made of guilt. I hadn't cried about Jude disappearing because I'd probably never stop. But standing there in front of her mum, I couldn't control myself any longer.

'I think about her every day since I last saw her,' I sobbed. 'I wear all these bracelets like she started to do because it's another way to remember her. I'm not going to take them off until she's back. And I check all the small ads in the papers almost every day in case she's left me a message. And when I was younger, I made these posters to try to find her.' I held out a piece of paper that she ignored. 'And I've been looking for her. There are so many websites out there. I spend hour after hour going through them, hoping—'

'Stop it, Enelle,' Mrs Dalton snapped. She'd had enough of my emotion, my guilt, my not being Jude. 'What do you want?'

I sniffed hard, scrubbed at my wet eyes with the back of my hand. *Urgh. Who cries in front of a mother whose life stopped the day her daughter disappeared? Who does such a thing? Me. That's who.* 'I wondered – I hoped you might talk to me about your family? I've been reading about genealogy and how family tree research can help you find people. I've done a few things, but I thought, if I could get some history about you and Jude, then maybe it might help to find her.'

Mr Dalton walked into the room, frowning. 'You say genealogy stuff can help find people?'

'Not always, but sometimes. I just want to try as much as I can to find her. If I find all the people who are related to her, it might be a clue as to where she went. She might know of some family that you didn't think to check, or friends of family. It's a long shot, as they say, but I want to try anything and everything to find her.'

'Of course you do,' Mr Dalton said. 'Of course you do, Enelle.' He turned to his wife. 'It might work, Lilani. When people die intestate, sometimes genealogy companies track down distant relatives using family trees and records so they can claim their portion of the will. I've never known anyone do it in quite this way before, but it might work.'

Mrs Dalton did not glance away from the television, but it did look like she was listening. Eventually she asked, 'You think this will help to find her?'

'It might. Or it might not,' I admitted. 'But I just want to try.'

'What do we have to do?' Mr Dalton asked.

'I just need you to tell me everything you can about your family's background. Names, dates of anything you remember, places where they've lived. I'll make some notes and then get on with it.'

'We'll do anything, won't we, Lilani?' Mr Dalton said. '*Won't we?*'

'Yes,' Mrs Dalton said despondently. 'Anything.'

# Now

## Nell

DNA, DNA, DNA.

It is all about DNA when it comes to looking for people. It's on all the TV detective shows as the thing that breaks the case, the thing that identifies people and brings criminals to justice.

I've been researching the Brighton Mermaid for ages, and I've been trying to find out about Jude's family, too, and in the background of this, I taught myself everything I could about DNA. I read everything available, I learnt how to decipher the code of DNA, how the sequences are rendered as numbers and letters. I learnt about autosomal DNA, the stuff provided by both your parents; I read about mitochondrial DNA, the genes provided by your mother, and all the women along her family line; I taught myself about Y-line DNA, provided by your father and all the men along his line. I read and researched and learnt what I could because I knew, one day, I'd be able to have access to the DNA databases similar to the ones the police had and I would be able to start searching myself.

Obviously when the tests became available to the public, they were too expensive for me. But I could wait.

I didn't have samples of Jude's DNA, nor of the Brighton Mermaid's, though. That was always the stumbling block, even as the price of publicly available tests came down.

I assumed they took DNA from the woman we found, and I knew they must have got Jude's DNA (probably from a hairbrush that had hair with the little bulb attached to the end) because the police forensics team tried to test our house for Jude's DNA at one point. But, like the fingerprints, her DNA showed up in the places where it should, because she practically lived at our home. Same with Dad's car, same with the shop. Shops. They tested all the shops, but only ever found her DNA in the one in Hove, where she constantly hung out with me.

For a long time DNA was like a shiny beacon, something I had no access to but something I was convinced would help me to find Jude and work out who the Brighton Mermaid was.

My mobile bleeps with the third 'He needs to see you' text of the day. I thought I'd bought myself more time at the weekend, but obviously not that much time. I'm going to have to go there. Even though—

'Miss Okorie, I'm so sorry to have kept you waiting.'

Shane's friend from the gym is called Craig Ackerman and he was keen to meet me the moment I called him yesterday. I'd suggested later in the week, but he managed to get a window in his schedule (his phrase, not mine) for today so I have come over to his offices just outside the city centre. His building is a very shiny thing: lots of clean lines and glass and magazines placed just so. There is uniformed security and a large reception desk on the ground floor, and the fifth floor, where his office is, has an impossibly neat personal assistant who sits outside his door, typing and answering the phone.

Craig Ackerman is older than me, by at least five years, possibly more.

'Take a seat,' he says but doesn't exactly point to any particular one. He has an expansive office, with a sofa, a side chair as well as his chair behind the large glass desk, and two chairs on the other side of his desk. And then, of course, there are the low cupboards, the side table beside the side chair and glass desk – all of them offer valid seating options.

I'm nervous, which is why I am internally babbling. I've never done this for someone who is a complete stranger before. When I started with the genealogy stuff, it was to try to work out if Jude had any family, no matter how distant, that she might have run away to. As time went on, I met a few people – online and in real life – who were searching for their extended family. They'd share what they were doing and I would help them by looking over what they had done and offering the insights that only a stranger can.

One woman, for example, who had been searching for her father's side of the family tree for a long time couldn't get past a certain point. They were all scattered across Sussex, mostly East Sussex, some in West Sussex, but only back three generations. I didn't have the family knowledge, the insight into family history and legend that she did, but those things, as it turned out, were dead-ending her search. I came at it by breaking down the family surname and searching for where each of those branches of the name originated in this country. Some had come over from Ireland and had settled along the Scottish border; others had settled in the Midlands. Once we had deconstructed her family name in a way she hadn't considered, her search took off again.

Craig Ackerman clearly realises I don't know where to sit, so he opts to go behind his desk. *Good choice, that man*, I almost say. *Let's keep this business-like if I'm going to do it properly.*

'So, how do you know Shane?' he asks when I have installed myself in one of the large leather chairs opposite his desk.

'He's sort of my brother-in-law – he's with my sister,' I reply. 'How do you know him?'

'Well, I don't really. I see him at the gym. One time he was watching a match on his mobile phone when mine had run out of charge, so he allowed me to watch over his shoulder. Firm gym friends ever since, even though we were rooting for different sides.'

Craig Ackerman is really quite posh. He is dressed in a suit that is clearly expensive but is quite modern in style and a royal blue colour. He has light brown hair neatly cut, light blue eyes and pale skin. I look him over, wondering what his genetic make-up will be. It usually shocks people to learn that how they look doesn't necessarily correlate with what is going on with their genes. They can be pale, pale skinned with blond hair and still find out they have 41 per cent Sub-Saharan African DNA; they can be dark-brown skinned with black hair and find they have 37 per cent Scandinavian heritage. DNA sneaks in from all over the place, and people are often floored because they've been looking in the mirror their whole life and seeing who they think they are; they've been bombarded with messages that say people X, who look like the one in the reflection in the mirror, come from Y. Then it turns out this particular person who looks like X comes from D, F, G and H, with the tiniest hint of a waft of Y, Z and A.

'Did Shane give you a rundown of what I'm after?' asks Craig Ackerman.

'Not really, no. He said it was something to do with a will?'

'Oh. I don't know why he told you that. I'm adopted. I would like to find out more about my birth family.'

'Do you have your adoption records?' I ask.

Craig Ackerman smiles. 'My dear, if I had them, what would I need you for?' He laughs. 'No offence meant.'

'None taken,' I reply, because in some ways it is a valid point. I reach into my large bag and take out my A4 sketchpad, which I use to make notes and start to draw a rough family tree to fill in. I also take out my voice recorder. I need to take an oral history of everything he remembers, everything he's been told – no matter how vague or gossipy – so I can get an idea of where to start.

The man behind the desk looks at the recorder suspiciously. 'Why on Earth are you recording me?' he asks.

'I'm not recording you as such. I like to get two versions of the history you tell me, in case I miss something in my notes.'

'I'm afraid I don't have much to go on,' he says.

'Doesn't matter. Any detail, no matter how small, can sometimes spark another avenue of research. Ready?'

He clears his throat a few times, picks up his glass of water and gulps a couple of mouthfuls before clearing his throat again. 'Ready.'

I hit record and pick up my pencil, ready to start sketching as he talks.

Craig Ackerman doesn't talk for very long because he doesn't have much to go on. He keeps apologising and I keep telling him it's fine. I need a challenge and it looks like this is it.

'Have you eaten anything in the last hour or so, Mr Ackerman?' I ask.

'No. May I ask why?'

I drop my notebook and recorder back into the folds of my large black leather bag and pull out the rest of my kit, which is my DNA collection pack. In a very large, clear polythene bag are fifteen buccal swab kits, rubber gloves, and several sheets of disclaimer forms, drawn up for me by a solicitor. Craig Ackerman's already lined face frowns at what I've just carefully laid out on his desk in front of me.

'What are you doing?' he asks.

'This is the other part of what I do,' I say. 'I take a DNA sample and send it off for analysis to various companies who will match you with anyone who could be a biological relative. I do all that for you. I send them off, and check the results, see which matches you have and explain them to you. I can also get in touch with any matches for you if you want. You obviously get a copy of the results and access to the account in your name on the various websites. But I do need you to sign an authority allowing me to submit these samples in your name, and a disclaimer to say you won't try to sue me if you don't get the results you were hoping for . . .' My voice peters away. 'You look confused, Mr Ackerman.'

'Craig, please, call me Craig.' The furrows on his brow deepen as he stares at the blue gloves on my hands. 'Shane did not mention that you took DNA samples.'

'It's most likely he didn't know. I don't really talk to him about what I do.'

The furrows deepen even more.

'Is there a problem?' I ask gently. 'The thing of it is, adding DNA to the search makes all the difference. I can do all the paper and hard-core genealogy research just fine, but DNA brings in another dimension and opens up even more avenues for discovery if you find a match. Which sometimes doesn't happen, I have to admit. And you can't do it with only DNA either, as the sample size out there is way too small. But old-school methods and DNA together are a powerful combination.'

'I see. What do I have to do?'

'Drink a couple of swigs of water to wet your mouth. Then use this giant cotton bud to swipe along the inside of your cheek.' I hold out the buccal swab, which does indeed look like a giant cotton bud, that I will store in what looks like an oversized test tube. Once I've taken the fifteen swabs, I'll send them off in different envelopes to different DNA testing companies. 'I'll bag them up and send them off.' He obliges with the water swig, but when it comes to the cheek swipe, he doesn't take the swab from me.

'Would you . . . would you mind doing the first one for me, so I can see what I'm supposed to do?'

'Open,' I say.

He opens his mouth and waits patiently for me to insert the swab and watches me the whole time, staring into my eyes while I move it around. Most people who ask me to carry out the swab for them look away, embarrassed that I am doing something that feels quite intimate. Not this man. He has that supreme confidence I often come across in successful businessmen – nothing seems to faze them.

Once I have the sample, I swiftly return to my side of the desk to put the swab safely in its glass tube. I slip the tube into the plastic bag and carefully lay the others on his side of the desk. 'I'm sure you can do these yourself now,' I say. 'And then once you've signed the papers, we're done.'

'You're most efficient,' he says.

I busy myself with getting the paperwork in order and wait for him to finish swabbing himself. I don't like Craig Ackerman. It's nothing he's done, he simply makes me uneasy. Having said that, I have to admit I spend a lot of time on high alert, feeling wary and unsure about people. Another hangover from the Brighton Mermaid stuff, I suppose.

'I generally send everything on Fridays, so once I post these off, I should get the DNA results in a month to six weeks. I'll let you know if I turn up anything else significant in the meantime.'

'It was a pleasure to meet you, Miss Okorie,' he says.

It hasn't been a pleasure meeting him, but I smile and say, 'Likewise. Thank you,' and exit his office as quickly as possible. In all these things, even with the people I find odious, I focus on the most important thing: another set of DNA results that will hopefully take me one step nearer to finding Jude and the identity of the Brighton Mermaid.

# Macy

'Shane, stop for a second, stop.'

'Wh-what's the matter? Am I hurting you? Am I too heavy on you?'

'No, no, it's not that. I just . . . This is the fifth time since Saturday.'

'I know, it's wonderful, isn't it? We've got our mojo back.'

'But why?'

'What do you mean, "why?"'

'Is it because of Nell?'

'What? No. Why would you say that?'

'You've . . . This . . . It's only been like this since you sorted things out with Nell on Saturday. You practically jumped on me when she left. Are you doing it because of her? Because of Nell?'

'Will you stop saying her name? Why do you keep saying her name when we're in the middle of making love?'

'Because I need to know if it's because of her.'

'No. A million times no.'

'Then why?'

'Because I love you. Because I want you all the time but it doesn't feel like you want me in the same way.'

'Of course I do. You repeatedly rejected me first, remember? That's where it started.'

'I rejected you because you called me Clyde one time. All right? It killed a bit of me and it took me ages to get the confidence up to make love again. I mean, we'd been together all this time and you called me by your ex's name at a crucial moment. That was hard. By the time I got over it, you didn't want to know.'

'Oh, I'm sorry, I'm sorry. I had no idea I'd done that. No idea.'

'It's OK now, I'm over it.'

'I really am sorry. But if it's any comfort, I know how it feels.'

'What do you mean?'

'You've called me Nell more than once. Usually when you're about to come. I know what you mean about it killing a little part of you each time.'

'Oh, Jeez. I'm so sorry. So, so sorry. I had no idea. You should have said something. I should have said something.'

'Do you think we're fooling ourselves here? That we're not really suited and we should just call it a day?'

'*I* think I love you. More than I've loved anyone in my entire life. *I* think I want to continue making love to you right now because it feels so good doing it with you. *I* think we're perfect for each other. And *I* think I want to marry you. That's what *I* think.'

'I think I love you too, Mr Merrill. And I think I want us to carry on making love. And I think I'll think again about marrying you.'

'I love you, Mrs Merrill.'

'Hey, I didn't say yes yet.'

'I know, but I'm just testing it out. Practising, if you will, for when I finally get to sleep with a married woman.'

*You already are, Shane*, I think. *You already are.*

# Nell

Maura Goodrich cries.

Since I arrived and laid out her final family tree, showed her where she fits into it, explained who is around her and before her, revealed the secrets of the people who share portions of her twenty-three pairs of chromosomes, she has not stopped crying. I sit beside her, not at all uncomfortable because this is often how people react, and wait for her to be calm enough to form words. When people see themselves on their family map, the upside-down tree on which they are a leaf of a branch, they become very emotional. Not all of them cry, but most of them pause for a moment, gather their thoughts, round up their feelings and then try to comprehend the vastness of it all. We seem to be tiny specks in the vast ocean of our DNA pool when it is all mapped out, and it is that – the literal relativity of it all – which takes their breath away.

'I knew it!' Maura says. 'I knew there was something they were hiding from me.' She sniffs and wipes her dribbling nose on her sleeve. 'I've always known there was this big thing that nobody talked about.' She sighs. 'I remembered my dad leaving for a while, like I told you, but they would always pretend I was mistaken or misremembered him going away on business. He didn't, he left and he went to live with another woman. Had a child with her.' She wipes at her eyes with her fingertips. 'Oh. The relief. I wasn't going batshit. I really do have a sister.'

Technically, she's her half-sister, but I know for many people, that detail isn't all that important. What is important is the connection they have out there. The other people who could be a part of their lives. It doesn't always work. They don't always find more people to expand their family and live happily ever after. More often than not, if a person hasn't actively gone looking – put their name on websites, submitted DNA, looked at records – they don't want to know. Most people who aren't actively searching have a life that may not be perfect, but certainly works for them, so they have no need for another person to enter their world. Those are the heart-breaking conversations. I usually tell them when I present them with their family tree so that I can tell them in person, hold their hand, offer a hug, remind them that they have other family to rely on. Or friends. That this doesn't change anything about who they were at the start of the search and who they could be. I also remind them that people often change their minds – they rarely find out this sort of news and decide they don't want to know for ever.

Happily, Maura's case isn't like that. Her (half-)sister had been floored. Brought up by her mum and stepfather, she had always been told that her father was unknown because he was a one-night stand. She'd been fine with that, apparently, but had put her DNA online in the hopes of one day meeting him. When she heard that she had a sister, she was over the moon. I wasn't sure how she'd receive the news that her mother and father had been together for the first year of her life, though. It wasn't my place to tell her, so I held my tongue.

'I want to meet her,' Maura says.

'She wants to meet you, too.'

'Really?! That's so wonderful. I'm so excited. I can't wait.'

'There are a few things to remember, though, Maura, before you meet Laura. You probably won't become instant best friends, or even sisters. She is, essentially, a stranger, so you have to bear that in mind. I will come to the meeting with you if you'd like me to, but you might want to take a friend or your boyfriend. Meet somewhere public, try to take it slowly and, most importantly, don't invest anything in the relationship that you're not able to lose. So if you're going to be hurt if she isn't who you think she is, then only expect the most basic things from her and the relationship. Does that make sense?'

Maura nods. She's not really listening. I'll have to repeat it all for her before I leave, but that's understandable. I'd be just as floored as she is.

*Ah, drat!* I didn't give Craig Ackerman the 'expectations' speech. I usually give it to everyone I work with, it's always best to under-promise than overpromise and have to eat humble pie when I find out very little or even nothing at all.

'All right,' I say with a smile. 'I'll tell you everything I found and then we can maybe call her.'

'That would be amazing!'

This is why I don't get horrifically upset and despondent when a search has no Jude or Brighton Mermaid connection. What I do helps people, it creates links and reveals connections to other humans. This type of work is rewarding even if it doesn't bring me any nearer to solving my two big mysteries.

'I have a friend,' Maura says while her eyes run over and over the family tree, 'he wants someone to track down some family for him, too. I said you were just the person. Shall I pass on your number to him?'

'Erm, if you've got his number, that'd be great.'

'Yes, wait right here, I'll go get it.'

Having a recommendation passed on is payment enough for me. Getting access to more and more DNA is vital for me right now. I need as many chances as possible to find that genetic link, that magic combination that will prove I'm doing the right thing. That I can solve these mysteries before everything blows up again.

# Macy

*Friday, 6 April*

Jude. Jude. Jude.

I keep dreaming about Jude, and she keeps echoing through my mind during the day. Every time I think about finding Clyde so I can start the divorce process, my mind skips back even further, back twenty-five years to that night and I have to think about Jude.

I don't remember the dreams, I just know, when I open my eyes, that she has inhabited every part of my mind while it floated in dreamland. Then, while I'm staring into the dark, her name repeats and repeats in my head, like a never-ending drum beat.

Jude. Jude. Jude.

I know she didn't run away. And I know who she was with when she disappeared. I can see it as clearly as though it happened yesterday. In twenty-five years I've forgotten so much – people, places, events and things – and still, I remember that night as clear as anything.

I remember . . . my bare feet on the textured carpet in my bedroom . . . my nightdress clinging to me in the hot stickiness of that night . . . the heat pulsing around me as I sat up because I could hear talking . . . the otherworldly feeling of being out of it as I went to my bedroom window and looked outside.

The world was asleep but they were not. They were in the street. I watched them. I watched them and I knew I could never tell.

Jude. Jude. Jude.

I often felt pushed out by Jude because she and Nell had known each other for so long.

Sometimes it felt like she was Nell's sister instead of me. But I liked Jude. I thought she was funny and kind and always had a great tale to tell. She was trouble, too. Everyone knew it. Even Nell knew it. Nell didn't care because she was her friend, but when I would listen at the door, sometimes I could hear Nell telling her off. Saying that she shouldn't have done this or that, telling her she was going to get them both into trouble. Nell was always loyal, and she would always stand by Jude, even if it meant getting into hot water, too. Nell *would* get into trouble as well, because our parents weren't like Jude's.

Our parents shouted and told off and took things away if you misbehaved. Our parents would sometimes smack if you got completely out of line. We always knew where we stood with our parents and we – for the most part – behaved. Jude's parents were mega laid-back. I think that was Mr Dalton. I heard Jude tell Nell how she and her mum would have stand-up rows, but it was always her stepdad who calmed them down. Mr Dalton always seemed like the most placid and unflappable person in the world. I remember one time I tripped and dropped a glass of water on him. It splashed all over his lovely grey suit and made him look like he'd wet himself. I was horrified and said sorry a million times. If that had been Daddy, he would have said 'Macenna!' in a cross voice because I was always spilling things and dropping things and knocking things over. He would have grabbed a towel and shaken his head and told me I had to be more careful. Mr Dalton just went, 'Oh, oops-a-daisy,' and then laughed.

Jude. Jude. Jude.

Being a parent now, I don't think Mr Dalton being so casual was a good thing. I didn't think so even back as an eleven-year-old.

Maybe because Nell only ever got into trouble with Jude, I kind of thought her parents needed to be stricter, should stop her doing exactly what she wanted whenever she wanted. When they found that dead body, when Daddy had to go to the police station to pick Nell up, I was certain that would be it. That Daddy and Mummy would ban Jude from our house as well as not letting Nell out ever again. It didn't work out like that, of course. Jude's parents only let her out to come to our place so she spent even *more* time with us. They were mostly in Nell's room, talking about the dead body and talking about Jude's bracelets and talking about what they could do to find out who killed her.

That was mainly Jude. She was the one who wanted to know who the woman was and how she was killed. Nell mostly wanted to forget about it. I could hear her sometimes, crying into her pillow, screaming away her fears. Nell thinks she hides her feelings so well, but I've always been able to see right through her.

Jude. Jude. Jude.

I sometimes think that what I saw that night was meant to be seen by Nell. If she had seen it, she would have done something different, I'm sure. She would have told, I think. She would have been brave enough to speak of it and not carry it around inside, making her bite her nails, cut her skin, keep a hundred little rituals that will help her to hide the truth.

I sometimes think, on nights like this when I can't sleep and when I do sleep I think of Jude, that my life would be completely different if only I didn't see what I saw that night.

Jude. Jude. Jude.

I sometimes think, on nights like this when I can't sleep and when I do sleep I think of Jude, that I should tell.

I know the end is coming. I can feel it fast approaching with every passing day. Nell taking a year off work to focus on this, the stuff in the newspapers, a call I had the other day at work asking if I was related to Enelle Okorie – are all the ticks of the time bomb that is going to explode. Maybe I should tell and detonate it now.

Maybe I should tell that I saw Jude at our house that night she actually disappeared.

# Nell

*Friday, 6 April*

'WATCH OUT!' shouts the man coming towards me as he raises his pointing finger.

I half turn to look where he's pointing and a hand connects with the middle of my back, violently shoving me. My arms go up as I fly forwards, then my body twists as my bag is ripped off my shoulder. I land awkwardly, pain spiking through my right elbow, hammering my right knee as they hit the ground first before the rest of my body. A moped whines into life suddenly and peels away as I lie motionless on the pavement.

Quick. So quick it takes me seconds to register what has just happened. Why my elbow hurts, why my knee aches, why I don't have my bag.

'Are you all right, love?' a woman asks while helping me up.

'That looked nasty,' says the man who shouted the warning, helping me up, too. 'Are you OK?'

I've just been mugged.

In quiet, laid-back Hove, I've just been mugged.

'That happened so fast,' the woman says. She's still got hold of my arm because I'm unsteady on my feet, shaky where I stand.

'Can't believe it happened,' the man adds. 'I saw him coming for you. I shouted. Did you hear me shout? I shouted.'

A small crowd is forming around us, people murmuring, talking about what they saw. Which probably wasn't much given it happened so fast.

'Do you think they got much?' a third person asks.

'Just my bag,' I reply.

'That's awful,' the first woman, who is still holding me up, says. 'I can't believe that just happened. Are you all right?'

'Yeah,' I say vaguely. 'I'm fine.'

'Do you want me to call the police?' the man says.

I shake my head. 'No, no.' I do not want him to call the police. The last people I want him to call are the police. Unless I have to, I have very little to do with the police. Most people won't understand why. I've been the victim of a crime and that is the first thing I should want to do. I can see it on the faces of those in the small crowd: *What does she have to hide that she doesn't want to call the police?* 'I'll call them in a bit,' I add to explain my aversion. 'I just need to get my breath back.'

'Don't blame you, love,' the woman says. 'That was awful. So terribly shocking.'

The outliers of the crowd start to drift away – it's not that interesting, I imagine, given that I'm not bleeding or hysterical.

'Thank you,' I say to the woman. 'You've been so kind.' I lean out of her hold now, and she seems as pleased as I am that I don't fall over.

'Do you want to go and sit down somewhere?' the man asks.

'No, no, I'm fine, honestly. I'd better get home and report my cards missing.'

'Do you want me to talk to the police with you?' the woman asks. 'Not that I saw much. It all happened so fast. One minute you were standing there and then you were on the ground and this guy in black was jumping onto the back of a moped holding your bag.'

So the moped did have something to do with it.

'It came right up onto the pavement,' the man says. 'That's why I shouted. Did you hear me shout?'

I raise my fingers and press them on my eyes. I feel sick. I can't believe this has happened. I mean, I've always known these things happen and I've heard people talk about having their mobiles snatched from their hands by people on mopeds, but I genuinely thought that was a London thing. Not a here thing. At all.

I've just been to the post office down by the Floral Clock in Hove and sent all the DNA samples I had to various companies, as Friday is generally my posting day. I then started for home and got halfway there before I remembered I hadn't sent off the consent and disclaimer forms to be lodged at my solicitor's, so I turned around and was on my way back to the post office when I was shoved.

'Are you all right?' the woman asks again.

'Yes, I'm fine.' I smile at her. It's just her and the man who shouted here now. Everyone else has gone. 'I'm perfectly fine. I just need a minute.'

I always carry my mobile in my pocket, and my keys, so they haven't got those things. But my purse was in my bag. My glasses. My diary, with the picture of Jude and me pinned to the inside cover. I can't get that back. I have so few pictures of Jude and I have no idea where the negative for that picture is. That's gone now. Out of everything, that's the biggest thing that's been stolen from me today. I can't replace it.

Despite my best efforts, despite me creating an extensive family tree and contacting almost all the people on it in the past ten years, I didn't find Jude and I didn't change Jude's mother's feelings towards me. There's no way she'll give me a picture of her daughter to replace this one.

I press my fingers onto my eyes again to stop them leaking tears.

That's why it's pointless calling the police. I can tell them what happened, but what can they do about the keepsake items with no value? How can they return the picture of me and my best friend at the circus down by the King Alfred on the seafront? How can they get me back the tenth-anniversary pen from The Super that I had at the bottom of my bag? How will they retrieve the stickers Aubrey gave me that I stuck on the back of my glasses case? The answer is that they can't.

I don't understand why someone would do this to me. Out of all the people walking down this street at this time, why did they pick me? It's not like I was closest to the edge of the pavement; I didn't have my mobile in my hand. It wasn't a designer handbag, just a big, black shapeless thing Macy gave me for Christmas.

Why me?

Out of all the other people on this road, why me?

*Bleep-bleep-bleep* goes my mobile in my pocket. *His* message tone.

No, it can't be because of that. Why would the Brighton Mermaid cause me to be mugged twenty-five years after I found her?

I'm being ridiculous. I know this.

I thank the woman and man for their kindness, reassure them I'm going to go to a café to have a strong, sweet tea to calm my nerves and then I'll call the police.

I'm being ridiculous if I think someone is out to get me. Of course I don't believe that. I haven't done anything to make someone get me in this way.

# 2013

## Nell

*Monday, 20 May*

'Are you Nell Okorie?' the man with black-framed glasses asked. It was late and I'd just finished closing up at the Super when he approached me.

My gaze swept over him in the orange glow of the street lamps. He had pale skin, brown hair, a face that looked familiar.

'Who wants to know?' I asked, poised to bolt. The road from here to the main road was slightly uphill, but I could make it. Once I was on London Road, there were pubs and restaurants that would still be open and I could dash into, hide in.

'Me,' he replied.

I took a step back and kept my eyes on him, watching for any sudden movements. 'And who are you?' I asked when it became clear he wasn't going to say anything else.

'Aaron Pope. John Pope is my father.'

He was getting his son to harass me now? The man was unbelievable. Now I knew where the DNA that made up his features came from, I could see his father plainly on his face.

'Right, well, on that note, I'm going to leave,' I said.

He stepped into my path as I tried to move past him and a flurry of fear flew from my stomach to my throat. Was he going to hurt me? John Pope had never raised his hand, but I didn't know anything about this man. He could be far, far worse than his father. He was taller than his father, and although slender, he looked muscular. Potentially dangerous.

He seemed to immediately recognise that he'd scared me so he stepped back again, gave me space. 'My father is . . .' he began.

Now there was a gap between us, the bite of adrenalin subsided a little – but I was still ready to run for it.

I waited for him to finish his sentence, but he didn't. He, instead stared off at a point over my shoulder. I'd seen that look before. Whenever something had happened to my father, I would escape as soon as I could to the bathroom to wash my face, hide my crying, and I would see that exact same look on my face in the mirror. Something had happened to John Pope. 'Your father is what?' I asked as gently as I could.

'He's in hospital,' Aaron Pope replied. He was still staring over my shoulder.

'Right. I see.'

That was the best I could do. I couldn't pretend to care what happened to John Pope.

I wasn't meant to think like that, of course. People like me, people who've been persecuted by people like Pope, are meant to rise above it, forgive, have compassion. I was done with that. The more time that elapsed between then and now, the less compassionate I became. The more adult years stacked up, the angrier I grew at the terrible things I'd learnt to be thankful for. When Dad would come back from police custody, battered and bruised with injuries that officers had – they said – inflicted in self-defence (even though Dad never had any cuts and bruises on his knuckles), I'd be grateful. *Grateful*. Because he was alive, because he hadn't become another of the many black men who died in suspicious circumstances while in police custody. John Pope had done that, and I could not feel any compassion for him. At all.

'For your sake, I hope he recovers soon,' I told my former persecutor's son.

I went to move on again and Aaron Pope spoke: 'Someone tried to kill him.'

If it had been anyone else, I would have been more surprised. But knowing what John Pope was capable of, knowing how persistent his 'above and beyond the call of duty' behaviour could be, the only surprising thing to me was that it hadn't happened sooner.

'Because of the Brighton Mermaid,' he added.

I used my fingertips to rub my tired, gritty eyes. 'Your father thinks everything is because of the Brighton Mermaid.'

In the orange glow of the street light, John Pope's son sized me up, looking me over as though I wasn't what he'd been expecting. 'I was on the phone to him when it happened,' he said quietly. 'He was talking about her, yes, but he said he was coming to see you because he had a piece of information that would change everything. He was saying that he'd been wrong all these years and that . . . that he'd made a connection that no one had noticed before. And then . . . and then . . .' His voice broke and his face creased as he hung his head.

I reached out to touch him, to comfort him – and then I stopped myself. He was a stranger – and worse, he was John Pope's son.

'A car hit him. It mounted the pavement and drove straight at him. That's what someone who was there said. It accelerated, hit him and then didn't stop.' He shook his head, as if trying to dislodge the memory of it. 'I was screaming his name, and I could hear him . . . I thought . . . I thought I could hear him dying. And I just kept screaming his name. I didn't even think to call an ambulance. I just kept calling for him.'

'You were probably in shock,' I said. 'It probably helped him to hear your voice.'

'Maybe. He's still in a coma,' he told me. 'He hasn't woken up after surgery yet.'

'It must be a really difficult time for you. How's your mother coping with it all?'

Aaron Pope glared at me as though I was winding him up. 'My mother left him years ago. She couldn't take it any more. He was obsessed with the Brighton Mermaid case more than any other.

She couldn't stay when he—' I realised, with some horror, that small shiny tears were rolling down his face. He tugged at his sleeves, pulled them down over his wrists and hands, trying to hide from what he was feeling about this.

I took him in again: he seemed damaged and fragile, like a cracked piece of porcelain that was yet to completely fall apart. I couldn't imagine what it must have been like to grow up with John Pope as a father. Someone that obsessive and hate-filled would not be kind, gentle and understanding at home.

'Mum left a while back.' He shrugged, trying to act as if he didn't care, but gave himself away by tucking his hands under his armpits – hiding again, trying to make himself less vulnerable. 'He didn't care that she left, not really. He always said you were the only person who understood his need for the truth.'

'Me?' I replied. '*Me?* Are you sure he said that about *me?*'

He nodded. 'Yes. You were one of the girls who found her. You wanted the truth as much as he did. He talked about how you were the only one who understood so much that Mum started to think you and he . . . *you know.*'

Aaron Pope took off his glasses and scrubbed his eyes dry before putting them in place again. 'Do you want me to drive you to the hospital, or do you want to drive yourself?' he asked. 'Assuming you have your own car.'

It was my turn to look at him as though he was winding me up. 'Why would I go to the hospital?'

'I know he's still in a coma, but you can still see him. The nurse told me he kept saying your name before they put him under.'

I frowned at him. He was serious. He actually thought . . . 'Aaron, I'm sorry, but no. Your dad . . . He . . . It wasn't how he said. It wasn't anything like he said at all. I'm not going to see him whether he's awake or not. It's just not going to happen.'

'But he's so ill; he's all alone. He'd want to see you.'

I sighed while searching for the right words. 'Look, when he wakes up, ask him to tell you the truth about what he did to me and to my family. Then you'll understand. Until then, I can't help you, I'm sorry.'

John Pope's son looked like he was going to cry again. He seemed desperate and bewildered. I almost changed my mind; almost decided to help him because he really was looking terrified. But I couldn't do that.

'I hope for your sake he gets well again,' I told Aaron Pope, and this time when I walked away he didn't do or say anything to stop me.

# 2015

## Nell

*Wednesday, 24 June*

Pope's son was waiting for me outside my workplace again.

It'd been a couple of years since he'd first shown up and he seemed to have grown up a lot in that time. Or maybe, he was simply looking normal now as opposed to how shaken and shocked he'd been back then. I had a feeling, the way he fixed his face and exhaled deeply before pulling back his shoulders and taking a large, courage-steeling breath, that he was going to tell me John Pope had died.

'Do you have five minutes?' he asked.

I didn't say anything, just stared at him. I wasn't ready to hear that Pope had died, that he had left this Earth without me proving that my father was innocent. I wasn't ready for Pope to have escaped without facing what he did.

'I'm assuming you remember me?' he said.

I nodded.

'Well, that's something. I just need a few minutes of your time.'

'OK,' I replied.

I led the way across the area in front of the supermarket, to the concrete bench flanked by large concrete planters.

'How can I help you?' I asked Aaron Pope. I watched people enter The Super, a lot of them seeming dazed and confused, not really relishing going in but needing to. Other supermarkets I'd been to – there was no way I was doing my weekly shop where I worked – seemed to have customers who were focused and ready, lists in hands, bags for life in pockets. Ours always seemed anaesthetised before they rocked up at the door, the general laid-back nonchalance of the London Road area seeming to infect everything they did.

'It's my father,' he began.

I teed up, *I'm sorry to hear that*, on my tongue, willed my brain to make it sound sincere and not *outraged* that my father never got to clear his name.

'He needs to see you,' he said.

'I'm— *What?*' I replied. 'Eh? He's not . . . ? He wants to see me?'

'Yes, he needs to see you,' Pope's son repeated.

'So he's not . . . ? Why does he want to see me?'

Aaron Pope nervously moistened his lips. 'He says he has more information about the Brighton Mermaid and your friend – Judana? He says he needs to tell you about it in person.'

The man was a joker. An absolute joker. 'That's not going to happen. I'm not going to see him. I don't care what information he has, I'm not putting myself in the same room as him.'

Aaron Pope looked momentarily defeated. 'If you're scared of him, there's no need to be. He can't hurt you. He's been partially paralysed since his accident so he can't harm you.'

'Not happening.'

Aaron Pope seemed to deflate, his face taking on a worn-out, defeated look. He was going to get it in the neck if he went back without me, I could tell.

'Did he ever tell you what he did to my family?' I asked.

Aaron shook his head. 'No. A few of his ex-colleagues said he went above and beyond the call of duty to try to solve the Brighton Mermaid case, especially when it was disconnected from the other Mermaid Murders. A few others hinted that he crossed the line a few times. But no, I never really found out.'

I pulled a bitter smile across my face and looked up to the sky. 'They're still peddling that "good cop doing anything he can to get justice" line, then, are they?' My tone was as bitter as my smile.

'Not that he was a racist bastard who got away with all he did because he was part of a system that is set up to always treat people of colour as guilty suspects first and foremost.'

I looked at Aaron Pope before returning my gaze to the sky.

'He called me a dirty little slut when all I'd done was find a dead body. He harassed my father until he nearly had a break-down, and my mother *did* have a breakdown. My sister is prob-ably still suffering from post-traumatic stress because of what she witnessed courtesy of your father. And he has stalked and harassed me for years. He used to follow me all over Brighton – I'd turn around and there he'd be, watching me. Until his accident, he'd been doing it nigh on twenty years . . . but he and his mates still think he was justified for all of it because he was a police officer.'

Aaron Pope sank even further in his seat. 'I knew it was bad,' he eventually said, 'because he wouldn't tell me. Usually he's fine with telling me what he got up to – proud of it, even – but he'd never talk about your family.' He threw his head back, looked up at the sky like I had just done. 'Jeez. I can't even imagine. I hate that he did that to you and your family. I hate it so much.'

I carefully studied the lines of his face, trying to see where the differences lay in his features compared to his father's. 'In all of this, I think you're the most special person of all,' I said.

He stared at me and said nothing in return.

'Because despite all that, despite believing me and not ques-tioning what I'm saying because you know it's true, and despite knowing what your father is like, you still want me to come with you, don't you?'

'Look, my father still has some friends on the police force, and he said . . . he said if you wouldn't come, I was to tell you that he has found a link between the Brighton Mermaid and the four other women that they called the Mermaids. Remember?'

'And?' I said this calmly, even though inside my stomach was turning cartwheels. There *was* a link? I had done as much research on Ralph Knowles, the man arrested for the murders, as I could. Everything said he was the one: there'd been complaints about him watching people; prostitutes said he'd got rough to the point of dangerous; he had a fondness for non-consensual strangulation; he had form for putting women in hospital; he'd been in and out of prison. But even though on paper he ticked many boxes that said it was him, his sheer lack of guile made me doubt if he truly was responsible. Whoever killed all those women had left very little forensic evidence behind – the killer was careful, meticulous, and Ralph Knowles had seemed to be anything but careful. He'd seemed positively reckless. He went around hurting people and doing a lot of time for his crimes. And now Pope had found a definite connection; he had proof that all the murders were linked?

'He said . . . he said he knows how to prove your father did it.'

Slowly, I rotated my whole body to face him. Aaron was staring furiously at the ground, his face pale and sickly. 'What. Did. You. Say.' My anger enunciated every single word.

'I'm sorry,' he mumbled. 'He said he'd talk to you or he'll talk to your father.'

I wanted to punch Aaron Pope in the face. Smack him so hard his dad would feel it; the entire Pope bloodline would feel it.

'I hate your father. I absolutely hate him.'

He lowered his gaze even further, but not before I saw 'me, too' dance across his face.

'Tomorrow night. At the small bit of greenery near here. I'll meet him there at six.' We could meet there because it was mainly populated by druggies and nicotine addicts – I wouldn't care if I never went there again.

'He rarely leaves the house. He spends most of his time in a wheelchair. It'll be hard to get him there.'

'I don't give a fuck,' I replied. 'He wants to start on my dad again, then he can come here and face me like a real man.'

'It'd be easier if you came to our house.'

'You think I'm going to go wandering into a house with him and you?' I retorted. 'Pope has meant me nothing but harm from the moment I met him so you *honestly* think I'm going to go somewhere that will allow him to do anything to me? It makes no difference if he's partially paralysed or not – he always got someone else to be physical for him.'

'I would never—'

'You're here, doing his bidding, so I don't care about your "I would nevers". I don't trust him and I don't trust you. Either he gets himself here at six tomorrow or I start harassment proceedings against him and you. His choice.'

Aaron Pope looked like he was going to throw up. If he was anyone else's son, if he hadn't carried John Pope's toxicity to me, I would have felt sorry for him and what he would face when he took that message back to his father.

*Thursday, 25 June*
'You know what day it is tomorrow, don't you?' John Pope said. 'You know what anniversary it is?' His voice hadn't changed, his manner hadn't altered. In his wheelchair he looked small and broken, but he was still the man he had always been.

I sat and said nothing.

'The boy here knows computers. He knows how to get into things. He helped me to start to piece together some of the information that I had. Someone broke into my house while I was at the hospital. Stole all the things I had about the Brighton Mermaid, about your friend. I can't remember what it was that I had. It was important. The boy told me I said it would change everything. I can't remember, it's gone. But the boy has found out some things. It's reminded me of other information – there was another link. We didn't pursue it because we couldn't find it on him. We looked in all his usual hiding places, but nothing turned up.'

I sat and said nothing.

'The strangulation, the lack of shoes, the repeated rapes, but the alibi that severed the link to the Brighton Mermaid. It wasn't Ralph Knowles. The other link they told no one about was the jewellery. They all had missing jewellery. Usually rings, but also earrings and a necklace. The Brighton Mermaid had two pieces missing, because your friend took her bracelet. They all had indentations on whichever finger the ring had been on; the forensic examiner said on darker skin, there was usually discoloration from long-term jewellery wear. One had a torn earlobe where the earring had been. One had a rash where the forensics people believed a necklace had irritated her skin – but there was no sign of it. Jewellery. They were all missing jewellery. Knowles didn't have it. He wasn't smart enough to hide it that well. Whoever did it took those things as trophies.'

I sat and said nothing.

'You have to find that jewellery, Nell. It's the only way we'll know for sure. You have to search your father's house until you find it. You have to find that jewellery or I will tell everything I know to those who *will* search and *will* find it. All they need is new evidence or a new line of investigation and they will open it all up again.'

He finished talking. Waited for me to speak to him; for me to answer his threat with acquiescence.

I stared at him, long and hard. Waited for my voice to calm itself so I would not scream, I would not swear, I would not give him the reaction he craved. He'd always wanted a reaction from me. I think that was why he'd kept coming for me over the years – because I would not react the way he wanted, I would not show that he had got to me.

Instead of speaking to him, I turned to his son. 'You have a way into the police databases?' I asked Aaron Pope.

'I don't do that,' he stated. 'Any more.'

'If you did still do that, would you be able to get me the DNA sequences for Jude and the Brighton Mermaid?'

'What are you talking about DNA for?' John Pope demanded. 'It's the jewellery. It's the jewellery that will solve this. Find the trophies he took and we'll have him.'

'But could you?' I asked Aaron Pope.

'If I still did stuff like that – which is illegal – then yes, I could. Possibly.'

'Would you be able to get me access to the files they have on Jude and the Brighton Mermaid?'

'No. Even if I did still do that, you can only go in a few times before they notice. And once they notice, they track you down and put you in prison. When you do that sort of thing to them, you don't ever escape prison.'

'Right.'

'But if I did still do that, I'd be able to get you the DNA and that would be about it.'

'Boy, take me home,' demanded John Pope.

'Give me your address,' I said to Aaron Pope. 'I'll come over and get the DNA files in a week or so. Is that enough time?'

'Yes.'

'Boy! I said take me home!'

'Do you write computer programs?' I asked.

'I own a software company,' Aaron Pope replied. 'So, yes.'

'Will you help me?'

'Yes.'

'You don't even know what I want help with.'

'I do. To get me and him out of your life. By solving the mystery; clearing your father's name.'

'And you'll help me?'

'In a heartbeat.'

'Why?'

'Because I want the Brighton Mermaid out of my life, too.'

'Boy! Home! Now!'

I stood up from the bench so I loomed over John Pope. His grey-white hair was slicked back, making him look like an ageing gangster whose minions denied him access to a mirror. He hated that I towered over him now. I could tell he hated everything about this meeting. The fact he'd had to come here at all would be bad enough, but the fact he was vulnerable in front of me, the fact that I didn't speak to him, the fact that when I stood I became a giant and made him feel insignificant – just like my dad had made him feel the first time he met him – was probably driving him mad.

'You stay away from my father,' I warned John Pope. 'I will look for Jude. I will follow all the leads you have with the Brighton Mermaid and the other women. I will do whatever is necessary to solve this, including being around you. *But you stay away from my father and my family.* Is that understood?'

He glowered up at me, his eyes burning with the white-hot hatred he had for me. 'Boy. Home. Now.'

That was John Pope speak for: *'Understood.'*

When I had his address on a slip of paper torn from the edge of the newspaper I'd been reading when they showed up, I said, 'I'll see you next week,' to Aaron Pope.

He nodded.

I didn't acknowledge John Pope before I walked away.

*Friday, 3 July*

The Pope house was a large red-brick place set in a horseshoe-shaped close with views out over the glittery green Downs. It had three good-sized bedrooms, another smaller bedroom, a decent-sized bathroom upstairs, and an eat-in kitchen with two large reception rooms downstairs.

'This is what I could get my hands on,' Aaron Pope told me. We were upstairs in one of the bigger bedrooms that he used as an office. 'Hopefully it's what you wanted.'

'Yes, it is.'

'What are you going to do with it?'

'Run it through the programs that I use. See if there are any relative matches out there.'

'Look.' He took the sheaf of papers stuffed inside a brown folder out of my hands again. 'If you're going to do this, you can't just use your normal computer. You need to create a private network, get hardware that is hard to hack, put up extra software protections.'

'Sure I do.'

'I mean it. You can't just put data out there that you've got through less-than-upfront means. If you wanted, I could write you a couple of programs to make your searching a bit easier, but only if you get the proper computer hardware.'

I surveyed Aaron Pope again. He didn't look so much like his father now that I'd spent more time in his company. It wasn't simply because he wore glasses and didn't have the scar – Aaron Pope was different and it reflected in the lines of his face. He didn't have the hard edges, the spiky attitude of a man who hated the world and expected the world to suck up his hatred and do as he commanded.

'Why would you do that? Write me some programs, I mean?'

'I told you, I want the Brighton Mermaid to be out of my life, too.'

'It's more than that.'

'Is it?'

I tipped my head to one side as I continued to study him. He was immediately uncomfortable with my gaze; worried, it seemed, that I would find out something by simply looking at him. 'Have you lived in Brighton all this time?'

'No. I was in London, for many years. Stayed after college. Came back two years ago.'

'What's your story, Aaron Pope?'

'What do you mean?' he asked, barely able to lift his head.

'I mean, why are you here?'

He frowned, but wouldn't meet my eye. 'I'm looking after my father. He needs someone to take care of him.'

F.O.G. He reeked of F.O.G. I knew I did, too. It was why I was here, in the house of a man I hated, working with him towards solving a mystery that he thought would prove my father guilty and I *knew* would reveal him to be innocent.

F.O.G.

Fear.

Obligation.

Guilt.

I'd seen it so many times: in the mirror; on the face of my sister; on the faces of my parents.

Fear.

Obligation.

Guilt.

It was why you went against what was best for yourself to do what was convenient for other people. It was why you wanted to say no but ended up going along with something that would make your life difficult. It was why I had seen flashes of true hatred on Aaron Pope's face when he talked about his father, but here he was obviously looking after him. Not flinching or even reacting when his father called him 'boy'.

Fear.

Obligation.

Guilt.

You see it on the faces of those caught in impossible situations, children who have been mistreated so long they automatically defer to the needs of their abuser.

I was wrong about John Pope, I realised. I thought he wouldn't dream of being physical because he didn't have the stature for it. I thought John Pope always got someone else to do that bit for him; it never occurred to me that if he had someone smaller than him, someone who loved him unconditionally . . .

'It's good that you're looking after him.'

'It's what anyone would do for their parent,' Aaron Pope mumbled. Poor Aaron Pope.

I hadn't yet sat down in his room because I had no reason to. I'd come to pick up the DNA file and then I was going home to start the long process of typing it into my computer in code form. After looking at him a bit longer, I pulled out the chair from in front of his large desk, neatly adorned with four computers, and sat down. 'Tell me about this computer thing, then,' I said.

'You really want to know?' Suddenly he could face me now we were talking about a neutral subject.

'Well, if I'm going to do this, I have to do it properly, don't I?'

Aaron Pope smiled. And with that smile it was clear – he looked nothing like his father.

*Friday, 20 November*

Aaron Pope came into his office and sat on the seat next to mine. He didn't speak; I continued to type, pretending I didn't notice he was pale and shaking, acting as if I hadn't heard his father shouting. Aaron Pope hadn't raised his voice once in retaliation to the words – as loud and clear as anything – his father had spewed at him. He must have stood there and taken it. Listened to all the hideous things his father had ranted at and about him but not fought back. F.O.G. Good old Fear, obligation, guilt.

This was what it must have been like when he was growing up, I realised. This, and worse, was what it must have been like for him.

The silence between us grew and grew, long minutes spinning themselves around us.

'You can talk to me if you want,' I said suddenly. I hadn't meant to say anything, I'd meant to keep my counsel, do what I had to do and leave, but I couldn't. I'd watched him from the corner of my eye, trembling, like I had done the first time his father had gone for me – and I had to do something, even if it was something as simple as offering to listen.

He stared at the screen and said nothing, but folded his hands under his armpits to try to hide how much he was shaking.

'Any time,' I continued. 'You can tell me anything at any time.'

He slowly turned his head towards me. 'I don't want to talk about it,' he said quietly.

'Don't want to or don't know how to?'

He immediately returned to looking at the screen.

'Like I said, any *thing* and any time.' I spun back to my screen, too. 'Any *thing* and any time.'

# Now

## Nell

On days like today, when the weather is clear, the sun has come up and the wind is down, John Pope sits in his garden.

So he doesn't have to deal with the stairs, his bedroom is downstairs in the second reception room, which lets out directly onto the garden.

He has a blanket over his legs, he has his radio on a wrought-iron table and beside that he has a bottle of whisky and a glass. It's not yet 11 a.m. but John Pope has a drink whenever he feels like it. If he doesn't get one, he rages at his son until Aaron gives in.

I stand in front of him and don't speak. Whenever he 'needs' to see me, I come but I do not speak until he speaks to me. We always do this. We always wrestle with each other to see who will give in first. He has time since he rarely has anywhere to be, but I am stubborn. Especially when it comes to John Pope.

He examines his nails in a theatrical manner; he snorts ugly-sounding phlegm to the back of his throat, spits it to the left of where I am standing, then returns to examining his nails.

I can feel Aaron's pain; his tension, it ricochets around him as he battles with himself not to step in and try to mediate, try to put an end to the atmosphere John Pope and I always create.

Every time he's tried in the last couple of years, it's ended badly for him. I still do this despite its effect on Aaron, partly because he needs to see that it is possible to stand up to his father. That just because his father demands something, doesn't mean Aaron has to give it or do it or say it.

'Time's running out, girly,' John Pope eventually says.

'No it's not,' I reply.

'I said you could have six months. Six months and then I would hand over everything to my friends. They would then start to reinvestigate your father. They would go through his life properly, thoroughly, forensically, like they should have done years ago.' He says this with relish, almost salivating at the thought of it. 'And you will be the one to start it off. You will search his house to see what you can find and if I don't think you've searched enough, I will call my friends.'

'We agreed a year,' I state calmly.

The searching using DNA and genealogy wasn't working fast enough for Pope. He wanted results; he wanted me to have found something by now. Two years was long enough, he said. He had given me an ultimatum: 'Find Judana Dalton, the identity of the Brighton Mermaid or anything tangible we can use or you search your father's house for the jewellery. And if you won't do that, I will turn everything over to the police, kick up so much of a fuss that they will have no choice but to talk to your father again.'

He will unleash hell upon my father, basically. I knew he would do it. And I knew that my family could not stand for that to happen again. Herstmonceux is their island, their escape from everything that began twenty-five years ago. They can be anonymous and safe out there. Dad potters in his huge greenhouse, Mum crochets and goes to church. Police coming back into their lives would be the ruination of them. He gave me six more months and I negotiated a year – but I know he is going to want something by the twenty-fifth anniversary in less than three months.

'Time's running out, girly,' John Pope says. 'Time's running out and when it's gone, you will help me.'

'A year. We agreed a year. I've taken a year off work. I'm doing it full-time. I'm doing all I can. None of this stuff happens quickly.'

'Time's running out. If I don't think you're moving fast enough, I will call it in.'

'They'll arrest you and Aaron for hacking into the police database,' I remind him.

'Small price to pay for catching the bastard who killed those women, isn't it, Boy?'

'I'm doing the best I can. I'm going as fast as I can. I've got more DNA results that should be back this week. I'll be able to—'

'Next time I call you, you come straight away, do you hear?'

'I come when I can,' I state.

'Make it sooner,' he replies. His gaze moves up from his nails to my face. It's 1993 again. Although I'm the one standing and he's the one sitting, the dynamic is back: he wants to break me – I won't let him; he wants me to cry – I'll never do it in front of him. 'If you know what's good for you.' *And your father*, he obviously adds silently.

*Go fuck yourself*, I reply in my head before I return to the house through the double patio doors.

He didn't *need* to see me, he just wanted to remind me who was in charge. Who could click his fingers and make me dance to that finger-clicking tune.

This is what happens when you make a deal with an evil man: if you don't work to produce results fast enough, he starts to reshape and reorganise the deal, he starts to threaten you with everything you fear.

I have to work faster. I've been putting off chasing stuff to do with Craig Ackerman because I found him so creepy. I haven't started a proper search on Maura Goodrich's friend, although I have sent off his DNA. I need to work faster, but not panic. If I panic, I will miss something and it could be a vital something.

'I'm so—' Aaron Pope begins but I hold up my hand because I do not want to hear it.

'I've told you before, Aaron, don't apologise for him,' I say. 'Just . . . just leave it.'

'You know he won't really call anyone,' Aaron says. 'Not until we have something more solid. He doesn't mind being arrested but he would mind losing face.'

Aaron is always doing this thing of trying to make everything better. I feel sorry for him because I know that's what his role in life must have been for so long. When he's working, though, when I watch him write code and programs, he's a different person. Transformed. His body is upright and strong; his face is focused and intense; he becomes the man he is when he is out of his father's orbit. He stops being the abused little boy whose father still torments him and he becomes Aaron Pope, adult, business owner, funny, thoughtful man.

'Bye, Aaron,' I say as I head for the door.

'Bye, Nell. When will I see you next?'

'Soon,' I reply. 'Really soon.'

# Macy

Every year, Daddy receives a Brighton postcard postmarked with the day that Jude disappeared.

The first couple of years I didn't know anything about them. When we moved to the middle of nowhere – also known as Herstmonceux, deep in East Sussex – one came in the bundle of mail that was forwarded from our old house.

I thought it was junk mail at first because it was a Brighton beach picture and on the back it was blank, except for the typed label addressed to 'Mr Okorie'. The original postmark said 14 July, a date I remembered well, but it had been posted in London. I thought nothing of it, really, until the next year, when it happened again. It came on a different day, this time not forwarded mail, but it was postmarked 14 July again – this time sent from Glasgow. The third year it happened, again a Brighton postcard with 'Wish You Were Here' on it, I went looking in Mummy and Daddy's room for clues because although the postcards always disappeared, they never turned up in the bin.

In the bottom drawer, under Dad's winter jumpers that he never wore, I found all the other postcards. Six in total by then. All of them Brighton postcards but sent from anywhere else.

I'm sitting at the kitchen table examining the postcard I 'borrowed' when we went to visit my parents a few weeks ago.

I've been too scared to get it out until now.

This postcard has five pictures of the Pier: the Pier from the front, the Pier from the beach side-on, the promenade leading onto the Pier, the Pier from a distance, and the telescope that sits halfway down the Pier. Across the middle it says '*Wish You Were Here*'.

All the postcards say 'Wish You Were Here' somewhere on them. Daddy has kept them all in the same place, just adding the latest one to the pile.

I was about to go back downstairs after being to the loo, when I had the urge to look to see if they were still there. When they were, I had another urge to take one so I could examine it properly on my own.

Is it a message or a threat? I suspect it's a threat. A sort of 'I know what you did' type thing. But that could just be me and my overactive, paranoid imagination.

'Hey, good-looking, what you doing?' Shane asks, coming into the kitchen. He's reading his phone and not paying attention to me, but quickly I slide the postcard under my laptop and look up at him.

'Oh, nothing.'

'Right, don't know if I believe that,' he says suspiciously and finally glances up from his mobile. 'Do you want me to pick up the kids today?'

I sneak a peek at his phone and see he has a sports page up. That's pretty much all he does on his phone – read sports updates, check the news.

'Yes, please,' I say. 'I have a lot of work on.'

'Great.' Shane comes to me and presses a kiss on my neck. 'I love you, you know. Can't wait to marry you.'

'Hey! I still haven't said yes, yet,' I call after him as he leaves the room again.

'You will!' he calls back on his way upstairs.

When I'm sure Shane is upstairs for a while, I slide the postcard out from under my laptop.

The postmark on this, the latest postcard, came from Glasgow.

When Shane goes to collect the children, I'm going to do my own detective work on two things: (1) Clyde, (2) the postcard.

(1) Clyde: I'm going to search for Clyde. I'd rather not look for Clyde, but I need to get divorced. It's always there, at the back of my throat, on the tip of my tongue, in the well of my chest – this need to tell Shane that I'm still married to the father of my children. *Our* children. Because they are his now.

Clyde was never really that interested in the children. Shane is all kinds of interested in them. It's been an odd eighteen months, and now we've got our mojo back, now we're connecting properly again, I think I do want to marry him. I do want him to know how much I adore him.

I just have to get divorced first.

Looking back, I cringe when I think about why I got married in secret. At the time I was convinced I couldn't trust any of my family since I knew they all had these huge secrets. I was going to get myself a secret too, I was going to show them. So we got married in secret and I felt nothing. Not happy, not triumphant that I'd got one over on them. Just nothing. Well, maybe a bit silly because my plan had fallen flat. It made it worse when Clyde left and I couldn't tell anyone about my husband leaving me. Well, I have to fix that. I have to find Clyde. Once I've started on that search, I'll start on number two.

(2) The postcard: I turn the rectangle over in my hands. Once I'm done with Clyde, I'm going to see if I can find anyone in the Glasgow area – where this postcard came from – who has a similar name or description to Jude. And I'm going to have a proper look at the actual postcard, see if there's any invisible ink, any impressions for rubbing, reactions to heat or something. Anything.

Because I suspect that the sender of the postcards knows what I know, saw what I saw, and they don't ever want Daddy to forget about that night.

# Nell

'Stop staring at me, Aaron,' I say.

Even though he is sitting slightly behind me while I type codes into his computer, I can feel his eyes on me. We've barely spoken since I arrived here and I've tried to shrug off his attention for a good half an hour, but I can't stand it any more. I can feel him avert his eyes, and his voice, when he speaks to mumble 'Sorry', is sheepish at having got caught.

My fingers pause over the keyboard and I wonder again if it's wise to come here when Aaron has developed feelings for me. It's hard to do what I'm doing without his resources, and since neither of us trusts email or virtual clouds, I have to come here. Sit in his office, and type in codes to see what comes back.

On paper, the Pope house is nice and cosy, a wonderful place to live. Since moving back in after his father's accident five years ago, Aaron has modernised and decorated the house, making it easier for his father to get around while bringing it into the present day. The walls are painted in a bright yellow to cheer things up; he has installed soft-pile carpets all over the house, to make it easier if his dad falls. There are wider doorways, larger windows to maximise light and virtually no sharp corners. Bold, bright artwork is hung on the walls, and the kitchen is full of modern, often wacky gadgets. Every room has a top-of-the-range screen and TV system. Aaron has done all he can to make the place bright and cheery, homely and welcoming, but the reality is that this house is sad, and it doesn't feel like it will ever be anything but sorrowful and damaged.

I start to type again, and then pause after a couple of minutes because 'You're doing it again.'

'I can't help it,' he says with a genuinely regretful groan.

On paper, Aaron is perfect. He has a line of light brown freckles across his nose; he has grooves behind his ears where his glasses dig in; he smells amazing. He is slender but muscular with it, and I'm always physically aware of him in not unpleasant ways. He is clever, he makes me laugh and I enjoy spending time with him. But the reality is, Aaron is John Pope's son. And no matter what, he will always be John Pope's son.

'You know I can't help it,' Aaron repeats. His expensive, ergonomic swivel chair squeaks slightly as he turns towards the door.

'Go and do something else while I do this, then,' I tell him. 'You don't need to sit here. I know what I'm doing.'

'I like sitting here. With you.'

I stop typing, throw my head back and press my fingertips onto my eyelids. 'Please don't do this, Aaron,' I say. For the past nine months or so, every time I've come here to input new DNA sequences into his computer, we end up having this conversation.

'Nell . . .'

'Just don't,' I insist. I don't want to have this talk with him again because I can already feel that it won't go the same way it usually does. His father threatening me again the other week has set me on edge. Has reignited the urgency with which I need to find a major breakthrough with what I am doing. I'm not feeling generous to the Pope men at the moment, so I know this won't be a conversation that ends with us pretending to move on from it. This time, I can feel that this chat will end badly for both of us.

'Nell, you know how I feel about you. I'm sure you feel something for me, too.'

'I like you as a person,' I state. 'Despite everything, you've become a friend. A good friend.'

'Why won't you give me a chance?'

'You know why.'

So far, so normal for this conversation.

'Look at me, please, Nell.'

This is the point where it's going to change. I can feel it in the air around us; it tingles along my skin, swirls butterflies in my stomach. This is the point where he's going to say something that will make me say something and everything will start to fall apart.

Slowly, I spin on my chair, away from the desk of computers, to face him. Aaron is wearing a plain black T-shirt today with dark green jeans. His pale arms are exposed, and I stare at them rather than risk looking at his face.

'Nell, look at me. *Please*.'

I lift my gaze to meet his eyes. And he stares back at me from behind his glasses, from behind the courage he's found to do this.

'I'm not my father,' he insists. 'I am nothing like him. What he did to you and your family is horrific. But I'm not him.'

'No, you are not your father,' I say. 'But you do his bidding, Aaron. *Always*. You never say no to him, do you? He wants to see me, you send me a text. And you keep sending them until I come here. If I don't come soon enough, you turn up at my home. You're not him, but he's got you behaving like him. And I can't deal with that.' I've never said that to him before because it does what I knew it would – it cuts him. I can see how every word slices at him, wounds him. That is the ultimate insult, telling him he is a proxy John Pope, and I don't want to hurt Aaron. I like Aaron. A lot.

'But I—'

I cut in with 'And anyway, I'm seeing someone.'

Aaron sits back in his chair, exhales deeply and looks vanquished – all the fight he had in him suddenly washed away.

I spin back to the computer. I have to take a few deep breaths before I type in the final sequences, but that wasn't so bad, we didn't get into it properly and we can spare each other that pain for now.

Aaron wrote this computer program to combine as many of the available DNA search databases as possible. Most of the databases that combine other databases online are for autosomal DNA, the DNA that you get from both parents. Aaron has created a computer program that combines mitochondrial (mother's female line), Y-line (father's male line) as well as autosomal DNA. Whenever I have new results or he adds new databases, I have to retype all the DNA codes I have into it because I need to make sure no one who might do what Aaron has done has access to the Brighton Mermaid's or Jude's DNA. They are not meant to be 'out there' and I do not want anyone tracing what we're doing back to us.

Aaron has also created a facial recognition program that is designed to match any missing persons images with images of people who have been found without names and identities. Neither of the programs he has created is strictly legal or totally illegal. Everything Aaron does for his dad and for me skirts so close to the line of legality that we never talk about it, and we certainly never send emails or texts about it.

'I'm going to leave for a bit,' I decide. It's too uncomfortable in here. Nothing of significance will come up on the computers anyway, it very rarely does straight away, so the best thing to do is leave, allow what we talked about to pass and then come back.

I grab my bag and move towards the door, but as I pass him, he takes my hand to stop me leaving. Slowly, Aaron presses his fingers between mine and then stands up.

'I'm not my father, Nell,' Aaron Pope says, still with his fingers threaded loosely with mine.

He raises his eyes to meet mine when I don't speak. He takes a step closer to me. 'I'm not my father,' he repeats. He moves to place his other hand on my face but I recoil so visibly he lowers it again. Instead he moves closer to me. So close it's obvious what he wants to do.

'I'm not my father,' he says again.

'Aaron—'

'I know you feel something for me. I just know it. And you won't even give me a chance because of someone else. You've told me in so many different ways without actually saying the words how he ruined your life. How everything you do feels like it's been done to spite him, to show him, to not let him win. And you won't give me a chance because of him. You're letting him do it again. You're letting him ruin something else for you.'

'I don't want to be involved in this life any longer than necessary, Aaron. You know that. You said it yourself, I want this over as soon as possible. That is why I gave up my job. I don't want this life any more.' This is what I've never said before.

'But once this is done we can move on from it,' he replies.

'I wish you'd understand, Aaron, I don't want to live like this. Your father . . . On top of what he did to me and my dad and my mother and my sister, what he did to you was unthinkable.'

Aaron looks at me as though I'm exaggerating; like I am twisting normal parental discipline into something it wasn't. 'What he did to you was *unthinkable*,' I repeat. And he pulls a face, dismissive and unbothered. F.O.G. Fear. Obligation. Guilt. It is making him minimise his childhood, creating a false trail of normality.

I do not want any of this any more. This is what has to change. Aaron and I both have to face up to the things we do out of F.O.G. 'Aaron, he repeatedly stuck your head in a bath of water because you said "damn". He beat you so badly he broke two ribs because you took a plate up to your room. He kicked you down the stairs because your whole class was given detention . . .' As I speak about the abuse he endured, things he's told me in unguarded moments, I see his face change: it drops the unbothered look and becomes haunted.

'I know you haven't even told me the worst stories,' I say now I know he's taking me seriously. 'You know what he did to you and worse, and still you're here, taking care of him. You'd escaped, you'd built a good life for yourself in London away from him and what he did, and now you're back here, living in the house of horrors you grew up in, taking care of the man who abused you.

'He has never apologised to you, has he? He has never acknowledged what he did or how being a policeman allowed him to get away with it because people kept looking the other way or giving him the benefit of the doubt. And I *know* he has never once said thank you, but still you're here. Because he had no one else, because your mother – who stood by and let your abuse happen – wouldn't do it. What you've done for your father, what you still do for your father, is amazing. But I don't want to be involved with him any longer than I have to be. If I gave you a chance, I'd end up around him for ever. I couldn't stand that.'

Aaron takes my free hand and rests it at the centre of his chest. His heartbeat is strong and solid; the vibration of a good person, a decent man. 'I'm not my father,' he says yet again as he holds my gaze. 'And I'd do anything for you, Nell. I'd do anything to be with you. *Anything.* I'd give up anything to be with you.'

*I'm seeing someone*, I say in my head as he moves even closer to me. *I'm seeing someone*, I silently repeat as his nose brushes against mine. 'I'm seeing someone,' I murmur as his lips are about to touch mine.

*Bleep-bleep, bleep-bleep* comes from the computer. It stops Aaron from kissing me and I pull my head away. A white box is flashing up on the screen. 'Match found,' it says. 'Match found'.

They were Jude and Brighton Mermaid codes that I just re-entered.

*Match found. Match found. Match found.*

# Macy

*Friday, 20 April*

I didn't find out anything about the postcard – there was no hidden message and no one in Glasgow that was anything to do with Jude as far as I could tell.

You can also buy those postcards online so you could get one from anywhere.

I did find Clyde, though, quite easily as it turned out.

He's living in South London with a woman who has four children. *Four* children. I'm not sure if any of them are biologically his, because their ages would overlap with the time he was with me, but I couldn't believe my eyes when I saw him standing in a photo with her and them. He had the hugest grin on his face and his arms around the other woman. They were the perfect family.

'Proud daddy,' the woman had tagged him in the picture. And lots of people had 'liked' the image. Lots of other people saying stuff about what a good father he was.

I wonder if she knows about me, about his three other children, the ones he's clearly not such a 'proud daddy' about?

I stand in the doorway to the kitchen and look at it again. I've been scrubbing since about midnight and nothing seems to have come out clean enough. I'll just have to do it again. And again. And again until I get it right.

# Nell

'What does this one mean?'

I move my index finger over two larger circles around one smaller circle, almost like a small bullseye, that are tattooed on Zach's chest. His tattoos are so intricate and delicate, yet bold and striking, I often feel I could get lost in them. They are a series of African symbols, called *Adinkra*, that he has had inscribed on his chest to create the larger picture. One of my favourite things to do is to point to a symbol and see if he can correctly name it.

'That is "greatness and leadership".'

'This one,' I say quickly, my fingers flitting over a chain link that looks like the cross-section of a squashed apple.

'Unity and strength in the community.'

'Right . . . how about this one?' The heart symbol, small and firm and perfectly formed, which is pretty obvious.

'Erm, that is "a call for patience and tolerance".'

'OK, was not expecting that. This one?' The symbol with one circle surrounded by four circles and five tufts.

'That is loyalty and adroitness, as well as the hairstyle of joy.'

'Right.'

I'm sitting astride him, and he takes my fingers off his body, pushes his fingers between mine like Aaron did earlier and I immediately feel a tidal wave of guilt crash through me.

'Aren't you going to ask about my hair or lack thereof?' Zach asks now that the whole hair thing has been brought up.

I look up from his chest and shoulder to his face. 'No,' I reply.

'You're not even curious?' he asks. 'Most people – especially women I've slept with – ask after meeting me more than once. I think you're the only person who has never asked or even hinted about it.'

'I am curious about it, but not overly. It's part of what you look like, so it'd be like me asking you why you have dark brown skin, if you know what I mean? I don't know you any differently.'

Zach places his hands on either side of my hips and his thumbs start to caress me. 'You're so different to other women I've met,' he says. His hands move up my body, skimming up my waist, over my breasts and then back down again. 'So very, very different. I can't get enough of you. I think about you all the time.'

I smile and swallow down more of that remorse that's been battling with elation since I left the Pope house. All through dinner at the Thai restaurant down on Market Street, and the drinks we stopped off for on our way back to Zach's flat, I cycled between fizzing with excitement at the connection I've found to the Brighton Mermaid, and being internally crushed with guilt that I almost let Aaron kiss me. In fact, if the Brighton Mermaid thing hadn't pinged I probably would have stood there and let him do it; not only that, I probably would have kissed him back. Yes, I'm only 'seeing' Zach, but I don't like the idea that I could, potentially, mess him about. I *like* him so much, I *lust* after him even more. I'm nowhere near the other L-word with him yet, but I could get there. And I hate thinking that I would let feeling sorry for Aaron get in the way of that. It's not like if I decided to give it a go with Aaron anything good would come of it. Any relationship with him beyond what we currently have would be dysfunctional from the off – a co-dependent meeting of F.O.G. minds. And I don't feel anything about him like I feel for Zach. Everything to do with Aaron is based around feeling bad for him about how badly his father treats him, not unfettered affection.

'I mean it,' Zach says. 'During the day I think about you. I wonder what you're doing. I see so many things, hear so many things that I'm usually bursting to tell you. It's ridiculous, really, when I don't know you, but there you go.'

I don't hear that sort of thing very often. Most of the men I have sex with are nice to me, and the ones who I have sex with more than once or even have flings with make it clear they like me, but they don't act like, to them, I am anything special, someone who is constantly on their mind.

'Tell me about your hair, then,' I say to Zach, to deflect from the continually blossoming guilt.

He uses the flat of his hand to stroke up the centre of my stomach then rests it on my chest, covering my heart. 'You *do* want to know now?'

'I think you want to tell me, which is why I want to know.'

'I suppose I do want to tell you.'

'Go on, then. Did you have hair before?'

'Yes. I had a lot of hair once. All over my body. I was actually really hairy.'

'And then?'

'And then it started coming out, mainly in the shower at first. Not much, but I started to notice a couple of bare spots on my head, a few spots on my chest. Then the "little bit" turned into a bit more, and a bit more until, over about six months, all my body hair and head hair fell out and didn't grow back. Then my eyebrows went and my eyelashes. That was the worst. When I exercise I get sweat in my eyes; I have to rinse my eyes out with eyewash every morning and night because they get full of the grit that's usually stopped by eyelashes and they dry out. At one point all my nails went, too. But that's stopped.'

'That sounds really tough.'

'I think the worst part was the eyelashes and eyebrows, not just for what I said about how it impacted on my eyes. It made me look weird. Before all of this happened I've shaved my head and I've let my hair grow out, never thought anything of it. So having no hair on my head wasn't anything strange, and no hair on my body was fine because no one sees that regularly. But the eyebrows and eyelashes, they made me stand out. I felt like a freak.'

I shift on him and he keeps his hand slightly left of centre of my chest, covering my heart. 'I don't think you look like a freak,' I say. 'I've always thought you're pretty damn gorgeous, actually.'

He blows a kiss at me. 'I don't care now, so maybe that's why you don't think I look weird. When it first happened, I felt so ashamed. I hated walking around because I could see people staring at me, double-taking, trying to work out what was wrong with me. My confidence took a huge hit and it's taken me a while to get some of it back. Like I say, I don't give a damn now.'

'Did you ever find out what caused it?' I ask.

'No, not really. It's an autoimmune thing, apparently. Not many people have what I have – alopecia universalis – where they lose all the hair on their body and eyes. They think it was stress, trauma, really. I was very close to my grandparents and they were taken from me quite suddenly.'

'What, they died?'

He nods thoughtfully, his lips pursed as though he is stopping himself from saying anything more. It's a very deliberate thing to say – 'taken from me' rather than 'I lost them'.

'Did someone hurt them?' I ask.

'Yes, someone hurt them. Killed them. It was a while back, but I think the shock of it took its toll without me realising. I've been tested for all sorts of things, and there's nothing wrong with me. The only thing I can really say that was significant was what happened to my grandparents.'

'Did they ever catch the person who did it?' I ask. I want to ask more but I don't. It doesn't really matter how or exactly when, it's enough that it happened and that it had such a profound and lasting effect on him.

'No, no they didn't,' Zach replies.

He has a faraway look in his eye that makes me think there is a lot more he would like to say but won't. He's not simply being cautious around me, I don't think; I suspect he keeps all of this stuff close to his chest, deep in his heart. This is something he doesn't talk about with anyone.

'Do you want to talk about it?' I ask. I could leave it, avoid the subject now he's being reticent, but then there'd be this unspoken 'thing' between us and I'd rather there wasn't. As much as possible, I want this relationship to be different to the others I've had. I want us to build something on a firm foundation; to be honest and open enough to ask questions. 'You don't have to, but I just want you to know you can if you want to.'

Zach smiles and shakes his head. 'No. I don't want to talk about it. I never want to talk about it. Too painful.'

'I understand.'

'You know what someone said to me once, though? About my lack of hair, I mean?'

'What?'

'I'd have a head start if I decided to become a criminal because I've got less DNA to leave behind.'

'Oh. Right.'

'Yes, that's what I said,' Zach says. 'I did point out I'd rather have hair and they told me I should try to look on the bright side of things, it'd make me happier eventually.'

'And they couldn't just say you'd spend less on shampoo or shaving gear?'

'*Exactly!* You're the first person to get it. Most people think I'm being oversensitive. But seriously, why would your first thought be that I'd get away with being a serial killer? I suppose someone like me does make people uncomfortable, so they do say strange things.'

'Maybe, but I think it reveals a lot about them, though. Is it going to grow back?'

'Probably not after all this time. I think they said if there isn't any sign of regrowth after the first year or two, it's unlikely to return.'

'Does it bother you? I know you said you don't give a shit now, but does it bother you?'

'Not much. Especially not when I pull a beauty like you who doesn't act like it's a big deal and who tells me in many ways that she thinks I'm gorgeous.'

I move his hand away from my chest and lean forwards, place my lips on his stomach and then slowly, carefully run my tongue up his body to his chest. Then I kiss him, slowly pushing my lips firmer and firmer onto his, until his mouth opens and our tongues meet. Zach pulls me down onto the bed beside him and our kissing becomes deeper. He climbs on top of me and stares down at me.

Again I'm struck by how open his face is without any hair, how it feels like I can see every part of him. I run my fingers over his face, relishing how smooth he feels, how without guile he appears.

He reaches under the pillow beside my head and pulls out a small silver square, slightly misshapen on the flat by the circle sealed up inside it. Up until now, we've always used these. At some point he went to get tested and he showed me the results. I went to get tested, too, and I showed him the results. Even though we've both been given a clean bill of sexual health, we've continued to use condoms.

I watch as he slowly tears open the small packet of protection. I've always thought of condoms as something to prevent pregnancy and guard against the spread of certain types of diseases, until recently, when I began to think of them as a whole different type of protection. I read something where some researchers had theorised that, through sperm, microscopic parts of the DNA of every man a woman has slept with stay inside her body, becoming a tiny little element of her physiological make-up.

It is just a theory, something the researchers put forward amongst other theories to explain why they found non-family DNA in women's bodies, but I was struck by it. I've always used condoms despite being on the Pill, because I've never been with a man with whom I didn't want some sort of barrier between us while we had sex.

This is why I am staring at the condom Zach holds. Would it be terrible if – potentially – a minuscule piece of Zach stayed with me for ever? Would it be so awful to share such an open, barrier-less intimacy with him? Maybe it's the guilt of almost kissing Aaron, or the excitement at having a chance to take a step forwards with my Brighton Mermaid search, but I reach for the condom and take it from him, drop it onto his bedside table. 'We don't need this,' I say, staring straight into his unadorned eyes.

He's surprised. 'You sure?' he asks. 'There's no pressure to do this, you know?'

*I'm sure*, I think. *I want this with you.* 'I'm very sure.'

He kisses me and I kiss him back as he slowly moves me into position underneath him. I place my hand on his face; his skin is warm and smooth under my fingers; our eyes are linked as he slowly enters me.

*I'm so sure about this and I'm sure about you.*

# Macy

*Sunday, 22 April*

'Please stop this, Macy,' Shane begs.

'Stop what?' I ask.

'Look around you, Macy. Look what you're doing.'

We are in the deepest hollow of the night, where darkness cannot find us and light is a dictator's mirage. I like this place, I do not have to do anything when I am here. Daytime will not be able to order me into the office; night-time cannot force me to lie down and sleep.

I look up at him from my place kneeling in front of the freezer. There was a spot right at the back that I haven't cleaned properly and I am doing it now. I'm also trashing stuff that's out of date. Stuff that is in date I am going to repackage and label so I know what is useable and what is for the bin.

'Macy, this isn't good for you. For any of us. The children are going to be up in a few hours and you've cleared out all the cupboards. Where are they going to eat their breakfast?'

'You're being ridiculous, Shane,' I tell him. 'All of this will be gone by morning. You know that.'

Shane pinches the bridge of his nose like he thinks it will help him understand. I'm glad he doesn't understand. Because I don't understand. How can Clyde be a proud daddy when he has three children he never sees, and he never pays for? How can he be a proud daddy with someone else? What was wrong with *me*? Why didn't he want me and our family life?

'I don't know what's set you off, but if you don't stop this, I'm going to call Nell, then I'm going to call your parents,' Shane says. 'You can't keep doing this.'

I notice how he said Nell before my parents. Is that what's going to happen now? Is Shane going to run off with Nell and be a proud daddy with her, too?

'Are you even listening to me?'

'Of course I am,' I reply. *I heard you say Nell.*

'I'm going to bed. I know this will be cleared up in the morning, but please try and get some sleep.'

'I will.'

'Promise?'

'I promise.'

As happy as he's ever going to be with that, Shane leaves. Probably to climb into bed and think of all the things he wants to do with Nell when he leaves me. They'll probably write 'proud daddy' in millions of languages next to their happy smiling photos.

'You'd better stay away from my sister,' I whisper. 'Or else.'

# **Nell**

'You're not going on your own,' Aaron tells me.

The woman with the close DNA connection to the Brighton Mermaid is called Sadie and she lives in Leeds. I've come back to Aaron's house today to make the call to the number she had emailed to me because I felt I owe it to him to be around while I pursue this lead. After Sadie and I arrange to meet tomorrow (another one who is very keen), I take her address and put down the phone. To be told by Aaron that I'm not going on my own.

I blink at him, surprised at the forcefulness in his voice – and the presumption that I will do as he tells me.

'I think I am,' I reply.

'You know nothing about this woman and you're just going to rock up at her house and have a nice little chat? I don't think so. She could be dangerous.'

'I know lots about your dad, I *know* he's dangerous, yet I still spend time here.'

'This is different,' he says. 'Anything could happen to you if you go there alone.'

'Anything could happen to me if I go there with you. What do you think you're going to be able to do that I can't?'

'I can't let you go on your own.'

'You're not "letting" me do anything. You're not the boss of me.' Despite what I'm saying, he is right, of course. I can't go on my own, but I'm not sure I want to go with him. We shouldn't spend any more time together than we have to. I can't ask Zach, though, and Macy would have a purple fit if I asked her. Hmmm . . . My world of trusted people is really quite small.

'I suppose we could go in separate cars,' I say.

'You think your comedy car is going to make it all the way up to Leeds?' He smirks. 'Good luck with that.'

'How dare you! Pootle can go anywhere she wants to.' Even I have to admit my very old, very little Mini would struggle with the journey. 'But, I suppose it would not be very environmentally friendly to go in separate cars. All right, we can go together if you don't mention "the thing".'

'What thing?'

'The thing, *the thing*. You know, what we were talking about when this DNA match pinged on the computer.'

'Oh, you mean me being in love with you?'

I roll my eyes.

'And me suspecting that you're in love with me but won't "go there" because of my father? You mean that?'

I clear my throat and pretend he hasn't just said that. 'If we don't talk about *the thing*, then we can go up there in your car.'

'What would you do if I did start talking about it? I mean, we'd be trapped in a car together for more than five hours – why wouldn't I try to talk to you about it?'

'All right, since it relates to the Brighton Mermaid, maybe I'll get your father to go instead. I can hire a car that will fit his wheelchair. I'm sure his personality will win over the brown-skinned people he is so respectful towards, and I'm sure a few minutes with him and they'll be telling us all about the family legends of people who disappeared. Yeah, I think that's the best way forward since you are so not like your father and wouldn't dream of imposing a conversation on me that I don't want to have.'

Aaron hangs his head. Every time he does that I feel like I am seeing child-Aaron responding to another telling-off by his dad; I feel like he is dying inside because he knows he could be in for a beating, and even if he isn't, that he is such a disappointment to his father. And every time I see child-Aaron, it kicks me in the stomach. I can't stand that he went through that. I can't stand that he is still going through that because his father may not hit him any more, but he still treats Aaron like the fifth-class citizen he believes him to be. I've never heard him use Aaron's name – only ever 'boy' or 'you'. He never says thank you, he never speaks to him in kind tones. He may not be able to physically hurt his son any more, but he's continued with his psychological abuse quite effectively.

I place my fingers under Aaron's chin and lift his head. 'Don't do that,' I say to him. 'Don't get that look on your face.' It's so complicated being around him; tangled and confusing. No matter what I might feel or could feel, he'll always be John Pope's son. 'Look, Aaron, let's just be friends, all right? It's the best way for both of us. We're good mates, aren't we? Let's just stick to that.'

'Yeah, fine.'

I want to hug away his misery, but I know even rubbing his arm to reassure him would cause more blurring of boundaries and more confusion – for both of us.

# Nell

I'm standing on the street corner near my flat waiting for Aaron to arrive. I'm a little early because I couldn't sleep last night. This is the first real breakthrough I've had with the Brighton Mermaid and my insomnia was well and truly out to play. I almost considered calling Zach to see if he was free, but then decided against it because I had to get up early to be here on this street corner.

Aaron pulls up in his silver car and it is extra shiny, as though he's given it a special polish after a special clean.

'Got enough stuff with you?' he asks, looking at my bags: the small rucksack, the snacks bag and the laptop bag. *And* the bag of bags as well as my post-mugging handbag, of course. I have a change of clothes, a blanket, a book, my laptop, some toiletries and a couple of mobile phone chargers. And slippers. Now, thinking over what I packed, I seem to have prepared myself to go and stay overnight at my parents' house, not to go and meet the woman who could possibly transform my life.

'Yes. You're lucky I didn't bring my pillow and duvet,' I say. He climbs out of the driver's seat and starts to load my stuff into the boot.

'Don't put the snacks bag or my handbag or the laptop bag in the boot,' I tell him. While he starts to load the back seat with all the bags, I climb into the driver's seat.

'What are you doing?' he asks when he returns to the front of the car.

'You didn't think I was going to let you drive, did you?'

'*Let* me drive? It's my car.'

'And it's my road trip that you've tagged on to.'

'Get out of my seat, Nell.'

'No.'

He stands with his hands open and his mouth frozen in shock. 'Get out of my seat,' he repeats.

'No,' I reply. I reach across my shoulder for the seat belt. 'If you're coming, get in. If you're not, you can call a taxi to take you home.'

'But it's my car,' he says.

'Yes, and I'm driving it.' I sigh. 'All right, if it makes you feel any better, you can choose the music. As long as it's not classical 'cos that makes me sleepy, and no heavy metal 'cos that makes me drive like a loony, and not country 'cos I can't be doing with that in my head.'

Aaron closes his eyes, pinches the bridge of his nose and sighs. I know what he's thinking when he makes his way around the front of the car and gets into the passenger seat. He's thinking the second we stop for a loo break he's going to take over the driving. Shame for him that I can go without stopping for hours and hours and hours.

Once he's clipped himself in, I turn to him and grin. 'Now, tell me, which one of these is the clutch?' I ask.

His eyes widen in horror. 'This is an automatic,' he replies. 'You have driven one before, haven't you?'

'Oh, chill out, Aaron, I'm just kidding.' I shake my head as I slip my replacement driving glasses into place and adjust the mirrors. 'You are going to have to lighten up – a lot, if this is going to be a fun road trip.'

One of those affection-filled smiles that he gets on his face when he's been staring at me appears. I whip my gaze away.

I force neutrality onto my face and sunshine into my voice when I say, 'Leeds, here we come.'

We arrive in Moortown, just outside Leeds city centre, around 12 o'clock. We stopped once at services near Leicester and Aaron was most disgruntled that I didn't climb out of the driver's seat to stretch my legs or use the loo. He refused to pass me any snacks or water and hung around for ages until he couldn't hold off any longer and had to go to the toilet.

Once he was out of sight, I got my snacks, ran around the car to stretch my legs, and got back in the driver's seat before he returned.

Aaron directs us along a road with red-brick, bow-windowed houses until we get to number 52, where Sadie, the woman who has a second-cousin DNA connection to the Brighton Mermaid, lives. She seemed nice on the phone, excited that her search had been linked to someone and that I was going to come up from Brighton to meet her.

I'm shaking as we stand in front of the white door with double-glazed yellow block glass in the panels. This reminds me of the terror I felt when I went to Jude's parents to ask them for their family history. I'd been shaking then, as well. Scared and nervous about what was going to happen when I knocked.

'I'm really nervous now,' I whisper to Aaron, who is standing right behind me.

'I am too,' he confesses. 'Which is ridiculous if you think about it.'

'I probably shouldn't have come here.' I swallow the nausea that's rising inside me.

I thought this was what I wanted; that I needed to find out who she was, who she could have been. I've had leads in the past, yes, but nothing as solid and concrete as this. I'd gone over and over the DNA matching, before I sent the initial email. I'd gone over and over it again after the phone call. There were 292 centimorgans across fifteen segments, which put her in the second-cousin category. Which meant that one of the Brighton Mermaid's grandparents was the brother or sister of one of Sadie's grandparents.

But nothing is certain until we do further testing and look at her proper family tree. It could turn out that Sadie has a stronger family connection than we first thought. Sadie could turn out to be a first cousin. Whatever it is, I am scared of what could come next. I haven't really, properly thought through what to tell her, either. I mean, she is only thirty; the whole Brighton Mermaid thing happened when she would have been about five. And I'm not sure how much it was talked about outside of East and West Sussex, really. It wasn't on the news for long, and most of the recent articles and speculation because of the upcoming twenty-fifth anniversary have been generated mainly in the Brighton area. So how much of what happened down there would have reached up here?

Also, will Sadie want to know that she is related to a dead body that was found on the beach all those years ago? And if she does, what will she do with that knowledge? I haven't thought it through at all. I don't want to lie to her, but it might be necessary to with-hold some information. But if someone did that to me, if they withheld information to get stuff out of me, how would I feel?

'Are you going to knock?' Aaron asks.

'I'm actually thinking of just running away, driving back to Brighton, and then packing up when I get home and going off to find a nice little hovel in the middle of nowhere to live in for the rest of time,' I reply.

'You don't skimp on being over-dramatic, do you?'

'I'm scared, Aaron. Really scared. And I don't even really know what I'm scared of.'

In response, Aaron reaches out and lifts the lion-shaped knocker on the door and hits it three times. 'We need to face our fears.'

'*Hiii!*' Sadie trills when she answers the door. She's so excited that I know, instantly, we're going to get on great.

Sadie's other half, Earl, sits in the corner of the room, glowering at us.

'Oh, don't mind Earl,' Sadie says when she ushers us into her immaculately tidy living room. Everything is in place and there is not one single item on a surface that doesn't need to be there. All the wooden surfaces are shiny and dust-free. On the phone, she told me she has three children – the oldest is nine. I have no children and my flat has never been this polished and pristine. 'Earl doesn't see the point in me doing all this so he's a bit grumpy that he had to take today off to be here.'

I smile at Earl and he practically scowls at me before shaking out his paper and then lifting it in front of his face.

Sadie pulls a face at him. 'He said it would be fine, you coming here, but I said you could be anyone, quite literally, you know, a serial killer or anything, so I needed him to be here.' She looks over my shoulder at Aaron. 'I see you did the same. Husband or boyfriend?'

'Just a friend,' I reply.

'Yeah, right,' she giggles. 'And I'm the queen of Jamaica!'

'Sore point, actually,' Aaron says. He clearly likes her too. 'Nell is seeing someone else and we're not allowed to talk about how I feel about her.'

Sadie throws her head back and laughs. 'And she made you drive her all the way here? Wow, you must *really* love her!'

'Erm, excuse me,' I cut in. 'I didn't make him do anything. He insisted on coming. And I drove, I'll have you know.'

Earl shakes his newspaper and tuts loudly.

'Come into the kitchen,' says Sadie, 'we can sit at the table. I've got all the stuff I've done out there.' She jerks her head briefly in her husband's direction. 'And we can talk without disturbing a certain grumpy someone.'

After she has shut the glass door leading to the large kitchen behind her, she says, 'Love the bones of him, I do.' She moves over to the kettle. 'Loves me too, despite all his grump. Tea?' She doesn't wait for an answer before she flicks on the kettle and starts cramming teabags into the spotty teapot that she's set out on a large tray with two large spotty teacups. 'Thing is, he'll be all ears later. He does find it interesting but he kind of tunes out because I do go on sometimes. Don't know if you've noticed.'

As she talks, she reaches into the cupboard above the kettle and removes another teacup and saucer. 'Sit, sit,' she says and gestures to the padded seats around the large dining table. 'I was watching one of those telly programmes, you know, where they get those famous people to trace family trees, and I thought, why don't I do that? Me mam, God bless her soul, doesn't really talk much about family stuff. There was some huge falling out and the family went their separate ways a while back. Don't get me wrong, bits of us meet up sometimes for weddings and stuff, but not all of us. They just won't get over it. No one can hold a grudge like the people in my family. I kid you not.'

On her dining table, Sadie has set out many piles of papers, her laptop and a couple of family tree books.

'Anyway, I watched a few of those episodes and I thought, you know what, I'm going to give it a go. I'm going to set up a huge family tree and find out who everyone in my family is. Obviously I had to do this without Mam's help 'cos she will not be involved. Then I watched *another* programme and they had these people who go around looking for people who have an inheritance. And that was it, I just had to do it. Not looking for an inheritance or anything like that. Just wanting to find more family.' She pours boiling water into the teapot. 'I wasn't even sure if I should do the DNA thing. His nibs said it was a waste of money but I thought, I might as well. If I'm going to do it, I might as well do it properly. It's really weird, isn't it? You send off this sample and then you get contacted by people who might be related to you. Or people like you two.'

I wonder if Aaron is as aware as I am that we haven't said very much. Sadie is a talker, which is great, really, because it's unlikely she'll ask that many questions, and I won't be as conflicted about what to and what not to tell her.

'So, where do you want to start?' Sadie asks when she sits down at the table. She places a cup in front of each of us.

Her eyes are dancing and she has a sweet smile on her face. She does have shades of the Brighton Mermaid – maybe the shaping around the forehead and eyebrow area, maybe the curve of the chin. There is something familiar about her.

And I decide in this moment that I'm going to tell her as much as I can. It's only fair, and I like her. Possibly stupid given I don't know her, but there's something endearingly open and honest about Sadie that makes me want to share all my information with her.

From my laptop bag, I pull out the purple plastic folder full of newspaper cuttings, my voice recorder and my notepad and pencil that I use to start sketching out a rough family tree.

'There's lots to tell you, but first, do you mind telling me as much of your family history as you can? Once we're done, I can tell you everything I know about the woman who could be your relative.'

Sadie claps her hands in glee. 'This is so exciting,' she says. She picks up her spotty teacup, sits back in her seat and begins to talk.

# Nell

'I really enjoyed watching you work,' Aaron says on our way back.

He insisted that he drive us home because I looked tired. And I am tired. My eyes are heavy and I have a headache that feels like my head is being slowly cleaved apart.

'You were so good at listening to her, and the notes you were making, I would never have thought to make myself. I was really impressed.'

'Thank you.'

'You should think about doing this sort of thing full-time. Getting paid for it.'

'No one pays people to look for their family tree. Not unless there's an inheritance or something involved.'

'Yeah, maybe. But I just think that is your true calling. You're so good at it.'

'Thank you,' I repeat.

We drive on in silence until: 'Have you ever been in love?' he asks.

*Why would you do that, Aaron?* I think. *Why would you try to take us there?* Instead of replying, I look out the window at the dark world.

'This isn't me talking about "the thing",' he says to my silence. 'It's just one friend asking another friend a question.'

*Have I ever been in love?* 'That's an odd question. I'm not sure what sort of answer you want from it, to be honest.'

'Just an answer. Have you ever been in love?'

I'm avoiding responding because if I look back over my life in any detail, I suspect I'm very likely to find that the reply is very possibly 'no, I have never been in love'.

'I was in love with Shane, I guess,' I say. 'In that young way when you think that what you feel is the most pure and intense love in the world and no one else has ever felt that way.'

'Shane who is married to your sister?'

'Yes, Shane who is with my sister. They're not married.'

'You've never really said how you feel about that. You just said your sister was with your ex. I didn't realise that you felt like that about him. It must kill you inside to see them together.'

'Not at all. It was over when I left for college and after the first month of thinking I would die without him, I was fine. More than fine. He tried to rekindle things when I finished college, but . . .'

'But . . . ?'

'I just didn't want to. I had no feelings left for him, basically. I sort of fancied him, and we did sleep together that one time – and you must never tell my sister that if you ever meet her. I'm really not proud of the fact that I let a temporary lapse in judgement take over and I did it with him.' I don't mention that it was seeing Aaron's dad that pushed me into it.

'What, when he was with your sister?'

'No, no, no way,' I say quickly. 'No, it was almost literally after college, when I was back living in Brighton. This was well over fifteen years ago. He wanted us to start dating again and I . . . There was nothing there. The sex had been all right, I guess. But I certainly didn't feel anything for him beyond nostalgia. I shouldn't have slept with him again. I might have more fond memories of him if I hadn't. That's why I said I guess I was in love with him, because doing that years later kind of muddied how I felt about him the first time around – when I'm pretty certain I did feel all that for him.'

Aaron checks his rear-view mirror and then side mirror and I think for a moment he's going to change lanes. But he doesn't.

Instead a look comes over his face, like he is trying to calculate something. 'No one else?' he asks suddenly.

No one else. Over the years, among the one-night stands and flings and short relationships, there's been no one else. It worries me. Am I incapable of love? Do I not know how to feel? Is that part of the problem with Aaron? We could fall into sex, we could fall into a relationship, but I would wreck it by not knowing how to fall in love. No, no, that's not right. I do know how to fall in love. I do know how to be in love. I must do. Most humans do.

'Zach, maybe.'

'Who's Zach?'

'The guy I'm seeing.'

'So you really are seeing someone?'

'Yes, I told you!'

'All right, all right. You can forgive me for wondering, given how things . . . Anyway, you haven't been seeing him for long, have you?'

'No, I haven't, but there's something about him that . . . I don't know, I like him differently to how I've liked other guys, and I think we could, maybe? I'm being very presumptuous – he might not even like me that much – but when we're together there's a spark that is kind of new and unique. I think sometimes when I'm with him that he's the guy I'm going to fall in love with.'

'I hope he is,' Aaron says. I know he means it on so many levels, and I do love him for that. 'And I'm sure he likes you that much. What's not to like?'

'What about you? Have you ever been in— OK, scratch that, have you ever had a girlfriend?'

'What sort of a question is that? Of course I have!' he replies.

'Well, I don't know, do I? You talk about your life growing up sometimes, and you talk about your life in London, but you never mention any women. You talk about your job, the company you started, where you lived, the holidays you went on, but it's always "I did this", "I went there", never "we" anything. I've always thought you lived the single-man life like I've lived the single-woman life.'

'I've had girlfriends,' he says. He is staring intently straight ahead and I'm sure he doesn't need to concentrate so hard, but he's uncomfortable talking about this. 'I had one girlfriend for nearly ten years.' He reaches up and pushes his glasses back on his face. 'We were engaged.'

'Bloody hellfire! Aaron, I had no idea. Engaged? What happened?'

'My father's accident happened. My father needed looking after and I had to move back to Brighton, back to my house of horrors, as you so rightly called it.'

'And she didn't want to move?'

'She did. She was all for it. She thought we could start a tech business down here, keep the one in London, too. She'd done lots of research and she was just gagging to live by the sea. But . . .' His voice peters out and his face looks grim. I understand.

'Was she a white English woman, your fiancée?' I ask him.

The intense staring is back on his face; his knuckles become yellow with the strength with which he grips the steering wheel.

'No, no she was not. She was British born, but her parents were Iranian.'

'And you could live your life, you could be with her, you could even get married – if you lived all that way away from your father. But you couldn't put her through being around him all the time, could you?'

'No, I couldn't. After I'd heard what he'd done to you and your family, I just couldn't put Lydia through that. I loved her too much. And the thought of him being like that with our children, too . . .'

I place my hand on his shoulder, briefly, to show him I understand.

'She is an adult, though. Don't you think you should have given her the chance to make that choice?'

He sighs and his grip on the steering wheel loosens, almost as though he is letting go of something I can't see. 'All right, let me explain it like this. My father calls my wife something out of my earshot, and she tells me. What do I do? I mean, she's already told him where to get off, and it's not made a difference to him. What do I do? Do I tell him what I think of him? Yeah, all right, I do that. And then what? I carry on living in his house and taking care of him and expecting my wife to do the same? What if it's one of the children, who won't be old enough to tell him where to get off? They'd be going out into the world and getting enough of that crap slung at them from all sides – home is supposed to be safe, not where your grandfather says nasty, vicious things to you.'

'In that case, you move out,' I say.

'Yes, I move out. I cut my father off. And then live for ever with the guilt that I didn't take care of my unwell father.' Fear. Obligation. Guilt. Shackles that are so difficult to unbind.

'You wouldn't have to cut him off, just—'

'Just still see him and basically condone how he behaves when he's vile about and to my wife and children. We talked about it for hours and hours, Nell, we tried to find a way around it. But the only way is if I cut my father out. And I couldn't do it. And I couldn't ask Lydia to even try living with it. She'd put up with enough racist crap in her life, the overt stuff and the covert stuff – I couldn't knowingly bring more of it into her life.'

'I'm sorry it didn't work out for you,' I tell him.

'I do understand, you know, Nell,' he says.

'Understand what?'

'When I look at it rationally, I understand why you won't even think about going out with me. It's the same as it was with Lydia only a hundred thousand times worse because I know what he put your family through. But then, I find it hard to be rational about how I feel about you.'

'This is "the thing" that we agreed not to talk about,' I remind him.

'I know. And I'm sorry, but just hear me out. Talking about Lydia has made me realise I need to back off. I didn't want to put her through all that horror and I don't want to put you through it, either. Even more so when I think of what he's already done to you, what he's doing now, holding this thing over your head. So, I'm talking about "the thing" so we don't ever have to talk about "the thing" again.'

I knew he'd get there, that he'd eventually understand what I've been trying to tell him during all the time he's been showing an interest in me: the outside world is scary enough, and John Pope made sure that it was terrifying inside my own home, too. And I've come to the point where I don't want to invite, no matter how obliquely, more of the terror-maker into my life.

'Thank you for saying that,' I mumble.

We're coming towards the end of the M23; we'll soon be on the A23 down into Brighton. I always like to look at the large stone Brighton gates, sitting tall and proud on either side of the road as you enter the city. Around us it is dark and there is nothing but fields. This part of the motorway has no lights and it feels like we are the only two people left in the world as his silver car moves us towards home.

'Did you get anything from Sadie?' he asks. 'I mean, I know you now know about the other branches of her family, and with their names you can start to look for them, but I mean, did you get anything else?'

'No. And yes.' I think back to how Sadie was. She seemed so free and open and comfortable with who she is. 'I kind of, in my mind, fit her personality onto the Brighton Mermaid's. Sadie is how I imagine the BM would be if I ever got to talk to her. You know, laughing all the time; talkative and friendly. Even though she was . . . you know, when we found her, so I had no sense of who she was. But I would love it if she was like Sadie.'

'So what are you going to do next?'

I pause for a moment to look at the Brighton gates, welcoming us back, telling us that on the other side of the gates we are protected.

'Well, I'm going to do Internet searches on all of the names she gave me, create a large family tree. From there, I'll come over to yours so I can use the proper facial recognition software to go through all the matching faces and names with the online records I can get access to. And then, hopefully, I'll get a few more things to work with. More names, more leads.'

'And what about your friend?'

Jude. What about Jude? I feel guilty. I've been so excited that I have a lead in the BM case that I've almost – only almost – forgotten I'm meant to be finding her, too. That soon it'll be twenty-five years since she disappeared – and the nightmare of my dad being accused of killing her began.

'I don't know. I'll just keep plugging away like I've been doing for years.'

Aaron pulls up outside my building and neither of us moves. We stare out of the windscreen. It's been a profound day in more ways than one. It began early and here we are back at home very late, one step closer to unravelling one mystery, and several steps beyond another thing we've been dealing with.

'I'll see you in a couple of days then,' Aaron says eventually. 'When you've had a chance to go through all your stuff.'

'Yes. I'll see you in a few days.'

Still neither of us moves. It feels like, after such a profound day, after such deep pronouncements, we need to say something more. Do something more.

'This is so crazy,' I say. 'I feel like I should invite you up or something.'

'I feel like asking you if I can come up.'

'And ask you to spend the night.'

'Together. Properly.'

'Having sex.'

'Making love.'

'"Making love"? Who actually says that?' I turn to look at him.

Aaron turns to face me, too. 'I do. Who actually says "having sex"? Like they're getting a root canal done or something.'

'I do. Lots of people do.'

'Lots of people say "making love", too. All right, what would you prefer? "Fucking"?'

'"Screwing"?'

'That sounds like you're putting together flat pack.'

I laugh. '"Making love" isn't so bad when you put it like that.'

'Neither is "having sex".'

'Yeah.'

'Yeah.'

We stare at each other in the dark of the car, both of us breathing hard, both of us with our lips slightly parted, our eyes linked. This is crazy. For the first time ever, I want Aaron Pope. I've always been aware of how attractive he is; I could even concede to a small crush. But right now I want to have sex, make love, fuck, screw, whatever with him. Right now I want to do the stupid, passionate, naked thing.

'We're not going to do this, are we, Aaron,' I state.

'No, we're not.'

'No.' I pull on the handle of the door and it pops open. 'No, we're not.'

I retrieve my belongings from the boot and the back seat and lean back to look through the open door. 'Goodnight, Aaron.'

'It's morning. Wednesday morning now,' he says. 'So, good morning, Nell.'

I watch him drive away until he turns at the end of my road and then I turn to my flat. As usual, when I'm stumbling home at this time from a night out, there are a couple of lights on across the different flats.

*Oh, Aaron.* I think as I drag my tired body, weighted down with my many bags, up to the third floor because the lift is out of action, again. *I wish things were simpler. Even if we can't get together, I wish, wish, wish, that he would get out of his father's orbit. I have to be there for now, but you are going to waste so many more years looking after the man who abused you.*

On my floor, I hit the timed light at the end of the corridor. Nothing.

I'm sure they only changed the bulb a couple of months ago. I hit the flat white circle again, expecting the light above to splutter into life this time. Nothing. Absolutely nothing. Three more hits, and still nothing. I have to accept it's not going to happen so I fumble in my coat pockets until I find my mobile. I flick on the torch function and move towards my flat, shining the torch in front of me. I will have to get on to the freeholder about the lift and the light and no doubt he'll dodge my calls and then somehow make out I've done something to break the lights and lift just to spite him.

At my front door I set down my bags, which seem to have doubled in weight in the dark and fug of tiredness, and reach into my other pocket for my keys.

My front door is ajar.

I pause in pulling out my keys and stare at the door.

*Did I leave it unlocked?* I wonder as I stare at the door. *No. I didn't. I'm sure I didn't.*

I stare and stare, my heart racing faster and faster until it is a painful juggernaut in my chest.

*I did not leave my door unlocked.*

I have four locks on my door and I remember securing each and every one of them before I went downstairs to wait for Aaron yesterday morning.

Slowly, carefully, I use the toe of my shoe to push the door further open.

As the door swings back, I notice the splintered wood from where it's been kicked open. But how can that be? How could someone kick open my door and no one in the other flats have heard?

I stare into the darkness of my flat, the torch from my phone making a small puddle of light by my feet.

I hear, *then* sense, the movement, and I'm about to raise my phone when the darkness suddenly comes alive and rushes at me at speed. I don't have time to react as a black shape barrels into me, knocking me aside, causing my face and my left side to slam into the splintered door frame, my head snapping back like I've been punched. I stumble back, the pain acute and sudden in my face, as I lose my balance and crumple.

In the darkness of the corridor, through the blurriness of my vision, I watch the darkness moving, running for the stairs at the end of the corridor, the only thing properly visible the white soles of its shoes.

# Nell

*Wednesday, 25 April*

This wasn't a normal burglary. That's obvious because pretty much everything of value – TV, DVD, cash, computer screens – is all still here, and the only things missing are the three hard drives from the desktop computers in my office. Also, whoever it was that came out of the darkness trashed my home. There are papers – everywhere. Every drawer has been opened and emptied, even the drawer in the white unit under the bathroom sink. The family trees have been ripped off the walls, the filing cabinet broken open and papers strewn about. It's obvious that whoever was here was looking for something, but I'm not sure what.

It's also now obvious that whoever pushed me over last Friday and stole my bag was doing it for a specific reason, and not simply to mug me.

I've been itching to tidy up. Pick things up. Straighten out things. Just get my flat back to how it should be. When I called the police, though, they said they would get to me as soon as they could, but not to touch anything, so I had to sit by the front door, my bags around me, my arm a big throbbing wedge of pain by my side, and my face stinging so much I kept thinking I was going to pass out.

'You really should go and get your injuries looked at,' the uniformed police officer says.

I'm allowed to sit on the sofa since it's unlikely they will get any forensic evidence from it. I actually preferred sitting by the front

228

door, because from here I'm at the epicentre of the devastation that has been wrought upon my home and it is making me feel worse, if that's possible.

'I will,' I mumble at the police officer.

'Is there anyone we can call to come and stay with you?' he asks.

I shake my head. Before I called the police I almost called Macy. My finger actually hovered over her number on my phone, but I decided against it. Aaron, possibly, but then that would be more line-blurring. And Zach I couldn't impose upon like that. So that was the end of that. 'I'll be fine.'

The forensics woman who is dusting for fingerprints is going over the television at the moment. She's working quietly, methodically, but for some reason it sounds very loud – like every touch of her brush is a canon firing, every lift of her fingerprint paper is nails dragged down a chalkboard.

'And you're sure nothing was taken except the computer hard drives?' the officer asks. The other police officer reappears from the bedroom area, and comes to stand beside him. The pair of them are dressed in black, short-sleeved uniforms, they have radios on their lapels, handcuffs on their waistbands, truncheons on the other side. And heavy black boots that I would have made them remove under other circumstances because I don't allow outside footwear inside my house.

'Yes,' I say. 'I had my tablet and my laptop with me.'

'Why do you have three computers, Miss Okorie?' the first officer asks pleasantly enough.

I've been waiting for this question, because they have seen the papers strewn around my living room and my office. All the papers and printouts and sheets I've pinned and stuck to my noticeboards have been ripped down, often torn in half or scrunched up before being thrown on the floor. The police officers will have looked at what these papers are, they will have seen that some of them are things that I, a civilian, shouldn't technically have. He was always going to ask, but he's going about it in a roundabout way.

'Because I have,' I reply.

'We do really need to know as much as possible so that we can help you,' he says.

I sigh. My face hurts, my arm hurts, my head hurts. *I* hurt. Not just the injuries. This, it hurts. This feels like someone has violated me, has taken the time to defile and degrade me. And that, quite simply, hurts.

*I think I need to move*, I decide. I close my eyes and try to move them to loosen the tension behind my eyelids.

'I look for people,' I say. 'I found the Brighton Mermaid twenty-five years ago. I look for who she is in my spare time. That's why I have three computers. I need them for different things.'

'I really think we should take you to the hospital,' the police-woman says.

'I'm fine. Truly. Just tired.'

'You're showing signs of concussion,' she replies. 'You're slurring your speech, not making much sense.'

'No, truly, I'm fine. I just need to lie down.'

'If you won't go to the hospital, then we'll take you to the station for the police doctor to look you over.'

Not happening. I am not stepping foot in a police station if I don't have to. 'OK. Hospital.'

They both look at me blankly. 'I said, hospital,' I repeat.

They look at each other then back at me. It takes a second or two for me to realise I'm speaking gibberish. I sound fine to me, but to them, it must sound like nonsense.

'Hospital. Hospital. Hospital.'

It's suddenly very hot, but I've wrapped my arms around myself because I'm so cold. I have concussion. I hate that the policewoman was right. I hate that—

# Nell

I wasn't even awake for the ride to the hospital in an ambulance.

I've never been in one before and I wasn't awake for it. I was awake though for the brain scan, for the bit where the doctors told me I have a tiny bit of brain swelling caused by the blow, and I was awake for the nurse patching up my eyebrow with thin white butterfly stitches.

I was also awake for the bit when Macy arrived.

She is currently pacing the cubicle, rubbing her hands over and over each other. She can't sit, she can't look at me and she can't really speak. She keeps starting at the sounds she hears outside the curtain. She hates hospitals anyway, but the fact she got called to come to one because her sister was being brought in by ambulance has pretty much awoken every single anxious nerve in her body.

If I hadn't been unconscious, I would have told them not to ring her. But she is down as my next of kin, and her number is one of the most recently called in my phone, although how the police got into my phone without my passcode I'd rather not think about.

'You wouldn't have told me, would you?' She sounds angry but she's not. She's hurt. And scared. *Terrified*, probably. Losing the people she loves is one of the things that strikes terror into Macy's heart. I'm the same, but Macy . . . she comes up with scenario after scenario about what could happen until they feel real, like they are actually going to happen. *This*, what is happening right now, will be one that she has played through many, many times. And it's come true. Which means the others could come true. 'You wouldn't have told me about this because you'd try to protect me.'

'It's not like that, I swear,' I say. 'It all happened so quickly. And I would have told you . . . eventually.'

'You treat me like I'm nine years old sometimes. You and Shane both. You can tell me stuff. I *am* strong enough to hear it.'

'I know.'

'So what do they think happened? Who broke into your house?'

She may *think* she wants to hear it, but the reality is, she doesn't. She just doesn't. If she knew I am in touch with Pope after all these years and that I regularly go over to his house . . . I have no idea what that would do to her.

'I don't know. The forensic lady said she usually has a good idea who does these things because the criminals usually work in a specific way. But this one was new to her. Especially since they didn't even go near the TV or the DVD pl—' *Should not have said that. Should NOT have said that.*

Macy, my pretty, clever, wonderful little sister, stops pacing and wringing her hands. She stares directly at me. Out of the two of us, she's the one who looks most like our dad. She has a lean face, soft cheekbones, big eyes and a soft, wide mouth. I look more like my mum, as my face is slightly rounder, my lips slightly plumper and my mouth not as wide. The way she looks at me now is the way Dad looked at me two days after I found the BM and I'd recovered enough from the ordeal to be questioned about what I'd got up to when I went out.

Dad kept staring at me until I told him every single detail about where I'd been, what I'd drunk, who I'd spoken to. Macy's going to do the same, I can tell.

She's my younger sister, I keep trying to remind myself when this sort of thing happens. I'm meant to be the take-charge one.

'Why didn't they take anything valuable like the telly or DVD player?' she asks.

'They did take my computer hard drives,' I offer rather pathetically.

'This is about the dead body, isn't it?' she says through her teeth. Mum's the one who talks through her teeth when she's angry. 'This is someone coming after you because of that dead body, isn't it? *Isn't it?*'

'Why would you immediately jump to the conclusion that this is something to do with all of that? Why don't you think it's something to do with the other cases I'm working on?'

'Other cases! Do you realise how delusional you sound? You're not some private detective, you know.'

'I know that.'

'Do you? When are you going to stop all this, Nell? You left your job and now look. You've been hurt because of that body. Because of *the Brighton Mermaid*.' She spits out the last three words because she never likes to say them. She never likes to romanticise what actually happened.

'You don't know that,' I reply.

'Yes I do. So do you.'

'Macy, you do realise that you're younger than me, don't you?'

'Nell, you do realise that you're older than me, don't you?' she mocks. 'And maybe it's time you started acting like a grown-up.'

'Because you do so well in the grown-up stakes,' I retort.

'And what's that supposed to mean?'

'It means . . . It means I've got a pounding headache and I need to go home.'

'Right, I'll go and find a nurse who can discharge you.' She starts to leave. 'We'll have to get a cab back to my place because I was shaking too much to drive.'

'No, you're all right. I need to go home, secure my flat. Make some calls.'

'You can't go back to your flat on your own after what happened.'

'I won't be on my own,' I say. *I'll have the large, solid memory of what happened to keep me company.* 'I'll, erm, I'll call my boyfriend.'

My sister lets go of the curtain and comes back to the bed. 'You haven't got a boyfriend.' I have hastily promoted Zach to boyfriend and I hope he won't mind, but needs must.

'I do.'

'You do not.'

'I actually do.'

'What's his name?'

'Zach.'

'Where does he live?'

'The apartments in town near Jubilee Library.'

'How old is he?'

'Forty.'

'What's his favourite food?'

'Saltfish and ackee.'

Macy folds her arms across her chest and harrumphs. 'If he's real, I want to meet him,' she says.

'He's real and you'll meet him soon enough.'

She stares at me with her head to one side for a long while. It really is like looking at my father. 'Please stop all this, Nell.' She says this quietly because she knows that's more likely to get through to me. 'You know, what happened happened. We can't go back on it. Can you just stop and go back to your job and do something else? Find a new hobby? This is dangerous.'

'The thing of it is, Macy, I can't quit and do something else. I just can't.' I can't tell her about Pope's ultimatum. How time is running out on me stopping him going after our dad.

'Why not?'

I wish I was feeling a bit better – more grounded, less light-headed – while we have this conversation, but it needs to be had, I realise now. I can't keep doing this in secret if I'm at risk. I drag my knees up under the blanket on the A&E bed and wrap my arms around them. 'Because the Brighton Mermaid stuff is basically who I am.'

'It's not,' she protests.

'Please listen,' I beg. 'It's hard enough to explain without having to wonder if you're actually listening to me or waiting to tell me I'm wrong.'

'Sorry,' she mumbles.

'Jude and I found her. And everything that has happened since then seems to have been about that. Jude disappearing, Dad being arrested, all those years and years of harassment. Even the fact that I can't settle down with anyone . . . It's all been about that night. I hate that it's true, but it is. I've tried so many times to do something else, be someone else. I almost didn't come back to Brighton after college because I knew as soon as I passed those gates, I'd be her again – the Girl Who Found the Brighton Mermaid. All this twenty-fifth-anniversary stuff doesn't help either. I just need to find out who she was. I just need to find out what happened to Jude. If I can find those things out, I can maybe start again. You know, lead a different life.'

'And what if you don't find out who she was, Nell? It's been twenty-five years – what's going to change now?'

'I don't know,' I say. But I *do* know what's going to change: Pope will set off the bomb that is reopening the investigation into our father, and I will be forced to leave Brighton. As selfish as it sounds, I will need to leave to stay sane.

'My life has been about her, too, you know?' Macy says. She lowers her gaze and traces her finger in circles along the edge of the blanket.

'Yes, I do know. And I'm sorry about that. I am so, so sorry that something I did has completely wrecked your life.'

'I didn't say it'd wrecked my life. My life isn't wrecked. I have three amazing children, I have a partner, a lovely home and a great job. Not many people can say they have that.'

I notice it even if she doesn't – the lack of adjective to describe her other half. 'Are you and Shane having problems?' I ask.

'No!' she shoots back. 'Maybe . . . Yes.'

'I had no idea,' I say.

'Well, why would you? He's, like, perfect and I'm a nutcase.'

'Don't say things like that about yourself.'

'I know what I do isn't normal. I know I shouldn't call you at that time on a Saturday morning, and that it isn't going to change how the week goes whether you answer or not. But I can't stop. There are so many things that I know I shouldn't do, but I can't stop doing them in case something terrible happens. I know that's not normal, but I can't seem to stop. I think Shane's getting sick of it. Sick of me.'

'Has he said something?'

'No, but I can tell. I mean he's asked me to marry him again, but he's so quiet and, I don't know, shifty almost these days. I thought for a time things were back on track, but no, he's always on edge again. It's only a matter of time before he leaves, just like Clyde did. And I feel powerless to do anything about it. I hate the things I do, the way I push people away or push their buttons, but I can't seem to stop it. It's clearly getting to Shane.'

'Or . . . Or it could be that he gave me the number of someone to talk to about doing some searching work for and he's worried how you'll react when you find out?' I offer knowing what her reaction will be.

'He *what*?! After all those conversations, after all the times he agreed with me that you should get a bloody grip and live in the real world, he does that? I'll bloody murder him.'

'"Get a bloody grip", huh?'

'You know what I mean,' she replies. 'I swear, he's as bad as you are sometimes.'

'It is my life, you know?' I say to her. 'I do get to choose what I do with it.'

'But it feels like you're wasting your life doing this.'

'Maybe so, but it is *my* life. And I've just explained to you why I do what I do. Can't you just accept it? And not give Shane a hard time for helping me?'

236

My sister mashes her lips together as she stares at me. She's having an internal battle about what she wants to say and what she should say.

'Look, Mace, this will all be over after this year. I will be done with it all. I just need to give it one last proper big try.' That's if Pope will even stick to the deal.

'OK, all right.' She shrugs – for effect, not because she doesn't care or even accepts that it's my life to 'waste'. 'I'll go and find the nurse to ask about you being allowed to go home.'

'Thank you,' I say and relax back against the bed.

'You'd better get on your phone.'

'What do you mean?'

'You better call or text your boyfriend so he can come be with you. You heard them earlier, you can't go home on your own, so either he comes to be with you like you said, or you come home with me.' She smiles sweetly, like she used to when she was a little girl. 'Your choice.'

# Nell

Zach comes through the glass doors of A&E almost at a run. Macy and I are sitting in the waiting area at the top of the long hill you have to walk up to get to the casualty department.

We've run out of things to talk about, mainly, I think, because she's been waiting for me to admit I don't have a boyfriend.

When I texted Zach and said I was at the hospital and could he come over at some point to drive me home, he called me back straight away to say he was coming. I asked, 'Aren't you at work?', and he said yes but he was coming anyway.

And here he is, dressed in a dark grey suit, white shirt and red tie. Looking impossibly handsome. He pauses in the door-way for a moment, looks around and then strides towards us when I call his name.

'Told you,' I mumble at Macy while her eyes nearly bulge out of her head.

'Are you all right?' Zach asks. I stand to greet him and he immediately wraps me up in a hug. 'What happened? Are you all right?' He loosens his grip on me slightly to look at my face. He does a double take when he clocks the swelling around my eye, my puffed-up lip, the thin white strips that are holding the skin above my eye together. 'Did someone *hit* you?' he asks.

'No, no. They shoved me aside while they were running out of my flat – the door frame did this.'

He hugs me again. 'What did the doctors say?'

'That I can go home as long as someone stays with me for at least forty-eight hours.'

'Done. We can stay at my place. I should be able to get a couple of people to cover my lessons.'

His concern and willingness to upend his life for me is both unexpected and surprising. 'Erm, that's not necessary,' I say. 'I just need a lift home.'

Zach is about to protest when Macy, clearly a bit perturbed at being ignored, loudly clears her throat. I step out of Zach's hold and point to my sister. 'Oh, sorry, Zach, this is my sister, Macy. Macy, Zach.'

Zach sticks his hand out and smiles. 'Oh, hello. Nice to meet you.' If he remembers that it was her who rang and rang the morning after the night we met, he doesn't let on.

'Nice to meet you,' Macy replies. It's her turn to double-take – when she realises Zach has no eyebrows or eyelashes as well as no hair. 'I had, erm, better be going then if you're going to take Nell home.'

'I don't think you should go home,' he says. He turns to my sister. 'What do you think?'

'I don't think she should go home if the place has been burgled. But she won't listen to me. The only reason she's not coming home with me is because she said you'd help her clean up.'

'Of course I will,' he says. 'But Nell, returning to a crime scene so soon after it's happened . . . It can really mess you up.'

I roll my eyes at them and then regret it because it hurts my head. 'Most people have no choice when they're burgled. It'll be fine. Besides, even if I do stay at your flat, I have to get some stuff from my flat.'

'All right, if you're sure,' Zach says, not looking convinced or happy about it.

Macy doesn't look convinced or happy about it either.

'It'll be fine, you two. I promise you.'

*

*The darkness comes at me from nowhere.*

*It runs at me with speed, pushes me down. I'm shaken by the fall, powerless to get up. The darkness throws itself onto my chest, landing heavily. It raises its fist, brings it down to—*

My eyes jump open.

And my face immediately smarts, the ache radiating down from my swollen eye socket to my jaw. I dared to look in the mirror earlier and it did indeed look like I had come off badly in a fight with someone bigger, stronger and more vicious than me.

It doesn't take a genius to work out what that dream was about.

Zach is still asleep and wrapped around me. We went on a flying visit to my home earlier. The police had made good on the promise to have the flat secured and I told him which bags to collect – the pile by the door – so I didn't have to go up there in the end. We rattled around his place, two people who are virtual strangers brought together by an unfortunate circumstance. And then to bed, where for the first time since I met him, sex wasn't on the cards.

It was nice to fall asleep like that and it's nice to wake up with him beside me. This is one of the things I've missed out on over the years – not having a regular companion means I rarely get to wake up beside someone, to have their warm skin next to mine, their breathing gently rocking my body.

Carefully I press my fingers against the battered side of my face. It's painful to touch and it's painful without being touched. I should probably get out of bed and take the painkillers they gave me at the hospital, but that would mean venturing into the darkness that extends beyond the bed to Zach's living room. Much as I'd like to, I can't do that. It took all my willpower not to ask him to let us sleep with the light on.

I close my eyes and sigh. Then I open them again because flashes of what my flat looked like – papers across the floor, stuff ripped off noticeboards, drawers hanging open, ornaments toppled, the gaping holes where the computer hard drives used to be – keep coming back to me.

It seemed so . . . *violent*. If they wanted the hard drives so much, why destroy the other personal stuff? That's before I consider why they wanted the hard drives, which brings me back to the violence of it all.

So many questions, very, very few answers.

My head is banging. Beyond the pain from my face, my head is aching with trying to work out who would do this and why. I'm sure it's linked to the mugging. But is it linked to Pope's accident? What if Pope was right and him being run over wasn't an accident? What if someone *had* tried to kill him?

And if they did try to kill John Pope, am I next in their sights? And why? To stop me hunting down the Brighton Mermaid's identity? To stop me finding Jude? Has whoever has done this been watching me all this time? If they have, what is different about now? Am I really that close to getting the answers?

The pain intensifies with the growing feeling of paranoia rattling around in my head.

The only person who has been around all this time and has meant me harm is Pope. Which wouldn't work, because unless he arranged to have the car drive at himself, it can't have been him.

There is someone else, of course. Someone who has been around all this time, watching, observing, waiting until I got too close. Someone who I would never think of as capable of doing anything to harm me, but who, if they were pushed, would have to do something to stop me.

Dad.

I immediately try to erase that thought. It's ridiculous. Despite his height and his build, despite his large hands and powerful laugh, he wouldn't harm anyone. Even when the police beat him up – more than once – he didn't defend himself. Despite what they said, his hands never had cuts on them, never showed any sign that he did anything but take the beating because he knew that doing anything else – including defending himself – could have fatal consequences.

When he was under attack he wasn't violent, so how could he do anything to the Brighton Mermaid? Or take away Jude? Or do something to me? He just wouldn't. My dad is not that sort of man.

I'm being silly. Panicking because I've been hurt. Lashing out with stupid, damaging theories because I'm scared. My dad wouldn't do that. I know him. We haven't been close in years, but he wouldn't do anything to Jude, he wouldn't have murdered those other girls. It just isn't in him.

Gently I take Zach's arm and pull it over my body. I want him as close to me as possible. I need him to remind me that I'm all right and that I don't need to start thinking ridiculous things just because someone attacked me. Zach moans gently then snuggles closer to me, nestles his face against my shoulder. 'Hmmmm,' he groans softly.

I close my eyes and focus on him. On being here. On being far, far away from all the rubbish that is starting to make me, for the first time ever, doubt my father's innocence.

# Macy

I'm better now. I think seeing Nell in hospital shocked me out of whatever state I was in before. It really is all getting too much, though. The thing with Clyde and his other family, the thought of what might happen if I tell anyone what I know about Jude.

The thing is, no one ever asked me. Not ever. It was like I didn't exist in that house; no one officially told me that she was missing and no one ever asked if I had seen her. Considering how close they knew Nell and Jude were, like sisters, you'd think they'd maybe ask Nell's actual, real-life, blood sister if she knew something. I might have told then. It would have been awful, given everything that went on without any real knowledge on the police's part, but it might have been an idea to ask me.

At that time I was mostly ignored. I think that was another reason why I was desperate to marry Clyde. He noticed me, he loved me, and he only ever wanted to be with me. I'd be with him now if I'd been willing to leave the children with my parents and take off. But how could I leave them with my folks, knowing what I knew? They were never with Mummy and Daddy unless I was there, too. I don't think anyone, not even Nell, has noticed that. Besides, I wouldn't leave them unless I had to. Unless it was best for them. Sometimes Shane hints – or even outright says – that the things I do are not good for the children. That my obsessions and rituals and anxieties will rub off on them, will make them grow up into anxious people, too. I know he's right and I know I don't want these feelings and behaviours for Willow, Clara and Aubrey. I want them to grow up safe and happy and secure. More than anything I want them to be secure in the world. To look at me and know they can implicitly trust me.

Sometimes, when Shane says stuff like that, it doesn't have the effect he thinks it will, it doesn't make me want to stop – it makes me want to leave. It makes me think the children will be better off without me.

But not today. I'm not going to leave them today. I watch them walk into school and I know I'm not going to leave them today. I just need to get a grip on everything. I need to stop obsessing over Clyde being a father to someone else's kids, stop worrying over whether to tell about Jude, stop thinking that something is going to happen to Nell.

Shane slings his arm around my shoulders, drops a kiss on my neck. We don't often do the school run together nowadays. Both rushing for work most mornings. But I used to love it when we'd all pile into the car together, talk loudly all the way there, often quizzing Willow on French or history or maths for her test that day, Clara reciting poems, Aubrey chattering about what went on in class the day before. They'd tumble out, happy and ready to face their school day. Shane and I would then slink off for a coffee together, or even home for a quickie before work. We've lost that.

'How's Nell?' Shane asks as we walk back to the car.

'She's fine. Her boyfriend's looking after her very well from the sounds of it.'

'Good, good, I'm glad.'

He doesn't colour up at the thought of Nell with another man any more. He actually seems unbothered by it. Maybe it isn't fake, the way he behaves nowadays about her; maybe they have properly sorted it out and he isn't planning on leaving me for her.

I still haven't had a go at him about giving Nell a 'client' number. I mean, what in the holy hell? He agrees with me that she shouldn't be focusing on that sort of thing, that the sooner she gets back to work the better, and then he goes and does that!

'Did the police say anything about catching them or getting her stuff back?'

'No, she said they were calling round tomorrow to get her full statement when she goes home.'

'OK, cool. Do you fancy a coffee, Mrs Merrill-To-Be?' he asks.

'Why yes, Mr Maybe-Okorie-To-Be,' I reply.

'Don't even think about it,' he says with a laugh. 'I am not taking your name, so don't even joke about it.'

'Yes!' I blurt out as I shut the car door.

'Erm, I don't think so, Macy – what would your dad say?'

'I mean, yes, I will marry you.'

'What? Really? *Really?*'

'Yes, really.'

Shane lets go of the seat belt he was about to clip in and instead leans across to bundle me up in a hug. 'I'm so happy, I can't tell you,' he says. 'I'm so happy. I wish I had parents or a family that I could tell.' He hugs me close. 'I love you so much, Macy. I'm so happy. So happy.'

I am, too. I know if I do this, it will stop me losing it over Clyde. It will give me something to focus on and it may well take my mind off the anniversaries that are fast approaching. I have a bad feeling about those two dates, so I need to focus on something else. Something good. Something that will help get us through the coming months unscathed.

# Nell

After three days away from the devastation, the flat looks worse, not better. There's an odd smell, like something has spoiled somewhere hidden, and there's an even stranger atmosphere. Almost as if the flat doesn't like that I abandoned it after something so awful happened to it.

I wanted to go back straight away because I knew the longer I stayed away the harder it would be to return, but I couldn't move. Zach kept looking after me, making me drinks, cooking for me, plumping up my pillows, letting me watch whatever I wanted on television. Like the sleeping-together-without-sex thing, I haven't really experienced this much devotion before. If I was being cynical I would think he is feeling guilty about something. But that's my paranoia from many, many years of having to deal with John Pope coming to the fore.

Zach is a good guy and he is looking after me. He had to nip to school a couple of times to take care of lessons and meetings he absolutely couldn't miss or couldn't get someone to cover for him, but mostly we've spent our time together in his flat, talking, reading, watching television and playing card games.

I almost lulled myself into a sense that he and I could stay like that for ever. But this morning, when Macy didn't ring at 5.17 a.m., I accepted that my life really is broken and I needed to go home and face up to what happened.

*It's only stuff*, I told myself as I pushed open the door, *try not to get upset about what's happened because it's only stuff*.

It is my stuff though. Things I've worked hard to buy and the way someone treated them feels personal. As though they have taken out the rage they feel for me on my belongings. They can't smash me so they smashed my stuff.

Zach makes a start in the living room while I go to the main bedroom to start putting things back together in there. I'll have to wash everything, of course. The fact that whoever broke in went through my underwear drawers, emptying them out, and basically touched items that are intended to touch my private parts, makes me feel dirty.

I stare at the bundle of black lace and black Lycra I've moved to the bed. A flash comes to mind of the shape of the darkness, standing over my underwear, sneering as it throws the items on the ground. I have to shake my head to get rid of that image – it has been conjured up by my imagination and most likely never actually happened.

I wish I could afford to bin them all. Remove them and the thought of the burglar's touch on them. I know most people would think I'm being ridiculous. *It's not as if you were actually wearing them at the time*, they'd tell me. But I feel like burning everything because not even cleaning everything down with bleach will erase the marks of this violation.

The intercom goes as I'm looking at the pile of knickers and bras on the bed, still wondering if I can possibly afford to replace them. I can't replace the flat, but maybe with something like this I will be able to.

'Do you want me to get that?' Zach calls from the kitchen.

'Yes please,' I reply. I grab the large wicker laundry basket that usually sits in the corner by the window, which was kicked over, and sweep the whole pile into it. I'll have to settle for washing them on a boil wash and not thinking about it. I am quite good at not thinking about things.

Zach appears in the bedroom doorway, looking sheepish and ever so slightly worried. 'It's, erm . . . it's the police.'

In the living room, the two police officers from the other day are waiting. They said they'd be back and now here they are. Standing in my home, looking as large and ominous as they did the day they had to rush me to hospital. I don't want them to be here. Now that Zach has miraculously cleared up the living room and piled all the paper up on the side, righted ornaments and polished things off, I don't want any more police involvement. I've actually decided to forget this. Pretend it didn't happen, act as though Zach and I becoming so close so quickly is a natural consequence of liking each other and not him taking care of me after something horrible happened to me.

'Miss Okorie, we just wanted to conclude the interview we began the other day,' the male officer says.

I wish I had enough guts to say it's all been one big misunderstanding and I'm sorry for wasting their time and could they please just leave. 'OK, fine,' I sigh, and indicate they should sit while I sit myself.

'I'll, erm, I'll just, erm, go and make some tea,' Zach says.

I'm guessing putting right the kitchen has given him an idea of where things are. 'I don't think there's any milk,' I say to him.

'Black tea is fine for me,' says the female police officer.

'Me, too,' the male officer adds.

Tea means they're sticking around just that bit longer. Great.

'How are you feeling?' the male officer asks when Zach has left the room.

'Fine,' I say tightly. I need to relax. I haven't done anything wrong and they are just doing their job. It's not their fault that as a young teenager I met a psychopathic police officer on one of the worst days of my life. 'Fine,' I repeat.

'We'd just like to take you through the events of the other night, if that's OK?' the female police officer asks.

'Yes. But I don't remember much, it all happened so quickly. I'm sure everyone says that, but it's true.'

The female officer takes out her notebook and pen. For some reason my heart starts to race when she does this. I really, really do not want to talk about it.

'Just tell us what you do remember, Miss Okorie. What time did you come back?'

I start to talk, to explain, and I can almost see myself. Walking back up to the flat, the broken light, the realisation that the front door is open, the splintered wood, the darkness suddenly rushing towards me . . .

They listen patiently, gently asking me questions to clarify this or that. By the end of it, once the tale is told, I'm trembling. It only happened a few days ago but it feels like I am dredging up something from a long, long while ago and at the same time reliving something that has literally just occurred.

I look to the living room doorway, surprised that Zach isn't back yet with the tea. It's not like he had to go out to pick the leaves or anything like that.

'Thank you, Miss Okorie. Have you had a chance to—' The policewoman stops talking when Zach enters the room carrying a wooden tray that I've actually forgotten I own, with four mugs of steaming drinks.

'Sorry it took so long,' he says. 'I had to wash out the mugs and boil the kettle a couple of times to make sure it was OK to use.' Considering how quickly he tidied the living room, it's a bit odd that he took so long to wash mugs and boil the kettle.

I look him over as he places the tray on the floor in the middle of the room and takes a couple of mugs to the officers. He seems different. Usually he's confident, self-assured, laid-back. But now he's ever so slightly on edge, a little nervous. Jittery.

All of us watch him hand me a mug and then take his mug and sit beside me on the sofa. In all the times I've seen him, he's never been like this.

'May I ask who you are, sir?' the male police officer says.

Zach looks at me and I watch worry skitter across his face. It's quick, but I notice it. This is not like the Zach I know. He looks back at the officers. 'Sort of Nell's boyfriend, I suppose?' he says, looking to me at the uplift of the question. 'Is that what you'd say?' he asks me.

*I have no idea who you are*, I think. *I don't know you at all. You could be anyone. You could be the person who burgled here for all I know.*

Maybe that's why he's been so caring – guilt that he did this to me. Maybe I've just spent the past few days being looked after by the man who put me in hospital in the first place.

'I, um, suppose so,' I mumble. Every nerve in my body is on high alert now. *At least I didn't sleep with him in the last couple of days*, I think. *At least I won't be looking back and needing to give myself a mental shower every time I think of the past couple of days.*

This is one of the worst things about what has happened – it's making me paranoid and mistrustful. Honestly, Zach hasn't done anything to rouse suspicion since I met him, but here I am deciding he's the person who broke in here.

'Were you here the night of the break-in?' the policewoman asks.

'Erm, no, no I wasn't,' Zach says.

'May I ask where you were?' the policeman asks.

Another set of nerves are set alight with that question. Not only because I have been thinking the same thing, but also because this is how it started with Dad. The police thinking it could be someone close to me and then running with it. Running and running and running until our lives were ruined.

'Erm,' Zach begins. I have never heard him say 'erm' so many times in one short conversation. 'Erm, I was probably asleep. I start work at seven-thirty in the morning, so I generally go to sleep quite early.'

'I don't suppose anyone can corroborate that, can they, sir?' the policewoman asks casually.

My heart feels heavy in my chest, my lungs feel like they are encased in cement. They shouldn't be asking him these questions, he's done nothing to arouse suspicion in them, not like he has with me. But that won't matter, they'll drag his name and his life through mud before they find that out. I can't bear it. I can't stand for this to happen again to someone I care about.

Zach locks eyes with the policewoman. 'No,' he says quietly, 'no, they can't.' Slowly he lowers his gaze and stares at the rug that lives at the centre of my living room. It is equidistant from the sofa, the television and the two armchairs the officers are sitting on. I spent a lot of time making sure of the equal distance between all those things because if even one was slightly off, it would bug me and bug me until I could change it.

Like their question will bug me and bug me. 'Why are you asking that question?' I say. I can't let this happen again. I'm not a fifteen-year-old this time around. I am someone with a voice and authority and I need to speak up.

'We're just trying to get as full a picture as possible of what happened,' the policeman replies.

Zach doesn't raise his gaze, doesn't raise his cup to his lips, he simply stares at the rug.

'Can I take your name, sir?' the policewoman asks politely. There's an edge there, though. A slight inflection on the word 'sir' that tells me what she's thinking.

I watch my sort-of boyfriend let out a small sigh. When he lifts his head he stares directly at the police officers. 'I'd rather not say,' he replies.

What and *WHAT?!*

I stare at him and feel the crushing on my chest intensify. Who is this man? Who have I got myself involved with? I lay there like an idiot and let him orgasm inside me without any barrier protection because I didn't mind the idea of a piece of him being with me for ever. I sat there like a fool telling Aaron that I thought he might be 'the one'. And now I've probably got to deal with finding out he's some kind of criminal mastermind or gangland boss or known killer.

'It would make things so much easier if you just told us, sir,' the policeman says. I notice both officers place their mugs on the floor beside their chairs, almost in unison, almost as though they think trouble is about to break out.

Zach looks at me, his expression a silent apology before he turns back to the officers.

'My name is . . . Detective Sergeant Zach Searle.'

# Macy

The engagement ring is beautiful.

Sapphire and diamonds in a white gold band.

'This and a few other bits are all I've got left of my parents,' Shane says. He's down on one knee and he's pushing it onto my finger. It actually fits, glides smoothly over both knuckles. (Clyde got me a jelly sweet ring that he ate after a few whiskys one night.) 'But you don't have to wear it and we don't have to use this ring – we can go and get something else if you want.'

'I don't want anything else,' I tell him. 'It's absolutely perfect.'

'I don't know what happened to my mum's wedding ring,' he says, getting to his feet. 'Disappeared in the crash that killed them.' I watch his face struggle with emotion; he stares down at the ground, trying to control himself.

One of the things that drew us together is the fact we didn't want to talk about our families. Me because, well, who is going to understand the craziness of my family history? And Shane because he has no one. Only child to parents who were killed in a car crash when he was nineteen. Every now and again I'll see how it hurts him, how he'll wish he had a Nell or a Mummy or a Daddy to share things with. He seems so lonely sometimes and I feel for him in those moments. Of all the unpleasant things I've felt in my life – ignored, overlooked, dismissed, undervalued – I don't think I've ever felt lonely. I can't believe I'm about to say this. Especially given what's happened to her but . . . 'Maybe you should ask Nell to investigate your family tree. See if you've got any other family out there.'

Shane's face registers surprise. 'No, no. Not my thing at all. I respect everyone who wants to do it, you know, go with God, but not for me. Too much potential for all sorts of cans of worms to be opened.' He pulls me into his hold. 'Besides, I've got you and the kids, I don't need any other family.'

I'm relieved, actually, that he's said no. Much as everything is cool right now between them, I don't want them spending too much time together. I don't want them to start to remember what it is they loved about the other one. I don't want to lose my fiancé to my sister, basically.

# Nell

'I'm working undercover,' Zach explains in the silence that follows his revelation.

He doesn't look at the two police officers who he has just handed his warrant card to, he looks at me while he talks. 'There's been some stuff that I can't talk about going on at the school and I'm working undercover there for the next few months. I am a qualified teacher, which is why I was able to do this assignment.'

*What in the holy hell?*

'I didn't mean to keep you in the dark. But obviously I couldn't tell you anything because I'm undercover. That was why I was so long before – I needed to get authorisation from my handler and her boss to tell you.' He looks at the police officers. 'All of you. They said I could if it was unavoidable. We don't know how far-reaching the stuff at the school is.' He returns to looking at me. 'I'm sorry I couldn't tell you. But this has nothing to do with us, Nell. It is completely separate.'

I listen to him talk and I'm aware that I'm not blinking because what he has said has made my eyes stay wide open.

*What in the holy hell?* I think again.

'When you were attacked, I thought what I'm working on had spilled over into my life away from the school. I was so worried, so scared for you. But it doesn't look like that's the case now.'

When he stops talking long enough for me to know he is waiting for a response from any of us in the room, I turn to the police officers. I force myself to blink a few times to make my shocked eyes work again. I need all of these people to leave. I need my home back. 'Are we finished?' I ask them.

'Erm, yes, yes,' the policewoman says. They seem more shocked than I am. They both stand. 'Call us if you remember anything else.' She holds out her business card and I stare at it like it's going to bite me. Eventually Zach takes it from her.

'You need to go with them,' I tell him when they move towards the door but he doesn't.

'Don't you want to talk?'

'No,' I state. 'I do not want to talk.' I shake my head. 'If there is one thing I do not want to do, it is talk.'

'At least let me help you finish straightening out your flat,' he says.

'I would like you to leave with your colleagues.' I can't stand to look at him, much less talk to him.

'OK, all right,' he says.

*Returning to a crime scene*, that's what he said at the hospital and I hear him saying it in my head now. No one talks like that unless they're a member of the police. I can't believe I didn't clock that at the time.

I follow the three police officers to the door, Zach grabbing his jacket and leather courier bag from the hook by the door. The others start down the corridor outside my flat but Zach rotates on the spot to look at me.

'Can I call you later?' he asks.

'Of course,' I say to him.

His face brightens and relaxes in relief.

'I'm not going to answer, but feel free to call as many times as you like,' I tell him before I shut the door in his face.

Cleaning, righting everything, putting my flat back together has proved to be more therapeutic than I thought possible. I've had to re-clean everything that Detective Sergeant Searle did, of course, because, well, I just can't stand the thought that he was helping me while simultaneously lying to me.

I'm appalled at myself for being so trusting and gullible. From the moment I met him to finding out the truth, I've been pretty open with him. Several times over the last few days I've been tempted to tell him about the Brighton Mermaid, about Jude, about the searches I have done and the searches I'm doing. I wanted to tell him about Sadie in Leeds, about Aaron and John Pope. He was looking after me, he was so selfless and kind when I hadn't really told him anything about myself or why I thought I'd been burgled and hurt, that I wanted to open up to him. We were close – I wanted to bring us closer.

And all along he'd been worried that what happened to me was his fault because he'd been living the ultimate double life. He thought that, and still didn't tell me the truth. Was anything about him true?

He could have a wife and children in London, for all I know. Well, that's if he is from London. I don't know London at all – he could have made up a place called Lewisham for all I know.

All those papers and printouts he picked up and stacked in the living room as well . . . He will have read them. He will know that some of the information on them didn't come through strictly legal channels. He could probably have me done for having a lot of that stuff in my possession. That was probably how he finally worked out that it wasn't down to him and I had got myself into trouble all on my own. How relieved he must have been to realise he was off the hook.

*When you make a mess you make a complete and utter mess, don't you?* I've told myself several times.

I stand in the middle of my living room, in the middle of my perfectly centred rug, staring at my flat. It's all fine now. You'd never be able to tell that someone trashed it the other day. In fact, this is probably the tidiest and cleanest it's been in years.

*I can't be here.*

When Zach was here, it was OK. I didn't mind so much. When I was cleaning up after Zach had gone it was OK because my mind was focused. Stopping has given me a chance to think, and thinking is not good for me.

I have nowhere to go, though.

If I go to Macy's, I'll have to explain about Zach. If I go to Aaron's I'll have to be around Pope. If I go to Zach's I'll have to deal with the whole big-fat-duplicitous-boyfriend thing.

*I can't be here, though.*

I don't feel safe. I haven't had a chance to get the locks changed. What if whoever broke in found some spare keys and comes back while I'm sleeping? What if the violence they'd visited on my stuff will now be visited upon me?

The knock at the front door makes me jump. Technically no one should be able to get in here without buzzing first, but people don't check, they don't challenge, they just let anyone wander in. That's probably how the burglar got in. They just waited and followed someone in.

The police said during our first conversation they'd spoken to all my neighbours and none of them had heard a thing. I creep to the front door and wait to see if whoever it is knocks again.

There is silence for a time. But I think someone is there. Lurking. Waiting.

*Bang-bang-bang!* The second knock is louder and makes me physically jump. I clutch at my chest, suddenly sick to my stomach.

'Enelle?' my father says. 'Enelle, are you in there?'

*Dad? Dad!* I unpeel myself from where I've been cowering behind the door and rush to open it.

'Daddy!' I say. 'What are you doing here?' It's taking all my strength not to grab him by the hand and drag him in and never let him leave. As nonchalantly as possible, I stand aside and let him in.

'Macenna called me,' he says as he steps inside. He has a large duffle bag with him. I've never really known my dad to carry any type of bag, let alone a duffle one. It clinks as he walks past and for one awful moment I have a flash that my dad is here to kill and dismember me. I am messed up. I am properly messed up. 'She told me what happened here.'

'Oh, that,' I say.

'Yes, that. Why did you not call us, Enelle?'

My father is looking at me like my sister looked at me with his face in the hospital the other day. I don't want to say why, so I kind of shrink a little and shrug my shoulders while opening my hands.

He holds up the bag. 'I brought some tools to change the locks.' He looks at the door. 'Whoever fixed it did a good job. I will change the locks and then we will have to see about getting you a new door, as well.'

I stare at my dad. He doesn't ever come to Brighton. He used to love it here, but after what Pope did, he had to leave for his and Mum's sanity. Over time, they've simply stopped coming here. If we want to see them, we go to their place. But here he is, for me. I think, sometimes, that I forget that my parents love me. What I did, who I brought into their lives, ruined things for them, but they still love me. They still care about me. You can love someone and not like them. You can love someone as a default and be inured to what hurts them. You can love someone and not be bothered by what befalls them. My parents love me and they care about me.

'OK,' I say. I want to hug him. I always want to hug my dad. I always want to be close to him and tell him I'm sorry and find out if he's forgiven me yet. Mostly, though, I want to hug him, to feel his arms, which are big and strong, around me, holding me safe, fighting away my fears. We're not like that, though. My dad's not like that. 'Do you want a coffee?'

'Yes, please.' He waits until I get to the end of the corridor, about to go into the living room, before he speaks again: 'We'll talk later about why you didn't call me, Enelle.'

He is going to tell me off but I don't care. My dad's here and I don't feel as scared any more.

'Do you ever see the Daltons?' Dad asks.

It took him a while to change the locks, but once he'd done that we sat in the living room, drinking black coffee and watching television. He went to cook us something but was dismayed by my empty fridge, poorly stocked cupboards and barren vegetable drawer. He'd side-eyed me, being a grocer's daughter who'd worked in a supermarket, with such woeful kitchen supplies, but didn't say anything.

'Not in a few years,' I reply.

'When was the last time?'

'I've seen them a few times out and about, but the last time I spoke to them was back in 2007, I think it was when I . . . I went to speak to them about finding Jude.'

'You found Judana?' My father is staring right at me when he asks this. And I can't look at him. I feel ashamed that I didn't tell him what I've been doing, even before John Pope became part of the process.

'No. I wanted to look for her. So I went to their house to ask about Jude's mum's family tree. I thought if I could trace all her relatives and find some that were missing, it would lead me to where Jude went.'

'I see.'

'It didn't work, obviously. I've found lots of other people over the years but not her.'

'I see.'

I finally chance a look at my dad. He is staring at me and it feels like he wants to tell me something important. His hair greyed a long time ago; with every arrest, every stint in custody, it greyed a little more, starting with a few streaks along the sides, until his head was covered in more grey than black, and then his hair was completely grey. Then white. It makes him look older than he is, more ancient than he acts.

'She was a nice girl,' he says.

I've been hanging around Pope too long, because the way Dad says that, it makes it sound like he *knows* she's gone; that she doesn't exist in the world any more.

'Yes, she is,' I say to present-tense her, allow her to still be alive in the here and now even if she isn't physically here. It sounds odd, and it is odd, if I think about it. I last saw Jude when I was fourteen. That means I don't actually know her any more. She's not a girl, she's not a teen. She's a grown woman with a life that doesn't involve me in any shape or form. The 'Jude' that Dad and I are talking about is past tense; she doesn't exist as that entity any more. Judana Dalton is alive, I just know she is, but Jude isn't. Still, I need to present-tense her, keep her alive.

'Go and pack a bag, Enelle. You cannot stay here alone tonight.'

'I'll be fine, Daddy, honestly.'

'Do not argue with me,' he says. 'Go and pack a bag.'

'But Da—'

'Yes?' he cuts in.

Why am I even bothering? It doesn't matter how old I get, my dad will always be my dad and he will always be the man who I have to listen to, no matter what. 'All right.' I'm secretly pleased, actually. I didn't want to stay here alone anyway, and right now, I don't have to.

*Thank you, Dad. Thank you so much.*

# Nell

*Wednesday, 2 May*

Dad tried to insist on coming up with me after he dropped me off, but I wouldn't let him. I am going to have to get used to coming back to the flat on my own, unless I want to move in with my folks (I don't) or I am going to go into my flat and never leave again (I'm not). Being away hasn't helped with the clock that is ticking in the background, I haven't been able to do many proper searches, nor visit any records offices. I have been aware all the time that Pope could pull the trigger at any moment and the idyll my parents have will be shattered.

I stand on the pavement and watch him drive away in his new black car before I turn my attention to my building. I loved this flat when I first came here. Despite its location at a dead end of a maze of roads, the converted factory is beautiful, stylish, spacious – all things that will be written on the seller's notes if I don't get over my fear.

This building is scary now. Everything feels threatening as I make my way inside. I jump when the front door clicks shut behind me, a reminder of the loud bang that came with the burglar leaving the building after he'd slammed me into the door frame. I have to take deep breaths as I climb the stairs, remembering that he was probably in my flat listening to my arrival, wondering if it was me and if he would be able to get out of there in time. On autopilot I hit the light timer light switch next to the stairs on my floor and wait for it to flicker on. Nothing. It's been over a week now and it still hasn't been fixed. It's dusk, so there is still light enough to walk around, but I'd feel safer if I could have a bit more light, be able to see something like my door being ajar from a distance.

Before I start down the corridor to my flat, I pause and take another deep breath. I can do this. I can honestly do this.

I take strong, bold steps. I can do this. I make it to my front door in no time. And it is fine. It is locked, it is secure. And there is a large brown box on my doorstep. I roll my eyes at the postie. They've done this before. Knocked, got no answer, got no answer from my neighbours, so they have just left the parcel on the doorstep. It's a good thing I don't order expensive stuff, I've often thought.

I put down my many bags (of course I didn't pack light) to unlock the door. So far, so uneventful. I do keep looking over my shoulder but that's normal. Wise. It is not the start of me turning into an even more paranoid wreck.

There is a bit of post behind the door, which reminds me I need to go and check my post office box for any DNA results. I dump my bags in the hallway then retrieve the parcel. It's not very heavy for such a big box, but there is a bit of weight to it. I resist the urge to shake it in case it's fragile.

I don't remember ordering anything recently. In fact, I know I haven't ordered anything recently because I'm still trying to claw back the money I overspent the night I met Zach, as well as the cash that was in my purse when my bag was stolen.

I place the package on the floor and get down on my knees to open it. There are no postmarks of any kind so it must have been hand-delivered. Probably Macy sending me a care package, although the label is printed with my name and address.

It takes an age to unpeel the tape holding the top flaps of the box together. When I finally get into it, I'm met with swathes of pink tissue paper. Definitely Macy. 'This had better be worth it,' I mumble. I pull it out, encountering more and more of it until I pull at a layer and it comes away, revealing my present.

On the bottom of the tissue paper-lined box is a huge dead rat.

# Nell

'Someone's out to get you, aren't they?' Macy says while pacing up and down her kitchen.

I'm still shaking, my mind quivering right along with my body. Hours later, and I can't stop shaking. I have to throw my arms around myself and rock to try to dislodge the memory every time I think about the rat's fat, lifeless body, its thick, ribbed tail flopped over its body, its throat glittering red where its jugular had been ripped out, its black, blank eyes. It's anchored there, though. I hate rats. They are the one thing about which I have what is bordering on a phobia. Alive or dead, I hate rats. And someone sent me one. Left it on my doorstep, wrapped up in an ordinary way. A warning. A reminder of what could happen to me. A pretty clear message that, yes, someone is out to get me.

I don't need Macy's version of I told you so right now. I don't need to hear anything except: *'Here is some good-quality alcohol that will erase the last seven hours from your mind.'*

'Someone is out to get you. And they're not going to stop until you're dead.' Her voice is wild and high – she's about to start screaming at me, I can tell.

'Macy, hush,' Shane says. He comes to crouch down beside where I sit on a kitchen chair. 'Can't you see she's traumatised?'

'Yes, I can see that,' she replies, her voice still uncontrolled. 'But *she* can't.'

Shane keeps going to touch me, rub my back maybe, then changes his mind as it would be crossing many, many lines. 'Macy—'

'No. NO!' Macy says, holding up her finger to hush him. 'Look at her. *Look at her.* If she could see herself she would stop what she's doing. She would just quit. But no, she won't. Even after this. Even after having her head bashed in she won't stop. What's it going to take? Huh? What's it going to take to get her to stop? Because this is all about her need to feel real or some shit like that. How real are you going to feel when you're dead?'

I slowly look up from the black and white tiles of the kitchen floor and face my sister. Standing there, dressed in her sensible pyjamas and faded navy towelling dressing gown, she's right in so many ways. In every way, actually. But being right doesn't mean being like this.

It's her anxieties, it's always her worries and fears and the things – big and small – she obsesses on that make her like this. Always. If I could strip away those layers of worries, unburden my sister of every single terror that pokes at her, creeps around inside her, I know she would be different to this. She would be the sister I love all the time.

'You're rubbish at being comforting, Macy,' I say to her, trying to magic up a smile. 'Absolutely rubbish.'

'This isn't funny!' she shrieks.

Shane leaves my side and dashes to her. 'Shhhhh, the kids,' he reminds her. 'You'll wake the kids.'

'I don't care,' she says and shoves him off her. 'In fact, I'm going to go and wake them up right now so they can get a good final look at their aunt who they love so much before she's murdered trying to solve a mystery the police haven't been able to solve in twenty-five years.'

'Stop it,' Shane says.

'No. I won't stop it.'

'I need to leave,' I decide. Me being here is going to break my sister. It was only a week ago that she had to rush to the hospital

– this is too much for her. I stand on my shaky legs, and pull around my shoulders the blanket my neighbours gave me earlier. I'm not a screamer, but I started screaming when I saw what was in the box. So much so my next-door neighbour, who I've always had a nodding relationship with, came tearing out of his flat and hammered on my door until I opened it. I felt bad because he was in his underwear and his girlfriend came out in a silk dressing gown with very little underneath it. They both baulked at the rat in the box and he valiantly pulled on a pair of jeans to go and dispose of it in the downstairs bins.

I had to sit on the floor of my hallway because I couldn't move and eventually the girlfriend brought me a blanket and some hot sweet tea because I was shaking so severely and my body temperature kept dropping. Even more eventually, I asked them to call me a cab and I gathered up the bags I'd taken to Mum and Dad's and I came here to Macy's. To be greeted with this.

I expected at least a little tea and sympathy before she started laying into me. But no such luck.

'No, sit down,' Shane says. 'Go on, sit down,' he adds forcefully when I don't comply. 'Sit. Now.' I do as I'm told. 'And you,' he turns to my sister. 'You need to stop this, *now*. I get that you're upset with Nell, and I can completely understand why – she's been reckless. But we don't turn on family, do we? No matter how stupid they've been and how much disregard they've shown for their own safety, we don't turn on them.'

'Erm, *thank you*,' I say.

This manages to stop Macy going for me verbally, but she continues to glare at me.

Shane carries on: 'This is all part of some weird sister stuff that I can't ever fully understand, and I know that it all began way, way back when, but you can't let this come between you. We're the only people that Nell has and we have to look after her, right? What else is she going to do? We're lucky, we have each other, but she has no one.'

'Erm, *thank you!*'

'Oh, that's not true, is it? Nell has a *boyfriend*,' Macy spits.

'Yes, yes I do, which is clearly where I should be right now. Silly me, thinking I'd come here and you'd be nice to me. Yep, I should have gone to my boyfriend's and not told you. 'Cos, you know, it's not like you'd make something that happened to me all about the effect it's having on you. Silly, silly me.'

'Nell, you're going nowhere,' Shane says. 'Macy, apologise.'

'I will not!'

'All right, if your sister walks out and you end up not speaking for years, just accept that it'll be on your head. No one else's.'

Immediately Macy starts to wring her hands. My head snaps round to look at Shane, horrified that he's just used one of her anxieties against her. Yes, she's being awful to me, but I can see where it's coming from and I can't promise I'd be any better in her shoes. If I step outside of myself and look at my situation from Macy's point of view, what I am doing is unintentionally recreating the horrific parts of our childhood for her. Having someone she loves violently ripped away from her is one of Macy's ultimate fears. I can understand – even in my traumatised state – why she is freaking out. And, even though she is being awful to me, I wouldn't dream of using another of her fears to stop her.

'There's no need to say that,' I say to Shane. 'I wouldn't cut Macy out, not for something I've caused.'

'No, he's right,' Macy utters quietly, her eyes slightly widened, her hands moving over and over each other like snakes in a barrel. I can see she's playing out the scenario now: she keeps being horrible, venting at me, and I walk out. I intend to fix things between us, she intends to fix things between us, but the hours become days become weeks become months become years and we will have lost time and something will happen to one of us before we can start to talk again.

'He's not right,' I reply. 'You've every right to be annoyed. I've brought all this to your door. Nothing's going to break us up. You know you're stuck with me for ever, right?'

She nods quickly; the strain of listening to me while her scenarios play in her mind causes lines of worry to stretch themselves over her face.

'I'm going to put some new linen on the bed in the spare room,' she mumbles. As she heads for the door, I jump up and take her in my arms. I don't like to see her like this. I don't like to think of all the worries that sit like boulders in my sister's mind.

Once she is out of the room, I turn on Shane. 'What the hell!' I snarl at him. 'What the actual hell! How could you do that?'

'I know, I know, but I had to get her to calm down.'

'Not like that. *NEVER* like that.'

'She was winding herself up and she was going to wake the kids.'

'*I don't care!* You *never* do that. She would have calmed down eventually. And it was me she was having the go at. I would never have used that against her no matter what she was saying to me, and neither should you.'

'And what if it's one of the children, eh? What if she's having a go at one of them and they can't stand up for themselves? Because she already does go over the top at some of the things they do, about their safety. She keeps them on a tight leash, won't let them do half the stuff their friends do because of her anxieties. She controls every single part of their lives and it's suffocating sometimes. But what if one of them does something exceptionally dangerous?' He raises his arm to indicate where she was standing a minute earlier. 'That is how she's going to react. That is the damage she's going to do to them. I just had to get her to stop.'

He's possibly right. I know Macy mainly only has a go at me when she thinks I'm being reckless, and I don't doubt that she and Shane get into it, too, but what if she does turn on the children or turn her worries into the children's fear and anxieties? As I told Zach, I wouldn't wish me on anyone. That goes double for children. The thought of messing them up like I am messed up is too scary to contemplate. Macy always wanted kids. Right from an early age. But what if she is passing onto them not only her creativity, her

268

warmth and generosity, but also her terrors, her continual fretfulness about safety, her angst about one of her own being harmed? It must feel like she constantly lives in a cage made with bars of angst, worry and unease. What must it be like to be a child watching your mother locked in such a cage? I don't know why I'm asking. My mother flitted in and out of a similar prison, well before Dad was first arrested – what John Pope did, though, shoved her into it, locked the door and threw away the key. I remember what it was like to grow up with Mum's anxieties at the forefront of everything we did.

I don't want those fears for Willow, Clara and Aubrey.

'I don't care, Shane. You may think it was necessary to ultimately protect the children, but don't do that again. Find another way to stop her next time. Not that.'

'I won't,' he says. Shane runs his hands over his face. He's showing signs of strain, too. I, with my various crises, am not helping at all. I can't imagine what it would do to them if they found out I was mugged a few weeks back. 'I'll go and help Macy with the room,' he says as he moves to the door. On the way out, he pauses to gently rub my shoulder. That's the first time he's touched me since we last slept together all those years ago. 'And I'll apologise. I'll apologise.'

Once I'm alone, I sit again and pull the blanket back over my shoulders. I'm not as cold, but the thick, chunky weave is comforting right now. I need something as close as possible to the sensation of having loving arms around me.

Something I've done is putting my life in danger and smashing up my family again. The thing is, I can't work out what it is.

# **Nell**

My face is almost back to normal and I just look like I've had a scrape. That's why I can do this for the second day in a row: take Willow, Clara and Aubrey to school. They all go to the same school, although in 2019, Willow will probably be going off to senior school, across the road, where Macy and I went.

Using Macy's car – with her permission, of course – to bring them up here is an odd sensation, almost like I'm having an out-of-body experience that has landed me in another life. This is the path I did not travel, but here I am doing the school run. Well, doing the school run in an ideal world. Because there is no way on Earth it's this simple. The kids mainly got themselves up this morning, came down for breakfast and ate it without the need for too much cajoling. Macy then set the timer – three timers, actually, to see if they could beat their personal bests when getting washed, toothbrushed and dressed.

'Shall I help?' I asked her.

She smiled at me and shook her head. 'That makes all competitions null and void.'

I'm not sure if she ever really wanted three children in four years, but that is what she has. And that is what she had to cope with when her ex walked out.

Back then, when I helped out, they were small so I'd take Willow to playgroups and classes, while supervising Clara and trying to pacify Aubrey. It was chaos, I had no idea what I was doing and I had to just get on with it as best I could.

Macy would sit in bed, almost zombie-like as she stared at a wall, or stared at a television screen, picking and picking at her nails. Several times I almost called Mum to ask if she could help or even just come to talk to Macy, but I couldn't do that to her. Macy would never forgive me for 'telling on her', as she would see it, when Mum and Dad had never liked him anyway. What was not to love? He was arrogant and thought he was far cleverer than he was. He got into fights in pubs and regularly ended up in debt because he liked a bet. He was sweet to Macy, though. Treated her like she was his reason for living, and was, as far as I could see, completely faithful to her. It was just everyone else he disliked and felt superior to.

And he walked away, it seemed, because he couldn't be bothered to be a father any more. Literally, just that. Over the years, Macy has let slip a few things about him and their relationship, and one night, in an uncharacteristic moment of sharing, she told me that he had – months before he left – asked her if she'd be interested in leaving the kids with our parents and going on an extended holiday. When she'd asked when they'd be back, he'd shrugged.

She was still taken aback when he walked out, though.

I pull up at a safe point on The Drive, which sounds like a small cul-de-sac-type street and is, in fact, a very wide, long road that would probably be classed as a dual carriageway if it went on for much longer than it does.

Willow opens the front passenger door while I open the back door to let out Aubrey and Clara. They all look cute in their various combinations of grey trousers, grey skirts, grey pinafores, white shirts and bright blue sweatshirts and fleeces. Willow is nearly my height. She throws her arms around me. 'Thanks for the lift, Aunty Nell,' she says with her smile that reminds me so much of her father. When he wasn't being an arse, you could see quite clearly how good-looking he was. Aubrey high-fives me, and Clara, for the first time since I came to stay, doesn't give me a side-eye as if trying to work out my angle.

I walk them to the main gate with Willow marching ahead because, at twelve, she doesn't need a chaperone. Clara drags her heels to keep pace with Aubrey and me, even though she clearly wishes we would get a move on. At the gate, they both hug me and then disappear into the school, without so much as a backwards glance.

Macy and I never talk about the time she couldn't cope. It's like it never happened sometimes. The children don't remember and our parents never knew. I eventually convinced her to go to the doctor and they diagnosed depression. It took a few more weeks for me to convince her to actually take the medication, but once she did, once she started to accept what had happened, she began to get better. I tried to convince her to speak to someone, to a therapist who might listen and unburden her of the things she could not say to anyone else. Even in her depressed state she managed to give me a scathing look that basically said: '*You first, love. You go get therapy for the way you live your life and I'll follow suit.*' I knew not to push it because, well, pot and kettle and all that.

'Cup of tea?' I call up to Macy when I arrive back.

She said she was going back to bed when I offered to take the children earlier and I had a moment of terror that my latest drama, so soon after the hospital one, would tip her into depression again. I know on a rational level that things don't work like that, that how Macy is is based on so many different factors, not just circumstance, but I don't want to be the cause of more distress for her.

'No,' Macy immediately calls back. 'I'm off to work in a bit. No rest for the wicked.'

'Cool beans,' I reply.

She's going to work. That's good. She's leaving the house. That's good. There's one less thing to worry about for today, at least. And all I can do is keep doing things that will get us to the end of the day intact. Or as intact as possible.

*

The house is empty. They are all at school or work, so I sit alone at the kitchen table with my closed laptop in front of me. I haven't even opened it since all this happened. Luckily, most of the files were backed up on here or on a USB drive I took with me, but the paperwork is another matter. They can't be easily replaced and the burglar made sure to rip and screw up everything they could. It's details like that, taking the time to do that, which make the whole thing so much more awful. It's vicious and unnecessary. It makes it personal. And dangerous. And leaves me wondering over and over what triggered it.

Is it the Brighton Mermaid? Is it my search for Jude? Or is it nothing to do with that at all? Could it be related to Craig Ackerman? He's a rich, powerful businessman – maybe someone is out to get him and I'm caught in the crossfire? It literally only kicked off after I met him. That would be the most logical conclusion. Especially considering I've been looking for Jude and the Brighton Mermaid for years now and I've not had anything like this happen to me. At the meeting with Craig Ackerman, something niggled me about him. I wouldn't be the only person who he has rubbed up the wrong way, so it's not outside the realm of possibilities that someone might be out to get him. Or someone might know a lot about his background and wants to stop him finding out any more, so they're trying to stop me.

I push the laptop away from me. What about Aaron? He has powerful computers; they have the programs he has written over the years and other things he has done for the search for the Brighton Mermaid and Jude. What if he doesn't tell me everything? What if one of the searches has thrown up something while I wasn't there and he's kept quiet about it and is now having to go back and erase all trace of whatever it is, which includes harming me? Which is ridiculous, as I watched him drive away after he dropped me off. There's no way he could have got into my flat before me.

Maybe it *was* Zach. This all started, too, after I met him. Maybe what happened to his grandparents has clouded his mind. He might even be using his undercover investigation as a cover for what he is really up to. Maybe the death of the Brighton Mermaid and/or Jude's disappearance is all connected to his grandparents' murder and he doesn't want me getting in the way. He didn't seem to blink at all when he saw all the papers that had been thrown around my flat, and he acted with so much guilt when he was looking after me. That can't have all been about thinking it was to do with his undercover assignment?

This is ridiculous. I am turning on people because I am scared. Because I am confused. Because I am certain someone is out to get me.

Instead of opening the laptop, I pick up my mobile. Maybe speaking to Sadie will help.

Her phone rings, rings, rings, rings, rings, rings . . . then: 'Hi! This is Sadie. Leave me a message or give me another call 'cos I might not listen to your message until much, much later which makes the whole message thing pointless, don't you think? Go on, call again. I dare you.'

Sadie makes me smile. Even her answering machine message is very 'her' – full of life and vibrancy.

I do as she instructed and call again.

*Ring, ring, ring, ring—*

'Hello?' a gruff voice says. Earl, I'm guessing.

'Hello, is Sadie there please?' I ask.

'No,' he says and then hangs up.

I stare at the phone in disbelief. 'No'. Just like that.

My heart starts to hammer in my chest. Shall I call back? Shall I leave it? I said I'd call her. Why is he answering her phone? He wasn't exactly overjoyed when we showed up; maybe he's trying to stop her from pursuing her genealogy research. Maybe he thinks

I'm one of those awful telephone marketers that is out to make her life a misery.

I bring up her number again and press redial.

He answers after the second ring.

'Hello, sorry, it's Nell,' I say quickly. 'I came to see Sadie the other week about her family tree? I was just wondering if I could talk to her.'

He doesn't say anything for a long few seconds. He's probably trawling through his memory, trying to remember who I am and whether he liked me enough to speak to me or not. 'No, you can't speak to her,' he eventually says.

'Oh, is she out or something?' I ask.

'No. She's in a coma. Someone knocked her down.'

I take a very long breath in, but no air enters my chest because it is tight, like an iron band has been clamped around it.

'What?' I ask.

'Doctors said she's lucky to be alive,' he says. 'Big car it was. Going so fast. People said it didn't even slow down. Just went straight for her. Mounted the pavement. Lucky to be alive.'

*Breathe, Nell. Breathe. Speak, Nell. Speak.* 'I am *so* sorry.'

'She can't talk to you,' he says. 'She can't talk to no one. Doctors still don't know if she's going to pull through.'

'I am so sorry,' I repeat quietly. 'Will you let me know how she is or when she wakes up?'

'Why would I?' he replies. And then hangs up.

Slowly, with a shaky hand, I put down the phone. In case I was in any doubt, it's quite clear: this is all about the Brighton Mermaid.

# Macy

*Sunday, 13 May*

Nell thinks I'm so stupid, that I can't see what's going on right under my nose.

It is Sunday evening and all the washing is done, all the ironing has been put away. We have had a roast dinner and everything has been washed up, dried and put away. The children's homework has been done. They've all had a hair wash and bath. They're all now in their rooms, reading quietly before bed.

All of this has been done by Nell. She has made this picture-perfect family Sunday happen in the sort of effortless way I've always thought is mythical. But this is the second Sunday that she has done this. As well as everything else she's done today, she's been bringing me cups of tea and glasses of water and plates of chopped fruit. She's constantly told me to relax whenever I've tried to help, and upstairs is a bath with bubbles and candlelight waiting for me to slip into it.

Nell thinks I'm blinkered, that I can't see what she's doing. She's become the cuckoo in my nest, doing everything better than me, not shouting at the kids at all, even getting Shane to chop vegetables earlier. And he didn't even complain when she told him to take the bins out. *Told* him, not *asked*. If I ever *tell* him anything, he rolls his eyes, replies that I'm not his boss and to ask nicely if I want him to do something.

Nell thinks I'm idiotic. That I don't know what they were really doing when she shut the kitchen door earlier because she'd 'accidentally' burnt something and the fumes were filling the house; that I don't know they were fucking each other's brains out. I bet they went to the pantry and had that quick, furtive type of sex Shane and I used to have when we had just moved in together and weren't sure which one of the kids was going to wake up first and come into our bedroom.

Shane thinks I'm so brainless that I don't know he's screwing her as often as he can and then he's coming to bed and doing it with me. He hasn't even noticed that I stopped wearing my engagement ring, that I haven't worn it since Nell arrived.

Nell thinks I'm so clueless. That I don't know she wants this, the life she should have had with Shane, and that's why she's being so super-efficient and super-amazing at everything. She wants my family and if she carries on being as perfect as she has been, then I think the rest of them are going to want it too.

# Nell

'Cup of tea?' I call to Macy as I return from taking the children to school.

I'm very nervous now about what could happen to members of my family. If someone has deliberately hurt Sadie, who is miles away, then I think anyone is in danger. I haven't told Macy, obviously. Nor Shane, who I fear may blurt it out and use it against Macy like he did the other week. That bothers me still. I keep looking back over our relationship and wondering if he was like this with me. I can't remember it, though. I remember how nasty he turned when I said I was going to go to college, like it was ever a possibility that I wouldn't go, but nothing like that, nothing so insidious and underhand.

It must be hard for him, living with someone who has multiple anxieties, and I'm hoping it was a one-off moment of frustration, but does that excuse what he said? I wrestle with that every day and I've spent the time I've been here trying to take on as many burdens as I can so Macy doesn't get herself worked up and I never have to bawl out Shane for saying something like that again. Because that is what will happen if he says it again – I will scream at him.

Macy doesn't answer my call up the stairs for tea. She rarely accepts a cup, she mostly says she's off to work and then leaves the house fifteen minutes later. It's unusual for her not to reply at all, though. Maybe she's asleep. Or, as is most likely, she's gone to work already. She's done that a couple of times – left the house while I take the children to school in Shane's people carrier.

I toss the house keys Shane gave me onto the side and head for the kitchen. Pope's threat is hanging over my head, and every day I get closer to detonation, but I'm still struggling with everything. I know I should go home, sort through the chaos of papers and start again, but I can't. For many reasons. Not just the fear of what might happen to my family if I'm not here constantly watching out for them, but also . . . I like it here. I like this life of taking the kids to school, cleaning up, cooking the evening meal, helping with homework, supervising bedtime. I feel useful. I feel I'm atoning for all the problems that my night out twenty-five years ago caused the people I love. Slowly but surely I'm making life easier for Macy and that means I am, in some way, making up for causing her problems in the first place. Yes, it was Pope who stalked and brutalised our family for years, who eventually caused my parents to move away, but it was me who brought him into our lives by finding that poor dead woman. And it was me who could have stopped everything that happened from happening by simply doing what Jude did and crying when Pope was being nasty and calling us dirty girls and dirty little sluts. If I had cried, if I hadn't defied him, things would have been different.

I move the bowls the children ate their cut fruit from and the side plates from their toast to the sink, and grab a cloth to wipe clean the table.

Zach has called and texted me several times. Every day, in fact. He wants to talk to me, he misses me, he'd just like the chance to explain. All fair enough – I miss him, I want to talk to him, I want to be with him – but dealing with him is way, way down my list of priorities.

Aaron has texted me several times, too. But not the usual 'He needs to see you' message, just 'Call me'. I'm sure he's turned up at my flat only to find I'm not there. Contacting Aaron, when his father isn't demanding it, isn't a priority. My family are who I need to take care of now.

On the side by the kettle is Macy's work pass. I frown at it. She never forgets it because she won't be allowed into her building without it. By the toaster are her car keys. She usually waits for me to return to take her car, but a couple of times Shane has got a lift to work so I've used his car and she has left before I've returned. But there's something odd about this. The car keys, fine (she could have got the train). But not the pass. She works in the big financial services building not far from Old Steine in the centre of Brighton. It would be a royal pain having to come back for it, especially without her car. I take my mobile out of my pocket and dial Macy's number. I'll drop it off to her.

When I press call, there's an almost dramatic pause and then I hear the tinny opening bars of Bob Marley's 'Three Little Birds' starting upstairs. Working on autopilot, I climb the stairs and go to Macy and Shane's bedroom. The sound becomes louder and louder as I approach.

In the bedroom, on the bed, beside a plain white sheet of paper, sits Macy's mobile with '**Nell calling** . . .' flashing on the screen while the phone vibrates and throws out the musical call tone.

I don't need to read the note to know what it says.

I don't need to pick it up and see what she's told Shane and me in her neat handwriting. It's obvious.

Macy has left home.

# **Macy**

### **To whom it may concern**

Yes, that's you and you. Nell and Shane. Shane and Nell. I have no idea who is going to read this letter first.

I've gone. Left. Departed for pastures new. I've left because it's obvious you don't need me around any more. Nell has taken my place rather expertly in the house and the kids have started to go to her with anything they want or need. They don't come to me and that's fine. I want them to be happy and if they're going to be happy with Nell, then I'm going to step aside.

I see you, Shane. I see you staring at my sister. You long for her, don't you? Just admit it. I asked you if it was you wanting Nell that made you try it on with me again and you said no. I actually think you meant it at the time. But let's be realistic. You only started having sex with me after I shut you two up in the kitchen and made you talk. I think, unconsciously, you wanted her and settled for me. Now it's a million times worse because she's here all the time. I keep wondering how long it will be before I walk in on you two at it.

I don't want to be worrying about that any more. So it's best I bow out now. Just be honest with yourselves about how you really feel about each other.

This letter was meant to be a lot more, I don't know, balanced than this. But I don't have much time.

Please take care of my children, Nell, I know you love them more than anything.

Macy

# Nell

'Why would she do this?' Shane asks.

We are standing at the foot of the stairs and he has read the letter a few times with his hand firmly over his mouth and his eyes blinking as though he's been repeatedly punched in the face. I called to tell him at work and he got a taxi home straight away.

He looks at me, frowning. 'You don't think I was trying it on with her because I really want you, do you?' he asks.

'No, I don't think that. And she doesn't think that, either,' I say. 'She was just upset and lashing out.'

He's looking at me with contempt and disgust. The feelings I have for myself. I shouldn't have come here. I should have used more of my savings, which I seem to be eating through at the rate of knots, to book into a hotel rather than come here. Rather than do this to Macy and her family. I didn't think. I just wanted to be around family, to fit in somewhere, to hide away from dead rats and lie-by-omission boyfriends. And, as a result, I've decimated Macy's life.

*This* is why Macy hates me. I know it is. She doesn't hate me all the time, but I can see it sometimes, a tiny flash of resentment will bolt across her eyes when she remembers something that happened as a result of me finding the Brighton Mermaid. She will be catapulted back to that time and then will detest herself for feeling that way, which will bring on a huge attack of her anxiety and self-loathing. It must have been torture for her to have to live with me. I am a nightmare.

'Where do you think she's gone?' Shane asks.

I shake my head. 'I have no idea.' When it comes down to it, I have no real clue about Macy's life. Does she have friends? Is there somewhere she goes to be at peace? Does she go to the gym or yoga class? Is she training for a marathon? All questions I have no idea of the answers to. We don't talk, I realise that now. My sister and I don't talk. We speak to each other, but it is all surface, super-ficial, because we do not know much about each other. And because she hates me, really. Not all the time, not even most of the time, but enough for her to not really share anything of her life beyond our visits. Enough for her to do this.

'We have to find her,' Shane says. He sounds desperate. Truly panicked. I'm wondering if he's thinking that whoever is after me is after her, too. '*You* have to find her.'

'*I* have to? I really don't know how.'

His face twists and he looks incredulous and furious all at once. '*You don't know how?*' he snarls.

'I honestly don't know how to find her,' I say quickly, to try to stop him getting more angry with me. 'I'm not an investigator, I just look for families and I find people who don't have a name to go with their faces. I use family trees and DNA and geographical connections. If someone's been gone a while I can maybe find them when they put down roots, start to leave a trail, but I don't know how to look for someone when they've deliberately gone leaving everything behind.'

'*You don't know how?*' he repeats louder and takes a step closer to me. 'Isn't that what you do now, Nell? Isn't that what you've ruined all our lives over? You find people. And you're oh so good at finding people,' another step closer to me, 'you're oh so pas-sionate about it that you just *had* to give up your job to do it.' Another step closer to me and I step backwards to get away from him. 'You *had* to make sure that the Brighton Mermaid and all the crap that goes with it is all any of us could think about and you're telling me that you don't know how? Did you even think about what all of this would do to Macy and the children? Never mind me, I'm not important, but what about them? Do you know how her anxiety and her OCD have shot through the roof ever since you told her what you were planning? And since you were burgled and then this, it's a wonder she stuck around this long.

'But none of what this is doing to us occurred to you, did it, Nell? Because you're selfish, you only think about what things mean for you, no thought for Macy and your parents and the children.'

Shane wants to take another step closer to me, I can tell, but he's restraining himself.

He's right. But I didn't foresee these types of repercussions. When John Pope made his threat, I knew I had to do whatever I could to stop him. I didn't think there would be other consequences, penalties that Macy would be forced to pay. I thought I was saving us all from what Pope wanted to unleash, but instead, I've sent Macy over the edge. She tried to tell me in the hospital and after the dead rat incident, but I didn't really listen. Her warning was not as loud and forceful as Pope's threat, but unfortunately it's been just as devastating.

'I'm sorry,' I say. 'I had no idea things were so bad. And that it was because of me. You have to know that I would never purposely do anything to hurt Macy, the kids or you. I'd never do anything to hurt anyone.'

Shane raises his hands and rubs them over his face. 'No, I'm sorry,' he says. 'I'm so sorry, Nell. I didn't mean any of that . . . I'm just panicking here, you know? I'm scared for her. She's been so unstable recently, and I didn't help the other week making that comment. If she's hurt herself—'

'She won't have hurt herself,' I cut in. I can't bear the thought of it. And she wouldn't. I just know she wouldn't. No matter how bad things get, Macy wouldn't hurt herself and leave her children. Just like I know she would never completely walk away from them without telling anyone where she's going. 'Do you know who her friends are?' I ask Shane.

He's staring wide-eyed into the mid-distance, shocked and shaken. I remember this nightmare. I understand a bit of what he is going through, what it's like to have someone walk out of your life and to have no idea what has happened to them.

'I think we'd better go to the police,' he says desolately.

'We will, we will, but first let's ring some of her friends.'

'How are we going to do that, exactly? I know hardly any of her friends. She doesn't go out, ever. Even when the school parents arrange nights out she doesn't go. I go sometimes, but she *never* goes. Same with work people.'

'Well, we've got her mobile – we can see who she's called and messaged the most.'

'Do you have her passcode? Because I don't. And her phone works on Touch ID anyway. And I seem to remember her saying the latest update meant we can't even download the phone's information onto a computer without her passcode.'

'Why don't you know her passcode?' I ask him, stunned.

'For the same reason I don't know your passcode and you don't know mine,' he replies. 'I trust her – I don't need to check her phone. She doesn't need to check mine. We have a thing called privacy. What are you saying, Nell? That our relationship is odd because we don't know each other's passcodes?'

'No, no, I was just . . . I just assumed if you're in a long-term relationship you know everything about each other including things like passwords, etc.'

'Well, you assumed wrong. When you get married or live with someone, you don't lose your identity, you know. You don't stop being a person who has their own life. Is that why you're still single, Nell? Because you're worried that you'll stop being your own person if you open up and trust someone?'

'No,' I reply.

'Right, yeah, sure,' he says.

'I'm so sorry for causing all of this,' I say.

'Hey, it's not your fault. I was just angry earlier, shocked. I'm sorry. This isn't down to you. This is all down to that policeman who made your family's life hell. Triggered a lot of Macy's anxiety, made you . . .' He stops talking, and his eyes widen again because he's horrified about what he was about to say.

'Made me what?' I ask, facing him full on.

He colours up, a red that makes him glow. 'Nothing,' he says.

'You might as well tell me,' I say. 'It's not like things are going to get much worse, is it?'

'Made you . . .' He sighs and I can almost see him cursing himself in his head. 'Made you so closed off. I think you've always been scared to let go and trust anyone and that's why you haven't had a proper relationship since, well, me.'

'You think I'm closed off?'

'It sounds awful when you say it like that. What I mean is, you always act like someone is going to stab you in the back or leave you. You don't allow anyone to get close to you. Not even Macy.'

'Is that what she thinks? That I don't let her get close to me?'

Shane's cheeks are still scarlet.

'It's not true,' I state, trying to keep the tears out of my voice. I won't convince him it's not true if I start crying. 'No, I haven't had a long-term relationship since you, but I'm not unusual in that. Loads of women are long-term single out of choice like me. And Macy is . . . I'm closer to her than I am to anyone else on Earth. She's everything to me. I can't believe she doesn't know that. After all this time, everything we've been through, she doesn't know that she's the only person I've ever felt close to.'

'Look, this isn't helping,' Shane says. 'I don't know how we got side-tracked onto this conversation. We just need to work out how to find Macy.'

I furiously blink back my tears, clear my throat. I thought Macy knew that she is the person I am closest to, that I have no one beyond her who I trust implicitly. But is that true? I haven't told her I am working with Aaron, that I am essentially controlled by Pope, that my ex-sort-of-boyfriend turned out to be a police officer, that Shane and I spent that night together after college. There are loads of things I haven't told Macy and yet I still think of her as my best friend, my closest confidante. Am I really deluded in all of this? Deluded in a way that neither Macy nor Shane are?

But Shane is right, none of this is helping. We have to focus on finding Macy. 'Let's go through the class list and call everyone on it if we can't get into her phone,' I say.

'Or go to the police,' Shane suggests.

'Or we can go to the police,' I agree. 'What would you say?'

'That she's gone missing.'

'All right, we'll say that a thirty-six-year-old woman has walked out leaving behind a note explaining why she left. If someone told you that, let alone if you were a police officer, do you think you'd investigate?'

'But this isn't like her. She wouldn't walk out on her children.'

Except she would and she has. Shane clearly doesn't know this. Only Macy and I know how low she got after Clyde left, how one time she disappeared for two days and I wasn't allowed to tell anyone, I just had to look after the children. But then, he said it himself: just because you're with someone, doesn't mean you know everything about them.

'Yes, I agree, but do you really think the police are going to see it like that? Look, if you get me the class lists, I'll go through and call everyone and then we'll see where we are. It might be that we have something solid to give to the police. Something one of them says might be enough for us to track her down.'

'I'm really worried that something's happened to her, you know?' Shane says.

'I know. But we mustn't think like that. We've got to stay positive until we know something else.'

'You're right,' Shane says. 'You're right.' He comes towards me, this time in a less threatening manner. 'I'm sorry . . . about earlier.

I shouldn't have said those things. They're not true. You're not selfish at all and you weren't to know how bad Macy's got recently. I don't think any of us has wanted to face up to it. When we get her back, I'm going to make sure she goes to the doctor and gets some medication.'

I nod. *Good luck with that,* I think. *You won't manage to persuade her to do that. But that's all pointless thinking right now. The most important thing is to find her and get her home.*

# Macy

I have not done this in an age.

I have not sat in a bar on my own in what feels like a lifetime. That lifetime that is being a mother. Even before I got together with Clyde I didn't go out much. Mummy and Daddy weren't exactly OK with either of us going out with friends after Nell and Jude found the dead body. And after Jude disappeared and everything that came after that, I didn't even bother to ask to go out.

I went to Brighton University so that I could live with my parents and didn't go out that often. I went out a bit, would sometimes stay out if things were extra fun, but mainly I was a homebody.

After I got together with Clyde, we went out a lot. We had a roaring social life that involved so many friends and going to lots of different places. He opened up my world. When I got pregnant, the partying slowed right down. Clyde didn't really seem to mind and we planned the next two to get it out of the way. It was exhausting, and I sometimes look back and wonder what I was thinking, what type of madness had taken over my brain to do that to myself. Love, of course. Love, the most crazy-making drug, had seized my brain and made me do that.

I would have done anything for Clyde. *Almost* anything, as it turned out. When he wanted me to leave the children to go on an adventure with him, I couldn't. Wouldn't. Actually, when it came down to it, I didn't *want* to leave them. I loved being with my children. I couldn't stand the thought of being away from them no matter how hard and arduous, draining and gruelling it was; I wanted to be with my children, always.

Oh, the irony – I wouldn't leave my children for their father, but I've left them for Nell.

I take a sip of the wine in front of me.

She's proved since she moved in that she's better at this than me, so I've left her to it. Everything I ever do is for my children, and if someone is going to be better at looking after them than me, if someone isn't going to foist upon them all my anxieties and worries and nervous habits, I have to give them the chance to be happy. They're my reason for living so it'd be selfish to stick around when someone like Nell seems to take everything in her stride. It was like that last time, too. When I told her Clyde had gone and she heard what I was actually trying to say and came straight away, she just coped. She stepped into my shoes without a moment's hesitation, a second's worry about what to do. She took over and she pulled us away from the brink.

My anxieties are slowly becoming out of control, I can see that. Shane can see that. Nell can definitely see that, which is why she took over again. I was being paranoid the other day when I thought she wanted my life. She doesn't. Of course she doesn't. She just wants to take care of the children. She just wants to keep us from getting too close to the edge again. She just wants to show them what normal is like. She just wants to push me out little by little until who I am in their lives has been diminished, which means the damage I can do them is diminished too.

I take another swig of wine.

Which is fine. Because I can do things like this. I can sit in a bar I've never been to in my life before and drink wine in the early evening.

I can spend the day getting my shoulder-length relaxed hair professionally put up, I can get my nails done and I can go for a facial. I've bought some new clothes, some new shoes and other new accessories to wear, too. I feel like a different woman. So I'm behaving like a different woman, sitting in a bar, having a drink on my own. The name – The King's Coats – doesn't sound that inspiring, and it's not much to look at, but it has panoramic views of the sea, and apparently the food is great.

This wine is going down well. *Really* well. Its tartness teases my tongue, slides down my throat. And it's making me feel all fuzzy and warm. I'm sure I'm smiling as I sit here. Smiling to myself and drinking wine.

Why don't I do this more often?

I *should* do this more often. I should have wine more often. When it was just me alone with the children, I didn't dare drink in case there was an emergency and I had to drive one of them to the hospital. Even when Shane came on the scene I didn't dare drink because he'd often have a beer or two and if I drank as well, there'd be no one to drive the children to the hospital if necessary.

But I've been missing out. Truly.

I pick up the bottle from its bucket of ice water and read the label again. I'm sure I've done that three times. I want to remember what it is, though. So I can have it again. Maybe I should take a picture of it? Genius idea!

I scrabble around in my bag, searching for my phone.

Oh. I remember. I left my mobile behind so they would know I was serious about leaving. No mobile. No picture of the nice bottle of wine. Boo!

'Hello, Macy,' the person who I've been waiting for says.

'Zach!' I say with a grin. 'Fancy meeting you here.'

# Macy

Every morning I wake up in Zach's bed, I have to reset my mind and remember that I am not at home and I don't have to listen for which one of them is up first, wonder how much longer I can linger in bed before I have to get up and start the day.

I roll over, and the weight of the wine I drank last night rolls with me. I'm glad he closed the blinds last night because I could not handle any amount of daylight right now. The downside, of course, to drinking is the morning after.

'Do you want to get some food?' I asked Zach the other day when he met me in the pub. 'I'm starving. Let's get some food for while we talk.' Before he could protest, I raised my hand and beckoned over the waiter who was standing at the bar using his pen to dig out his ear. Once upon a time that would have had me walking out of there, disgusted and horrified by what the chef was likely to be doing behind closed doors, but not that day. Not after wine, not after feeling like a different woman, not when Zach had actually shown up.

The waiter brought us menus but Zach didn't even pick his up. 'What's going on, Macy? You said you wanted to talk about Nell?'

'Yes, I do,' I replied. But I was put out. Why did he have to bring her up within six seconds of sitting down? 'But not right away.'

He put his head slightly to one side. 'How did you get my number? You implied in your text that Nell had given it to you, but she didn't, did she?'

'Her mobile gave it to me,' I replied.

'You went through her phone?'

'No. Not really. She put it down for once and left the room and I got your number from it.' Of course her passcode is the day Jude disappeared. 'I had to talk to you. I had to find out why you dumped her. Is it because she's sleeping with my other half?'

Zach stared at me really hard for several minutes, it felt like. I had to keep taking lots of sips of my good buddy white wine to counteract the potentially sobering effects of that stare. 'What are you playing at, Macy?' he asked. 'You go through your sister's phone, you have a makeover so your hair, your clothes and your nails make you look exactly like her, and now you're trying to what – make me jealous? Make me angry? Hurt me? By saying that about her sleeping with someone else. Are you having some kind of breakdown?'

'How dare you,' I said to him. 'I'm just trying to . . .' What was I trying to do? I'd wanted to talk to Zach because it would hurt Nell. Even though they were clearly not together any more, I'd seen how she was with him. She liked this guy a lot and I wanted to hurt her like she'd hurt me by taking over my life rather than talking to me about what I was doing wrong. 'I'm just . . .'

Zach sat back in his seat and folded his arms. I did the same. Just so he'd know that he wasn't the only one who could look serious and authorit-ta-ta . . . and serious.

'How much have you had to drink?' Zach asked eventually when I kept looking at my wine glass because I wanted more but I didn't want to be the first person to unfold their arms.

'Only the one . . . *bottle*,' I replied. 'Before this one.'

He shook his head and I crossed my arms even tighter and huffier just so he knew that I didn't care if he disapproved. 'I didn't dump Nell,' he said. 'I . . . I kind of neglected to tell her some stuff about myself and she's refused to speak to me or see me ever since.'

'Huh!' I unfolded my arms because I really needed wine. 'She's one to talk. I guess she never got around to telling you that she's slept with my other half, Shane.'

He looked sceptical.

'It's true! She went out with him when she was about eighteen.'

'So more than twenty years ago?'

'And after college, too. Although neither of them will admit it.'

'She's slept with him while you and he were together. Is that what you're saying?'

'Well, I haven't got any proof of that, but if you saw them together you'd know instantly that it's not as straightforward as they make out.'

'Why am I here?' Zach asked tiredly.

'*So I can get back at Nell for taking my children away from me,*' I almost said. Even though I didn't actually know that was what I was doing until that moment, I almost told Zach that. 'So I can ask you if I can stay at your place.'

'What? No.' He drew back, horrified and disgusted at the idea. 'Absolutely not.'

'I've left home. Nell was staying with us and it got too much for me with her and Shane and not knowing what actually went on between them. And Nell kind of took over, doing everything for the children, and I couldn't take it any more. I've left them. All of them. Even the children, who are my whole world. But I couldn't cope any more.' I wiped at my teared-up eyes and my now running nose. 'I had to get away. I have nowhere to stay where they can't find me. I need a break from Nell and Shane.'

The muscles in Zach's jaws rippled as he listened to me talk, and they rippled when I stopped talking and they continued to ripple as he was deciding what to do. I could see why Nell liked him. Even without hair he was very good-looking. Handsome. Wholesome. 'All right, you can stay for a few days.'

'Thank you!' I said, relieved.

'But I'll have to tell your sister where you are.'

'No! I don't want anyone to know where I am. If I wanted them to know, I would have gone to my parents' house. I just want to be free of them all. I just want to be Macy alone for a bit. If you tell her, I'll leave and disappear.'

'Macy—'

'I'm serious,' I cut in. 'If I get even a hint that you've told her, I'll disappear and no one will ever hear from me again.'

'Fine, fine. You can stay. And I won't tell Nell. I won't tell anyone where you are.'

As far as I know he's kept his word. And he's let me stay. He doesn't like me being here, though, I can tell. Last night starts to seep in and I cringe. He's going to like it even less after last night.

He was right, the other day, I looked ridiculous with my Nell makeover. I don't know what I was thinking, really. So I kind of ditched that stuff in favour of his clothes. *'Not even Nell wore my clothes,' he said when he came home from work and found me in a pair of his boxers and a T-shirt, cleaning his flat.*

'Come on, Zach, it's Saturday night,' I said last night. 'Have a couple of drinks with me.'

'I think you're drinking enough for the both of us,' he stated without taking his eyes off the television.

That evening's foray into Zach's wardrobe had resulted in me donning one of his casual checked shirts and knotting it under my breasts. Paired with the only pair of jeans I'd brought with me, I had to admit I looked good for a mother of three.

Zach was sitting on the armchair at this point. He'd begun the evening while I was clearing up after dinner sitting on the sofa, but when I dropped down beside him he immediately moved to the armchair.

I rolled my eyes and stuck out my tongue at him. He was no fun. Literally the opposite of fun. It was Saturday night, for goodness' sake. Didn't he understand that women like me – mothers of three

– didn't get that many Saturday nights off? Didn't he understand that women like me – mothers of three – didn't often need to drink so much to drown out the voices in their heads of their children asking when they're coming home? At first, I'd been drinking because I was enjoying it. Now I needed it to help me forget about my children.

I leant across to pick up the remote control and whoops! I dropped half the glass of wine all over my front. Urgh! What a waste of good wine. I put the wine glass on the floor without knocking any more over and then slowly unknotted the shirt and then undid the buttons. I slipped it off and was tempted to suck the wine off the front, but that would be way too crazy, even for me.

'Look what I've done!' I said.

He half turned to the sofa and then whipped his head away. 'For pity's sake, Macy, put some clothes on! And stop this!'

'*What?*' I could hear myself whine because of the wine. 'I dropped some wine down my top, that's all.'

'That's not all and you know it. Macy, I've had enough of this. I had reservations about you coming here, but I didn't want you staying out on the street. You're Nell's sister, I know how much she cares about you, so I don't want anything to happen to you either. If you don't stop this behaviour, though, you can leave.'

'But—'

'But nothing! I'm not going to sleep with you. And don't pretend that's not what you've been angling for to get back at Nell. Whatever you think you'll achieve with this, it's not going to happen. So stop all this crap before I'm forced to ask you to leave. And I *will* ask you to leave and I will *not* worry about where you go.'

With that, he got up and left the room, taking my dignity with him.

I felt terrible, truly awful. The only sane thing to do in that situation was to drink some more. And hopefully the humiliation would go away, too.

\*

'I'm sorry,' are the first words out of my mouth.

Zach has his back to the kitchen door and stiffens when he hears my voice. 'It's fine,' he says without turning round.

'It's not fine,' I say. 'It's so far from fine. I'm so sorry. I'm missing the kids so much and it's making me act out.'

'Why don't you just go home, then?' he asks.

'Because I shouldn't be there. Nell is just better for them. She gets them, she can do all that stuff they need without breaking a sweat. She's perfect for them and I'm not.'

'You're their mother. And I'd imagine it's easy to do all that stuff without breaking a sweat, as you say, when you know it's not permanent. When you've got day after day after day of the same thing, I can imagine it getting pretty wearing, and not being at your best all the time.'

'Maybe you're right. But I don't feel ready to go back yet. Is . . . is it OK if I stay here a bit longer? No more funny stuff. I swear.'

'All right, you can stay here a bit longer. I think you should let me tell Nell where you are, though. She and Shane must be going out of their minds with worry.'

'I'll think about it.'

'Macy, seriously, I really think you should think some more about going home if being away from your children is going to have this big an effect on you.'

'It's not just that, though . . . can I trust you with something?'

'Sure.'

'I feel terrible, all the time. I was married to this guy, the children's dad. And he left me. I found him again recently and he's got this whole new life with another woman and four children. I don't know if they're his but either way, it makes me feel terrible. I just feel so inadequate. That I did terribly by my children by not being good enough that he stayed. I mean, it's all there, every picture she posts of him she says he's an amazing father. I just . . . Why couldn't he be an amazing father to *our* children? What was wrong with *our* family?'

Zach turns around to look at me. 'Well, first off, never believe what people write on social media.'

'I know, I know, but when you see the photos and read stuff like that, it's hard to believe it's fake.'

'And second of all, every guy I know, *every single one*, who is described as an "amazing father" is a tosser.'

'You think?'

'I *know* it. Women only wax lyrical like that when a guy does something so mundane but needs praise to make sure he, at some point, does it again. All the millions of fathers who pull their weight and parent their children are never described as amazing because they do stuff for their kids without needing accolades. What would Shane need to do to make you describe him as an amazing father?'

'I don't know.'

'Have you ever had cause to describe him as an amazing father?'

'No.'

'But does he do all the stuff a father does without needing you prompting him all the time?'

'Yes.'

'There you go. Your ex playing happy families on social media doesn't mean it's real. The best indicator of future behaviour is past behaviour, I've found. You don't know what's going on beyond the computer screen.'

'I suppose.'

'Look, Macy, I know you don't want to, but think about going home. You need to be with your children. They need you, too. There is nothing wrong with you.'

'Yeah, I'll think about it. I'll definitely think about it.'

I like Zach. I can absolutely see why Nell liked him. He's so decent. I wonder what it was that made her break up with him. I feel I can talk to him about anything. The other thing that's been on my mind, that has been keeping me away from home and from Nell, of course, is the stuff with Jude. I was heading back to that place where I wanted to tell Nell to hurt her. Just to show her that what she was doing was dangerous for all of us.

'Is there something else you want to talk about?' Zach asks.

*Tell him*, a voice in my head says. *Hear what it sounds like out loud. Get it done now so when you do eventually tell, it won't be so alien.* 'I . . . well . . .' *Have you lost your mind?* I ask myself. *You can't tell him that. You can't tell anyone that.* 'Nothing.' I shake my head. 'Nothing.'

From the expression on Zach's face, I'm sure he doesn't believe me.

# Nell

*Sunday, 27 May*

'No way, not going to happen,' Shane says. He's keeping his voice down because the children are asleep upstairs, but I can see it's an effort to do so. He's incredibly angry and I think he wants to cross the room, grab me by the shoulders and shake me. Hard.

'Shane, it's the only way.'

'Don't you understand me? No.'

I press the palm of my hand onto my forehead and rest my elbow on the table. I've had this headache since Macy disappeared. Actually, probably since my face was slammed into a door frame and I had a brain scan to check I didn't have any real damage. It seemed to abate for a few days, twinging every now and then when I am stressed, peaking when the rat incident drove me from my home – but it'd started to go away. Now, with an additional layer of stress on top of trying to work out who is out to get me and why, this headache is a permanent fixture in my head.

'Shane, if you think about it, it's the best plan.'

'They're my children and you're not going to take them away from me, not without one hell of a fight.'

Wearily, I get up and go to shut the door over properly. Ideally we would have talked about this before the children came home from school on Friday, or at any point over the weekend, but Shane has not worked from home since Macy disappeared and was barely there over the weekend. Except at 5:17 a.m. yesterday, when I could hear him lurking outside my bedroom door, waiting for Macy to call. She didn't call and he eventually went away. I've hardly seen him so I've not had a chance to have this chat, but it is a conversation that needs to be had.

'No one's taking the children away from you.'

'What do you call this plan of yours?' Shane snarls.

'I call it taking the children to spend the half-term holidays with their grandparents, since there's no one else who can look after them.'

'What about you? You can look after them. You haven't got a job, remember?'

I observe my sister's partner across the kitchen in a cool manner. I'd forgotten how good-looking he is: tall and slender, with an easy smart-casual dress sense, his brown-blond hair messy but stylish. I haven't looked at Shane properly in years. Not since I found out he and my sister were together. I would look at him, sure, but I wouldn't see him, not properly, not like I am right now. And I'm looking at him like I am right now because he's just said something that has made him a tosser in my eyes. Not the man I used to go out with, not the guy who has wanted to marry my sister since he met her, but the guy who has just basically said he thinks I should be free childcare.

'Don't be an arse, Shane,' I say. Since Macy disappeared, I have stepped up the looking-after-her-children role while Shane seems to have stepped back – way, way back – from it. With half-term coming up, I need to get them away from here. I've always felt they were safer at school, and not with me when someone is trying to harm me. I can't have them with me all through the holidays. And even if I didn't think being around me was dangerous, why should I? 'I do have a job,' I state. 'It's just not one that pays at the moment. I've not done much in the past couple of weeks because of what happened to my flat, and then Macy disappearing, but I need to get back to it.' *I need to get back to it before Pope forces my hand.* 'And I need to know the children are being looked after properly.'

'Look, I know it's not ideal, but you can't just dump them with your parents and think that's going to solve anything.'

'All right then, you take the week off,' I say.

'I can't.'

'Why not?'

'I don't know what it's like in your world,' Shane snaps, 'but in this house, all the bills, the food on the table, comes from my wages. If I don't work, our family doesn't eat or have somewhere to live. That's what a proper job does – not what you've been doing.'

'I've earned the money to pay my mortgage and everything for the next year, Shane. I earned it and then I saved it up. That's why I'm not being paid for what I do. And I don't know why I'm justifying myself to you. This situation is simple: you can't look after the children during half-term, I can't look after the children during half-term, my parents will do it.'

We're talking as though Macy doesn't exist. Neither of us has mentioned her since we found out that she had taken a three-week leave of absence from work, and had told the children she was going on a special trip and would call them when she could. So it wasn't a spur-of-the-moment thing; she planned this. She wanted out and laid the groundwork with the important people – the children – to make sure it happened with as little disruption to them as possible. She also sent the children a postcard saying 'Missing you lots and will be back soon' that arrived yesterday.

It was a Brighton postcard, postmarked Gatwick, so she was still in the area. Knowing she is safe and made provision to do this meant we didn't go to the police and we didn't talk about her. I suspect Shane is worried as well as angry with her for doing this, whereas I am just relieved that she is OK. All right, I'm a little bit angry, too.

'It's only for a week,' I tell him.

'It's not going to be for a week because it's not happening. And that's final.'

'I really want you to be all right with this, Shane,' I say carefully. I stop looking at him and stare instead at the area near his feet while I continue to try to press my headache away. 'I really want you to agree to this without . . .' I stop because I know how this will come out, how much it will hurt him. And I don't want to hurt Shane. I don't want to hurt anyone. I never do. Not even Pope. And I *hate* him.

'Without what?' he asks.

I have to look him in the eye when I do this. He has to know I'm serious, that, as unpalatable as it is, this is the truth of our situation and I will invoke it if he doesn't agree. 'You and Macy aren't married. You haven't formally adopted the children. I . . . I am legally their next of kin, not you. Macy made me their legal guardian years ago, and I get to decide what happens to them over you.'

He stares at me for long, long seconds. What I've just said is like a body blow to him, like I've just discharged the whole voltage of a Taser into his most vulnerable parts. '*You fucking bitch,*' he says quietly, viciously. '*You fucking, fucking bitch.*'

I have to look away. His words don't hurt me, they bounce off me like raindrops off an umbrella – it is the betrayal and wounding on his face that cut me up inside.

'Five years, five long years I've been providing for those children, loving them, bringing them up, and you're basically saying I mean nothing and you get to decide everything. You *bitch.*'

'Shane, it doesn't have to be like this. I just want them to spend time with my parents. Give us both a chance to—'

He waves his hand as if to dismiss what I am saying like a king dismisses a lowly courtier. 'Do what you want, Nell. You're going to anyway. Just don't be surprised if I'm not here if you decide to bring my children back.'

He leaves the room without looking at me again.

I close my eyes and give in to the headache. Give in to the pain of it, which is basically fuelled by the tears I've been trying not to shed since I read Macy's note and realised how much she hates me. Now Shane hates me, too. I don't even bother to wipe away the tears. Right now, crying is the only thing I can do that doesn't feel wrong.

# Nell

*Monday, 28 May*

Dad's smile is something I haven't seen in years.

He does smile, obviously, but when the children run through the door, throwing down their backpacks and kicking off their shoes while heading for the kitchen, his face glows with the radiance of his smile.

'Wash your hands,' Mum calls to them as they hit the kitchen, aiming for the rack of freshly baked cheese and leek scones. The house is filled with their divine savoury scent and I take in a few lungfuls, feeling comforted at once. When Dad had to give up his shops and they moved here, he chose this place because of the substantial size of the garden. It allowed him to cultivate the soil to grow vegetables and to have a large greenhouse to try to grow more tropical fruits and veg. I think Dad feels sometimes like he gained this when he lost almost everything else, and he would love to share it with someone. Mum is so not interested and, I can tell, frets about the cleanliness of Dad's hands after he's been working in the garden. I'm sure the children will have a great time here and Dad will have a wonderful time teaching them about gardening and growing food.

'Come into the greenhouse, Enelle,' Dad says after he has grinned and grinned at his grandchildren.

'Put that down and go and wash your hands!' Mum shrieks.

'But we don't need to,' Willow says.

'We were only in the car,' Clara adds.

'And we all went to the toilet and washed our hands before we got in the car,' Aubrey explains.

Whereas Dad is going to have fun, Mum is probably going to be more than a little stressed out with keeping on top of their hygiene. But that will do her good, too, I'm sure.

Dad's place to talk is his greenhouse. It was the stockroom at the Hove shop when we still had it, but in recent years it is this large place with real glass panels. Those real glass panels can be controlled so when he is growing stuff that needs to be protected from direct sunlight he can dim the place with the flick of a switch.

'Where is your sister, Enelle?' My father asks the second the greenhouse door has shut behind me. He is staring at me like he knows everything about what I've been doing and is waiting for me to answer his question before he rains down hell on me.

'I'm sorry, Daddy. I don't know where she is,' I say.

My dad looks me over, from head to toe, then back up again. I've let him down. It's clear on his lined face, imprinted on every crease that has developed since he walked into the police station to pick up his daughter twenty-five years ago.

'Is this something to do with what you've been doing all these years?' he asks.

I shake my head. 'I don't think so.' Beyond what I told him about looking for Jude and talking to the Daltons, Dad has never really asked me what I'm doing. He has always been interested in my work at The Super, he has always asked if I had a significant other, he's even asked if I was thinking of becoming a mother, but he has never asked what I have been doing. 'She was upset with Shane and me, mostly me, and left.'

'Did you have relations with Shane?' he asks.

My eyes become like beach balls in my head, they widen so much. 'What do you mean?'

'I know you and Macenna think that your mother and I live on a different planet to the pair of you, but before we were parents we were young people too. I have seen how Shane looks at you some-times. Did you have relations with him?'

'No, Daddy, *no*.' I cringe at the idea that my dad would think it, let alone ask me about it. And I can't stand for him to say the word 'relations' meaning sex again. 'I went out with Shane nearly . . .' I try to calculate it in my head so I don't inadvert-ently tell my dad I had sex when I was sixteen '. . . Nearly twenty years ago. But nothing since then. Macy thought we might still have feelings for each other, but we don't. At all. If you've seen Shane look at me, it's awkwardness. We both feel odd around each other after all these years. But he loves Macy. She's the only one for him.' I shudder at the idea that my dad thinks I would do that to my sister. 'I wouldn't do that to her. I just wouldn't. He wouldn't, either. Everything is a mess. But not *that* much of a mess.'

'Tell me about this mess,' he says. This is the first time, the *first time* I've had a conversation with my dad. We talk all the time, but I'm usually keeping stuff from him, by trying to project the image of being a good daughter. I've never really spoken to him before like he is another adult who I can open up to. This is what Shane was trying to say – I am closed off to most people. I can't be honest with most people because there is always something I have to hold back. Not the normal way people hold back, not the polite way of not overwhelming others with too much information about your life, but this is almost calculated. Every conversation I have is nec-essarily modulated and controlled so as not to reveal too much about myself.

'I can't. Not yet. Not all of it,' I say to my dad.

'Why not?'

'Because . . . I just can't, Daddy. I'm trying to sort all these things out, and things keep happening that make it harder.' *Those things, of course, being someone trying to harm me and John Pope hanging a threat over my head.*

'Go to the police,' Dad says simply.

For him, after all he went through, to say that must mean he can see how serious it is, despite all the minimisation I have done.

'I can't. I've nothing to take to them.'

'Let them decide that,' he says. What strength must it take for him to say that to me? I always knew my dad was the strongest person ever, and he's proving it to me once again.

'I will, Daddy, once I have things clear in my mind I will think about going to the police.'

My father stares at me. He's going to say something else, something profound and life-altering, I can tell by the way he hesitates, the look in his eye, the way his face is set. 'Be careful' is what he actually says. 'Take care of yourself.'

I'm disappointed, and also mollified. This is probably what it's like to converse with me – you know there is something big I could say, something huge I'm often on the verge of saying, and then I pull away. 'I will,' I utter.

'We will take care of the children. Even if it is for more than a week.'

'Thank you. Macy might contact you, and you can tell her that the kids are here.'

'I will.'

'Right, I'd better go back and help Mummy with getting them settled in,' I say.

'That's a very diplomatic way of putting it,' Dad laughs.

He reaches out and puts his arm around my shoulders, then briefly, very briefly squeezes me towards his body. The second time I remember my dad initiating that kind of physical contact. The first time was when he took me home from the police station.

# Nell

'Nell! Oh my— I've been going out of my mind with worry about you.' Aaron practically grabs me through his front door and holds me in his arms. 'Are you all right?' he asks.

He doesn't let me go and, for a moment, I forget who he is enough to fold my arms around him, rest my head on his chest and relax. This is what I miss about being with Zach. I miss someone holding me, comforting me. I didn't have it for very long with him, but I miss being held like it was something that happened every day of my life. I've slept around not only because of what Pope called me, but to have human contact. I wanted another's touch, the chance to simply be with someone.

Aaron's hands move on my body – one to my lower back, the other to the back of my head – like he knows that's where I love to be held, like he's done this before. He takes a huge breath in and then sighs to release it, almost as though this is everything he's ever wanted.

I need, right now, to have someone make me feel like this – to have someone make me believe that I am wanted and I am not a screw-up. I snuggle closer to him and he holds me tighter. After a few seconds I pull my head away and look at him. He gazes down at me.

Against my body, I can feel his breathing become shallow and fast, as though he is trying to control himself.

*Go on, then*, I think, because it's clear he wants to kiss me. *I'm not going to pull away. Go on, do it.*

His eyes search my face, looking for a hint of doubt, any indication that I don't want this. What he sees makes him release me and step away instead of kissing me.

He clears his throat and runs his hand through his hair, and I lower my gaze. Embarrassed. I'm completely mortified that Aaron realised that I would allow him to kiss me, I would probably let him take it so much further, but it would *all* be driven by him. I wouldn't be enthusiastic about it, I wouldn't be desperate to be with him, not like I was for those few minutes in the car when we came back from Leeds. It must have been obvious from my face that I would be going along with it because I need someone to make me feel better.

'Where've you been?' he asks. 'I've been so worried about you. You just disappeared and didn't answer your phone. Someone at your flats said you'd moved out after you'd been burgled and attacked by rats or something.'

'I've been to Messed Up and Broken via the scenic route of Completely Screwed Up My Life.'

'What? What are you talking about?' Aaron says.

'Everything has gone wrong since we came back from Leeds.'

'Tell me about it – someone tried to run me over last week.'

'What? Are you all right? What happened?'

'I was coming back from the train station. I'd just got to the end of the crescent as you turn into this road and I heard a car suddenly speed up. It took me straight back to what I heard on the day my dad was run over. My first instinct was to run, but instead, I stopped and stepped back. Then I turned and ran for it in the direction I came from. I looked back briefly and saw the car mount the pavement and swerve to just where I would have been if I had carried on walking or run for it.'

My whole body feels weak at the idea of what could have happened to him if he hadn't heard his dad's accident on the phone. Those traumatic few seconds on the phone five years ago have probably saved his life.

The iron girdle is back around my chest. *Breathe, Nell. Breathe. Speak, Nell. Speak.* 'Someone did the same to Sadie,' I manage. 'She's in a coma. I haven't rung back. I'm too scared in case she's died.'

Aaron slaps his hand on his forehead and takes another step backwards. 'What's going on, Nell? What have we stumbled into?'

'I have no idea. I haven't even told you what happened to me.'

'What, that story your neighbour told me was real?'

I explain briefly what happened and as I talk, I start to get a tingly sensation all over my body. What if Macy didn't just leave – what if she was stolen? Magicked away like Jude was, never to be heard from again. No. No, the note sounded like it was from her, it was in her handwriting and only she would have said that I was taking over her life.

'I'm so glad you're all right,' Aaron says, and I'm sure he shoves his hands deep into his trousers pockets to avoid touching me.

'I'm not sure I am, actually.' I close my eyes, to try to picture the family tree printouts from my flat. Were the Brighton Mermaid and Jude ones still there? I can't remember. I open my eyes again in frustration. There is something there that I have found that I don't realise I have found. *What is it?*

I have almost all my files on my laptop and on a USB drive that never leaves my person. I am bothered by the stolen computer hard drives, but not from a data point of view, because all of that is long gone. When Aaron and I started to work together, and he told me about computers, he'd made me buy some that were unhackable if I was careful. I needed a special key fob to open them as well as a password. If anyone attempted to break into the computer or physically take it away to work on, everything would be erased. He also showed me how to set up a private virtual network for accessing the Internet. And when we did email it was through a service that is based in Switzerland and is virtually unhackable.

Our only vulnerabilities really are the text messages, but that is why he keeps them short: 'He needs to see you' and, latterly, 'Call me'.

When Aaron started talking about all this stuff, I thought he was not only unrealistically paranoid but had also managed to convince himself he was the star of an espionage drama that he was trying to drag me into. I also thought he was being rather free with my limited funds. But it didn't hurt to be a bit more cautious about what I did online and I'm glad, right now, that I did go along with it, because it looks like he was right all along.

'I have to go back to my flat,' I say. 'I have to see if there are files missing. At first I just thought everything had been trashed, but now I'm thinking some of it might have been stolen.' I shake my head. 'I took most of them with me, though, to Leeds.'

'You're acting as though any of this normal,' Aaron says. 'It's not. None of this is normal.'

'Let me think, let me think,' I say, closing my eyes again. The reason why I ended up being able to help other people with their searches was because I could stand back and see all of their problem and which roadblocks needed to be navigated. I need to think about all of this like an outsider would.

My problem has always been that I am too close to the Brighton Mermaid, to my missing best friend, to deconstruct the problem. I've always believed that it wasn't my dad so it must have been someone else. But then, is that being fair to my dad? I've always been so desperate to keep him out of it, what if he is at the heart of it? No, no, I'm doing it again. I'm centring these searches on me and those close to me. I need to step back.

'Aaron,' I say, opening my eyes, 'who did you tell that we were going to Leeds?'

'No one,' he says.

'I didn't tell anyone. We never emailed or texted about it, I only did the searches on my private network after I started it here on your virtually unhackable computers. So, who did you tell? Or are we dismantling your computers to find the bug, seeing as mine are long gone?'

'I didn't tell anyone,' he insists.

'Where did you tell your father you were going that day?'

'Well, obviously I told him. I thought it would get him to back off about the six-month thing. It was something tangible, what he was asking for. I mean I didn't tell anyone other than him.'

'I believe you,' I say. 'But who did *he* tell?'

'No one. He hardly sees anyone; even most of his old colleagues have stopped coming by to see him. He won't have told anyone.'

Sometimes Aaron forgets who his father is. I step around him, heading straight for the garden patio, where Pope sits with a blanket over his knees. Today his radio is on, tuned to some talk channel, and a book has been left face down beside his glass of whiskey.

'Who did you tell about Sadie in Leeds?' I say to him.

He looks up at me with those sharp blue eyes. He looks at me how he always looks at me: disgust coated with fascination, like oil slicked on the surface of water.

Pope hasn't demanded an audience with me today, so he reaches for his glass and looks to the right of me to pretend I don't exist. It's usually fine when he pretends I'm not there, when he doesn't bother to speak to me, but what he's done has hurt someone, has ruined my life, almost got his son killed. Today he has to speak to me on my terms.

I step into his line of vision, closer to the table, and then I snap off the radio to halt the droning chatter that is filling the air. 'Who. Did. You. Tell.' I want to clap my hands in his face to get him to focus.

He cuts his eyes at me and then sips his drink.

'I know you don't care about anyone but yourself, so I won't bother telling you that the woman we spoke to in Leeds is in a coma after someone ran her over. I won't tell you about how someone broke into my flat and then sent me a dead rat so I can't live there, but I *will* tell you that someone tried to kill your son. I know that doesn't bother you, because it's not *you* after all, but if they try again, and they manage to hurt him next time, you're going to end up with no one to take care of you. 'Cos even if he's "just" injured, he won't be able to fetch and carry for you.'

As I thought, that gets his attention, enough to make him focus on me while he sips his drink.

'Who did you tell?' I ask again.

'Just a couple of my friends.'

'You were never going to give me six months, were you? Certainly not a year. You were just waiting for something that would allow you to try to kick off an investigation, weren't you? You made an official call, to what, the cold case team? They probably just ran a few checks to see if you were wasting their time.' I shake my head. 'You bastard,' I say quietly. 'You absolute bastard.'

I look at Aaron. 'He's done it. He's pulled the trigger and now it's out there. The police now have a link, a name that might help them identify the Brighton Mermaid. Which is probably why whoever is doing this had to get rid of Sadie. They had to stop her from talking to the police, potentially giving them a name that might reveal who the Brighton Mermaid was. Because if we find out who she was, we potentially find out who she was with before she died. Your father couldn't wait, no, he had to go off half-cocked. That's why we're all under attack. We don't know enough yet to do whoever the killer is enough damage, but we know enough for them to want to stop us.

'And the worst part is we have no idea who it is. In other words, for whoever killed the Brighton Mermaid and all those other mermaids, it's open season on all of us. And *he's* done that.'

Pope doesn't say anything. I'm not sure if he doesn't want to condescend to speak to me or if what I've said has shaken him up. But I'm scared because what he's done has meant literally anyone out there knows about us and we are all in danger.

'OK,' I say to Aaron, who is visibly shell-shocked. He probably didn't believe his father would do something like this. 'Right, since this is a panic situation, clearly we're going to have to go a bit further than we intended. I'm going to my flat to see which of my papers are still there and which are missing. When I come back, you'll have to—' I stop talking and glare at Pope. 'Sorry, almost made the same mistake again there. Come on, I'll tell you on the way to my place.'

'I need your help, Boy,' Pope says without even looking at his son. He is only speaking because he knows Aaron will do whatever he wants him to whenever he wants it. Not any more. I've had enough of Aaron being treated like that by this man. I know Aaron will have, too. I've seen him change over the last couple of years. He's grown stronger; he's started to see a life away from his father.

'He can't help you right now, he's busy,' I say.

'Boy, I need you to stay here.' Pope is scowling at me, his simmering hatred fuelling this attempt to dismantle me.

The only thing that is going to be broken here is Pope's hold over his son. Aaron is on the road to doing it – he just needs a hand to keep going.

'Didn't you hear me?' I repeat, as though he is hard of hearing. 'He can't help you right now. He's coming with me. If you needed his help so badly, you should have thought of that before you started shooting your mouth off and making it necessary for us to now travel in pairs.'

'*Boy* . . .' Pope says, threateningly, telling his forty-year-old son not to defy him. 'Boy . . .'

'Come on,' I say to Aaron.

Aaron doesn't move. The fear on his face is apparent, his body is almost rigid with the terror of going against his father. I hold out my hand. He can do this. He can walk away. Even for just a little while. He can do this: he can start to cut the cords that bind him to his abusive father. And I will help him.

# Nell

There is stuff missing from my files.

The way everything had been strewn around, screwed up, ripped and thrown, I hadn't really thought it might have been to try to hide the fact that things had been stolen along with the computer hard drives. I haven't had a chance to go through it since Zach did the initial living room tidy-up, and I did the office, and we both just piled stuff together and stacked it up. Having been through it now, I see that the stuff that's missing is specific. As I suspected, it all relates to the Brighton Mermaid and to Jude. Every scrap of the stuff relating to the other mermaids that were found along the coast is also missing, probably because I didn't take them to Leeds with me. I'd wanted Aaron to get me their DNA profiles, too, but it was too risky. He said he would do it, but I could tell he knew the second he did, it'd trigger an investigation that would lead right to him, so in the end I said we'd work without it. If we got any further with the Brighton Mermaid we'd go to the police about the others.

The person who broke in spent a lot of time gathering that information from the stuff I had.

Aaron has been sitting very quietly on my sofa, having a private, near-silent breakdown while I go through my papers. He was mute on the drive here, his eyes wide and fixed on the road ahead, his skin pale and clammy as though he had just been through a severe shock. Which, I suppose, he has. I was shocked and reeling a little, too. I'd never spoken to Pope like that before, so I can't imagine what it must have been like for Aaron to just walk away.

Right now, on my sofa, with his eyes wide and his mouth shut, I think Aaron Pope is trying very hard not to rock to soothe himself.

'There's stuff missing,' I say, although I'm not expecting an answer. I'm saying it to say it out loud, a point of aural reference so I can look back in a while and remember that I said there is stuff missing. 'Quite a bit of it.'

I took a lot of paper files to Leeds with me, but not everything. Some of the newspaper cuttings, the ones with more in-depth reporting, have been stolen. I'd highlighted sections on some of them, like the fact her vest top was from a shop only found in Birmingham. The police didn't have the resources to send someone up there to show her picture, but they'd faxed over the artist's impression and spoken to someone on the phone, Pope told me, and no one had recognised her. He said they'd even persuaded a local news programme to do a mention about her along with the drawing, but no one had called in. Not even the usual cranks who called in for every police appeal. I'd managed to get the local newspaper item which ran at the same time, but that is missing.

I'd also done so much research on her tattoo. The police hadn't been able to find the tattoo artist who inked her 'I am Brighton' mermaid. It was so distinctive, so unique, the type of thing you would have to detail on a passport, but no one had recognised it. I'd also printed out many pages of tattoo chat forums where I'd asked lots of questions about the style of art and the potential copycat artists who might have done it. All of them had led nowhere, but I'd kept a record of those searches, hoping to come back to it at some point. All of that is gone, too.

Everything relating to Jude is missing, as well. The photo of her that I'd pinned up. The photocopied pages from her diary that were in the original police reports that Pope passed on to me. All of the family tree stuff I have done, the contacts, the relatives I've found and been in touch with, the branches of family that have appeared along the way. Even though Mr Dalton has no blood relationship to Jude, I still put him on the family tree. And though it made it more complicated, trying to find out about his branch without that much information from him, I did the best I could. I did the best I could and Jude's tree started to reach its natural end with nothing really to show for it. And yet, those years of painstaking work have vanished from my flat just like Jude disappeared from my life.

Which means there must be a stronger link between what happened to Jude and what happened to the Brighton Mermaid than I thought.

'There's stuff missing,' I repeat to the dust floating in the air, because Aaron is clearly not going to snap out of his near-catatonic state for a while.

Is it really only those two files? All the others seem to be there. Maura Goodrich's friend's file is still there, I just saw that. But what about Craig Ackerman? I still don't have his DNA back and I haven't found out much about him. He said, when I took his family history, that his parents weren't keen on him tracing his birth family so he couldn't talk to them about what they knew. He hadn't applied for his adoption records, which is where most people start when they are tracing birth family. And he wasn't thrilled about giving a DNA sample. He didn't protest, but I saw the surprise flash across his eyes when I mentioned it.

I look down at the papers spread out all over the living room floor and frown before I get down on my knees again and look through them. His information, what little there was of it, is missing, too. If he is something to do with this, if he harmed Pope all those years ago when he thought he was getting too close, then he's always known about me. About Macy. About Shane. It would be easy to get talking to Shane, get an introduction. Try to find out what I know. But why after all this time? What has changed to make him take such a risk? Was I getting closer and I didn't realise it?

Is there something that made him decide he had to meet me? Because looking back, his story is flimsy. The people who I have met who want to find birth parents have done some stuff themselves. Craig Ackerman had done nothing. But why would he meet me? Did he think I'd tell him what I know about the Brighton Mermaid and then he could decide how much of a threat I am to him? If that's the case, the DNA must have panicked him. *He must have been trying to get it back.* Does that mean he fears he might have left some DNA behind at a crime scene?

*Hang on, hang on.* I get to my feet, so quickly it brings Aaron out of his trance enough for him to frown at me. I go to the fridge-freezer in the kitchen.

When I was waiting for the police, I did touch one thing – the fridge. All the stuff had been emptied out, the freezer drawers opened and partially emptied, and I couldn't stand the frantic, panicked bleeping of the 'door open' alarm any longer, so I'd closed it. Didn't tell anyone, just put as much back into the drawers as I could, shut them and went back to sit by the front door to wait for the police.

I have a two-bedroom flat and I live alone, but I have a large fridge-freezer. In the freezer, in the compartment used to make ice, I store DNA samples. You wouldn't know it because it has an inbuilt ice-tray with an insert you remove. Once the ice is made, you twist the handle and the ice is dispensed into the compartment below it. I have ice made, but I never use the compartment below because it is the perfect size to store the buccal sample tubes. It's a bit eurgh if I think too deeply about having other people's DNA where I store food, but generally I don't think about it.

I have some of Craig Ackerman's DNA in my freezer. The backup samples I always keep in case something goes wrong. Well, something has gone wrong. Horribly wrong in a way that I could not have predicted. I need to know who Craig Ackerman really is.

'What are you doing?' Aaron asks from the doorway of my kitchen. I pull open the freezer door. The ice compartment wasn't disturbed when I shut the freezer door. Maybe whoever trashed the flat, who took those specific files, didn't think to look in the ice-cube tray or, if they did, didn't think to look *underneath* it. Maybe, maybe . . .

I pull out the ice-cube box and unclip the upper tray. They're still there, six sample tubes from the last DNA samples I collected, six sample tubes with my writing on the labels, each with their little swab end, sitting in stasis, waiting to be taken out and tested. I usually don't need these backup swabs; I usually keep them six months until all the results are back and then I dispose of them. Three of them belong to Craig Ackerman.

'I'm seeing if I still have Craig Ackerman's DNA swabs,' I reply.

'Who?'

'The case I was working on a few weeks back, remember? The guy who was adopted and wanted to find his birth family, see if he had any other siblings or anything? Remember I told you that he hadn't done much?'

Aaron's face tells me that he has no idea who I mean. 'What's he got to do with anything?'

'All of this started happening not long after I met him. I didn't think much of it, didn't connect him and all the weird stuff, but since his files were taken with the Brighton Mermaid ones and Jude's ones, it must be related. No pun intended.'

'Maybe we should just leave it all alone,' Aaron says tiredly. 'It's too much, all of this. We've wrecked our lives and maybe we should just let it all go.'

What is this 'let it all go' nonsense? 'And then what, Aaron? How are we supposed to tell the people who are trying to run us down and sending dead rats that we've decided to let it all go? Stand in the middle of the street and scream it out in the hope that whoever's doing this hears us and stops trying to kill us?'

'I don't know if I *can* do this any more,' he says quietly. 'Before, when I was helping you and writing computer programs and going through the results with you, it was all a bit odd, a bit out there, and a way to get the whole Brighton Mermaid thing out of my life. But it wasn't serious. Not like this. I could even tell myself my dad had an ordinary accident. But someone almost killed Sadie. They tried to kill me. They hurt you. This is too much. I don't live in this kind of world.'

'Aaron, whether we want it or not, we're in this. Right in the middle of this. Your father put us there a long time ago and we've kept ourselves there for whatever reason. But there's no way out of this now. We're here, and we have to see it through to its conclusion.'

'We really don't,' he states. 'Look, I'm going to go home. See if I can make it up with my dad. Try to put all of this behind me. I think you should do the same.'

'OK,' I say to Aaron. What I want to do is scream at him that pretending it's not happening won't protect him; that if he goes back to his dad now, when not even four hours have elapsed since he made a stand, he's going to be his father's lackey for the rest of his life. But I can't do that. I can't be like Pope. I have to leave Aaron to find out the truth all by himself. I thought I was saving him earlier, but maybe I just pushed him too far, too fast. 'You do what is best for you.'

'I don't know what's best for me, Nell. Haven't you worked that out yet? I do things because of other people, because of my dad, because of you. I'm never sure what's best for me. But I'm scared. I think we could both end up really hurt, like Sadie in a coma, or worse. I just want us to both walk away from this thing while we still can.'

'I can't walk away from it. I have to see this through to the end.'

Aaron rubs his fingers over his forehead, looks pained. Eventually he lowers his hand and sighs. 'What are we going to do?'

'You don't have to be involved in this, I can do it alone.'

'Where would the fun be in that?' he replies flatly. 'What are you going to do?'

I hold the three tubes in the palm of my hand. 'We need these processed properly so we can find out who Craig Ackerman is and why he's brought all of this into our lives.'

'How are we going to do that? I don't think I'm going to be able to persuade Dad to get one of his mates to help us.'

'I'll find a way,' I reply.

*Oh, don't worry, I know someone who'll help us*, I think. *I just have to ask in the right way.*

# Macy

*Monday, 28 May*

I'm hoping that Zach is right about the fakery of social media, and that nobody should need to call someone an amazing dad because he does those things by default. I've been thinking about it and I'm hoping those things are true, and that Clyde didn't just leave because there was something wrong with our family. Not that I'd wish a lazy-arse fecker on anyone, I just don't want to have been the reason he left. I want it to be something about him.

I was normal with Clyde.

Well, as normal as I could ever be, I suppose. I didn't do half the things I do now and he still left. That's what's galling, I suppose. I'd clawed my way out of my teenage years, not completely unscathed but all right, met Clyde which seemed perfect and then it wasn't for ever.

I should probably go home because I can't stay away for ever. That's what the logical part of me says I should do. But the other part of me, the part that sees what I'm like, knows I should actually keep my distance. I don't want my children to turn out like me. I wonder, sometimes, if this is another aspect of how my mind works, my new obsession. I think I can control how their lives turn out, how their mental health expresses itself by not exposing them to me. But what if me not being there is what will send them over the edge? It was loss that started this off for me. I know it. I can't stop it, but I know it. First the loss of Jude, then the loss of Daddy as the man I knew him to be, then the loss of our life in Brighton.

I got better. Much better. Then Clyde was lost to me and suddenly it was all back. I had to find ways to make the world understandable and controllable and clean. I like things that are clean.

I stand at the door to Zach's bathroom. It's clean for now. I'm not sure which he prefers, actually, my drinking or my cleaning. Yesterday he came in from work and stood very still, looking around, and then went, 'Well, OK. Thanks for cleaning, Macy. I, erm, appreciate it.'

He didn't look like he appreciated it.

'It's cleaning or drinking,' I explained.

'Well clean away, Macy. Clean away.'

I can see why Nell liked him so much. I really can.

# Nell

'I couldn't believe it when I got your message,' Zach says when he opens the door. 'And now you're here. I didn't think I'd ever see you again.'

I really wish seeing him didn't give me an almighty kick in my chest and stomach. I look him over and those kicks begin to pummel my heart. '*I miss you,*' I want to say. '*I really, really miss you. I know we weren't together for long, but I miss you so much.*' I have better things to think about, though, so I shove those feelings away, force them under the rug like an uncomfortable truth that needs to be hidden and ignored at all costs.

'Like I said, I need your help.'

I am all business. Even when he steps back and lets me into his flat, and I see the little silver coat hooks on the wall where I'd usually hang my bag, and the large framed map of Africa and its islands – each country a different colour, the River Nile a bright red line that snakes through eleven countries – that I almost always stopped in front of to gaze at. I don't stop, I don't indulge myself in the nostalgia of it, I stay focused. I remain all business.

'Look, I know, and she's all right,' Zach says.

'Pardon me?' I reply.

'You want my help to find your sister, right?'

'Macy? You know about Macy?'

'Yes. I, erm, yes.'

'How?'

'She called me. But she's fine, that's the main thing. She's fine.'

'No, that's not the main thing at all. The main thing is: *what the hell?!* The main thing is: why did she call someone she has met for a total of five minutes? And the main thing is: why on Earth didn't you tell me?'

'I don't know why she called me; she said she got my number from your phone and said she wanted to talk about you. I figured if you didn't want to speak to me directly, you might do it through your sister – so I met her.'

'And why didn't you tell me?'

'She said she would disappear completely if I told you I'd spoken to or seen her. I didn't want that. I knew you wouldn't want that, either. So many people – women – go missing every year and I didn't want that to happen to Macy, or for you to have to deal with it.'

There is more. Much, much more.

'Where is she?' I ask. His face is broadcasting loud and clear where she is.

'Right this second, I don't know.'

'But . . . ?'

'She's been staying here. In the spare room.' He adds that last statement like it will make any of it any better.

Is this what it's been like for Macy with Shane? Does she feel like someone is slowly slicing away pieces of her heart? Is that why she decided to sleep with Zach – to make us even? 'Did you sleep with my sister?' I ask him. I know the answer – I just want to know if he's low enough to lie about it.

He does not look away or seem uncomfortable when he instantly replies, 'No, I did not sleep with her. Or anyone else since you, in case you're wondering.'

'But . . . ?'

This time he does glance away and wither a little more before dragging his gaze back at me. 'But it's been complicated. She's not in a good place. I think getting away from it all has been good for her, but she's still struggling.'

I nod. 'Right, so in other words my sister's tried it on with you a few times and you're not sure how much longer you'll be able to resist her?'

'I'll be able to resist until the end of time,' he says firmly. '*You* are all I want.'

'I don't have time for this,' I say. 'Sleep with her if you fancy it. It might clarify that what you do is nothing to do with me.'

'I don't fancy it,' he responds.

I redirect my gaze to the framed Africa map. The shape of it reminds me of the outline of his tattoo, the time I spent tracing my fingers over the little *Adrinka* symbols, questioning him about them. This hasn't exactly gone the right way. I was meant to forge some kind of truce between us before I asked for his help. The Macy Factor has blown that out of the water. I may as well just ask.

I reach into the inside pocket of my jacket and pull out two of the buccal sample tubes I have left of Craig Ackerman's DNA. I've kept one back, just in case. 'I don't quite know how it works, but I need you to take this to your mates in the crime lab and get it analysed for me. And then run it though the police databases to see if it matches any crimes on there. Or missing persons reports. Or anything, really.'

Zach glares at what I am holding out to him as though it has insulted him, and then he looks up at me. 'It doesn't work like that, Nell. This isn't even my district. Since they found out I was here things have blown up, all kinds of hassle has come raining down because we were carrying out an investigation in their area without telling them. And it looks like we've been essentially accusing them of being involved in something because we kept it quiet. I can't just waltz in and start demanding DNA analysis and database searches.'

'Do it through your London station, then, I don't care. You need to make this work for me. Please.' I can feel tears building up behind my face, stinging my eyes. '*Please.*'

'No, Nell, I really can't. I have no idea whose DNA that is. I put it into the system and, despite what they say, it could very well end up staying there. Someone innocent could be irreparably damaged by me doing that, or it could allow someone to walk away because their DNA shouldn't have been entered by other means into the system in the first place.'

The tears start and I'm not able to stop them. 'Someone's trying to hurt me, Zach, possibly even kill me and if you don't help me, they may very well succeed.'

# Nell

It took a bit more to convince Zach to help me. He took me into the living room of his flat, let me cry for a bit and then asked me to tell him everything.

I eventually did tell him everything, even about Aaron and his work on the computers, the not-so-legal parts too, before Zach would agree to see what he could do.

'I need to see you,' he said when he called me this morning.

The urgency in his voice scared me and elated me at the same time. I was right, about Craig Ackerman, which made me relieved that I wasn't going crazy. I was right about Craig Ackerman, which made me scared that I'd brought this man into my life.

We've arranged to meet at the Peace Statue on the seafront. I like this statue, probably more than any other in Brighton and Hove. She was erected around 1912 and she stands on a globe, holding another globe in one hand, an olive branch in the other, her beautiful wings fully extended. There is something calming and hopeful about the Angel of Peace, the way she sits on the border of Brighton and Hove, almost as though refereeing the differences between the two towns, while holding them together by reminding them that without the other they wouldn't be a city at all.

I suppose I suggested it because it's a fitting place to meet. When we were little, Macy and I would run here, leaving our parents behind, the first one to touch the plinth on which she stood the winner of the imaginary prize of Most Important Girl in the Okorie home. I was older, bigger and faster, and I was supposed to let Macy win, spare her feelings and prove I was the more mature sister. Most of the time I did just that – held back, gave her the chance to get there first. *Most* of the time. Sometimes pride, competitiveness, sheer bloody-mindedness would take over and I would beat her by a mile. I would use my height, my strength to leave her far behind. To be fair to Macy, before all the stuff that happened, she was always secure enough in herself to never question her wins or losses, she just took it as part of the consequences of playing a game with me. That's what I miss about Macy from before the first arrest: she never seemed to worry too much about anything, she was able to throw herself into life and took whatever happened – good or bad – as part of what living was all about. The Peace Statue is part of our shared history that I can look back on fondly.

Meeting Zach here is fitting because I want peace with him.

I haven't told Aaron yet about this. I can't, because he went back to his dad the other night and I couldn't risk him blowing it by confessing all to Pope in an attempt to curry favour with him.

I'm here early so I stand in the queue and buy myself a cup of coffee from the café beside the Peace Statue. Summer is here and with that, with the warmer, longer days, and fragrant air, and beautiful seascape, comes more people. More people who want to soak up Brighton, who want to immerse themselves in Hove, who start to convince themselves that they could actually live here.

You can tell the people who live here and those who have come on a day trip, or who come for a few days but now consider themselves one of us. They wear too many layers and carry bulging bags; they think their small, foldable umbrellas will be enough to match the wind on the seafront when it gets itself even a little riled up; they stop and take pictures every few seconds with a camera or simply with their eyes.

The people who are visiting see and *notice* what us who grew up here very often take for granted.

I stare at my coffee for a long time before I decide to go back, queue up, get a number and then wait for it to be called to get Zach a coffee, too. I've just finished stirring in a second sugar when he arrives. He stands at the base of the statue, a handsome man with a look of dread on his face.

'Here,' I say to him in lieu of hello and hold out his coffee.

His face registers surprise. 'For me?' he asks.

I nod. 'Two sugars.' I wonder if he realises that the coffee is actually my way of saying, *'I miss you.'*

I wonder if I should take his pointed 'Thank you' as *'I miss you, too'*?

'So, what was so important you couldn't say it on the phone?' I ask him to stop him staring at me. I don't mind it, so much as realise it's highly inappropriate to be going off on any type of tangent at the moment. Someone is trying to harm me – kill me, as I said to Zach – I shouldn't get distracted.

Zach seems disappointed, and looks away. 'Let's walk,' he says.

'You've got something awful to tell me, haven't you?' I say as we set off towards Brighton.

'Look, I shouldn't have done this. Don't ask me how I got it done, but quite a few people could be in serious hot water if anyone finds out. Which kind of makes what I found even more contentious.'

'I don't get you. Did you find Craig Ackerman has something to do with the death of the Brighton Mermaid?' I've been going over and over this. How the two are connected. If his date of birth is accurate, then Craig Ackerman would only have been twenty-six or so when she died. Was he really a killer that young? That doesn't seem possible to me.

'No,' Zach says after a sip of his coffee. 'Well, there was no match, nothing to connect him to that case or to your friend Jude. In fact, we have nothing at all about him in any of the police crime databases.'

'What? Nothing? Nothing at all? That's not possible. I'm sure there must be something. Anything.'

Zach shakes his head, avoiding eye contact while he does so. 'Honestly, Nell, he doesn't even have a parking ticket. He's a model citizen.'

'I was so sure . . .' I can't believe this. Why would whoever broke in take his files along with Jude's and the Mermaid's? 'You could have told me that on the phone,' I say. 'Why the need to meet up?'

Zach takes a huge gulp of his coffee and clearly, from the way his face contracts, it scorches his tongue. He's obviously trying to avoid saying something.

'You know DNA, how it works, don't you?' he finally says.

'Yes.'

'Look . . .' Zach sighs. 'There was nothing in the databases about him. But when we ran his DNA through all the systems, something was thrown up. We found a link on the Y-chromosome line, a high incidence of short tandem repeat polymorphisms, with someone else on the criminal database; the number of matching centimorgans and alleles suggested a half-sibling connection.'

Time is starting to slow down. I can feel it. The blood in my veins is dawdling on its journey around my body, the breath in my chest is taking ages to go in and out, my heart is taking an age to contract and expand for every single beat. I know what he's going to say.

'Craig Ackerman's half-brother is called Shane Merrill.'

I have to stop walking. Like time, my whole body has slowed down and slowed down until it is now at a standstill.

'Why?' I manage. My brain has slowed down, too, and I'm finding it almost impossible to function. *Why is Shane in the database? Why would he lie to me about who Ackerman is? Why would he try to harm me?*

'Why is Shane Merrill in the database?' Zach rubs his hand over his lash-free eyes and then runs it over his hairless head. He looks absolutely agonised at what he's having to say. 'He's a . . . he's a convicted rapist. He was convicted on DNA evidence.'

My body is trembling and I feel my knees wanting to give way. This can't be happening.

'I haven't told Macy yet. Technically I shouldn't even know.'

I'm quivering. Like I do after I've drunk too much and my body can't physically take it any more; I'm shaking like I did when John Pope interrogated me in a police station and called me names.

Zach still looks uncomfortable, troubled, though. Now he's unburdened himself he shouldn't look so . . . *burdened*. He comes to stand in front of me. 'Look, there's no easy way to say this, but I did some checking and I'm so sorry. Macy told me about you and him and . . . a couple of the accusations that weren't pursued by the CPS were around the time you and he were together.'

# Macy

*Friday, 1 June*

**From:** Macenna Okorie
**Sent:** 01 June 2018 10:53
**To:** Clyde Higgson
**Subject:** Divorce

Clyde,

I'd like a divorce, please.

Can I have your address – a work one will do – to send you the petition? It can be very quick as we haven't lived together for more than five years and were never really financially linked.

The children are fine, by the way.

Macy

# Nell

*Friday, 1 June*

I've always felt fortunate that the first time I had sex I had an orgasm. Two. It wasn't painful, he was nice to me, he told me he loved me. My first time had been as ideal as you could get, I thought. And now I am finding out the first man I slept with was, at that time, a convicted rapist.

I can't move for the horror of that.

Zach has helped me to a nearby bench.

'I'm so sorry, Nell,' he says when many minutes have elapsed and I have sat with my face in my hands thinking about how fortunate I have always believed I've been to have a positive first sexual experience. And how that is now sullied and disgusting because of who he is and what he has done to another woman. *Women.* More than one. He has raped more than one woman. 'I really wish I didn't have to tell you.'

When I take my hands away and look down at them, I'm shaking again. 'There has to be some mistake,' I say. 'It has to be some other Shane Merrill. That's the only thing I think it could be.'

Zach stays silent. He stares into his cup and waits for me to get a grip. Of course it's Shane, of course it is.

'After the burglary, after the dead rat, after poor Sadie, I didn't think it could get much worse,' I state.

'Is it really a surprise, Nell? Think back over your relationship – is this *really* a surprise?'

'Yes,' I reply. 'It is. He was nice to me. Lovely to me, even. He didn't treat me badly. That's why a part of me is still wondering if this is all some huge mistake.'

It's plain on Zach's face that he doesn't believe me, and if I wasn't there, if I hadn't dated Shane, I wouldn't believe me, either. 'I swear, he treated me really well. He was nice to me, he was gentle, he never raised his voice, never forced me to do anything I didn't want to do.' I shake my head. 'And anyway, do you really think I would have let him near my sister and her children if I had any clue about this? Or if he'd ever forced himself on me? He treated me really well.'

'Did you ever say no, though?' Zach asks. 'I know you say he never forced you, but at any point did you actually turn him down when he wanted sex, or go against anything he didn't want you to do?'

I feel like he's interrogating me. Not overtly, not even subtly, but the conversation has definitely shifted to something that you wouldn't discuss with a boyfriend – ex or otherwise – or even a friend. It feels like I am being made to account for my connection with a suspect.

'I suppose not,' I reply carefully now that it feels like I'm talking to a policeman, a detective sergeant, no less. For all I know, they may be building a case against Shane for something and I've unwittingly helped, while screwing myself over as I'll never know who is out to get me and why.

'You don't have to talk about it, if you don't want to,' Zach says. 'But I'm just asking, really, because you were very young when you and he were together. A lot of young people, girls particularly, don't often say no to their partners. They only really see what the man they love is like when they say no to him. You say he was nice to you, he treated you well, but did you ever have occasion to say no to him or to go against what he wanted? Because that's generally when the real him comes out.'

*When I went to college*, I think but don't say. *He turned nasty when I decided to still go to college. He called me names, said vicious things, implied that I was gagging to go out there and shag around, that I was a dirty girl, a dirty little slut, just like Pope had called me. I was devastated, but then I twisted it in my own head, I made myself understand: he was upset, he loved me and I was leaving him, of course he was going to act out. That's how you respond when someone you love hurts you. That's what I told myself at the time. That's what I tell myself today. Except it always felt like it was beyond normal hurt and upset; he wasn't just expressing his feelings, he was trying to hurt me, diminish me, make me do what he wanted by any means possible.*

It's my turn to stare into my coffee. I never did say no to Shane, if I think about it now. Not about anything.

Mainly, though, because we never argued, never had a cross word. I was so enamoured with him and how he had transformed my life by being someone I could spend time with now that Jude had left. That aside, I adored him. He told me all the time how much he loved me. He held me like I was something precious; he looked at me like he couldn't believe his luck.

And, if I am honest, truly honest, all of those things made sure I never went against him. I had no voice, no power to be normal with him. I was young, naïve, desperate to never be alone.

Now I have to look at our relationship through the prism of what he was doing to other women at the same time. I can admit that I saw him whenever *he* wanted – not once did I ever ask to see him because I would never dream of making a demand on his time in that way. If he didn't suggest the time to meet up next, I would just leave it and try to get on with schoolwork until he showed up again.

Shane was my first and he controlled everything – *everything* – about our sex life . . . about *my* sex life. It was beyond having the sex he wanted whenever he wanted. I was never allowed to decide when or how I orgasmed. That was always down to Shane to decide, Shane to provide.

If I tried to touch myself during sex, he would always take my hand away and keep it away. I wasn't allowed to do that, *that* was something for him to do. If I wanted to have straight sex with no oral sex from him to me first, he would make sure that he finished first without me orgasming, almost as though I had lost my chance because I said no to how he wanted me to come. My trip into ecstasy was always something he 'gave' to me. I remember him telling me more than once that it made him unhappy to think I might be masturbating alone because he loved to see my pleasure and so my doing it without him there felt like I didn't need him. He didn't actually tell me not to do it, but he made sure I – young, naïve, desperate to not be alone I – would comply and never masturbate without him.

Shane was lovely to me . . . and everything I did, especially when it came to sex, had to be centred around him. But really, is that on the same spectrum as what Zach is saying he is accused of? No, not accused of – convicted of.

'What did he do?' I ask Zach.

When he's silent and seems to seek solace in his coffee for far longer than is necessary I know it's bad. It's the kind of bad that will feel like someone has graffitied the inside of my mind. Eventually, he turns his head to look at me because I am staring at him, watching the burden settle onto his features again.

*I thought I was going to fall in love with you*, I think as we stare at each other. *I thought we had a future. The future.* Zach observes me like he thought the same about me, hoped our futures would intertwine enough for us to have a shared life together.

He clears his throat and then focuses over my shoulder at some point in the distance. 'Do you really want to know, Nell? *Really?*'

'No, I do not want to know. But I have to know for my sanity.'

'All right. Again, I shouldn't be telling you this, it's not something I should know. He was first accused in 1991.'

'But he must have been only twenty then,' I cut in.

'I know. He denied it at first, but the DNA evidence said otherwise. So he then said it was consensual. The jury didn't believe him, but the judge took pity on him as he was a studious young man with a bright future ahead of him and handed him a very light sentence. With good behaviour and time served, he did less than a year. I'm getting all of this from the records, so this is my take on what I've read and heard.'

'But there's more?' I ask.

'Yes, there's more. Look—'

'Just tell me, Zach. I'm a big girl, just tell me.'

'To the outside world, it looked like he learnt his lesson from that first conviction. He came out of prison a reformed character, he attended a perpetrators' course, all the while protesting his innocence, and then went straight. Got a job, settled down to a normal life, got himself a girlfriend.' Zach points at me. 'But in reality, he had just learnt to use a condom, found out how to skew other forms of DNA collection. Especially since back then it was still quite new when used in forensics.'

'How did he do that?'

'It's nasty stuff, stuff that eats away at your soul. It gave me pause and I've been dealing with this sort of thing for years. I don't think you should hear it. And even if you want to hear it, I don't want to say it out loud. It's the sort of thing that haunts me. But suffice to say, he was never convicted again. He was arrested a few times, accused even more times, but there was never enough evidence and he managed to cast far too much he-said-she-said doubt to secure anything that the CPS were happy to proceed with.'

Was it Shane with the Brighton Mermaid, then? With the others? Did he do that to all those women? Did he kill them? But where does Craig Ackerman come into it? Why would Shane bring him into all of this, by sending me his way, especially if he doesn't have anything criminal attached to his name?

'How many women were there?' I ask Zach.

'You don't want to know, Nell, you really don't.'

'I do. I really do.'

'There were enough, all right?' he snaps. 'There were enough of them for me to not understand why they didn't manage to find a way to get him off the streets. He is absolute scum. But he chose his victims well, I suppose. Most of them had breakdowns, those being the ones who actually went to the police. But part of me wonders if they just didn't think it was worth it back then. If, because Shane's victims were the type of young women who were routinely disbelieved and dismissed, the police just let it go.' He rubs his hands over his eyes. 'I'm sorry for snapping at you. This whole thing has made me incredibly angry and it's not like I can do anything about it because it's not my patch . . . I hate to think of all those girls and young women who didn't get anything close to justice because no one cared enough.'

Zach hasn't told me anywhere near everything. And Shane was doing this while we were together. While I was in his bed, while we were, I thought, having amazing sex, he was off doing this as well.

'Is it my fault?' I ask. 'Was I just not enough for him and he had to go off and do that?' Zach will be honest. Even if he doesn't want to say it, he will find a way to tell me if it was.

He takes his hand away from his face and frowns at me. 'No, no, of course not,' he replies. He snakes his arm around me and pulls me close. 'It was not you at all. You know as well as I do that sexual assault and rape is nothing to do with sex, it's all about power and control. It's not your fault in any way, shape or form, and he started well before he met you.'

'But if I was enough for him, shouldn't he have stopped when he was with me?'

'It doesn't work like that, Nell. If he's pathological enough to be doing that in the first place, no one, no matter how wonderful they are, is going to stop him.'

I like being held by Zach. It's comfortable and familiar, something I grew used to very quickly. We sit in silence for a long while, mainly because I know when I speak again this magic will be broken and he'll be a police officer and I'll be someone who has deep emotional ties to a prolific criminal.

'I don't know how I'm going to tell Macy all of this. It'll destroy her,' I say as I sit up, out of his hold, away from his heat.

'I know,' he mumbles. 'I'll tell her if you want? I'm used to delivering bad news.'

'No,' I say and shake my head. 'I have to tell her. I owe her that. I can't believe he's been sneaking out and doing that all these years. It's mind-boggling.'

'From what I could see, it doesn't look like he's done it in a while,' Zach says.

'But you just said he was pathological, so why would he stop?'

'I don't know. In fact, I don't know that he has, but there have been no reports in years of assaults that fit his MO, most notably what he does to skew the DNA harvesting and the theft of jewellery.'

'Theft of jewellery?'

'That was something he always did, since the very first time, and not something he's likely to have changed – he steals a piece of jewellery from each of his victims. Trophies, if you will. He either rips it off them, or scares them into giving it to him. He often goes for things that mean a lot to them: antique rings, lockets and the like. If they have nothing like that, he'll take whatever they have – even if it's just a cheap plastic watch, a hairclip or a lock of hair. Anything. No one has really complained of that in years. Even if the other circumstances seem similar, that seems to be missing.'

'Jewellery,' I mumble. This is what Pope said had linked the mermaids. Each of them had an item of jewellery missing. So it *was* him. He did do it.

I feel like I've been punched again. Shane is a rapist. Shane, who I spent two years sleeping with, is a rapist. Shane, my sister's partner, is a rapist. Did he move along the coast, doing what he did? But to cover his tracks, did he start to kill? The Brighton Mermaid was the earliest type of these bodies to be found – was she his first and it escalated from there? Is Craig Ackerman his helper as well as his sibling?

'Do you know something, Nell?' Zach asks me.

'What would I know?'

'You've got that look on your face that says you've just worked out something. What is it?'

I look over my once-upon-a-time paramour, the man I could have loved, the man I could still fall in love with if I stop holding myself back. I could tell him, let him in, but I know I'm going to do that really annoying thing I do that my dad does, too: I'm not going to tell. It's too soon. I don't want to say it to Zach and for it to become swallowed up in what could become a much bigger investigation.

'I can't tell you,' I say.

Zach pushes his tongue deep into his cheek and his eyes harden. 'Can't or won't?' he eventually says.

'Both. I don't know what there is to tell, but if I did, I still wouldn't tell you. I'm sorry. I know you've gone above and beyond with all this, but I've just got a couple of things to work out first, then I can tell you. Maybe. Possibly.'

He shakes his head in despair because he knows whatever he says won't make a difference. 'You're going after him, aren't you?'

'No,' I say. And I'm not. I'm going to go after those trophies, the jewellery he stole. They may not link him directly to the Brighton Mermaid and all the other mermaid-like women that were found, but there will be items from the other women. The ones who didn't become mermaids, the ones he brutalised and stole from but never got justice.

'Oh, Jeez,' Zach sighs. 'I shouldn't have told you. I should have known that telling you would do nothing but make you go towards him, not away from him.' He shuts his eyes and shakes his head. 'He's dangerous, Nell. Stay away from him. If he's the one who's after you right now, then that should tell you how deadly the man is. For all we know, the reason why he hasn't had any complaints made against him recently is because all his victims are dead.'

'I'm not going after him.'

'Look, tell me whatever it is and it may be enough for me to trigger an investigation, historic or current.'

'I can't do that. If I do that, and they go and talk to him, it might tip him off and allow him to cover his tracks.'

'Nell . . . Promise me. Promise me you'll stay away from him.'

'I promise you, I will stay away from him.'

Zach closes his eyes again and holds himself very still as though listening for something, possibly the lie beneath my words. 'All right,' he says when he opens his eyes. 'Give me your phone.'

'Why?'

'Just give me your phone.'

I do as I'm told.

'Please put in your passcode and then get up the "find my phone" or "find my friends" bit.'

'No way!' I say and snatch back my handset. 'That means I have to sign in to location services and the cloud and I don't do that.'

'I will sign in to my cloud on your phone so I can find you.'

'No way!'

'It's that or I go and have an "off the record" chat with Shane. Your choice.'

*Trapped.* Once I've made sure nothing will automatically upload to his cloud, I give him my phone ready for him to sign in.

'Text me,' he says as he types into my phone. 'When you get into trouble – because it's a given that it'll be *when* you get into trouble – text me "H", just that, "H", and I will come and find you.'

'I won't need rescuing because I'm not going to do anything stupid.'

As he hands me back my phone, he glances at my adorned wrists. 'And get rid of those bracelets,' he says. 'They're too noisy, they'll get you into trouble.'

'I'm not going to do—'

'Keep in regular contact.'

'Honestly, I'm—'

'"H", just send me "H", and I'll come find you,' he repeats.

'Honestly, Zach, you're worrying for no reason. I'm going nowhere near him.'

I mean it as well. I absolutely mean it.

# Nell

*Saturday, 2 June*

I've never really been in Macy and Shane's bedroom before.

I came in a few times to leave clothes on the bed, to find the note that Macy left when she ran away, but not properly. I'm standing in here now, looking around and wondering at the secrets it holds.

In the time since I saw Zach, I've felt nothing but sick at the thought that my sister and I have both slept with someone like Shane. Macy's children have grown up with him as a father figure for over half a decade.

I lay in the middle of my bed last night, wide awake, so many different thoughts firing off in my brain, connections and revelations lighting up pathways across my mind like the lights coming on after a blackout.

Shane and the Brighton Mermaid.

If it was him, then so many things would make sense. It would mean that he came for me, wooed and dated me because I was one of the girls who found the Brighton Mermaid. When I left for university, and then wouldn't get back together with him, he must have got with my sister to stay close. Not for me, but to find out what I knew.

If it was him, then he must have done all those other things: the mugging, the dead rat – he knows how bordering on phobic I am about rats.

If it was him, then I've slept with a serial killer. My sister has slept with a serial killer. Every time I think that, an almost uncontrollable nausea rises inside.

But what if it wasn't him? What if Shane has nothing to do with the Brighton Mermaid and it's all a coincidence that those files were taken and he used to steal jewellery from the women he . . . he . . . I couldn't even think it, the thought was so horrible. What does Craig Ackerman have to do with it? Maybe it's all him. Maybe Shane is being controlled by Ackerman and he has tried to protect Macy, protect me in all of this. Maybe being with Macy transformed Shane but Ackerman had some dirt on him and Shane had to play along or lose everything.

These doubts, these connections that could be coincidences, are the reason why I need to find those trophies. If I find them, there may be DNA on them that will link them to any of the other mermaids, and then I'll know.

I wanted to come earlier, but I had to go over to Mum and Dad's to check on the children, seeing as neither Macy nor Shane was around and I hadn't seen them all week.

I stand at the door to their bedroom, just inside the threshold, with my shoes on. I know Macy doesn't allow shoes in the house, but I can't be here for long, I can't be taking my time to unlace my shoes and then lace them back up again. From what I can see, Shane is away for a few days – there was a lot of post behind the door when I came in and the house doesn't look like it's been lived in at all.

Their room has a large bed, neatly made, of course, and everything is immaculately tidy. Macy and Shane are both neat freaks, and that was one of the first signs of Macy having a breakdown – she stopped picking things up and didn't care. Even now, with Macy gone, Shane has kept their bedroom pristine. I look around at the room. If Shane is who Zach has told me he is, then he will keep his trophies near to give him a constant thrill. Like an alcoholic taking a sneaky tot of their favourite tipple right in front of everyone – they get the hit of alcohol *and* the added kick of no one knowing what they're doing.

Where would he hide them? I face the bed, a big, ornate sleigh bed with a thick mattress. Surely he wouldn't put them in there?

No, any cut or slit in the mattress could be seen by Macy. As I am looking at the bed, to the left is a bank of white wardrobes with a combination of drawers, cubbyholes and sliding sections for accessories. I remember when Macy was designing it, how happy she'd been because it was her dream come true to have space and room for everything.

I stare at the wardrobes. It seems too obvious but people talk about hiding things in plain sight all the time. Maybe he's put the items in Macy's jewellery drawers? No. For someone with Macy's OCD tendencies, she would notice. And she isn't really a jewellery person; I sometimes think she refuses to wear it as a way to mark out how different we are.

I miss the familiar jangle and tinkle of my bracelets on my wrists; without them, I don't sound like me. But Zach is right, they make me conspicuous.

I don't sound like me without my bracelets, but I can hear my heart. It's racing in my chest. I don't know when Shane will be back and I do not want him to find me here. Not in the house, and definitely not in his bedroom. My heart, its loud, drumming beat, is like a timer counting down the seconds till he comes home. On both sides of their bed there is a set of drawers, small, white, with small chrome handles. Not in there – too much chance of Macy finding them.

Maybe under the carpet, under a loose floorboard?

To the right of the bed, in the huge window bay, is the big old leather love seat in front of the large shutters. Those shutters were another thing that made Macy so happy; another dream house item she was able to tick off her list. She picked an antique silk colour instead of white after having me go over and over and over the samples with her.

I feel so sad about this house. That period when she was doing it up, picking out the decor and planning each room, was the one time in our lives that Macy and I were pure friends, totally sisters. We worked together without any animosity hanging over us. I was her sounding board and she was the most excited I'd ever seen her. This house and its contents are about to be ripped away from her. Once she finds out about Shane, she won't be able to live here.

This is why I am here, why I need the trophies. Not just to solve the mystery of the Brighton Mermaid and the other mermaids; I will need them to prove to Macy that this isn't just about me trying to ruin her life. Again. She will convince herself that it wasn't Shane, and if it was, it is all in the past. If I have the trophies, I will have something solid to show her. But where?

I'm sure they're in here. They are somewhere that he can control access to. Only Macy is really in here on her own and no one I know goes through their own bedroom on a regular basis. If it is tidy and clean and comfortable, you very, very rarely search through every nook and cranny.

I look at the light brown leather love seat – large, squat and dominating the window bay. It was Shane's from before I knew him. He's cared for it, treated the leather to keep it soft and new-looking. He's had it reupholstered a couple of times to keep it use-able, I'd guess. I seem to remember, back in the day, he told me that his parents had given it to him. He kept it in his tiny bedroom then, too. It was ridiculous, squeezing it into his bedroom in his first flat. When I slept with him when I returned from university, it was in that flat's bedroom too.

*The love seat.*

Everything else in this house is new. He used to joke sometimes about how he had nothing left from his old life when he moved in with Macy. 'She's made me get rid of it all – except my car and my love seat. And even the car's going to be upgraded to one that will fit all of us in.' I knew he was exaggerating. Yes, he got rid of all his things when they moved here together, but he hadn't seemed bothered about any of his other possessions except this thing that has been in all the bedrooms of his that I've been in.

The trophies have to be in the love seat.

The light brown leather is so soft, the filling gives way immediately when I climb onto the seat and start pushing my hands down the sides of the base cushion. Nothing, not even a stray coin or pieces of fluff. He obviously clears it out regularly to make sure no one takes too close a look at it. Next I move behind it and then shove it forwards. The stitching at the back is very secure, nothing out of place, nothing that suggests there is an extra flap or secret compartment back here. It must be underneath. I move round to the front of the seat, push it back into place, being careful to line up the foot marks exactly where they have indented the soft, pale carpet. Then I get down flat on my back and slide my hand under the seat. I run my fingers along the smooth, slightly cold material underneath and nothing seems out of place. Along the edge, I can feel the straight, hard frame of the seat, then my fingers catch something. A patch of material that is folded over like a hem.

My heart almost stops in my chest.

I didn't *believe* Shane had trophies from the crimes he's committed, keepsakes from his assaults, which would further cause his victims distress because that missing something would always be on his victim's mind. These items were an abstract concept that I knew deep down I'd never really find. My fingers open the seam, which is held together by Velcro, and slip inside. I have to withdraw my fingers and then push my whole body closer and my shoulder further under the love seat to be able to put my fingers deeper into the cavity.

There is something definitely there. Definitely. I push my fingers deeper inside, reaching for it, almost there . . . almost there . . . A sharp pain shoots through my index finger as it scrapes against something, probably a piece of exposed spring.

'Ow,' I mutter and have to jerk my hand out.

The end of my finger has been punctured and a bead of blood has formed on my fingertip. 'Great,' I mutter to myself and put the finger in my mouth to stem the blood flow before it starts to drip – it'd be perfect if I bled all over Macy and Shane's lovely cream carpet.

I suck at the little cut until I'm confident it's stopped enough for me to take my finger out of my mouth. I examine it again, a tiny hole right in the centre of my finger that is quite painful for something so small and innocuous-looking.

*Click.*

I'm about to put my arm back under the seat when I hear it. The very definite but extremely quiet click somewhere in the house. Shane. He's back. And he's creeping around. He must have seen the light in his bedroom and been wondering who it is since the rest of the house is in darkness.

I jump up and turn to the love seat, check that it's in the right place before I face the door.

'Nell! What on Earth!' Shane says. 'I thought you were a burglar or something!'

He's suddenly there and my heart is suddenly in my throat. He has crept through the house super quietly and at super speed.

'What are you doing in my bedroom?' he asks when I don't speak.

I can't speak, of course. I can't really look at him, either. When I looked at him, properly, for the briefest of microseconds before, I had a flash of the Brighton Mermaid's face, twisted in terror, petrified with pain. He did that. If not to her, then to other women.

'I, erm, I was looking to see, erm, if, erm, if there was anything here that might tell me where Macy is,' I say. I can feel heat rising through my body, causing my head to throb and my heart to pound. I have to get out of here.

'You still haven't heard from her?' Shane asks.

Considering the last time he spoke to me he called me a *fucking, fucking bitch*, he's being quite normal. When I took the children to my parents' place, he didn't speak to me at all, he just hugged the kids and told them what a great adventure they were going on and how much he loved them and would miss them. That's what's so

350

hard to fathom in all of this. How he could be so normal, so *loving*, and be a prolific criminal at the same time? I forget, I always forget that people are rarely ever just one thing. They aren't all good, they aren't all bad, they have different sides to them. Only truly terrifying people can separate out the different aspects of their lives as effectively as Shane, though, surely?

'No, erm, no.' I have to clear my throat a couple of times and take a deep breath. Being so near him is making acting normal very difficult. It feels like I'm under an interrogation lamp and the heat radiating off the lamp is making me wilt. I can feel my fingertip throbbing and I have to put it in my mouth to remove the blood that has started to pool again.

'Are you sure that's all it is?' Shane says, stepping into the room and towards the wardrobe side of the bed.

I take a step in the direction of the door, the opposite way from him, heading for the exit via the window side of the bed.

'What do you mean?' I ask with my finger still in my mouth.

He nods at the bed. 'You sure you're not wanting to, you know, for old times' sake?'

The pounding of my heart increases tenfold. 'With you?' I say, lowering my hand from my mouth.

Shane takes another step closer to me. 'Yes, of course, with me.'

I shake my head, pretending my breathing isn't difficult. Fear. I'm actually scared of this man. Terrified of him. I have good reason to be, but I didn't think I could be so physically knocked by it. I take a step towards the door while trying to widen the gap between us. I don't want to be trapped on this side of the room with him. If I can get to the door, I can run.

'No, I don't want to, *you know*, with you,' I say with only a slight amount of the disgust I feel at the idea of it.

'Oh, come on, Nell, I've seen the way you look at me,' he says. He's moving closer as he speaks and I'm trying to manoeuvre myself further away but towards the door at the same time. I can hear my breathing, now that I don't have the jingle of my bangles,

I can hear my heart and I can hear my breathing and they both sound ridiculously loud. I'm sure he can hear it. I'm sure he, like other predators, can sense my fear. I'm sure he's going to pounce because he can hear I'm struggling to breathe.

I shake my head because I can't speak. I'm concentrating too much on breathing, on the door, on escape.

'Nell, it's all right, I know.'

I have to look at him then and the flash of the Brighton Mermaid's face bolts across my mind again. 'Know what?'

'I know you want me just as much as I want you.'

I shake my head. My chest . . . it's so tight. I won't be able to run with my chest this tight.

'Are you all right?' Shane asks. In microseconds he's crossed the gap between us and is standing right beside me. 'You don't look very well.'

The whole world tips suddenly. Like I am standing on the deck of a ship that has abruptly dipped to one side. Shane catches hold of me because, of course, the whole world hasn't tipped, only I have. I'm not surprised I don't look very well because right now I don't feel very well. Surely it can't just be fear that's doing this to me?

'Whoa there, Nell!' Shane says, peering at me, concerned. Once he has steadied me, he doesn't let go. He keeps a tight grip on my bicep with one hand then with the other hand takes my bleeding finger. 'Looks like you've hurt yourself,' he says. He smiles. It's a smile that chills my very soul. Before I can do anything, he raises my hand to his lips and runs his tongue along the palm of my hand. I rip my arm away from him, before I can assimilate the sensation of his mouth on my body. He has a strong hold on me, though, and it takes a huge effort to free myself.

'Looks like you've hurt yourself doing something you shouldn't have been doing,' he says.

'What?' I manage.

'Looks like you've hurt yourself putting your hand in places it shouldn't be, Nell.'

'What . . .?'

'Oh, poor Nell, looking in places she shouldn't,' Shane says, still holding onto my bicep.

I want to run, but I can't. My body will not move. I try to shift my legs and they are stuck firm to the floor. I try to pull myself away from him and my arms are immobile. My head is swimming, my vision wobbly, and my chest so tight my heart can't beat.

'I'm not stupid, you know, Nell,' Shane says quietly. 'I would never leave my precious things unprotected.' He leans in so close I want to flinch away but I can't. 'You'll be asleep in a minute, Nell. Be the good girl I know you are, don't fight it.'

'Wh—'

'What did I do to you? Nothing. You did it to yourself. You shouldn't go putting your hand in places it doesn't belong.'

I look at the cut on my finger and it's bleeding again, the blood sitting on the tip of my finger like a small, expanding ruby. My throat is dry, my eyes heavy and impossible to keep open.

'Close your eyes, Nell. It'll all be so much better if you just close your eyes—'

# Macy

'Have you heard from your sister?' Zach is the personification of worried. That's the only way to describe the look on his face and the way he holds his body – it is like someone has sculpted him to appear that way. He practically pounces on me when I return from a walk down the road to pick up some takeaway.

'Why would I have heard from her? She doesn't have my new number, unless you gave it to her.'

He shakes his head. 'Of course I didn't.'

'But you *have* seen her?' I ask.

'Yes, I saw her yesterday. But I need to find her. She's missing.'

I doubt she's gone missing, because she'd never leave the children. Or would she? When Zach looks this concerned, maybe it's not a given that she wouldn't leave them. After all, I did, and I would kill for them.

'What about my children?' I say to him. 'Where are they?'

'With your parents.' He says that like it's no big deal. Well, it *is* a big deal, it's a huge deal. Why are my children with Mummy and Daddy? I never leave my children with my parents without me being there. Not after the Jude thing. The only people I know I can trust 100 per cent with them are Nell and Shane.

'What? Why are they with my parents? Where's Shane?'

'That's the second question I was going to ask you – do you know where Shane is?'

'Why would I know where Shane is? What the hell is going on?'

'Look, it's really complicated, all right?' he says far too dismissively when we are talking about my children. Obviously they haven't been able to get in touch with me, but he can't just say 'it's complicated' when the most important people in my life aren't being cared for by the people I thought were better at it than me. When they are, in fact, somewhere I'd rather they not be.

'Don't tell me it's complicated. Tell me what's happening with my children.'

'To be honest, I don't know. All Nell said was that she'd left them with your parents for half-term.'

'Half-term? They've been there a week?' *Damn you, Nell.*

'She said they were fine, they were having a brilliant time with your mum and dad. And that's all I know. But right now, I have to focus on finding Nell.'

'How are you going to find her? You're a teacher.'

'Not exactly,' Zach says after screwing up his face. 'I'm a police officer. Working undercover. Well, I was. Look, I haven't got time to explain it all but I think your sister is in trouble.'

He's police? No wonder Nell wanted nothing to do with him.

'I don't understand what's going on here, Zach.'

'Like I said, it's complicated. The important thing is, your sister is missing. It's possibly something to do with the Brighton Mermaid. It's possibly not. I've tried to track her phone and the last place it gave off a signal was at your house. I've been there and there's no sign of her. Or your husband. I need your husband's number.'

'He's *not* my husband. And have you thought that maybe they're "missing" together? Dumped my children with my parents and have gone off to some love nest somewhere?' They obviously took my advice in my note about getting together. *I might have known.*

'They haven't. Well, if they are together, they're not *together* in the way you're suggesting. I need you to give me his number.'

'Why do you need his number?'

Zach hesitates, obviously unsure of what to say, how much to divulge. 'Tell me!' I demand. I've had enough of this. Enough of Nell and Shane and now Zach keeping secrets. Someone needs to start being honest with me when it is about my children. They can have all the secrets they want as long as it doesn't include Willow, Clara and Aubrey.

'All right, look. While doing Nell a favour, I found some stuff out about your hus— about Shane. Some terrible stuff. Nell wanted to tell you about it herself and I'm pretty sure she wanted some evidence before she did that. She wouldn't tell me what she was going to do exactly, but I think she went looking for said evidence. I told her to keep her phone on, I put a tracker on her phone – it was the best I could do to keep her safe. But damn it, her phone was turned off at your house a couple of hours ago, and it hasn't been turned on since. I think something has happened to her.'

'What terrible things?' I feel sick. Zach is saying Shane has done something to my sister. But that can't be right. That definitely can't be right.

He glances down at my hands, then back up at my face. I'm probably wringing my hands. If I'm not, I want to be. Because I am scared. I am very, very scared. What he's saying is making the clawing, cloying panic that lives with me, that sits on my shoulder, whispering in my ear about all the things that could and do go wrong, roar; it is screaming at me about how this will turn out.

'Look, it's best that we don't panic,' Zach says gently. 'We just need to do everything we can to find Nell. OK?' He lays a hand on my shoulder to calm me, and my panic detonates like a neutron bomb. Zach wouldn't touch me unless things were dire! The terror burns inside me, liquefying every part of me. *She's going to die. My sister is going to die. And the man I have kept in her life all these years is the one who is going to kill her.*

'She's going to be fine,' Zach says. 'She'll be fine.'

'You don't know that,' I say. My fingernails, recently manicured to be short and painted a deep blood red, claw at the knuckles of the opposite hand.

Zach watches me for a couple of seconds, then reaches out to still my hands. 'She'll be fine,' he repeats. 'We just need to find her. Only we can do that. OK? Does your hus— does he have any type of phone locator on his mobile?'

'I don't know,' I reply. Zach hasn't let go of my hands. I know it distresses people when I do things like that, but I can't stop. It's the only way to get the stuff inside, out. 'I don't know about his phone. We don't really talk about it. Why would we? We both just go out and use our phones. We've never lost them or anything so it's not something I've ever thought about. He has two phones – one's for work. But I don't know anything else. I don't know, I don't know.'

'It's fine. It's fine.' He closes his eyes and tips his head back. He's thinking but I need him to be talking. To be explaining what is going on.

'If she's missing, why don't you just put an all-points bulletin out for her?'

'That's what the Americans call it, over here it's a APW, All Ports Warning. And I can't just do that unless I have very good reason. And no, me thinking she's missing isn't a good enough reason.'

'What are we going to do?'

'Right.' Zach lowers his head and looks at me. 'OK, I need someone to check on his phone for me. I know people in London but no one down here.' He takes a firmer hold of my hands suddenly and I guess it's because he's about to say something that will upset me. 'Do you know someone called Aaron Pope?'

I shake my head quickly. 'The only person I know called Pope is . . . No. No. Is he related to . . . ?'

'Yes, he is.' I try to pull my hands away from Zach but he clings on tightly. 'I have to go and see him. He's the only one I know of down here who has the skills to help me find Nell while at the same time keeping it under his hat.'

'I don't understand. I don't understand what you're saying.'

'I need to find Aaron Pope's address and to go and see him. He will help find your sister by helping me to find your husband.'

'*He's not my husband!*' I scream at him. I shove him off me. 'And why would he help you find Nell?'

'She's . . . she's been working with him, trying to find out who the Brighton Mermaid is.'

The Brighton Mermaid. THE BRIGHTON MERMAID. My whole life has been dictated by that woman, even though she's been dead for twenty-five years.

'Look, Macy, I don't have time to stay here and explain it to you. I have to find out his address and then go to see him. If you want me to tell you everything, you'll have to come with me and I'll explain it all in the car. But I can't delay. I need to find your sister, do you understand? Everything is going to be fine, but I need to get moving to make sure it is.'

'I don't want to be anywhere near that man,' I state.

'I understand,' Zach says, 'but I need to go and see him. OK? You'll be all right here, won't you?'

I nod. I need to ring my parents anyway. Find out how the children are. I need to clean up Zach's flat – it's not as pristine as I would like it. I need to—

Zach is staring at my hands. 'Right, OK, look, I can't leave you here like this. You have to come with me and wait in the car or something. Get your coat and shoes back on, while I find out this guy's address.'

I'm not really hearing him. The sea is rushing into my head. Filling up my brain. I just want this to stop. I just want all of this to stop.

# Nell

'I can't believe you've got us into this mess,' one of the voices says.

I'm moving. We're moving. I'm lying down and my head is swimming, my mouth is filled with slime, and my whole body is moving. I want to open my eyes, I want to scream through the gooeyness coating my tongue, but I don't dare. Not when there are voices and I'm probably in a car or a van being taken somewhere. I know the voices. One is Shane, the other is Craig Ackerman, except he doesn't sound as posh as he did when I met him.

'I didn't get you into this, *you* got *us* into this.'

'How? How did I get us into this?'

'Why did you have to give her a DNA sample? That's what started all this.'

'I didn't know she was going to take DNA samples. You didn't tell me that, did you? "Oh, she's giving up her job to find out who the Brighton Mermaid is, you need to keep her occupied. You need to get close to her, see if she remembers seeing you that night." Well, you didn't fucking tell me that she took DNA, did you?'

'You could have put her off.'

'Oh yes, I spin some ridiculous story about wanting to find out if I have any birth relatives and I'm going to say no to a DNA swab? How's that going to work? That's why I've been trying so hard to get them back.' Something slams against something solid. 'This is all your doing. All your doing.'

'How is it my doing? If you hadn't killed Sirene, none of this would be happening.'

'Sirene! Pah! That was always your problem, Shane, always remembering their names, talking to them.'

*Sirene*. Her name was Sirene. Poor Sirene. She's been without a name for twenty-five years because of them. And all along they knew it. They both knew who she was.

'You were always acting as though they were anything other than what we needed them for. If she hadn't run away, I wouldn't have had to do what I did. She had everything: somewhere to sleep, food to eat, we even gave her clothes and make-up. But she still ran away.'

'She was just scared, like the others.'

'Yeah she was scared. She was *really* scared.' Craig Ackerman's voice sounds like that was the best part for him – her being terrified.

'Yeah, Craig, and you getting off on that is what caused all this.'

'No, if you'd just let me kill that bitch back in '93, this wouldn't be happening.'

'It wasn't only me who wanted her alive.'

*There's someone else involved.* Someone else who knew about me and wanted me alive, but who? And why?

'"It wasn't only me who wanted her alive"! *You're pathetic.* You've been whipped by her for years. You were supposed to keep an eye on her, find out what she remembered, what she knew, not start shagging her.'

'You've been at it too long, Craig. You don't understand what it's truly like to have real power. The power I've had over her all these years, it doesn't compare to the other things we do. The way she looked up at me all doe-eyed and innocent, willing to do any-thing – *everything* – for me as I took her that first time. That's power, that's control. Terror is nothing compared to devotion.'

'No, mate, until you've looked into a girl's eyes and watched that moment, that exact moment when she realises what you're going to do, that she's not going to get away or be rescued, you don't know power. And until you've held her in your hands, squeezing, watching as the horror in her eyes at what's going to happen changes to the realisation of what is actually happening . . . Until you've watched and felt that, you don't know power.'

Craig Ackerman is going to kill me. He has nothing in him that will stop him doing that. And Shane won't stop him. No one will stop him. It sounds like it's only the grace and favour of the person they are obviously working with that has kept me alive so far.

How many more of them are there out there? How many of them are there in this group that torture and abuse young girls? Because that's what it sounds like – they take women, they abuse and rape them and then, it seems, kill them.

Craig Ackerman is going to do that to me.

My head hurts. A hangover-like feeling I haven't had since that first night with Zach. *Oh Zach.* If I hadn't been so stubborn, he may well have been there when Shane and his half-brother came for me. I want to groan, to shift to see how much of my body I can move after what I was dosed with, but I have to stay still. I don't know when we're going to stop, when they're going to actually start with the killing.

'He's going to let me kill her this time,' Craig Ackerman says. As the fog shifts, I'm starting to hear the subtlety in their words, the inflections in what they say. Craig Ackerman sounds almost gleeful at the prospect of killing me. 'He has to let me kill her this time.'

'He won't,' Shane says. 'You know she's special.'

Craig Ackerman snorts, a sound laced with disgust. 'They're all *special.* She just didn't end up in a room like the others.'

'She didn't end up with your hands around her neck and left in water like the others, you mean?'

'There's still time.'

'He won't let you.'

'He'll have no choice.'

'What does that mean?' Shane asks. Shane sounds scared, I can hear that now. I can also hear how he masks his fear with forced bravado, clipped words and strong statements so he sounds like he is on par with Craig Ackerman. He must be terrified of his brother.

'It means I'm going to fix our "investigator" problem before he arrives.'

'You can't kill Nell.'

'There we go again: *whipped.*'

'I'm not. She's not a runaway like the others. People will notice if she disappears. They will ask questions. They will track down all the places she's been.'

'Well then, you shouldn't have taken her, should you, Shaney?'

'I wasn't thinking properly. When she passed out I had to get her out of there. Macy could have come back at any second.'

'Oh yeah, the *sister*. Whipped by her as well, aren't you?'

'Macy is nothing like Nell. She's been easy to manipulate and control over the years. She has all these fears and insecurities that I've played on. Keeps her in line.'

'Didn't you say she'd left?' Craig Ackerman sneers. 'Can't have kept her that much in line. And Nell took the kids away. *Whipped*, mate, you're totally *whipped*. And now you've created this "Nell problem" that I'm going to have to deal with.'

'You can't kill Nell.'

'What did you think was going to happen when you called me? She knows about us, you think she's going to keep quiet?'

Shane says nothing.

'You're not going to keep quiet, are you, Nell?' Craig Ackerman calls. 'I know you're awake. I heard your breathing change. You know all our plans, what we've been up to. And you won't be a good little girl and keep it all to yourself, will you? You've got a big mouth and a misplaced sense of justice. And an idea that you deserve to tell anybody whatever you want.'

I don't say anything, don't move. He's bluffing. He can't hear my breathing above the sound of the engine. He's trying to scare me, probably trying to scare Shane, too. I can tell it annoys him that he doesn't have complete dominance over Shane yet. He needs that if he's going to get him to go along with killing me before the person they're *both* scared of turns up. He needs Shane on the back foot before he starts to say whatever he needs to get him to kill me.

'Don't worry, Shaney, you'll get another chance with her. We'll tie her up and you can do whatever you like with her before the end.'

*That* was for my benefit. To get me to show I'm awake, to scare me with the knowledge of what is coming when they eventually stop the car.

'We're not killing her,' Shane says.

'Your choice, Shaney boy, but if you want to do it one more time with her, she doesn't get to live. No one believed the other girls but they *will* believe her, you said it yourself. So if you do her, we kill her. Your choice.'

'We're not killing her,' Shane repeats, but his voice sounds much less certain of that.

'Remember what you said about her first time?' Craig Ackerman says. 'Remember the look in her eyes? When she would do anything for you? Imagine having that power, that control back. Hasn't it been torture all these years, being around her and not being able to claim her as is your right as her first? Listening as she talks about all those other men she's let inside her body? You said she was easy, slept around, didn't seem to care who stuck it to her. Aren't you sick of her giving it away to everyone except you? You do her, we kill her so she doesn't get to do that with anyone else again.'

'We're not . . . We're not . . .' Shane stutters. He can't say it. It's not even that he can't say it and sound convincing, he just can't say that they're not going to kill me because he's thinking about it. Craig Ackerman has found it, that weak spot in his armour that will let him in, that will make Shane think about killing me. I knew he would find it, but I didn't realise it would be so quickly.

'You'd be her first ever *and* her last ever. Wouldn't that be something? Her first and last. Everyone in between would be washed away with that act.'

Shane says nothing. He's thinking about that. It's the sort of thing that would appeal to him, I can tell. It's not about being with me, I know that. It's Shane's obsession with being important. That's why he didn't want me to go to college. It wasn't just to keep an eye on me, but to make sure he was my number one.

'You want her again, don't you?' Craig Ackerman asks.

I don't hear his reply if he gives one but I guess he's said yes when Craig Ackerman says, 'I don't blame you, bro, I can see the appeal. I wouldn't mind a bit myself.'

*'You don't touch her,'* Shane snarls.

'I wouldn't dream of it, she's yours. When she came to my office, you should have seen how she was, though, all pouty, pushing her chest out. Gagging for it, she was. She made taking the DNA sample . . . Let's say it raised my blood pressure. But mate, I know she's yours. I'm just saying I can see the appeal: she's well put together.'

Shane is silent again.

'He can't get here for another couple of hours, he said. So when we get there, you've got two hours with her. Think of it: two hours to do whatever you want to her.'

Shane doesn't speak and Craig Ackerman leaves him to sit with his thoughts and for a time the only sounds I can hear are the purr of the engine and the whoosh of the wind passing us by. I'm guessing, as I haven't heard any other cars or sirens that we're heading into the countryside. I can't open my eyes to find out where I am, and from how uncomfortable I am, I'm guessing I'm on the floor of Shane's people carrier, although I'm not sure how they managed to get me into the car without anyone seeing.

I need a plan.

'So we're agreed?' Craig Ackerman says after he has given Shane enough time to think about what he'd like to do to me, but not enough time to start having doubts about the price he has to pay for those two hours. 'You do her, I make sure she doesn't tell anyone about it. And we tell him that it was an accident? Agreed?'

Shane is going to rape me; Craig Ackerman is going to kill me. I have to think of it like that. I have to keep the horror of what they're planning right at the front of my mind so I can prepare for flight or fight. Because it's not going to be like it is in the movies: no one is going to come riding in to rescue me and neither of these two are going to suddenly find a conscience where they decide not to hurt me.

Power and control are such strong drugs for these two and they are in their thrall. Craig's narcotic is killing people, women in particular. It's clear and apparent in his voice. It probably started out with having power and control over the bodies of young women, being able to force himself on them whenever he wanted, but after he killed Sirene, the Brighton Mermaid, he seems to have got a taste for it. He seems to like it. More than like it, I can hear in his voice how he *craves* it. He is desperate to kill me. He probably has been since he watched me standing with the Brighton Mermaid.

Shane gets his kick from the power-and-control narcotic by controlling sex. He is right, he did have my utter devotion. I thought he was the perfect boyfriend, an absolute gentleman, and that he completely adored me. But my devotion fed his habit; he was gripped with getting the drug-like high of having a girl live her whole life around him. That's why he lost it so completely when I kept on the path to university – I was stepping out of his control and that drove him insane.

They're both power-and-control junkies and I'm the source of their next fix.

*But*, I think hopefully, *Shane might not agree. Shane may decide he'd rather not if it means I end up dead.*

'Agreed?' Craig Ackerman repeats, a bit more forcefully.

Shane says nothing.

'*Agreed?*'

'Agreed,' Shane replies, and seals my fate.

# Macy

In the car, Zach encourages me to call my parents.

I can't because if I speak to them and speak to the children, the dam inside me might just break. I don't want to cry on the children and I don't want to speak and ask questions that will let Mummy and Daddy know I'm appalled that Nell has left the children with them. She doesn't know what I know, but still, she was meant to be looking after them, not dumping them and going off.

When it becomes clear that I won't be calling my parents, when I sit hunched up in the passenger seat, my head resting against the door, staring into space, Zach starts to tell me what Nell's been doing all these years. Who she's been doing it with.

'I can't believe . . . Why would she do that with him of all people?'

'It's mainly his son.'

'Well, that's all right, then! Oh, come on, what was she thinking?'

'From what I gather, she was trying to protect you and your parents.'

'Yeah, right. Noble Nell. I don't believe it for one second. She's been obsessed with that whole Brighton Mermaid thing for years and she's ruined all our lives because of it.'

'It's not like that, Macy. She told me that Pope was threatening to start harassing your father again. He gave her an ultimatum: he'd get the investigations on the Brighton Mermaid and

Jude's disappearance reopened by any means unless she found something tangible to prove your dad didn't kill her and didn't kidnap Jude.'

That cold tingling takes over. Every time I hear the name Jude. Even people who are not her cause this reaction. I wish I could tell Zach, tell Nell, tell anyone what I saw that night.

'She could have told me.'

'No, she couldn't. She couldn't have told anyone in your family. She told me what Pope did to you all. She's been desperate all these years to make amends for bringing Pope into your lives.'

'She shouldn't have done it. I don't care what he threatened, she shouldn't have done this. This makes a mockery of everything we went through.'

'Are you ever going to forgive your sister?' Zach asks.

'What for?'

'For being Nell?'

'That's a ridiculous thing to say. How can I forgive her for being who she is?'

'I don't know, but the hatred you have for your sister is going to drive you crazy,' he replies.

'I don't hate my sister.'

'Yes you do, Macy. It's apparent in every conversation you have about her. You resent her. And that's the sad thing: no one, *no one*, knows more than Nell how much she messed up by sneaking out that night. And no one, *no one*, hates Nell more than Nell does. Your sister—'

'You love her, don't you?' I cut in.

'I don't know her.'

'You love her, don't you?'

'No, I don't . . . But I was starting to.'

'Do you think it was the same for Shane? That he loved her so much? Do you think he's obsessed with her and that's why he's taken her?'

'No. Macy, it's not like that at all. I have to tell you about Shane. It's not going to be easy listening. In fact, most of it is bad, but you have to hear it. You have to know how serious this is.'

I brace myself. Or, rather, I think I brace myself. But what he tells me is nothing like 'bad', it is *horrific*. It is a horror story, a relentless nightmare that I cannot wake up from.

# Nell

*Saturday, 2 June*

The road is bumpy now.

We've come off the motorway-type roads, we've moved along normal roads and now we've turned onto something more off-the-beaten-track towards, I assume, the final destination. Is this where they deliver the girls they take? Is this where they meet the man they are both so obviously scared of?

There is a slight incline, as though we are driving up a shallow hill. Maybe we're somewhere in the Downs. Those green and pleasant hills that I often stare out at when I'm in Aaron's house. They are beautiful to look at, but for me, being stuck out here in the dark is what nightmares are made of. I have many types of nightmares; finding out Jude ended up like the Brighton Mermaid is the main one, but being alone out here is one of the worst. Alone in blackness, with unknown dangers coming from any angle and no way to escape – that terrifies me.

The van rattles from side to side as they start to slow down, and the spike in my stomach leaps up to my chest. I have to do this. I have to do this or I will not survive.

'She still asleep?' Craig Ackerman says.

'Must be. Never known Nell not to be talking if she's awake.'

They haven't spoken for the last part of this journey; they've been quiet, contemplative, probably thinking through what they're going to do.

'What did you give her?'

'I told you, I didn't give her anything. All my stuff is protected. Drug-laced spikes – if you touch one without gloves, it's sweet dreams. I can't control the dose. Her puncture looked pretty deep, though. Probably why the drug worked so quickly.'

'Well, you're going to have to carry her in. She is yours, after all.'

'Fine.'

The engine is turned off, the keys taken out of the ignition. They leave the van at the same time, slamming the doors behind them.

I open my eyes, blink to get my bearings, listen to the crunch of footsteps on gravel, taste the terror on my tongue, feel the fear crawl through my veins. I hear the click of the back door being opened, the dull swoosh of it being pulled back. I close my eyes again and wait for the sensation of Shane leaning over me, his hands reaching for me, and I kick out. Aiming low, low enough to hit that soft spot.

When he cries out and staggers back, doubled over and clutching the space between his legs, I know I got him where it will truly hurt. Craig Ackerman is by the front door of the big old farmhouse that they've brought me to and this is it, my two-second window to do what I do best. What I haven't done in years, but haven't forgotten how to do.

Run.

The ground is uneven and crunchy underfoot, and I stumble when I hit it. But it takes a microsecond to steady myself, to force myself upright and then to start running.

I make it off the gravel driveway, through the gap in the hedge and then stumble out into the fields that surround the farmhouse. In this inky blackness, in the distance, I can just about make out shapes – bushes, hedges, a line of trees far, far down over the fields. I need to get to the trees. If I can get to the trees, I can hide.

*Thud, thud, thud, thud!* The world around me is full of their footsteps, moving across the earth, chasing me down.

My legs are stiff from where I've been lying in the same position for so long, and they protest as I try to pick up the pace, attempt to run faster over the uneven, soggy ground.

*Thud, thud, thud, thud!* The noise . . . the vibrations . . . They sound horribly closer now.

*Thud, thud, thud, thud!* There's a fire in my chest where my lungs should be, and my eyes are struggling in the darkness as it constantly changes the shape of the horizon. But I can't stop, I can't even slow down, I have to keep moving.

*Thud, thud, thud, thud!* Nearer and nearer.

*Thud, thud, thud, thud!* I need my legs to go faster. I need them to call up the muscle memory of when I used to do this, when I had to literally run for my life. I can do this. I *have* to do this. I have to reach the trees. I'll be safe there, I'll be able to hide there.

*Thud, thud, thud, thud!* fills my ears. *Thud, thud, thud, thud!* They're right behind me. *Thud, thud, thud, thud!* My ragged breathing, the whistle of the wind, the creak of my bones are all drowned out by it. *Thud, thud, thud, thud!*

I have to go faster. I have to—

Suddenly I am flying, knocked over by force.

Craig Ackerman. He threw himself at me and I tumble, winded by the way my body slams to the ground.

I try to move again, but he's on top of me, crushing my chest with the weight of his body, folding his hands around my neck with the anger of a man who doesn't like people who defy him.

'This is what *she* did,' he snarls at me as he starts to squeeze. 'This is why. She couldn't just accept it, she had to run. She had to try and tell.'

He's going to do it, I realise. His hands are warm, heavy, deadly around my neck. He's going to do it and there's nothing I can do to stop him.

'Get off her!' Shane is suddenly shouting. 'Get off, get off, get off!' He tugs at Craig's arms, extended and rigid as they lock onto my neck, tightening and tautening, closing and shutting.

'You promised me!' Shane shouts. 'You promised me I would get a chance. You promised me!' He sounds like a child pledged a first go of another child's favourite toy, but who has had the offer taken away and is making his displeasure known. 'Let her go! You promised!'

Blackness is creeping in at the edges. With the hands around my neck and the weight on my body, I can't hold on any longer. I have to keep fighting, I have to—

Suddenly he's off me. He releases my neck, and is off my body.

As I cough and gag and splutter, rolling on the ground to get my breath back, I have to remember that this is simply a pause. Once Shane has had his 'go', Craig Ackerman will be finishing what he just started.


There is another car in the driveway by the time they march me – each holding on to one of my biceps – back up to the grey-brick farmhouse with a slate-grey roof, and white sash windows.

I stare at the car, blinking and blinking at it.

I've seen that car before. It's the latest in a long line of this person's cars that I've seen since I was a child. The first was a beige Citroën. The second I can't remember. The bright red one with the square frame, a Volkswagen, was Jude's favourite. She used to pretend it was her car and planned to get one the second she had saved up enough money from her Saturday job. The fourth, a white Peugeot, was my favourite. I stare at the car, a brand-new black Volvo with leather seats and chrome roof rack.

Slowly the car door opens and the light comes on, illuminating briefly the person inside.

This is 'him'. This is the man who they are both scared of, who has stopped me from being killed all these years.

He stands in front of his car, his head on one side, and looks at me for many long seconds before he speaks.

'Hello, Enelle,' he says.

# Macy

Aaron Pope looks like his father.

I wonder if he's like his father in other ways? If he can look at you and make you feel insignificant, unclean, unworthy? If he relishes that moment when something he says breaks you down enough to cause tears? Nell never cried. Not that I witnessed, anyway. She stood up to him and I could see, even when I was sobbing and falling apart, he hated that. I wonder if this man is like the one whose face he almost shares.

'Can I help you?' he asks when he opens the door to us. He doesn't sound like his father. He sounds softer, nicer. But that means nothing, really. He keeps looking at me, puzzled, wondering if he knows me. I'm enough like my sister to trigger that in him.

'Are you Aaron Pope?' Zach asks.

The man at the door nods slowly.

'My name is Detective Sergeant Zach Searle. I need your help.'

'I don't know how I can help you, officer.' He is still looking at me, his eyes slightly squinted, his mind obviously whirring.

'I'm looking for Nell Okorie.'

'Nell?' he says, seizing on that word like it is a precious jewel. Another man clearly in love with my sister. 'She's not here. I don't know where she is.'

'No, I didn't think she was,' Zach says. 'I think she's in trouble. She told me you help her with computer stuff. I need you to trace a phone number for me to see if I can find her.'

The man in the doorway looks wary. 'I can't do that.'

'Of course you can,' I say. I point to Zach. 'He's not working with the police right now, you won't get in trouble. He just wants to find my sister before someone hurts her.'

'You're Macy?' he says.

'Yes.'

'And you're Zach?' he asks. 'The guy Nell was seeing?'

'Yes.'

'All right, then. I'll help you, but I haven't traced a phone in ages. It might take me a while.'

'I hope not,' Zach says, obviously forgetting what he was telling me before. 'I don't think Nell has much time left.'

# 1993

## Nell

*Monday, 26 April*

'I think your dad is the best because he's just so cool about everything,' I said to Jude.

Jude hung her head over the edge of my bed, her two plaits stuck up on each side of her head like ears.

I sat at the top of the bed, resting my head against the wall, next to a poster of Maya Angelou's 'Still I Rise' poem. Jude had given it to me for my thirteenth birthday and I'd felt bad because I'd only got her a friendship bracelet.

'I don't think there's ever anything you could do that would make him angry. Not like my dad who gets cross all the time.'

'Your dad's not angry,' Jude said. She lifted her legs up a little off the bed and I was sure for a second she was going to slip off and conk her head on the floor. 'He just tells you off. Mine never tells me off. Sometimes I want to do bad stuff and keep doing it until I find the thing that will make my dad tell me off.'

'You can have my dad to tell you off if you want.'

We both cracked up laughing because my dad was always telling Jude off – no chewing gum, why didn't you do your homework, no shouting in the house. Sometimes Dad acted like Jude was his third daughter.

'I'd love to be able to do whatever I want,' I said dreamily. Even when Jude stayed out till late at our house and my dad had to drive her home, or she forgot to do her homework, or lost bits of uniform, her dad wouldn't shout. Her mum would get cross and tell

Jude to do better and she would want to stop her going out, or coming to my house; but her dad would say, 'No, give the girl some freedom. She's growing up and needs to make some mistakes for herself.'

I'd love it if my dad was like that. I could get things wrong and not worry about being told off, losing time with Jude, not being allowed to leave my room until I'd finished all my homework.

'See, I think my dad not telling me off means he doesn't care.'

'Of course your dad cares about you,' I said, aghast.

'But he's not interested in me,' Jude said. We often talked about our parents. I'd told her how nervous and on edge my mum was, how strict my dad always was, but this was the first time she'd said anything like this about her stepdad. 'I think, if it wasn't for the fact I had to be with my mum, he wouldn't even know if I was there. He's only interested in Mum.'

'Do you really think that's true?' I asked.

Jude put her legs down and threw her arms back beside her head, pressed the palms of her hands onto the floor. Her body was arched, a perfect curve over the edge of my bed. She was the best gymnast in our school and she had been in primary school, too, but she never got to do any competitions because her parents never got around to signing the forms. That made me think – was she right? Did they really not care about her that much? Dad and Mum wouldn't have approved of me doing something sports related instead of something academic, but they wouldn't let me miss out for the sake of not signing forms. Jude's mum and dad were always off out with friends, going to dinner parties, the theatre, the cinema. Sometimes, they went away for the weekend and said Jude could stay on her own or come and stay with us. I loved it because I got to have my best friend around all the time. But was that what Jude meant, as well?

'Yes, I think that's true,' she said.

'Well, like I said, you can have my dad to tell you off, if you want. I'm sure he won't mind, he seems to *really* enjoy it actually.'

Jude laughed again. 'I love your dad,' she said. 'He's like the best man in the whole world. When I get married, I want him to be exactly like your dad.'

# Now

## Nell

*Saturday, 2 June*

'Aren't you going to say something?' asks the man who has just exited the car.

I can't speak to Frazer Dalton, Jude's stepfather. How can I speak to the man behind all of this? How can I do anything but stare in horror at what this all means? If I could get away from the other two, I was thinking, I would have a chance. I would be able to get a message to Zach, I would be able to convince the police to open a new case. But if it's *him* – he who has drinks with senior police officers, and moves in legal circles – behind it, then what chance do I have, even if I do get away? There's clearly never been any DNA or forensic evidence that would connect him to any of it. It would literally be my word against his.

'Take her inside,' he tells the other two, who have become almost meek in his presence.

Craig Ackerman moves first, tugging me to get me to move while Shane's fingers slip away. I look at Shane, wondering why he isn't moving too, and find he is petrified, frozen to the spot, looking at Mr Dalton with absolute terror daubed across his face. I have never seen him so small and, quite obviously, terrified.

'I didn't—' Shane says.

'I'll deal with you later,' Mr Dalton interrupts, his voice as stern as a whip.

Shane looks at his feet and nods.

'Move,' Craig snarls and tugs me harder, practically dragging me to the front door of the farmhouse, which is sitting open.

The farmhouse is comfortable, cosy. The furniture is not new, it is well used as though someone lives here but not regularly. We come into the hall through a vestibule, to the right side of which there is a toilet and small laundry area. Dark green wax jackets hang on the pegs beside the door, three sets of rubber boots sit beneath the coats.

Craig Ackerman pushes me through the doorway on the left, into the large kitchen. The floor is a slate-grey stone, the work surfaces are a pale wood and there is a large farmhouse sink that he forces me past into an area that is a dining-cum-living room. It is long and extends far beyond the depth of the kitchen, which means, I'm guessing, there are bedrooms downstairs – next to the kitchen – as well as up the stairs.

I'm forced on past the large oak kitchen table with six chairs around it, and into the living room area. It has a matching cream, green and pink flowery sofa set as well as a large green beanbag.

'Don't move,' Craig Ackerman says as he virtually throws me into an armchair against the back wall.

I'm so tempted to throw my arms up in the air and wiggle my bottom back and forth against the seat, just to show him I'll move if I want to. It won't change the outcome, so what will he actually do if I do 'move'? But I don't 'move'. There's really no point in antagonising him.

From beside the television, Frazer Dalton pulls up a leather chair and sets it in front of me. He sits back and looks down on me from on high, a king staring down at a disloyal subject, pondering what to do with her.

He takes a deep breath. 'What am I to do with you, Enelle,' he asks rhetorically. 'I've never wanted to hurt you.'

*Do you want me to be grateful or something?*

'I'm sure you must have a lot of questions,' he says.

I can only think of one question right now: 'Where's Jude?'

Is she one of the ones who ended up a mermaid, left in water, robbed of her dignity and a precious piece of jewellery? Is she somewhere that no one has found yet?

'I have been hoping for many, many years that you would be the one to tell me that,' he replies. 'I've been very disappointed, to be honest, that you haven't. I've watched you find so many different people over the years, but never Judana. I was sure that even if you didn't find her, she would contact you at some point. But no, she never did.'

I look at Shane, standing on Mr Dalton's left, and then at Craig Ackerman, standing on his right. How did he end up with these two? How did they end up with him? What is it that they do? The way they were talking in the car, it sounded like . . . it sounded like they were terrible people.

'What are you going to do with me?' I ask him.

'I don't know, Enelle, I really don't.' He shakes his head sadly.

'Did you kill Sirene?' I ask him.

Craig Ackerman and Shane exchange looks, aware now that I was awake in the back of the van.

'Sirene? Who is she?'

'The Brighton Mermaid,' I say. I stare directly at him because I sense fear is something all three of these men thrive on. I cannot show fear – that will make this whole thing a lot more satisfying for them. 'You know that.'

'I have never killed anyone,' he states. 'I find that sort of thing distasteful, to say the least.'

'You and Shane both, apparently.'

'Shane and I are nothing alike.'

'I suppose not. Shane likes to see fear and possibly devotion. You don't like that, do you?'

'What do I like, Enelle?'

I look over Mr Dalton, as he'll always be to me. He is a neat, well-put-together man. Nothing is out of place: his brown-blond greying hair is neatly cut as always; his skin is well cared for although lined with age; his clothes are immaculately cleaned and ironed; his shoes are polished to a shine. He is all about order, control, image. What do I think he likes?

I think he likes to control women. No, not women. They present too much of a challenge; are by their definition his potential equals. He likes to control girls. He likes to be in control of every little thing they do. He likes to break them down, remove any semblance of will or spirit until he has their complete obedience. He thinks he is a superior being. He thinks he is above everyone and everything and he believes he is in control. I think he likes to employ all sorts of methods, try out all sorts techniques to achieve his goal of ultimate obedience. That is what I think he likes.

'I don't know,' I say. 'I don't know what you like.'

Mr Dalton treats me to a ghostly, terrifying apparition of a smile. 'I like to study the human condition and use it in a positive way,' he says. 'I like to see what limits a person can be pushed to, how you can deconstruct a person's personality to become the better, more compliant version of themselves. You can take a person, hold their life in the palm of your hand, and shape it at will. Turn them into who you want them to be. That is what I like, Enelle. I like to create people.'

'By "people" you mean "girls", don't you? You wouldn't dream of doing any of that to a man your age, would you? It has to be someone who you think is weaker than you, right?'

'Teenagers and young women are the ripest for picking, yes.'

'Where did Jude fit in with all of this?'

He sits forwards, folds his hands together and leans on his legs. 'Judana was my greatest project. I had her for years, I could study and shape her from an early age. She had to understand how unwanted she was, how inconvenient she was most of the time. You and your family, you interfered, a lot more than I would have liked, kept boosting her by providing her with a place to go, but with careful handling I was getting there. I wanted Judana to feel exactly like the burden she was. And then, when she was broken down, when she truly believed she was worthless, *I* would build her up. I would shape her to be at my beck and call. She was meant to leave, but I would help her. Give her a place to stay, away from her mother and away from your lot. She was to be the ultimate specimen of what it is to create someone. In time, she would help me to create more girls like her. I invested substantially in Judana and she disappeared before I was ready.'

'You . . . you *wanted* Jude? To have sex with?'

'Nothing so base, Enelle. She would be the lynchpin to my plan to create the type of companions that men like myself need.'

'You wanted to create women who are willing to wait around for men to come to them? What's wrong with them having mistresses?' He looks at me as though I am simple, that I haven't been listening. 'Oh, right, that'd be too much like hard work. Talking to them, having them expect things like consent, conversation, respect. You want girls who won't answer back, who will put up with whatever you throw at them because they've been trained to expect nothing more.'

'You make it sound sordid. I invest in people, Enelle, and I *always* get a return on my investment.'

'What about Sirene? What sort of investment was she?'

'I help runaways, Enelle. The girls who learn they are not important or wanted at home. I look after them, care for them, give them somewhere to stay.'

'How do you meet them?'

'Why would I tell you everything, Enelle?'

'Why wouldn't you? I'm guessing you don't get much of a chance to talk about what you've managed to do.'

'The world is full of places where the unwanted go. I find them and make them feel wanted.'

'Then rape and kill them, let's not forget those small things.'

'I do not kill people,' he says.

'What do you need these two for? I don't understand. If you spend so much time breaking the girls down, and then recreating them, what do you need these two jokers for?'

'I can't be here all the time. The girls need to be allowed to go to the lavatory, to be fed, given water . . .'

'Raped . . . killed . . .'

Mr Dalton rests his face on his hand and then looks at me as though trying to work me out. 'I have always had a soft spot for you, Enelle. There's something very earnest about you and the way you live your life. It would make me ashamed if you were my daughter, how sexually uncontrolled you are, but I like you. I truly believed you would be the one to find Judana for me. But alas, that doesn't seem to be the case.' He sighs. 'What am I going to do with you, Enelle? I really do not know.'

'You could let me go?' I say. 'That's a valid option. It's not like anyone's ever going to believe me against you, are they?'

'As your father found out, though, Enelle, mud sticks. They may not believe you, but they will start to look into my life a bit too closely for my liking.'

Mr Dalton has grey eyes. They are like steel and they are cold. I look directly into them, and he looks directly into my eyes. 'You've only got one option then, haven't you,' I state. He finds killing distasteful, but that doesn't mean he won't allow it. And that doesn't mean I shouldn't confront him with the reality of this situation.

He looks away first. For a man who thinks he is a superior being, I'm surprised he does that. But I guess he hasn't been confronted by someone who has known him practically her whole life and who is seemingly on a level to understand what he must do if he won't let me go.

I appear to be fine, pragmatic and stoic, even, about what they will have to do, but I am not. I am jelly inside, terrified. I keep hoping that something will happen to save me, and then I keep remembering that is not possible.

'You, watch her,' Mr Dalton says to Shane suddenly. He gets to his feet. 'If you think you can do that without causing another big problem for me to solve.'

Mr Dalton's disdain for Shane is very clear on his lined face. He tips his head to the door, nods to Craig Ackerman, who follows him down the length of the kitchen/living room and out of the house.

'I suppose they're going to work out what to do with me once they kill me,' I say to Shane.

'None of this needed to happen, Nell,' he replies. 'What were you doing? Why were you in my house searching through my things?'

It's good that he's asked me that. It means he doesn't know that I've told anyone else, except for maybe Aaron, who Craig – I presume – tried to kill.

'I wasn't searching through your things. I was looking for the set of keys you have to my flat.'

'I don't know what you're talking about,' he says.

'I realised a couple of days ago that the locks had been undone before the door was kicked in. That's why there wasn't as much damage and the police were able to get someone to easily patch it up. I guessed that the only person who would have keys to give to the burglar would be you. Probably copied from the set Macy has. I worked out it was you from the dead rat. You're the only person who knows about my pathological fear of them, besides Macy.'

'I had to get you to back off,' he says. 'Why wouldn't you just back off? When you were living with us, taking care of the kids and the house, you were happy then, I could tell. All you had to do was keep doing that and forget all that other nonsense and it would have been fine.'

'You killed someone, Shane. It's never going to be fine.'

'I didn't kill her,' he snaps. 'I didn't kill any of them.'

'Them? So there was more than one?' They *are* connected, the women they found along the coast.

He shakes his head. 'Just shut up.'

'I heard what you said in the van, you know? I know you were going to let him kill me just as long as you got "a go".'

'Shut up.'

'What would you be doing to me right now, Shane, if Mr Big over there hadn't turned up?'

He doesn't reply.

'Did you have it all planned out? What you'd do, before Craig killed me?'

'Stop it.'

'What are you even doing with those two, Shane? How did you get involved in all of this?'

'Just stop talking, Nell.'

'Why should I?' I say. 'They're out there, now, planning how to kill me and what to do with my body. Why should I shut up?' I sit forwards in the seat. 'You said it yourself, I never stop talking. Why would I stop talking now?'

Shane doesn't say anything.

'Look, just chat to me, please?' I say, my voice small and scared. 'I'm more than a little bit scared about what's going to happen to me. Just talk to me. Help me understand. Was it all fake between us? Craig said you'd done it to keep an eye on me – did none of it mean anything?'

'You don't understand, do you, Nell? It was me that kept you alive. Craig wanted to kill you, and your friend, but I said no, I'd get close to you and find out what you knew. I made sure you didn't keep on trying to find out who the Brighton Mermaid was. Because you know what? Craig wouldn't care if Dalton got angry. He would have killed you and then would have taken Dalton's anger. I stopped that. I saved you.'

'How did you get involved with all of this?' I question. 'How did you even meet Dalton?'

'He was my solicitor. I was accused of stuff I hadn't done. He got me off, made it all go away.'

'And taught you how to get away with it after that?' I realise. That's why nothing ever stuck to Shane after his first conviction – Dalton had coached Shane on how to get away with his crimes.

'I hadn't done it, any of it. I didn't need to be taught to get away with it.'

'What about Craig? You always said you had no family. Why did you lie when you have a brother?'

'He's my half-brother and he found me. My dad left his mum before I was born, and he tracked him down and then tracked me down. He thought it'd be best if no one knew we were related when . . . He just thought it would be better.'

*It'd be better that no one would link them when they began doing what they did with Dalton.*

'What happened with poor Sirene?' I ask. 'Why did she end up like that?'

'Because she ran away. If she hadn't run away . . .'

'Where did she run away from?'

'Nell, you don't understand what . . . Sirene was a runaway. She had no one. We took her in, gave her a place to stay, food to eat; we took care of her.'

'What did she have to give in return?'

Shane doesn't say anything because whatever he says will sound terrible because it *is* terrible.

'You all just forced yourself onto her whenever you fancied it, right? All as part of Mr Big's plan to break the girls down. Repeatedly raping her so she was broken.'

'It wasn't like that. We all have needs. She needed a place to stay – we had other needs.'

'Did she know that's what she was exchanging for her "needs"? Or did Dalton – and I know it was him because I can see how he would get a runaway to trust him – did he just charm her into a place where he kept her prisoner? I bet it wasn't just those two, either. I bet *you* did terrible things to her as well.'

'I didn't. You know me, Nell. The others might be like that, but I'm not. I was nice to her. I looked after her. I made sure she was all right.'

'Oh, I bet you did. You were the nice one, the one who talked to her, patched her up if the others hurt her. I bet you were wonderful to her to get what you wanted. Did Sirene look at you how I used to?' I ask. 'Were her eyes filled with devotion and adulation because compared to the other two, you were "nicest" to her?'

'You don't know what you're talking about. I was good to her.'

'Were you? Or did she just cry less with you? Did she not suffer much physical pain so she could keep the tears inside when it was your "go"?'

'Shut up.'

'Because I think it was probably worse with you, actually, Shane. I think she probably saw really quickly who charming Dalton *really* was after he had started his process of breaking her down. You can't fail to see what a creep Craig is. But not with you, I don't think. I think you were nice to her, I think you talked to her and spent time with her, and that's what made you the worst of the three of you. Because you were nice, she probably kept thinking, kept hoping, that you'd save her, you'd unlock the doors and set her free one day. Yes, you talked to her, found out her name, whispered sweet words to her, probably made sure you didn't hurt her too much when you raped her, but really, you were worse than the others because all you were doing was messing with her mind. Making sure she was so utterly confused—'

'JUST SHUT UP!' he screams at me, puce with rage. 'SHUT UP! SHUT UP! SHUT UP!' I can see he is restraining himself from physically hurting me. 'JUST SHUT UP!'

I lower my gaze and sit back in the seat, breathing as hard as I was after I ran away earlier. I probably shouldn't have done that, riling a dangerous man is never a good idea, but I couldn't stomach his nice-guy act any longer. He actually believes what he is saying. He honestly thinks that he isn't as bad as the other two because he emotionally manipulated that poor young woman.

'You know, they're probably out there right now, planning how to kill you as well as me,' I say conversationally when Shane has resettled himself in the chair opposite me.

'Are you trying to get into my head, Nell? *Really?* You're an amateur.'

'I'm not trying to get into your head. I'm merely pointing out an obvious truth: all of us here know that they're going to kill me, so why do they need to go off and discuss it? *I* know it's going to happen, *you* know it's going to happen – so stay here, talk about it freely. You all take pleasure in the fear and intimidation of women anyway; why would they deny themselves the pleasure of watching me fall apart as they discuss putting an end to me? Dalton said it himself, he likes to break women down, he likes to watch it happen. So what possible reason could he and Craig the killer have to go away and have a secret discussion all alone? Hmmm . . . let me think. Could it possibly be that they've decided the lame duck who has caused them all the problems they're having tonight needs to go too? Hmmm?'

While I've been talking, Shane's face has been drawing in, his eyes widening while he moistens and remoistens his lips. It's slowly dawning on him that I might be right.

'They wouldn't do that to me,' he says suddenly, shaking the thought out of his head.

'No, course not. They wouldn't betray or kill anybody. It's just not in their nature.'

Shane stands up, and turns towards the other end of the room, where they left. I'm glad I've managed to trigger his paranoia. If I'm not getting out of here alive, then I'm at least taking Shane's mental well-being with me. And it's one for Macy, who he said he's been manipulating all this time.

I sound brave, like I've assimilated what's about to happen, but I haven't. I wonder if it was like this for Sirene and the other mermaids? If they knew deep down what was going to happen to them in the end, but kept on thinking someone would save them. For someone to save me, people need to know where I am. No one knows where I am, and by the time Zach starts to look now I don't have my phone, it'll be too late.

I look over the suddenly jittery form of the first man I ever went with, my sister's wannabe husband. At least he's feeling as scared as I am. Probably more so, because I can't picture it in my head how they're going to do it, but he's seen it many, many times – he will know what they're capable of and how they do it.

The back door bangs shut behind the other two as they return to the farmhouse and come through into the dining area, down towards the lounge.

'Take her upstairs,' Dalton tells Craig. 'Tie her up in one of the rooms and lock her in. We'll sort her out later.' He then focuses on Shane. 'You and I need to have a serious talk about what is going to happen next.'

'No,' Shane says suddenly. He moves to stand between me and Craig. They're both roughly the same height and build, and being near to each other, I can see they've both inherited the same traits – forehead shape, brows, angle of cheekbones and shape of lips – from their shared father. It's amazing that I didn't see it before. 'Leave her alone.'

Craig looks back at Dalton and I don't need to see his face to know he's given Dalton a 'told you so' look. He's clearly told Dalton that Shane might not be compliant in what happens to me, and they've discussed what to do about it.

I was only half playing when I said about them plotting to kill Shane, too. But it seems I was right. The way Craig and Shane are squaring up suggests that Craig wouldn't think twice about harming his sibling.

I know Macy hates me sometimes, and it's a real, genuine, palpable hate, but she does also love me. She does care about and worry about what happens to me. There is a connection between the two of us that is unspoken and real. There seems to be none of that between Shane and Craig. I wonder if that's because they didn't grow up together. I wonder if it's because they've been linked mainly by this thing they do, and this thing they do is so dangerous that they're always checking if the other is watching their back or actually examining it for where to stick a knife in.

'If you want to talk about what's next, then you do it with her here,' Shane says. 'He's not taking her anywhere on his own.'

Dalton's anger flashes first in his eyes like the igniting flame of a furnace, then settles down on the set of his jaw, the clench of his lips. 'What happens next is what always happens next,' he eventually says to Shane.

'Neither of you is touching her,' Shane replies.

'All for one, Shaney, and one for all,' Craig states. 'That's the way it's always been. So we're all complicit, we all have as much to lose, none of us are going to start telling on the others.'

'*Neither of you is touching her,*' Shane repeats in a dangerous voice. 'She's mine.'

Dalton is still angry; it rests there on his face like a mask. 'Shane, I didn't want this to happen. I don't want to hurt Enelle, touch her in that way. It wouldn't feel right. But you caused this mess and we now have to do as much damage limitation as possible. There's too much to lose.'

My heart has been beating fast and loud since I was in the back of the people carrier. It has been loud in my head, louder than my ragged breathing, but now it picks up pace. The danger of this stand-off is flogging my heart like it is a racehorse that is being whipped into winning a championship race.

I look at the three men in front of me, each of them examples of the horror of humanity, each of them ready to hurt each other and do me harm.

Even if Shane was doing this for the right reasons – to save me – and not because he believes he owns me and doesn't want anyone else touching his property, I don't think much of his chances. Not against his brother. There's a crazy, uncontrolled wildness in Craig Ackerman that is fast manifesting in the tensing up of his muscles, his dangerous stance, his clenched fists.

My heart. It's beating so fast, getting faster and faster, it's actually agony. It feels as if it's going to race itself into flatline.

I throw my arms across my chest and gasp loudly at the pain that has just clawed through me.

I curl forward, and Shane looks round at me, and with his eyes off both of them, Ackerman decides to pounce.

# Macy

John Pope's son doesn't say much. He alternates between the two screens he uses, completely focused. We went straight upstairs and I'm standing here wondering if his dad is in the house. Zach said this is his house and that Nell told him that his son is his carer. He must be in the house somewhere. Possibly downstairs in the room off the hallway that had its door closed.

I hate that Nell came here because she was scared of what Pope would do if she didn't. I don't know why she didn't tell me. All right, I *do* know why she didn't tell me. But it must have been so lonely for her. She doesn't act like it. She always acts like she's OK with everything and that she's just wafting through life looking for the identity of the Brighton Mermaid, searching for Jude, and nothing gets her down.

I hate that Nell came here and was in the same house as that man.

I hate that that man's son is the only person who can help us right now.

Aaron Pope slams his fist down on the desk, so hard the keyboard lifts up, as do a couple of pens and scraps of paper. 'I can't do it,' he virtually growls in utter frustration. 'I can't get the triangulation to work.' He forces his hand in his mouth and bites down, hard, while glaring at the large screen in front of him. He's panicked, I can see that.

Zach hasn't said much either because he's panicked too.

I know panic.

I know how panic can change you. How it can stop you thinking, from properly feeling. I know how panic twists every little emotion into something giant, transforms every single breath into a cage of barbed wire that mangles itself around your very being. I know what panic is like, how it can metaphorically kill you. In this case, panic is going to kill my sister. I can't let that happen.

I crouch down beside Aaron. 'Tell me about Nell,' I say to him.

He blinks at me behind his glasses, obviously trying to focus on me after staring so hard at the screens. He shakes his head: *I don't understand.*

'Tell me about Nell,' I repeat. 'I don't know her. She's been coming to you and working with you for years and I didn't know that. There's so much I don't know about her. Tell me about her.'

'We haven't got ti—' Zach begins and I hold up my hand to shush him. Neither of them knows panic like I do. I know what I am doing.

'Tell me about Nell.'

'Erm.' He flops his hands up and shrugs his shoulders. 'She's odd, I guess. Funny in a strange way. She's private. She's kind. She's caring. She can be annoying. I don't know. How is any of this helping?'

'Tell me about Nell.'

'I don't know what you want me to say.'

'I want you to tell me. What has she been doing here all this time? Tell me how she works, how she thinks, how she would solve this problem. Tell me about Nell.'

'I don't know. She would . . . she would . . .' A light suddenly comes on in his head. A light that would not have come on if he was still panicking. 'She would look for something else. Or she would combine something else to make what we need. I need to . . .'

He pushes his glasses back up his face and returns to the computer, pulls the keyboard towards him and starts to type. 'I can't get the triangulation to work, I can only get two points on each phone, so I'm going to combine the points on both phones. They will hopefully—'

He stops talking when the computer pings. The map on his screen stops being a map of the whole of the south coast and instead suddenly zooms in on one area. 'Hopefully one of those two points will act as a third for the other phone. Which is what it's done. There. He's – well, his phones are here.' He points to the computer screen with his finger. On the map it looks like a sea of pale green surrounded by the white lines of largish roads. 'I'll get an aerial map up.' He clicks a couple of keys on his keyboard and an aerial photo of the area appears. The pale green is replaced by dark green fields, the white lines become grey streaks. There are green hedges, boundaries of different fields, but very few buildings. And what buildings there are seem too spaced out.

'Do you know this place, Macy?' Zach asks me. 'Do you know of any reason why Shane would be out there?'

I shake my head. 'No. I've never been there. I've never . . . no. No.'

'If he's taken her out there, then there's only one reason why,' Aaron says, voicing what we're all thinking. 'We have to get there.' His fingers start to work on the keyboard again and he comes up with a postcode for the area, and a partial address, since the area where he managed to narrow Shane's phones to is small on the screen but quite large in real life. 'When we get nearer, if Macy calls him, I'll be able to pinpoint his exact location.'

'No,' Zach says. 'I have to call this in now. I have reasonable grounds to ask them to go and find Nell.'

'Good. But I'm going, and you can't really stop me,' Aaron says. He gets up from his seat and grabs the piece of paper that he's scrawled the postcode onto.

'Me too,' I say. 'I'm going too.'

'All right, all right,' Zach says. 'We'll all go. But you have to do exactly what I and the other police officers say. All right?'

'Yes,' Aaron says.

'Yes, fine,' I say.

'Right. Let's go.'

# Nell

*Saturday, 2 June*

The world has exploded: the air is full of shouting and the sounds of flesh hitting flesh, things being slapped, snapped, broken. I pull my legs up and watch in horror as Shane and Craig roll on the ground in front of me, a two-headed creature, writhing and roiling, fighting itself.

I thought Craig was stronger, more dominant, that once he had pounced it would be a done deal. But Shane is stronger, more vicious than I could ever have imagined. I watch them, then I look up to see Dalton.

He is horrified. He stares at the two fighting forms, not knowing what to do. When he inflicts violence, it is on young women, girls without strength, people who don't fight back. But I bet he doesn't see them as people. He sees them as tools, objects that are there for him to experiment on, break down, force himself on, dispose of once finished.

Everyone in Dalton's life is a pawn, something for him to control. This is horrific because this is not what he was expecting. This is out of his control.

This is also my chance to run again.

I don't need to think this twice, don't wait for them to stop fighting, stop taking chunks out of each other and return their attention to me. I jump up and then jump over them, landing awkwardly before I start to run for it.

'No you don't,' Dalton says. I thought he was too shocked, too immobilised by the fight to notice. He grabs my arm and tries to restrain me. I try to pull my arm free, but he has me firm.

'No, *you* don't,' I reply, and then stamp hard on his foot. Bring the flat of my hand up hard against his nose, then claw at his eyes. He isn't expecting any of these assaults and lets me go when my hand connects with his face.

I run again, not thinking how long it will take for Dalton to recover. What I did won't hold him back for long, so I need to move. I run the length of the room, turn at the large kitchen island and head for the door.

'She's getting away!' Dalton roars as my fingers connect with the Yale knob and I rip the door open. The night air is another assault – cold, bracing, a shock after all the heat fear has created.

I don't stop, as I run from the farmhouse, the gravel crunching underfoot like old autumn leaves. I have to make it to the trees this time. I can't get caught again. If I get caught again, it's all over.

I am over.

My shaky legs carry me as far as the fence, before the world is suddenly illuminated. First the bright white of headlights, closely followed by flashing blue as cars bump their way up the dirt track towards the farmhouse.

I stand frozen, watching them approach. Hoping against hope that I am awake. That this isn't a hallucination brought on by the after-effects of the drug I unknowingly absorbed when I pricked my finger. The cars keep on coming, the lights brightening up the whole area around the farmhouse the closer they get and the more of them that pull up next to each other.

Automatically I throw my hands up. I don't want to get mistaken for a criminal. I don't want to be damaged and hurt before they can identify that I have nothing to do with the men inside. I hear those men come tearing out of the house behind me and then stop when they see who has joined us up at their secluded location.

I have no idea how they got here, or who they have come for. But I don't care. I'm not alone up here. I am not going to be violated by three men then disposed of like I am not human.

That, for me, has always been the worst part of the Brighton Mermaid story, and the stories of the other mermaids: they were not treated as though they were human. It was what Jude was so angry about with the Brighton Mermaid too. They seemed to be just bodies. Things to talk about. Things to ponder and 'solve'. But not real humans who needed dignity and respect and consideration for simply having existed. Whatever happens next, I will not be 'just' a body that shows up or even that is never heard from again. Whatever happens next, people will know who I am.

There is a silver car at the front that I do not recognise, but inside I see her. Macy. Or someone who looks like Macy. I narrow my eyes to shield them from the headlights and try to look again through the windscreen. *Macy?*

The door opens and she climbs out. The other door opens and Zach climbs out. The back door opens and out climbs Aaron. Three people I have never been more pleased to see in my life.

I move to run for the car, for Macy and safety and the chance to be on the other side of the line. The other cars stop and start to spill out police officers, people who have terrified me for more than half of my life because of what one of them did to my family all those years ago.

'DON'T MOVE!' a voice barks and I immediately stop, raise my hands again. I keep my hands up, the breath catching and catching in my throat, not moving to my chest.

The police officers swarm forwards like black ants rushing towards sugar, avoiding me, a roadblock in their path, and heading for the goodies behind me. Grunts, growls, groans, the sound of handcuffs – a sound I've heard far too many times in my life – securing. I don't move. I don't move at all, not until three men are being marched towards police cars, until other police officers are heading towards the house.

When it's clear they have everyone they need, and that they are going to leave me alone, I lower my arms. I close my eyes, I take a huge breath in and I let the fear take over. She's by me in an instant, her arms are around me the moment after and my sister is holding me, propping me up while I break into a million tiny, terrified pieces.

'It's OK, it's OK, it's OK,' Macy hushes. 'I'm here, I'm here, I'm here.'

# Nell

*Sunday, 3 June*
I'm fine. *Now.*

Before, I was hysterical. So hysterical, unable to stop crying, that I had to be given a sedative to calm me down. I've slept a little as a result of that and I'm fine now.

That's the main thing. I'm absolutely fine. Zach and Aaron are in the waiting area outside and only Macy is allowed to stay here with me. A police officer has taken an initial statement and I'm supposed to relax until I'm discharged. There's only one thing wrong with that idea: the second I relax, everything that has happened comes rushing in and despite the medication coursing through my bloodstream I can feel the hysteria rising again.

I hate that. I hate that I wasn't sanguine and quipping, throwing my arms around my sister and my friends, joking about how they came together to save me.

Instead, the whole thing hit me full-on when Macy put her arms around me. The absolute terror I'd felt since waking up in the back of Shane's people carrier had twisted itself around my very core, had spread its tentacles through every vein, smashed into every heartbeat, compressed every tiny breath.

*I thought I was going to die.*

I thought I was going to die; that I was going to be murdered and would end up like the Brighton Mermaid, dumped somewhere, a nameless body that people would think about in passing, that someone would write a piece about twenty-five years in the future wondering if anyone would ever be able to put a name to the body.

I wasn't only crying about that. I was breaking down because so much of my life has been about the Brighton Mermaid, in ways I couldn't even begin to understand – Shane, Mr Dalton, Aaron, even Zach, in the end, had become about the Brighton Mermaid.

'Talk about déjà vu,' I say to Macy once the police officer has gone. She's been very quiet, staying close to me, but not saying much. Avoiding eye contact. She has been straightening the edges of the bedclothes I was sitting on, but she seems to have a lot of her nervous tics under control.

'Yeah,' Macy says. She closes her eyes, sighs, then says: 'I'm so sorry, Nell.'

'Funny, I was about to say the same to you,' I reply.

'What are you sorry for?' she asks.

'What are *you* sorry for?'

'I asked first.'

'And I asked second.'

'Bloody hell, Nell, I had visions of us having a big emotional heart-to-heart where we sort out our differences, where we cry about you-know-who and you-know-who both being evil and we resolve to move on as the best of sisters. But no, we can't even *start* the conversation, let alone actually have it.'

'All right, I'm sorry for ruining your life. Back then and in the present. I'm so sorry that we're not closer. That what I did has resulted in you feeling bad for so long. And I'm so, so, *so* sorry for bringing *him* into our lives.'

'You didn't have to say all that, you know,' Macy responds. 'You didn't ruin my life in the past *or* in the present. I mean, it wasn't until Zach asked me why I didn't like you . . . Actually, he asked me when I was going to stop hating you and I was shocked that someone else could see that. And that it was true.'

I stop looking at her and stare at the curtains that surround my little cubicle in casualty. I knew it, but it hurts to hear – it blasts another crater into my already devastated heart. I'm going to start crying. And I don't know if the sedative I'm on will be enough to stop me becoming hysterical again.

I don't want to become hysterical again.

I want to be in the fuzzy glow of not feeling very much at all.

'I don't *really* hate you,' Macy says quickly. 'I just thought I did. And because I thought I did, I kept finding things you did to prove that I did. I don't hate you, Nell. I love you. I adore you. You're who I want to be like. You're basically my hero. My very, *very* flawed hero.'

'You're just saying that,' I say, trying to sniff away the tears while wiping my eyes.

'I thought . . . I don't know what I thought consciously. It's just felt for so long that the whole world runs around after you. Mummy and Daddy weren't the same after Daddy was arrested but they still did everything they could for you. And in my eleven-year-old brain at the time, all the horrible stuff that was happening to our family was all your fault. I kind of clung to that. And when I met . . . *him* and I found out that you and he had been together, it felt like I'd, well, that I'd finally get to be like you. To have what you had. He was so lovely and so committed that I knew that finally, *finally* I was going to be the centre of attention. But no, he was clearly still into you.'

'He wasn't.'

'Will you not interrupt me!' she says crossly. 'I'm spilling my guts here, I don't need you stopping my flow.'

'Sorry. Keep going.'

'I *thought* he was still into you. I didn't realise it was because of . . . uh, I just can't even think about it . . .' Macy taps the side of her head, as though trying to dislodge any thoughts of Shane. 'I don't hate you. I mean that, you know? I don't hate you. I love you. You always seem so capable and with it. Men are just falling in love with you left, right and centre while I . . . One guy left me with three kids, and the other one made a very good show of being with me, but he was never really there.' She picks up my hand, slips her fingers through the gaps between mine. 'I want us to be proper sisters. To put all this other stuff behind us and just, I don't know, be proper sisters.'

'What are proper sisters?' I reply. 'It's not like we're enemies or anything, is it?'

'No, but we don't talk, we don't connect, we don't spend any time together.'

'Yes we do. It's just we've spent a lot of time with all this unsaid stuff between us, and me keeping secrets and doing stuff that I couldn't tell anyone in our family about because of the upset it'd cause, and you thinking Mum and Dad prefer me to you and me thinking you're so close to them in a way I could never be, and you being resentful and me being resentful that you're resentful but kind of understanding it as well . . . Wow, we have a *lot* of sister issues to work out, don't we?'

My sister grins at me. This must have detonated every single one of her worries and anxieties, but she's hiding it well. My poor sister. She's been living with all of this her whole life. At least I was a bit older, at least I could start to assimilate what was happening with what I knew of as an imperfect world. She couldn't. She went from what I remember clearly as living in a place where people were good to each other, or they got along with each other. You turned on the news and there was sometimes a terrorist attack that was removed and distant from us, there was sometimes a killing that made all the headlines, there were police appeals, there were wars in different countries, uprisings and revolutions. It was always so far away, completely removed, and then all of this came crashing into our lives and never really left. And Macy had to integrate that into her life. The way she did it was through her behaviours, her ritualistic ways of self-soothing.

'So, what you going to do about those two sitting out in the waiting area?' Macy asks. She runs her slender hands over and over the sheet on my bed, trying to smooth out the creases.

'What do you mean?'

'Zach and Aaron. Both of them are *clearly* in love with you. What are you going to do? Who are you going to choose?'

'Oh, you mean who am I going to choose between the secret policeman and the son of the man who persecuted my father?'

Macy smirks. 'To be fair, both of those things kind of helped to rescue you.'

'Yeah, well, there is that . . . It's not true, you know,' I tell her.

'What isn't?'

'What you said about men falling in love with me left, right and centre. It's not true. It might seem like that, but it's not. They may like me, but that's because they don't know me. It's easy to be all gooey-eyed over a person you want to fuck or you've fucked a few times. It's much harder to fall in love with someone who you've seen every side of. The truth of the matter is, what you think is love from these blokes is the desire to fuck me and the inkling that I probably will sleep with them because I am, as Pope called me all those years ago, a slut.'

My sister transforms in front of me: her eyes seem to catch fire, her face becomes angry, her body is rigid with rage. 'Never say that! Never say that about yourself!' she snaps. 'You are not a slut! I don't care how many people you sleep with, you are *nothing* like *he* said. Nothing. Never say that again. OK? *OK?*'

I draw back, surprised by the strength of her reaction. 'OK . . . OK, I won't say that again.'

She calms down again, the fierceness draining away in an instant. 'But don't try to get out of it: which of those two are you going to choose?'

'I don't know. Give me a break, sis, I've got bigger things to worry about.'

'Ah-*ha*!' she says as though she's caught me red-handed committing a crime.

'"Ah-ha" what?'

'You didn't automatically say Zach, which means Aaron must be in with a bit of a chance.'

'I'd really, *really* like it if we changed the subject now.'

'Nell and Zach and Aaron sitting in a tree, K-I-S-S-I-N-G,' my sister starts to chant under her breath. 'But who's she kissing first? Who's she kissing first?'

'Enough, you! Can you go and find the nurse? I really want to go home.'

When she disappears behind the curtain, I lean back and close my eyes. And even though I'm sedated, even though I'm safe and I'm fine, tears slowly crawl out of my eyes and down my face.

# Macy

I couldn't tell her the truth about Jude at the hospital.

I couldn't tell her because I'd never seen her like that. She completely fell apart out there and I'd literally had to hold her up. I think the three of us who knew her were completely shocked by her breakdown. She's always been the epitome of strength and resilience – nothing seems to get Nell down for too long.

Even when they'd given her drugs to calm her down, I could see that she was teetering on the edge of hysteria again.

That's why I couldn't tell her.

We're in her flat – neither of us even thought about going back to my house – and I'm standing in the doorway, watching her sleep. She was zombie-like when they released her from hospital. Zach drove us home; Aaron sat in the front beside him while I sat in the back with Nell. She thanked us all and refused to let either of them help her upstairs.

I've never thought of Nell as fragile, that she could hurt so deeply. She looked broken when I told her that I hated her. And it wasn't true. I didn't hate her, not properly.

I have to tell her, though. The mystery of the Brighton Mermaid is solved, but not the stuff about Jude.

Jude. Jude. Jude.

Nell needs to know.

The best thing to do would be to leave it until tomorrow morning, when we're both awake and we can do something about it.

But it's burning a hole in my tongue, just like it has burnt a hole in my life since that night I saw her. Since I saw my sister's best friend get into my dad's car and disappear into the night, never to be heard from again.

As I stare at my sister, noting the lines of her face, her eyes open.

I wonder how long she's been awake while I've been standing here. She told the police officer in the hospital that she'd pretended to be asleep for most of the car journey to the farmhouse so she could listen to what they were saying.

I walk into Nell's room as she pushes back her purple duvet and slowly, almost painfully, pulls herself upright. I sit on the edge of her bed and stare at her.

'What's the matter?' she asks me.

I sigh. What's she going to do when I tell her? Will she shout at me? Will she call me a liar? Will she believe me? For years I haven't believed me. For aeons I've pretended something else happened.

Jude.

I open my mouth to tell her and the words jam themselves sideways in my throat. The word. The name.

'Daddy does that, you know,' Nell says. She doesn't sound like she was asleep at all, not even groggy from the drugs they pumped into her earlier. 'He looks at me like he wants to confess something, something terrible, and then changes his mind. What do you want to tell me?'

'Daddy,' I say. It's the only word I manage to force out from the words plugging up my vocal cords.

'What about him?'

'Jude.'

She's giving me the Nell hard stare now. She's connecting things in her head and then she's throwing them away because that would mean I am saying something she can't bear to contemplate.

I don't even realise I'm wringing my hands until Nell puts her own hands over mine and tries to still them.

'Tell me,' she says. 'Tell me about Jude.'

Jude. Jude. Jude.

I close my eyes. Behind my eyelids I watch Jude reach for the handle of the car, pull it open. She looks back, over her shoulder, as though someone is chasing her, and then climbs in. My eyes fly open again.

'Tell me,' Nell repeats.

'I saw . . . I saw Jude get into Daddy's car the night she disappeared. Something woke me and I got up, looked out of the window, and I saw her getting into Daddy's car. He drove her away and when he came back he was alone.'

Nell takes her hands away. She closes her eyes and lowers her head as agony claws its way across her face. 'Do you think he took her and killed her?' she asks.

When I don't reply, she moves her gaze up to look me full in the face. 'Do you?' she repeats.

I want to say 'No.' I want to say 'Of course not.' I want to say 'That's the most ridiculous idea on Earth.' But if the last twenty-four hours have taught us anything, it's that you never know. You just never know.

'I don't know,' I reply to my sister. 'I just don't know.'

# Nell

*Sunday, 3 June*

Dad is being jumped on by his grandchildren when Macy and I arrive.

He is flat on the floor in the living room and the children are treating him to piley-on, jumping on him and squealing in delight. I've never seen Dad like this with the children, but I don't recall ever really being around them all at the same time. I think I've spent a lot of time distancing myself from them, from all of them.

Mum is sitting on the sofa, with her crochet, obviously pretending none of this is happening. I can imagine this sort of play is like a mallet on the xylophone of her nerves. She (and to be fair Macy) will be seeing all the dangers that could befall them as they roll around on the floor (hitting a head on the fireplace hearth, catching a limb on furniture, falling awkwardly) and she is clearly doing her best not to scream at them to be careful or to stop it.

I'm proud of Mum for that, at least. It's probably been challenging for her all week, but she's clearly been trying.

'Since when did you have a key to Mum and Dad's house?' I ask.

She shrugs. 'Since always.'

'How come?'

'I used to live here, remember? When you were off in college, this was our family home.'

'But they've changed the locks since then.'

'Probably, but I just asked for a key. You mean you didn't?'

'No.'

'Oh.'

'MAMA!' the children yell when they hear her voice and look up. They leave their helpless granddad on the living room floor and barrel towards her, almost knocking her over when they make contact.

Macy bursts into tears. Big fat tears that course down her face, while she tries to gather her children together in her arms that aren't quite wide enough, while kissing and hugging and kissing and hugging and kissing and hugging them at the same time. While Macy reacquaints herself with her offspring, I stare at my dad.

It must show on my face, that I know. That I know he was the last person to see Jude on the night she disappeared. It must show because as he sits up, we lock into eye contact, something we haven't done in twenty-five years, I realise. My father looks into my eyes, I look into his. A small, regretful smile materialises on his lips as he breaks our visual link and gets himself up. He doesn't look at me again as he brushes himself down because he knows it's time for us to have that conversation we didn't have twenty-five years ago, around the time my best friend walked out of my life, never to be seen again.

The three of us go into the greenhouse when it is dark. When the house is full of warm, fragrant dinner smells and the children's voices have finally been quietened by sleep (they've made Macy promise she will be there when they wake up, which added an extra fifteen minutes to bedtime), we head for Dad's place for talking. He switches on the lights in his greenhouse and the plants seem to glow extra green. He goes to the far side of the green-house, to his fuchsias. They were Jude's favourite plants. Even though she didn't like pink, she loved them. I wonder if Dad grew them for Jude.

After what he did to her, he grew them for her so he could never forget.

'D— Erm, what happened to Jude?' I ask. I want to call him Daddy, to be normal with him, but I know after this conversation I won't be able to call him that again. I probably won't be able to call him anything. I'll probably want to erase all memory of him from my mind. I've been trying that with Shane; I hope I'll succeed with my father.

'I saw her at the house,' Macy says. 'The night she disappeared, I saw you with her. She got into the car and you drove her away.'

*Were you having an affair with her, Daddy?* I want to ask. *Did you get her pregnant and have to get rid of her?*

'Why did you not ask me about it then, Macenna?' he says.

She shrugs.

*Because she was scared the truth would be too horrible to hear.*

'Judana came to the house that night,' Dad says. 'She did not want to wake anyone else up and was throwing stones up at Enelle's window . . . She was in a state.

'She almost ran away when I opened the door and whispered to her to come in. After hesitating, looking up at Enelle's window a few more times, she did.

'I took her into the kitchen and sat her down. Your mother was working that night and the pair of you were asleep. Or so I thought, Macenna; I did not realise you were awake. I asked her what the matter was and she wouldn't tell me for a long time.

'Eventually, I made her coffee and I sat down and waited for her to talk.'

# 1993

# Jude

Nell's dad had always been the coolest dad. He was like a proper dad. Nell never really got that. She didn't live with my dad so she didn't realise what it was like to know that someone just didn't want you around.

But he loved Mum. Everything was always about Mum. I heard them doing it sometimes and it made me feel sick. I don't think Mum would have done it if she knew I could hear, but I always thought my dad wanted me to hear. Every morning after they'd done it he'd make a special point of asking me how I slept.

Nell's dad, who I always wished was my dad, sat me at their kitchen table and made me coffee. He asked me to tell him everything that was the matter, what had made me come there at that time of night. I couldn't speak. I didn't think he'd believe me. He said nothing for a long, long time. And I sat staring into my coffee, turning over and over in my head what had happened. A few days earlier, I'd been getting my bag out of the boot of my dad's car and saw something glint down the side. I'd managed to get it out with a nail and found a small, silver mermaid charm. Like the kind that comes off a charm bracelet. Like the kind that comes off a charm bracelet that girl was wearing that I had taken. I'd spent a lot of time looking at that bracelet, examining it, and some of its loops were open, so some of the charms were missing. And this looked like a charm from that. Of course, it could have been from anywhere, anyone, so I'd pretended it was no big deal. Pretended

I could forget about it. I'd wanted to tell Nell but she was already so freaked out by everything, she looked like she spent the whole night crying sometimes, that I knew she would completely lose it about this. So I took the charm, and I'd kept it and I didn't say anything to anyone.

And then, that night, while Mum was at work, I'd heard voices outside. I was meant to be in bed asleep, but I'd been lying fully clothed in bed, thinking about the girl we found, about the charm, about what to do, when I heard two men talking. They were quiet, but they were there. I'd crept out of bed and had gone to the window. My dad was in the back garden, smoking with someone else. I couldn't see his face properly at first, but then he turned around and I saw him.

I had to jump back in absolute horror. I'd seen him that night on the seafront, when I was going to the phone box to call the police. He'd smiled at me and he had such an awful look in his eye that I'd thought he was going to attack me so I'd started walking really quickly. He hadn't followed me, but he did watch me, and I remembered his face because of how scared he'd made me feel. With that and the charm in my dad's car, I'd known that they were both involved. They'd probably killed her. I hadn't known what to do, so I'd waited until they had gone out to come to see Nell. To see what she thought I should do.

I couldn't tell that to Mr Okorie. He probably wouldn't believe me. But he was waiting for me to speak, so eventually I said, 'It's about my stepfather. My dad.'

Mr Okorie's face drew in on itself in a way I had never seen before. Did he know? Did he suspect?

'Has he . . . has he been inappropriate with you?'

That floored me. I thought him and my dad were friends – why would he even ask that?

'It's all right, Judana,' he said in his deep voice, 'you can tell me. I will understand.'

I didn't say anything, because he hadn't been inappropriate with me, not in the way Mr Okorie meant, but I did suspect him of doing something awful or being part of something terrible.

'Would you like to go to the police about it?' Nell's dad asked.

I shook my head. Not after that policeman. I didn't want to see him ever again. I didn't want to be around him ever again. I'd always been a little scared of the police, I think most people are, but he had frightened me. And because none of the other police officers had stopped him, nor been nice to us in any way, I couldn't stand for it to happen again. It might not be that same policeman I talked to, but none of the others made me feel safe, either. And if I was accusing my really respectable dad of something . . . 'No, Mr Okorie, I don't.'

'Judana, you have always been like a daughter to me,' Nell's dad said. It was true, of course. He did treat me like Nell and Macy, he told me off, he helped me with my homework, he was openly disapproving of some of the things I wore, he acted like he loved me. He was like a dad should be, I thought. 'I will do anything to protect you as I would Enelle and Macenna.'

All this time, I'd thought I didn't really have a dad who cared, and I did. I honestly did. 'What do you think I should do?' He didn't know what I was really asking about, just what he thought had happened, but I wanted him to give me an idea of what to do.

'The only thing I can think of if you don't want to go to the police is for you to move in here. Stay with us. I will protect you.'

I shook my head. 'My mum wouldn't stand for that. I'd have to tell her why. And if I tell her why, then she'd expect me to go to the police. But I can't stay at home either.'

'Judana, think again about going to the police.'

I had to get away from here. That was the only answer. If I was away from here, I could think properly about what to do. How to let the police know about my dad. 'I think I need to leave. That's the only way.'

Nell's dad looked so sad and tired then. 'Where would you go?'

'I don't know. Just away from here.'

'Judana, I cannot let you go out into the world on your own like that. I wouldn't allow Enelle or Macenna to do so; I cannot let you do it, either.'

It was the only way. I'd have to run away if he wouldn't let me go. 'Maybe . . . I think, well, I *know* my mum has a cousin who lives in France. Maybe I could go there.'

He didn't believe me. 'Give me the number of this cousin and I will call them to arrange everything.'

'I do have the number, but if you ring them, they'll . . . probably . . . ring Mum and tell her I'm coming. It'll . . . it'll be easier if I can just show up and then beg them to let me contact Mum in my own time.'

'Judana . . .'

'Please, Mr Okorie, I just need to get away for a bit. I can't think here. I just need a bit of time. A bit of space.'

'I do not want you to leave, Judana. I would prefer it if you went to the police.' He studied me for long seconds. 'You are going to leave whatever I say, aren't you?'

I nodded.

'Is there really a cousin in France?'

I needed to leave. France seemed good. It was out of the country, I didn't need to get on a plane to get there. I'd need money and a passport, though. I'd have to sneak back to my house to get both.

'Judana, is there really a cousin in France?' he asked again.

I didn't like lying to Mr Okorie, but . . . I nodded.

I wasn't sure if he believed me completely, or if he told himself I was telling the truth to stop me from just running away and ending up God knows where, but he sighed again. Looked even sadder.

'I will give you all the money I can get my hands on,' he said. 'Do you have your passport with you?'

I shook my head.

'I will give you Enelle's passport and drive you to Newhaven to get the ferry to France. No one will check the passport too closely. Where does your mother's cousin live?'

'Calais. No, no, I mean Dieppe. Where the ferry comes in. I have the address in my address book.'

'Call your mother's cousin from the ferry port when you arrive and call me, too.'

I shook my head. 'I can't do that, Mr Okorie. I can't let anyone know where I am. Not at first. He'll come and find me. I just know he will.'

Nell's dad was silent for a long time. He was thinking it all over. 'I know he will,' he finally agreed.

'Can you . . . can you just not tell anyone where I've gone or that you've seen me? And I promise, when I'm ready, when I'm less scared, I'll get in touch. I promise. I promise.'

I didn't want to leave. I wanted to have the life I thought I would live, as best friends with Nell, getting a proper boyfriend, passing my exams, going to university. I didn't want to leave but if I wasn't going to go to the police then I had to, because I couldn't live in a house with my dad and pretend.

Mr Okorie stood as though he had a heavy burden on his shoulders. 'I will have to leave you in Newhaven to be sure to be back before the girls wake up if I am not going to tell anyone you were here,' he said before he left the room.

I got up and washed up my cup. I rinsed it out, dried it and put it away. No one could know I'd been here.

'Judana, we will miss you,' Nell's dad said in the car. We'd stopped off at his shop to get the takings that he hadn't banked and now he was driving us to Newhaven.

I was crying. I'd started the second he turned on his car engine and I couldn't stop. I would miss Brighton. I loved the place so much. It was where I belonged, where I would always belong, but I probably wouldn't see it again.

'If it does not work out with your mother's cousin, always know that you can come home to us. The Okories will always have a place for you.'

He kept talking, telling me how much they cared about me, how he wanted me to stay, and for me to come back if I ever had any doubts. Or to call him and he would come and get me.

At Newhaven Ferry Port we got out of the car. It was a large white building that I thought looked like a giant four-storey shed with windows.

'Take care of yourself, Judana,' Nell's dad said. My life would have gone so differently if he'd been my dad.

'Thank you, Mr Okorie,' I said through my tears.

Nell's dad did something I would never have expected him to do – he hugged me. Put his arms around me, held me close, kissed the top of my head. 'I'm proud of you, my daughter,' he said before he let me go.

That made it all right, suddenly. He was proud of me and I knew that meant I could do this.

'Send me a postcard to let me know you are safe,' Mr Okorie said before he left. 'Do not write on it and do not post it from where you live. I would simply like to know that you are safe.'

I nodded.

And I watched him drive away knowing he would do everything in his power to keep me safe.

# Now

## Nell

*Sunday, 3 June*

'Judana was like my daughter,' Dad says to us. 'I wanted her to be safe. When the police were looking for Judana and her mother didn't mention a cousin in France, I realised that Judana had lied to me. But I would still do the same. She needed to be away from Mr Dalton.

'I have never like Mr Dalton,' he continues. 'That was why I very rarely allowed you to stay at their house, Enelle. And why I encouraged Judana to spend so much time at our house. I noticed how he looked at you girls in unguarded moments. I did not like the way he was with girls at all. I knew Judana's father would have wanted me to do the best for her.'

'But you could have told them at any time that Jude was alive and that you had helped her to get away to keep her safe,' Macy blurts out. Sometimes I forget that she was so very young when all this began. That she sometimes still sees the world like that.

Over the years, with what I've seen going into and during adulthood, I look back and I realise why we were treated like that. I suspected it at the time, and Pope skewed what was actually happening, but the reality is, as two black girls, we were suspects until all the evidence proved otherwise. We were not automatically witnesses or automatically victims: we were suspects from the moment those police officers arrived at the beach and saw what we looked like. John Pope wasn't the worst of them, he was simply more upfront about how everyone else was treating us and thinking of us.

'They would not have listened to me, Macenna,' Dad says. 'Not without evidence of what he was doing.'

'They wouldn't, Macy. Not against someone as respected as Jude's stepfather. You didn't see how that policeman changed when Mr Dalton walked into the room when he was interrogating us. Daddy had already told him to leave us alone, but it was only when Mr Dalton walked in that he stopped. There's no way they would have believed Jude against him. Not without iron-clad evidence. And you know what? From all the stuff I read in the police files, no one ever even looked at Dalton as a suspect in Jude's disappearance – that's how convincing he was at playing Mr Respectable.' We haven't even told Dad everything that has happened in the last twenty-four hours. That will devastate him. That Jude probably knew what her stepfather was up to and hadn't trusted him enough to tell him.

Macy's eyes are filled with tears; I can barely see for the tears swimming in my own eyes. She nods in understanding. 'Oh Daddy,' she says, sounding like she is that eleven-year-old watching from her bedroom window. She throws her arms around him. He went through so much, endured all of that for a young girl. For us.

My poor dad. My poor, poor dad. I move forwards, towards him. Macy has always been one for throwing herself onto him, hugging him, not giving him a chance to be naturally resistant to physical contact. I could always see his discomfort and I always respected that. But today I think it's allowed. Today he doesn't hesitate before he wraps an arm around Macy and another one around me.

Holding us close like I hope he held Jude before she left all those years ago.

# **Nell**

Dear Jude

I'm going old school here and writing you a letter with good old-fashioned pen and paper.

Your mum said you'd been in touch and that she was going to visit you so I could give her a letter to pass on, if I wanted. I did very much want. I know she's not coming back, by the way. I could tell by the way she was talking that the visit is going to be permanent. Good on you both and I hope it's nice having her with you after all this time. She's going to need a bit of looking after, now she knows what her husband was really like. We're all still reeling with everything so I can only imagine what she must feel.

I've told your mum a lot of what has happened, so I'm updating you here, if that's all right? Well, tough really if it isn't!!!

Firstly, the Brighton Mermaid is called Sirene Greene. She was there on Sadie's family tree and once I had her name, it was easy to find her family who live in Sutton Coldfield, near Birmingham. They'd been looking for her for many years, and had been to Brighton more than once, before she was found, because she was obsessed with the place. They didn't know about her tattoo, though. She'd run away to become a pop star after her mum and dad said she should forget all such nonsense and concentrate on her studies. She was seventeen when she ran away. She saw an advert for a singing contest in north London and had asked her

421

parents for the money to get the bus. When they said no and to stop all of those ideas while living under their roof, Sirene had decided not to live under their roof any more.

They thought she would come back. The police weren't too interested as she was seventeen and had run away a couple of times before, so they too assumed she would be back. By the time her family realised she wasn't coming home, the police said she was eighteen, an adult, and therefore allowed to disappear if she wanted. I'm guessing she ran into Mr Dalton somewhere along the way.

Her story is so sad. I spend a lot of time thinking about her. Her mum showed me lots of photos of her and we talked a lot about her. It was nice to hear about her and I think her mum was comforted to know that someone out there was interested in who she was beyond the lurid headlines about how she was found and the men responsible for her death. I felt awful for her, but she did say she and Sirene's brothers were relieved in a way to have finally found her. And that they could now take her home. Her name 'Sirene' means 'mermaid', you know? I never thought to search that in all those years.

I'm guessing you saw some of the press coverage, which is why you got in touch with your mum? They couldn't have loved it more that the mystery was solved just in time for the twenty-fifth anniversary. It took some doing, but my family managed to stay well away from all of that despite some of the journalists' best efforts.

Sadie is slowly recovering. They were actually talking about turning off the machines at one point but she pulled through. She's absolutely thrilled that it was her information that cracked the mystery. You'd love her if you met her, she's hilarious and so generous-spirited. I can't tell you how relieved I am that she's OK. What's nice is that she now has Sirene's family to be in touch with.

Shane, Craig Ackerman and Mr Dalton have all been remanded into custody without bail. I think you know that? Once they were arrested, Shane sang like the proverbial canary. I suspect it was his revenge for them plotting to kill him but they couldn't shut him up. He confessed to anything and everything; told all about the other two. After Shane had stolen their jewellery, Ackerman had killed all those women and left them in places where Ralph Knowles, the man originally charged with the murders, had been, to basically stitch him up. Dalton was the mastermind who concentrated on breaking the young women he lured into his world. The CPS person I spoke to reckons it won't come to court in the end – she thinks they'll all plead guilty, especially because they're going to start looking for the girls Ackerman didn't kill. The ones they held and broke down to be playthings for other men.

I have to confess I feel sick every time I think about it. I'm still freaked out that I had Shane so wrong. As I keep reminding myself, though, no one is all evil. Sometimes I do have to go and shower, just to get the memory of my time with him off me. I think Macy's the same.

Speaking of evil, remember that awful policeman? John Pope was his name. Lots of things have happened to him over the last few months. First of all, he was arrested for perverting the course of justice. His son, Aaron, shopped him. It probably won't stick, but the fact he was brought in for questioning where he used to work was mortifying for him. When I asked Aaron why, he said that he blamed his dad for all those other mermaids dying. He said if his dad hadn't been so terrible to you and me, you might have felt safe enough to go to the police with what you saw. As well as that report, he's also reported his father for historic child abuse. There are hospital records and the like for that, so either way, Pope is going down. Something has switched in Aaron, and it's been incredible to witness. I was so pleased for him that he's finally unshackled himself from his father in such a decisive way, but he has a long journey ahead of him. He's not going to be all right overnight, no abused child ever is once they free themselves of their abuser, but he's on the right track. And I applaud him for it. I love him for it.

Oh yes, one last note about John Pope. When it was revealed that Dalton was one of the men responsible, John Pope remembered what it was that he had found that led to him being run over. He had discovered – through the misappropriated files – that Ralph Knowles, the man they originally arrested for and charged with the Mermaid Murders, had been represented years ago by Dalton. He'd thought it was too much of a coincidence, especially since there'd been an anonymous tip-off about Knowles in the first place. But rather than tell anyone in the police force and get them to investigate it, he'd wanted the glory for himself – he called Dalton and started asking him seemingly innocuous questions. Dalton twigged that he was onto something, so sent Ackerman after him. That was the problem all along – Pope could have been a good policeman if he wasn't such a vile human being.

Macy says hi. She's moved in with our parents in Herstmonceux. She just refused to go back to the house or let her children go back to the house. I had to pack up everything for them (Zach and Aaron helped), although a lot of it she wanted to trash because they were reminders of Shane. The house is now for sale because, for her, the Brighton dream is over. You know what, though? After their week living there, I don't think she'd have got her children to come back to the city anyway. They love Mum and Dad's huge garden and they spend loads of time running around in the countryside. She's told them that Shane did something very wrong and against the law so he had to go to prison. It was that or keep trying to hide newspapers and news from them. She's also getting divorced. She sat me down and explained she'd got married in secret and how sorry she was that she didn't tell me before, and asked if I would be able to forgive her. ''Course,' I said.

'Why don't you look more surprised?' she asked.

'Because I already knew,' I replied. 'Macy, I spend a lot of time searching through official records. I saw your marriage notice form and I saw your wedding certificate.'

'Why didn't you say something?'

'Because you didn't want me to know. Can't wait till you tell Mummy and Daddy about it though.'

The upshot is, Clyde is giving her the divorce she wants and she's moved to the middle of nowhere and they're all loving it.

Zach, my ex-sort-of-boyfriend, has gone back to London, back to his wife and kids. Joke! He has gone back to London but there is no sign of a wife or kids! He is waiting to hear if he still has a job. What he did, unofficially accessing those files on Shane, is usually grounds for instant dismissal. The CPS are still considering his case and we're hoping that given the result of what he did (solving lots of murders), it would not be in the public interest (the official term) to pursue a conviction at this time. In other words, do it again, matey boy, and you're out. I think they're being particularly harsh on him and keeping him waiting because he refused and continues to refuse to name the people who actually went into the files for him. I didn't realise what he did was so serious and I love him for doing that for me.

Who else do I need to update on? Well, me, I suppose. I have a new job. Sort of. I'm an official consultant to the police on unidentified people. I'm basically working on the other four mermaids that were found along the coast. Primrose, Maia, Celia and Jody. Shane gave the police their first names, so I'm following it all up with going through records, building family trees using all the DNA databases, including the police one. Primrose, Maia, Celia and Jody. I want to find out who they are so their families can finally know where they are and they can be more than just 'mermaids'.

I've mostly recovered from what happened at the farmhouse. I get scared sometimes, especially when I'm in my flat alone, but I'm dealing with it. I have a friend stay over whenever it gets really bad. I'm hoping the CPS lady is right, though, and I don't have to testify. But you know, that aside, I'm happy.

Well done if you've got to this point, Jude!

I just want to finish by saying I missed you all these years. I sort of understand why you don't want to be in touch directly. But I missed you. And I think about you. And I hope you have love and happiness and joy in your life.

With all my love,
Nell x

# Macy

Nell said she was bringing someone to Sunday lunch, but she wouldn't tell me who it was. 'Is it your boyfriend?' I asked hopefully.

'I'm not answering that question, Macy,' she replied. And I knew it *was* her boyfriend.

I've been asking her who out of Aaron or Zach she's going to choose for weeks now. And she won't answer. She's been to stay with Zach a few times in London and they're 'just friends', apparently, but when I ask her where she sleeps she says in his bed – 'it makes talking all night easier'. And since Aaron moved out of his dad's house, he's apparently stayed a few times at Nell's place. Again, just as friends, even though I'm pretty sure he sleeps in her bed, too. I've told her more than once that she needs to decide who she wants because it's not fair on them – they need to be free to find other people. She always says she doesn't want to talk about it. Until today, when I think she's bringing whoever she's chosen to lunch.

Which is why I'm standing here at the living room window, waiting for them to arrive. I don't know which one of them I'd prefer because they are both decent guys. Aaron did an amazing job finding Nell, and it was a real act of bravery reporting his dad for perverting the course of justice *and* for what he did to him in the past. Zach did an amazing job finding Nell, too, and he did take me in when I had nowhere to go. So, possibly, Zach has the edge with me.

I see Nell's red mini with its chequered roof turning into the street and then slowing down until she pulls into Mummy and Daddy's driveway. After she turns off the engine, she opens the door and climbs out, still wearing her driving glasses. In the passenger seat is what looks like a large basket of flowers. She pulls the lever on her seat and folds the seat forwards so the person in the back can get out. Then she moves to the other side of the car, opens the front door and retrieves the flowers.

I grin when I see who has climbed out of her car. Zach. She chose Zach. I'm pleased. Rather than shut the passenger-side door, though, Nell balances the flowers on one arm and pulls forward the car seat on that side, too. Seconds later, Aaron climbs out.

Ah, I see. I see who she's chosen now. Nell. She's chosen Nell.

Aaron says something and the three of them laugh.

I'm pleased. I'm pleased my sister has chosen herself. I'm doing the same by starting the process of getting proper help to heal myself. I'm doing all I can to be kind to myself, I'm learning to forgive myself for allowing Shane into my life, and I'm dealing with my anxieties in a clear and upfront way.

I watch the three of them talking in the driveway. Zach says something that makes Nell scowl comically and Aaron crack up some more.

It's lovely to see. It's lovely to see that after twenty-five years of carrying the burden of the Brighton Mermaid's legacy, my sister is finally happy.

# Nell

*Sunday, 28 October*

# Dear Nell

# Thank you.

# J x

# Acknowledgements

**Hurrah! I get to say thank you to all these wonderful people . . .**

The ones who help make this book happen: Ant and James; Susan, Cass, Hattie, Charlotte, Rebecca, Emily, Aslan, Jason, Emma, Becky and everyone else at my publishers; Emma D.

To the ones who help to keep me going: my lovely family and friends, G, E & M.

To the ones who buy the book: You.

*And a special thank you to Graham, for the police advice.*

ALSO FROM DOROTHY KOOMSON...

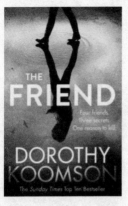

**What secrets would you kill to keep?**

After her husband's big promotion, Cece Solarin arrives
in Brighton with their three children, ready to start afresh.
But their new neighbourhood has a deadly secret.

Three weeks earlier, Yvonne, a very popular parent, was almost
murdered in the grounds of the local school – the same school
where Cece has unwittingly enrolled her children.

Already anxious about making friends when the parents
seem so cliquey, Cece is now also worried about her children's
safety. By chance she meets Maxie, Anaya and Hazel,
three very different school mothers who make her feel
welcome and reassure her about her new life.

That is until Cece discovers the police believe one of her new
friends tried to kill Yvonne. Reluctant to spy on her friends but
determined to discover the truth, Cece must uncover the potential murderer before they strike again . . .

arrow books

'Do you ever wonder if you've lived the life you were meant to?' I ask her. She sighs, and dips her head. 'Even if I do, what difference will it make?'

In 1988, two eight-year-old girls with almost identical names and the same love of ballet meet for the first time. They seem destined to be best friends forever and to become professional dancers.

Years later, however, they have both been dealt so many cruel blows that they walk away from each other into very different futures – one enters a convent, the other becomes a minor celebrity. Will these new, 'invisible' lives be the ones they were meant to live, or will they only find that kind of salvation when they are reunited twenty years later?

arrow books

ALSO FROM DOROTHY KOOMSON...

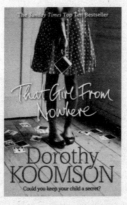

'Where are you coming from with that accent of yours?'
he asks. 'Nowhere,' I reply. 'I'm from nowhere.' 'Everyone's
from somewhere,' he says. 'Not me,' I reply silently.

Clemency Smittson was adopted as a baby and the
only connection she has to her birth mother is a cardboard
box hand-decorated with butterflies. Now an adult, Clem
decides to make a drastic life change and move to Brighton,
where she was born. Clem has no idea that while there
she'll meet someone who knows all about her butterfly box
and what happened to her birth parents.

As the tangled truths about her adoption and childhood start
to unravel, a series of shocking events cause Clem to reassess
whether the price of having contact with her birth family could
be too high to pay . . .

arrow books